THE MATE GAMES BOOK THREE

# POSSESSION

K. LORAINE

USA *Today* BESTSELLING AUTHOR

MEG ANNE

Copyright 2022 © Ravenscroft Press

ISBN: 978-1-951738-86-0 (Paperback Edition)

ISBN: 978-1-951738-84-6 (Hardback Edition)

Permission requests can be sent via email to:
authors@themategames.com

Cover Design by CReya-tive Book Cover Design

Photographer: Wander Aguiar

Model: Theo

Edited by Mo Sytsma of Comma Sutra Editorial

*For Sarah, the president of the tripod fan club.*
*Save a tree, ride a Viking.*

"The language of love is like that, possessive."

— HOLLY BLACK

# POSSESSION

# AUTHOR'S NOTE

Possession contains sexually explicit scenes, as well as mature and graphic content that is not suitable for all audiences. **Reader discretion is advised.**

Welcome to The Mate Games, a detailed list of content and trigger warnings is available on our website. For those of you who prefer to go in blind, keep reading.

# CHAPTER
# ONE
### ALEK

*Two months ago*

K*ærasta.*

I still couldn't believe that word left my lips. Sunday wasn't my mate. I didn't have one. Fated mates were rare and precious. The fact that my parents found each other was the stuff of fairy tales. The odds of lightning striking twice for my family were less than zero. But here I was, uttering an endearment I'd never been called to speak before.

At least she had no idea what it meant.

The fuck of it all was I wasn't even supposed to be here. Tor had been slated for the mission. As the twin with a perpetual hard-on for following the rules and proving himself, he'd been the clear choice for this military assignment. Which made it even more surprising when Cora, the Satori matriarch blessed with glimpses of the future, told

We'd learned early on never to question one of her *feelings*. So there'd never been any doubt I'd take her advice. Even though I didn't have any interest in this kind of responsibility.

Every few months, a Novasgardian would be sent to Earth for a full trip around the sun to learn and report back on any magical or technical advancements. We never wanted to be caught unawares when it came to growing powers in the supernatural world. Not after the casualties Novasgard sustained in the battle against a foe who'd been left to his own devices for far too long. These last twenty-five years we've been much more involved, increasing our visits to Earth, refusing to ever let another enemy rise to such heights.

I only had to make this work for one year. Gathering intel on the future leaders of the supernatural Families at Ravenscroft shouldn't have been hard. They were ripe for the picking, all full of misplaced pride and puffed up like peacocks showing off for their future mates. Easily distracted, ready to boast about their power. I'd have them filling my book with intel before my time here was half over.

But then *she* happened and everything stopped.

Gods, if she was my mate, how the hell was I supposed to leave her?

My limbs vibrated with an unfamiliar sensation. Was this . . . panic? My breaths were strident and labored, as though I'd gone twelve rounds with a wyvern and it was winning.

*Kærasta.*

The word echoed in my mind again. *Mate. Beloved. Destined.*

Fuck.

2

Hands shaking, I pulled the spelled mirror out of my pocket and ran the tip of my finger over the runes etched into its frame. They lit up as my skin passed over them, the magic sparking to life once all ten of them were activated.

My mother's concerned face appeared within seconds. "Alek? I didn't expect to talk to you today. What's wrong?"

"How did you and father know you were mates?"

She blinked. "*That's* why you called?" Relieved laughter escaped her, and she ran a hand through her hair. The slight quiver of her fingers betrayed her own nerves. I'd worried her by calling out of the blue.

"I'm sorry, Móðir. I . . . I didn't know what else to do."

Her frown returned and she peered out at me, eyes searching. "You never need to apologize for calling me. What's got you worried about mates?" Then her eyes lit up, excited by the possibility. "Have you met someone?"

Swallowing through a throat tight with nerves, I tried to put my thoughts together into some form of coherence. But I also didn't want to give her false hope that I'd bring home a daughter-in-law either.

"I'm just curious . . ."

She raised a brow, not buying my bullshit anymore now than she had when I'd been little. "Curious. About how to know when someone is your mate. Well, for your father and I, we knew immediately. Not that it was easy. Recognizing you've found your mate is only the first step. Earning your place beside them is something else entirely."

"So there was no doubt?"

"No. Our eyes met, and something in our souls shouted 'mine.' But it took us a while to get from there to where we are now. For Odin's sake, he wouldn't even be tempted when I walked out in only a—"

3

I held up a hand. "Okay, that's enough detail. I don't need to know more about . . . that."

"The point is, once we found each other, even before we came together, we couldn't be parted."

"What would have happened if you were?"

She laughed, long and loud, wiping a tear from her eye when she finally caught her breath. "That's funny. You've seen your father in the midst of one of his rages. Do you think he would have allowed that to happen? I mean, not even death kept us apart." Her eyes got dreamy and she bit her lip. "One could argue death is what brought us together. How else do you explain a ghost being brought back to life after decades only to find their soulmate?"

"Sounds like destiny."

"Exactly. And I learned to never fuck with fate. Trust me. Besides, if you found your mate, why would you *want* to be parted? True mates are a rare and wonderful gift."

Knowing I was getting dangerously close to spilling a secret I wasn't ready to share, I asked, "What if fate deigns to give someone more than one mate?"

She was quiet for a second, and my heart beat frantically as I waited—with no little dread—for her answer. "I've never seen it, but your father once explained to me his ancestors' belief about the soul. How it can split into many parts only to come back later. Perhaps twin flames are not the only kind. Fire spreads and burns. Why couldn't a soul have more than one mate?"

*Is that what I am? A missing part of her soul? Are all of us? What are the odds Sunday would find her mates at the same time in the same place? What does fate have in store for her that requires more than one?*

"Alek? You've gone quiet, minn son."

4

I shook my head to clear the troubled musings. This was more than I bargained for. "It's a path I hadn't considered."

"We are rarely prepared when fate comes calling. All we can do is adapt. Just look at your father. He threw every plan he had aside the second his soul recognized mine. And when our bond was threatened, he fought a seemingly unwinnable battle to save it. One does not walk away from the promise of true love, Alek. Rather, we do anything in our power to keep it. Remember that, perhaps it will lighten those heavy thoughts of yours."

I didn't know how to respond. Instead of telling me I was making a mistake, she'd only reaffirmed my instinct. Sunday was my mate. She was the other half of my soul, and I was one of the missing pieces to hers.

And now that I've found her, how am I supposed to walk away when my time in this world is up?

If my mother was right and this *is* fate, then the answer is I won't.

Not by choice.

~

*Present day*

USUALLY THE SIGHT of my homeland brought with it a wave of peace. Not today. The blinding snow, early morning sun, and chilly air only served to emphasize that I was no longer in England with Sunny.

Just the thought of not being beside her sent panic roaring through my veins. I shouldn't have left. It wasn't too late. If I could get back through the portal . . .

"Peace, son."

I spun out of my father's grip, glaring at him with an anger that was not borne out of my emotions. At least not entirely. It felt like a creature had been set loose, and it was his anger, his need for blood, that was driving me.

"Should we remove his restraints? He seems calm," my uncle Finley said, his eyes filled with apology as his gaze swept over the shackles on my wrists.

"No. Not yet. You know how the bloodlust can be. We need to be sure before we set him free."

"I'm fine. Let me go." Even as I said the words, I knew they were a lie. I was anything but fine, but if they let me free, I might be able to get back.

The portal continued to shimmer beside me, a beam of moonlight shining down on a fuzzy figure I knew to be Sunday. Every cell in my body urged me to go to her. To protect her.

I took a step toward the opening between realms.

My father, the bastard, tracked my move.

"Close it," he ordered.

"No!" I roared, taking another step. But the portal was already closing. "Sunday!"

"Sorry, mate," my uncle said. "There's nothing for it."

I rounded on him, chest heaving. "You fucking asshole."

"Run." The word was a harsh growl from my father. Not directed at me. "Now."

My uncle shook his head. "One day I'll learn to stay away from berserkers." Then he opened himself another portal and disappeared. Likely knowing he'd never be able to outrun me.

"Coward," I spat.

"Aleksandr, be calm. This is right and safe for all of you."

The final shimmers of the portal faded, and a searing pain snapped through me, deep into my chest, leaving behind a cold and hollow chasm. She was gone. Taken from me by my own flesh and blood. Fury burned in the pit that remained where my heart should have been.

Violence was the only language I knew.

Where my father, my hero, had once stood was now only an enemy. My muscles rippled, swelling in a now-familiar sensation as my beast took hold. The shackles they'd foolishly thought would contain me broke with a quick twist of my wrists, falling away silently into the freshly fallen snow.

"What have you done?" I threw myself at him, my fists aimed at his face.

He caught both with his open palms, stopping me with a strength that surpassed my own. "Alek . . . you don't want to do this."

"Yes, I fucking do."

I lashed out with my leg next, trying to sweep his feet out from under him. It was only because he was distracted trying to restrain me that I caught him off guard and knocked him flat on his back.

He grunted, black bleeding into his irises, snuffing out the icy blue. "Stop this."

I growled, low and deep, beyond speech. I jumped on him, cocking back my arm and preparing to smash my fist straight into his jaw.

"I said stop. This." With a mighty roar, my father launched me into the air, using the force of his powerful arms and legs combined. I flew back and slammed into a tree, hard enough it may have hurt if I wasn't so energized by rage and pain.

The crack of the tree echoed through the forest, sending

birds flying through the morning sky, fearing the disturbance, knowing better than to stay. Monsters lived in these woods.

Today, that monster was me.

I pushed myself up, the metallic tang of blood filling my mouth. I wiped a hand across my lips, and it came away crimson. The sight of it only made my need to destroy stronger. I spat out a mouthful, the red drops profane against the purity of the snow.

A boulder the size of a small car sat to my left. Without stopping to consider whether it was even possible, I grasped it, muscles shaking not with strain but barely suppressed fury as I hefted it up out of the frozen earth.

"Alek . . ."

But I didn't care for my father's warning. He was the reason my bond had been severed. He stole my mate from me, and now he had to die.

I hurled the stone straight at him.

A look of unmitigated rage crossed his face. His eyes bottomless pools of black as he bared his teeth and snarled. Without blinking, he caught the massive rock and tossed it back to the ground as if it was no more than an inconvenience. "It's not nice to throw things."

The earth shook even as the stone sank into the ground. "You took everything from me."

"You are a child throwing a tantrum. I will not speak with you until you learn some control."

"Then this is the last time we will speak, old man."

Pain lanced my father's features. "Then you leave me no choice."

Before I could even register his next move, he raised a hand up to the heavens. The cloudless sky turned black as pitch a second before thunder rumbled in the distance.

The flash in his eye was my only warning before the bolt of lightning came down, forking before touching his hand and coming straight for me. All I knew was pain, then darkness, and finally . . . relief.

# CHAPTER
# TWO
SUNDAY

**T**ears tracked down my cheeks as I watched Alek step through the portal. In the blink of an eye, it disappeared, as though he had never existed, as though he hadn't taken a piece of me with him. Grief and anger swelled, breaking me open until I was nothing but a tempest of white-hot fury.

I raged, thrashing in Caleb's hold as I tried to chase after Alek, even knowing it was too late. He was gone. Somewhere I couldn't follow.

The emptiness was unbearable.

"*A stor*, you need to calm down."

"No, you just let them take him."

Wrath boiled to the surface, and before I could stop myself, I slapped him. Needing someone else to hurt the way I was hurting. Needing an outlet for this all-consuming rage.

I'd never been so furious in my entire life.

Caleb staggered back, but even seeing the pink imprint of my hand on his cheek wasn't enough to satisfy the beast in me. With a scream of primal fury, I spun around, eyeing the pile of demon bits on the ground. Still shrieking, I grabbed a dripping torso and hurled it blindly. Nothing helped.

I reached for another piece of demon, but a hand with the strength of iron shackles caught me around the wrist and yanked, pulling me roughly into a hard chest. The scent of incense met my nose. Caleb.

His hands lifted, cradling my face.

"Look at me, *a stor*."

My ruined tattoo ached from where Chad had dragged the dagger through it. The connection I felt with Alek was gone, broken, severed. The uncontrollable urge to destroy the world around me had my body on edge, the lust for blood and revenge making my limbs shake.

"I said, look at me."

My gaze found Caleb's, and I fell into the drowning pools of his sapphire-blue irises. Calm bled through me as the fury burning in my veins evaporated. We didn't speak. I couldn't. All I knew was the pure peace of being held by Caleb's power.

"What the bloody hell is going on? I've heard of raining cats and dogs, but I draw the line at body parts." Noah's voice broke the suspended moment, calling my attention back to the chaos around me and the spot where he burst through the brush. His gaze locked on mine and immediately turned serious. "What's happened? I smell your blood, but it looks as though they've been dealt with."

"They have," Kingston answered, coming to my side. "Are you all right, Sunshine?"

"No. Of course I'm not fucking all right. They took him away from me."

Kingston scrubbed a hand over the back of his neck, bruises already forming around his throat. "Maybe they were right to. You saw how out of control he was. He didn't even recognize me, Sunshine. The look in his eyes . . . fuck, I thought it was lights out for me."

I swallowed, knowing he had a point, but I was too pissed to care.

"We have to go get him. He can't be gone. Help me find a way to Novasgard." I turned back to Caleb. "You know a way, don't you?"

He nodded. "Aye, I know of a gateway, but even if you could open it, you can't go after him."

"Yes, I fucking can."

"No, *a stor*, he left willingly. You can't bring him back if he doesn't want to be here."

And that was when it really hit me. He hadn't been taken by his father against his will. Alek had walked through that portal and left me by his own choice. He *left* me.

All the desperation to go after him disappeared, replaced by a soul-weary ache.

"What did I miss?" Noah asked, looking between us, a deep crease forming between his brows.

"Alek turned into a berserker," Caleb said. "We haven't figured out what set him off yet."

"Fucking Chad," I spat. "He planned to sacrifice me."

"Why the bloody hell would he do that?" Noah's outrage was impossible to miss as it twisted his features.

"He wanted to take my place as Alpha."

"Bastard," Noah snarled.

"He got what he deserved," I said, violence lending my voice a sharp edge. I couldn't seem to get a rein on my emotions; I was too raw. Everything was at a ten.

Kingston's hands ran over my arms and down to my hips as though he was checking me for additional injuries.

13

Then his palm rested lightly on my lower belly as he locked eyes with me, silently asking, '*Are both of you okay?*'

Caleb sucked in a sharp breath, clearly aware of what Kingston was doing. Noah, ever observant, noticed as well.

"What's going on?" Noah's voice was low and controlled.

So much for keeping things secret for now. Alek's semi-willing capture changed everything. My men needed—deserved—to know. Especially since I was planning on going after Alek while growing one of their babies inside of me. They were going to have some feelings about that. But they needed to understand why it wasn't going to sway me. And before long, they'd both sense the changes in my body.

I may not have a way to Novasgard yet, but if that blond asshole thought he could just steal one of my mates without repercussions, he was seriously mistaken. I'd tear a hole in the universe if it meant I could bring Alek back.

"Dove. What are you keeping from me?"

His question hit me like a shock from a live wire. It brought me back from the edge of fury. I locked gazes with him, his molten amber eyes making me all at once calm and terrified. The sensation had me reeling. Nausea rolled through me, but I swallowed it down.

Kingston's arms tightened on me, and he nuzzled into my neck, whispering against my skin, "It's all right, baby. I'm right here. You're not in this alone."

Gulping, I glanced between Caleb and Noah, anxiety tightening around my heart like a fist. "I'm pregnant."

"*We're* pregnant," Kingston corrected.

"Oh? Are *you* growing the tiny human?"

"Wolf."

I shook my head. Leave it to Kingston to choose this moment to throw down the gauntlet. I had to admit it made me feel better, that sliver of normalcy. Especially when my eyes returned to my vampires. Neither had so much as blinked. Caleb stared at me with a tortured expression, as though he already knew, and Noah looked like he was about to be sick.

Great.

I stepped forward, reaching for Noah, but he flinched away. "Noah."

"I . . . Sunday . . . fucking hell, this can't . . . You . . ." His panicked eyes stared into mine. "It can't be mine."

All the air left my lungs, those four words breaking something inside me. I knew not all of them would take the news as gleefully as Kingston had, but a part of me hoped they'd at least be okay with it. But actively rejecting our baby? That was pretty much the worst-case scenario.

"So you can fuck her but not take responsibility for what comes next? You fucking coward. Can't you see this isn't what she needs from you?" Kingston's low growl rumbled through my body.

"Jesus, Mary, and Joseph, what a fecking disaster."

"She was supposed to be protected. She took suppressants." Every word that left Noah's lips sent accusation flying toward me.

"I did. And if you were that worried about knocking me up, maybe you should have used a goddamn rubber." I couldn't look at him right now; it hurt too much. So I turned to my confessor, steeling myself in case I found nothing but contempt staring back at me. "Caleb?"

"What have we done?"

"Keep it together, Priest. It's not like you fathered the kid."

I stiffened in Kingston's arms.

"You didn't tell him?" Caleb asked.

"You told me not to." I hated the tremor in my voice, the tears blurring my vision. They'd just shattered me more thoroughly than I thought they ever could. I hadn't realized how much I wanted their acceptance and support until they'd denied me.

Kingston's hold tightened around me as my words landed. "Fuck you both. She deserves so much more than this from you. She's not your little cocksleeve to use and throw away when you're done with her."

It wasn't exactly a bouquet of roses, but it was right there among the most romantic gestures I'd ever experienced. Especially coming from Kingston. He'd promised me I could always count on him, that he would never walk away from me, and he was proving it right here and now.

"You don't understand the implications," Caleb said. "This is so much bigger than the five of us."

"Abomination," Noah whispered, his complexion sallow, eyes haunted. That single word sent a chill down my spine.

A protective growl escaped Kingston, one I'd never heard from him before. "Our baby isn't an abomination. Say it again, and you won't have a tongue when I'm through with you." Before any of us had a chance to respond, Kingston scooped me up into his arms. "Come on, Sunshine. You don't need those two spineless fucks. You know I'm all in. And we already know it's my pup you're carrying. Let them tuck tail and run. I'll never let you down. I know what it fucking means to be a mate. And once we get the Viking back, you know he'll be right there beside you too. They're lucky he's not here now. He'd have torn them to shreds for that bullshit they're spewing."

He might have been speaking to me, but his words were aimed at the two vampires behind us.

"Sunday, wait. I—" Noah called after us, but I just shook my head and buried my face in Kingston's warm chest.

"Too little, too late, leech. From now on, consider yourself relieved of duty. We don't need you. Any of you."

I couldn't respond. It was too painful, and I was busy fighting against the tears clawing at my throat. But Kingston held me together, kept me from falling to pieces. He pressed a kiss to my temple and whispered, "I've got you, baby. I'll take care of you. Always."

# CHAPTER
# THREE
## THORNE

This was wrong. Everything about it. I couldn't let her leave thinking I was angry with her for what we'd done. My fingers twitched as I tensed, ready to blur to her side, but a strong hand landed on my shoulder, anchoring me.

"Leave her be. You and I have other matters to discuss." Something in Caleb's cool voice stopped me.

"I can't just let her think I abandoned her."

"You know what happens to hybrid babes. To their mothers."

I did. That's what had me so upset. If I'd done this to her, if I was the reason her life was now at risk . . . I'd never forgive myself. I could survive a lot of things, but not losing her.

"We need to make a plan."

I snorted. "It's bloody late for that. She's already pregnant. The odds of it being one of ours . . ."

"It can't be mine."

"Why?"

"Because . . . fecking hell, I don't know why. I've already

ruined her, desecrated her. I can't have done this to her as well."

My lip curled up in a cruel smile. "Denial won't save you now, Father."

"It won't save you either, Blackthorne."

"I guess I'll see you in hell then."

Caleb bared his teeth at me. "Aren't we already there?"

I raked my hands through my hair. "I can't believe we were so reckless. How did this even happen?"

He raised a mocking brow. "Given the state she's in and your eager participation, I don't think you require my help explaining it to you."

"But she was on suppressants. She wasn't even in her fertile period when we were together, for Christ's sake."

"Do not take the Lord's name in vain."

"Oh, spare me your judgment, Priest. You, of all creatures, don't get to sit atop a self-righteous high horse when you stuck your cock in her the same as the rest of us. Except I haven't broken any vows by loving her. You can't say the same."

Caleb's eyes tightened. It was his only outward reaction to my spiteful words, but I knew they cut deep. "Your youth is showing, Blackthorne."

"What the fuck is that supposed to mean?"

"I mistakenly believed you meant it when you said you loved Sunday and would want to work together to find a way to save her. But apparently you care more about throwing a tantrum than you do taking responsibility for your part in this mess." He turned and started walking away.

"Where the fuck are you going?"

He answered without looking at me. "Someone around

here has to be an adult. Since you seem incapable of it, I guess that leaves me."

I flipped him off. Childish? Perhaps. But it felt bloody good.

"Good riddance," I muttered, taking two steps in the direction Kingston and Sunday had gone before coming to a halt.

*Abomination.*

I shuddered. I may not care for the self-righteous prick, but he was right about one thing. Hybrid births were problematic for a myriad of reasons. Not the least of which was their low survival rate and the havoc they played on their mother's bodies. And I was already in enough trouble with the Council. If they found out about the babe . . .

My hands balled into fists.

Even if the child survived, the Council had been hunting them down and killing them for centuries. Rarely did they grant clemency. My aunt Briar was one such exception, and that was only because she'd been turned, not born.

Fear formed an icy pit in my stomach. If anything happened to Sunday because of me . . . I didn't know what I'd do. I couldn't even meet the sun and end it all because of the blood running through my veins. I was as near to immortal as it got. Perhaps I could get Kingston to do the job; he'd seemed eager enough. He'd probably rejoice if given the opportunity to kill me. Not that I blamed him. I'd do the same if someone hurt her the way I had.

The look on her face when I'd reacted to the news would forever be burned into my mind. I'd crushed her, unintentionally. But the instant the word pregnant was uttered, all I saw was Death riding in on his pale white steed. Coming for her.

Because of me.

If I'd known there was a chance of getting her pregnant, I would have taken every precaution available to me. But I'd checked. She hadn't been fertile. A small voice whispered in the back of my mind. *Perhaps it isn't yours.*

But the sick, slithering feeling in my belly refused to latch onto the hope. I'd known I was going to kill her from the moment I first laid eyes on her. I just hadn't planned on doing it this way. I'd been a fool to think I could have her and keep her. The stars weren't on our side, proven only by the events leading up to this moment. Nothing had worked out in our favor yet; why would they start now?

There was only one person I could think of who might know how I could save her. I couldn't think about the child. My priority was my mate. She could have more children, but I would never have another Sunday.

My hands shook so fiercely I struggled to dial Lucas on my phone. I finally managed after the third attempt. As I stood in the moonlit woods, surrounded by entrails and blood-soaked dirt, I waited for him to answer.

"Nephew, this is an unexpected surprise," my uncle said, his voice not holding his usual sarcastic bite.

"I . . ." I had to clear my throat to get through the anxiety tightening everything in me. "I've killed her."

"Already?"

"Oh, sod off. This isn't a joking matter. Sunday's pregnant."

"That's my boy. Virile and unstoppable. Your father will be glad someone is carrying on the Blackthorne name."

My uncle's lackadaisical manner was both infuriating and calming. This was Lucas's way. And while I appreciated it on most occasions, I really needed him to be serious right now. This was a literal matter of life or death.

"I think you're missing the point. Sunday's a wolf. I'm a vampire. Any child of ours is doomed."

"Oh, nephew, I'm so sorry. I forgot she was a shifter."

Unbridled emotion hit me like a stake straight to the heart. The thickness in my throat grew unbearable as tears swam in my eyes. I was going to lose any hold I had on my control right here and now.

"I can't lose her. She can't die. Tell me she's going to be all right, Lucas."

My uncle's voice was far gentler than I'd ever heard. "I can't promise you that. But we will do everything in our power to save them both. When the time comes, bring her to us. We will help her through it."

"If she dies . . . I won't be far behind." Even if I had to beg Kingston to kill me, I'd follow her into the next life.

"She wouldn't want that, not if she's your true mate."

"I don't care. Don't pretend you wouldn't do the same if it was Briar on the line."

"What if the baby survives? Don't you want to be there to raise your child?"

"I want it all. Desperately. Nothing would make me happier than building a family with Sunday, but not at the cost of her life." This should be a time for celebrating. Instead things were strained and her life was in danger.

"I lost Briar once to death. All I could think about was the time I wasted not being with her. I would have given anything to have those moments I let slip through my fingers. Don't be a stupid git because you're afraid."

"You're right. Thank you, Uncle."

"Anytime. I'm always here if you need me."

I hung up, not really feeling much better as his words tumbled through my brain. Was fear enough of a reason to be separating myself from her right now? Could I live with myself if something happened and I'd wasted the time we could have had? Would I survive if I started to care about the baby only to lose it? To lose them both?

In another life, I would have been proud to have filled her with my child. Even now, knowing she was at risk, the thought of her belly swelling as the baby grew safely in her womb sent a wash of pure male pride through me.

I couldn't get too attached to the baby. Not while working to find a way to save them. But I wouldn't abandon Sunday. That's all I seemed to do when things were hard. Run. I wouldn't do it again. She deserved better than that.

I was her mate. It was time to start acting like it.

It was time to prove I'd do anything to save her.

# CHAPTER
# FOUR
## SUNDAY

*Two Days Without Alek*

Moira linked arms with me as we rushed out of our last class of the semester. We saved the worst for last . . . theology with Caleb. If it was awkward attending class with my professor before he possibly knocked me up, it was absolutely unbearable now. Especially after the way he reacted to my pregnancy. He was always my dark knight, my protector, even though we couldn't be together in public. I hadn't expected him to jump for joy, but I also, deep in my heart, never thought he'd turn cold.

In one terrible night, I'd been abandoned by three of my mates. Maybe not in the same way, but it was abandonment all the same.

Even though I had Kingston, my heart ached for everything that was missing. Instinct still screamed for me to find Alek, bring him home to me, make him see what a mistake he'd made. But the truth was, he didn't want to be here. Whatever his reasons were, it had been his choice to go.

I refused to let my thoughts continue to dwell on any of my other mates. Kingston was safe territory; they were definitely not. Maybe I'd been wrong to put my faith in them.

"Brr, it's colder than a witch's tit out here," I grumbled, shivering dramatically as Moira cuddled into me.

She cupped her breast. "Can confirm. It is, in fact, colder than a witch's tit. In case you were wondering."

I couldn't help but laugh. "Sounds like a personal problem."

She shrugged. "Ash doesn't complain."

"Are you excited to go home and see her during the break?"

A little of the light left Moira's eyes. "It's harder to see her when she's home. Her parents make things uncomfortable."

"You're welcome to join Kingston and me with his family."

"So you're really doing that, then?"

"Where else would I go? The headmistress is locking down the campus for a magical cleansing, and I sure as shit don't want to go back to my pack and spend the holiday by myself."

"You don't think things will be different now that you can shift? Well, maybe not at the moment with the no shifting while pregnant thing, but you know, in general."

"I'm sure they will be, but I don't want to be surrounded by people who refused to love me when I was at my lowest. I'd rather spend time with the people, or at least one of the people, who always accepted me as I was."

My belly fluttered with nerves at the thought of going

to the Farrell estate. The last time I'd seen Kingston's parents, I'd rejected their son. I was hardly daughter-in-law of the year material. And bonus, I was showing up with a bun in the oven that may or may not be his.

Moira gave me the sweetest hug before releasing me and staring into my eyes. "Thanks for the offer but, I'll pass. I do *not* want to be the third wheel in that particular sandwich."

I opened my mouth to correct her metaphor, but gave it up. Not worth it.

Warm arms wrapped around me from behind, the earthy scent of Kingston washing over me and immediately soothing something deep inside my soul. "Mmm, you look better than you did when you left this morning, Sunshine. You're fucking glowing."

"That's frostbite," I snarked. "It's fucking freezing out here."

Kingston's chest rumbled against my back. "Guess that means I should get you home and underneath me, I mean, a blanket. There's a reason wolves are pack animals. We keep each other warm."

"I swear to the goddess, if I have to hear you talk about puppy piles one more time, I'm going to hurl."

"Don't get jealous, Belladonna. You could always be my little spoon," I teased.

"Bitch, I'm the big spoon, and you know it."

"*I'm* the big spoon." Kingston nuzzled my neck and then scraped his teeth over my mark, making me suck in a sharp breath as need careened through me.

"Technically, Alek is the biggest spoon." As soon as his name left my lips, my smile vanished.

Look at that. I'd gone a whole five minutes without thinking about Noah, Caleb, or . . . Alek. The slowly healing wound I could feel but not see around my heart broke open again. I knew it was impossible, but I wished there was some way to contact Alek, even if only so I could be sure he was okay.

As though summoned by my thoughts, I felt it the second Noah's gaze landed on me. My traitorous body responded, the hair on the back of my neck lifting and my heart picking up speed. Instead of giving in to the keening need begging me to look at him, I turned the other way.

"Dove . . ."

"Fuck off, knobhead. She doesn't want to see you right now." Moira's fierceness eclipsed her size a hundred times over. And I didn't stop her, even though the bond between Noah and me begged me to acknowledge our connection.

"Nice one," Kingston said, holding up his hand for a high five.

Moira eyed his palm with distaste. "Nope."

He shrugged and wrapped his arm back around my waist.

Noah tried to catch my eye one more time. "Sunday . . . please. You don't understand—"

"You heard the witch. Fuck off. Sunday doesn't need you anymore."

I lost the battle to keep my gaze off him and finally looked up. Grief flashed in Noah's eyes as they met mine, and he hesitated for another moment before sighing and walking away.

Kingston must have felt my muscles tense up again because he spun me around in his arms and pressed a kiss to the tip of my nose. "I have a surprise for you, Sunshine."

He'd used similar means of aggressive affection to combat my melancholy every time my mind wandered to

30

my missing berserker. Or to Noah's less than enthusiastic response to my news. And Caleb's . . . Calebness.

I had to give it to the wolf—it was effective.

"You go on ahead, Sabrina. I've got this. Don't worry about leaving a light on. She won't be back tonight," he added with a cocky wink.

"What did I tell you about that nickname, Alphahole?"

"Don't be mad. You know I'm your favorite."

"Only because the others are fuck-ups or totally MIA. It's not like the bar is very high right now."

"Aw, don't be like that, Elphaba."

"If you don't knock it off with the pop culture witch references, I'm going to put an itching hex on your underwear."

"Don't you dare come near Jake. Sunday would never forgive you."

"I thought you were leaving."

"I'm trying, but you won't go away."

Moira huffed. "Fine. *I'm* leaving. Don't go and get yourself pregnant . . . oh, wait." She snickered and blew me a kiss.

"You know there are a lot of other ways I could get myself into trouble besides that."

"I know, sweetie. You've done them all. It was only a matter of time before you went for the obvious choice."

"Get out of here, Elphie." Kingston leaned close, whispering in my ear, "Close your eyes and trust me?"

I nodded as Moira grumbled and walked away from us.

"What, no broomstick?" Kingston called after her. "I thought everyone deserved a chance to fly."

Moira gave him the finger as she stomped off.

"You're really on top of those Wicked references. You a secret musical theatre nerd?"

He started humming the chorus of *Popular* as he lifted me into his hold and headed forward, walking at a steady pace. "So what if I am?"

I wrapped my arms around his neck. "Look at you. And here I thought I'd learned all your secrets."

"I just want to make you smile. Now close your eyes. You'll spoil it if you see before we get there," he growled playfully.

"I don't like surprises."

"Yes, you do."

"Not anymore."

His lips brushed my forehead. "You'll like this one. I promise."

I pursed my lips but grudgingly obeyed. Knowing Kingston, he was probably right. He'd been on a mission to keep me as happy as possible these last couple of days. I didn't think he'd risk doing anything that might have the opposite effect.

A few minutes passed before we came to a stop, the cold flakes of snow landing on my cheek picking up their pace as a storm threatened overhead. I shivered.

"Okay, Sunshine. Open your eyes."

He set me on my feet, and I stared at the old but well cared for carriage house in front of us. Confusion had my brow furrowing. "What is this?"

"Surprise. We're home." His voice held a nervous edge like he was worried I wouldn't like it. "At least for the rest of the year."

"Home?" I stepped forward onto the walkway that led to the front door. "This isn't mated pair housing. Those are apartments. This is a whole ass house."

Color tinged his cheeks, and he ran a hand along the back of his neck. "We have the leech to thank for that. He pulled some strings and forked out a lot of dough to have the contractors get this place converted for you in time."

"In time for what?"

"Your birthday. It's kind of from all of us, even though he footed the bill. The rest of us gave input on the inside— even the priest. Even though it's temporary, we wanted you to be comfortable."

Tears pricked the corners of my eyes, stinging as emotion welled and clogged my throat. "I don't know what to say."

"Say you'll stay."

"We don't need so much space anymore. It's just the two of us."

He slid his palm over my non-existent bump. "Three."

I pushed his hand away, not wanting to draw attention to my belly. Just because the guys knew didn't mean I wanted everyone else to know yet. Something in me warned that this was a secret I needed to keep as long as possible.

My heart ached that Kingston didn't correct me and say the others would be back. As much as Noah and Caleb had hurt me, I didn't want to be without them permanently. And even though I hated it, it had been Alek's choice to go with his father. Though a part of me knew the decision wouldn't have been so easy for him if he'd known about the baby. Surely when he came back he'd want to be with us. Family was everything to my Novasgardian.

*If he comes back.*

Shoving the thought away, I forced myself to smile as I gestured to the house. "Show me?"

Kingston took my hand. "I thought you'd never ask."

The instant I walked through the door, I was soothed by the familiar scents of my mates. They'd all been here.

Echoes of their distinct markers filled the space, some only a ghost, others strong and alive.

"There are four bedrooms so the others can have their own space while they sleep."

I cocked my head and stared at Kingston. "The others have to sleep in their own rooms? Where are you sleeping?"

"With you, of course."

"Cocky."

"Confident. Besides, as far as I'm concerned, they need to re-earn their place in your bed."

"And you get to decide that for me now?"

"Daddy perks."

"Oh, don't tell me we've got matching daddy kinks now."

A low hum of approval radiated from him. "I don't know. You've never called me daddy before."

Arousal punched through everything else I'd been struggling with, and this time I welcomed it. "Show me the bedroom, and maybe I'll try it."

Kingston started dragging me toward the stairs. I couldn't help but laugh. So much for my tour. We were walking so fast I was only just able to make out the completely open floor plan with its kitchen in the back and living room in the front. The space was bright, airy, and warmly lit. Definitely inviting.

"Is that . . ."

It couldn't be.

Kingston stopped only long enough to follow my gaze. When his eyes landed on the fur rug in front of the fireplace, he grinned. "Sure is. I know how much you enjoyed it. And I'm pretty sure our pup was conceived on it. Only seemed right we brought it home."

The reminder of him claiming me and giving me his

knot for the first time sent a flood of slick straight between my legs. I sucked in a sharp breath as his attention returned to me, nostrils flaring as he inhaled deeply.

"You know what? Fuck the bedroom. I say we christen this rug all over again." His voice was low and rough as his eyes burned with need. "I want you so fucking bad, Sunshine. You're wet for me. Don't try to deny it."

"I'm not. I couldn't if I wanted to. My wolf won't let me."

He grinned and leaned down to kiss me. "Good."

"How do you want me?"

The heat in his gaze melted my fucking panties. He walked toward the rug, peeling his shirt off on the way and tossing it over one of the sofas. Turning to face me, he pulled off his belt and then slowly unbuttoned and shucked his pants. He held my gaze as he dropped to his knees, his cock hard and jutting between his spread thighs. A bead of clear liquid sat at the tip, and I licked my lips instinctively.

"How about this time you tell me how you want me?" As he asked the question, he took the discarded leather belt and fashioned a binding around his wrists, pulling it tight with his teeth.

A belt could be dangerous in this situation for humans, but not when a powerful shifter used it this way. It was more symbolic of his submission than anything else. He could easily destroy the leather with one flick of his wrists.

"W-what?"

"Use me, Sunshine. Have your way with me and make me yours. Let me prove to you I'll never leave."

Once again, Kingston showed me how well he understood me and my heart. There was no hiding from him what the loss of the others was doing to me, and he was trying to put me back together in the only way he knew how.

"What do I do?"

Flashing me a wicked grin, he bowed his head, adopting a completely submissive—and absolutely mouthwatering—pose.

"Own me."

She stared down at me with hunger lighting her eyes, but a flicker of unease hid in those depths as well.

"What's wrong, Sunshine? Is the little girl afraid of the big bad wolf?"

Her lips quirked and she lifted her chin. "Me? Afraid of you? Never."

"Then prove it. Get that sexy ass over here and take what you want."

"I've never . . . I mean. I'm not sure how to do this."

"Sunday, you and your wolf have been trying to top me since day one. Now's your chance."

The sight of her teeth biting her plump bottom lip had a lightning bolt of need shooting straight to my balls. Jesus fucking Christ, if she didn't have mercy on me I was going to lose control and mount her right here. Fuck letting her take the reins.

"You really want me to take charge," she breathed.

"If you think you can. So far, you've shown me I'm the

That got to her. Unease banished. All I had to do was tell her she couldn't, and now my girl was showing up.

"Shouldn't you have a safe word or something?"

I smirked. "You really think you're going to take things further than I can handle?"

"Safety first."

I only had to think on it for a second before settling on my answer. "Lilacs."

Her expression softened, and she closed the distance between us, grasping my hair in her fist and jerking my head back before leaning down and stealing a kiss. It was over as quickly as it started, her voice exuding Alpha power when she said, "Eat me."

"Yes, Mistress. Do you want to save these clothes, or should I tear them off with my teeth?"

"Teeth. Now."

"As you wish."

I sat up on my knees and leaned forward, pressing my nose between her thighs, inhaling her fucking intoxicating scent. My cock jerked, and I swear I came just a little when my girl threaded her fingers in my hair and rocked forward.

My wolf took control, and in mere moments her clothes were ribbons on the floor. She stood over me, naked and dripping and fucking perfect.

"Good boy," she moaned as I slid my tongue along her slick folds, parting her gently before finding her swollen clit. I loved the way pregnancy made her taste. I wanted to fuck another baby into her right after this one was born. Twins next time.

With the hand fisted in my hair, she held me against her. I could feel her balance shifting, but it wasn't until her foot pressed on my shoulder I'd realized what she was doing. I hummed in approval, the change in her position opening her up so I could feast.

"Suck my clit, make me come so you can drink me down."

Goddamn, my Sunshine could talk dirty. I didn't need her to tell me twice, but I wished I hadn't bound my wrists so I could grab her by the ass and hold her still.

Using the tip of my tongue ring, I alternated between flicking it over her clit and humming, using the pressure and vibrations to send her flying over the edge, making her come hard and fast all over my tongue.

She shuddered and cried out, the sound of cracking wood above me registering but not distracting me from my goal of pleasuring her until she told me to stop.

"Enough. Fuck. Kingston." Her breathy cry of my name wasn't the most erotic thing I'd heard from her, but damn if it wasn't close.

"Did I satisfy you?" I asked, keeping my gaze trained on the floor as she backed away. I was ready for a reward for being her good slave.

When I'd started this, it had been about helping her reclaim some control, but now that we were fully in the scene, I was just as into it as she was. More, even. Who knew power exchange could be so fucking hot? The anticipation of what she'd do next and when I'd get to come had my balls aching with need.

"You did. That tongue piercing of yours is a gift. Now stop talking before I gag you."

I had to fight back a groan.

"Hmm, you know, that's not the worst idea I've ever had." She leaned down and picked up a strip of her torn fleece-lined leggings. "Did I ever tell you about the time

Father Gallagher blindfolded me and watched me make myself come?"

A low growl left me before I could stop it.

She smirked. "Jealousy looks good on you." Then she strolled around me until she stood behind my kneeling form. "He took away my sense of sight, told me what to do to myself, barely fucking touched me, then came all over my cunt."

My hips jerked, cock searching for her warm, wet sheath. I could smell her slick as she wrapped the fabric over my eyes. Fuck, it was all over the blindfold. I didn't know how I was going to last. I was a stiff breeze away from coming all over myself like a fucking teenager.

"You like how I smell, don't you, pet?"

Pet? Fuck. Yes.

"I do, baby."

She caressed my hair, giving it a sharp tug and whispering in my ear. "Call me Mistress when I'm owning you, pet."

"Yes, Mistress."

I couldn't see through the thick material covering my eyes, but holy hell, could I *feel*. Her fingers traced my mark, dancing over the skin like the wings of a butterfly. The sensation sent goosebumps across every single inch of my flesh that wasn't rock hard and straining. I leaned back in search of more, needing her body against mine, but she denied me.

"On your feet," she commanded.

It was tricky to maneuver with my hands bound and eyes blindfolded, but I did it. She rewarded me with another low, throaty purr. "Good boy. Now take two steps back."

There was a moment when my wolf balked, not liking

that it couldn't ensure we were safe, but my trust in my mate prevailed. She wouldn't ask me to do anything that would hurt or embarrass me.

The backs of my knees hit the hard chair behind me after exactly two steps.

"Sit."

I sat.

"Spread your thighs."

I spread them.

"Hands to yourself, pet. I'm going to play with you now."

I could hear the soft thud just as her hands landed on my knees, shoving my legs further apart as she settled between them. Her hair brushed my inner thighs, the tendrils feeling like the finest silk sliding across me. And when the strands slipped over my cock, I bit back a moan of pure need.

Fuuuck me. This was heaven. No, it was hell.

*Don't come. Don't come. Don't come.*

Then she took just the tip of me in her mouth and sucked. Hard.

Stars exploded behind my eyes.

"Fuck, Sunshine." My hips kicked forward in search of more.

She lightly scraped her teeth along my sensitive flesh. "Mistress," she corrected. "And if you speak again without permission, you won't get to come."

My entire body tensed in protest, my arms straining against the leather at my wrists.

"Be a good pet, Kingston, and I promise I'll take care of you. Do you trust me?"

"Yes, Mistress."

She kissed the head of my cock, her tongue darting out

to taste me. I swallowed a groan. I could picture her on her knees with my most prized body part at her disposal. A jolt went through me as her teeth caught the ring piercing my head and she tugged.

"Remember your safe word?"

"Yes, Mistress."

"You'd better use it if you need it."

I nodded just as she cupped my aching balls and squeezed while she brushed her lips over my crown. The slide of her tongue across the slit sent tingles shooting through me, collecting at the base of my shaft, swelling my fucking knot.

She purred, clearly pleased with herself. Fuck, so was I. I was so far gone, I was damn near in rut. If that happened there was no knowing what I would do.

She repeated the move, this time letting go of my balls and sliding her hand further back. My legs shook, my body breaking out in hot and cold shivers, not sure if I wanted her to stop or if I never wanted her to stop. I'd never thought about anyone touching me like this, but it was the most erotic moment of my entire fucking life.

"Stand. I want to see all of you."

I wasn't confident my knees would work for a moment, but the idea of disappointing her had me on my feet, awaiting her next command.

Her cheek brushed the side of my cock, warm and soft, and then she pressed a gentle kiss to the base. But she didn't stop there. As though she knew my every desire, she moved downward, sucking on my already tight balls one by one, taking them into her wet mouth and applying gentle pressure before letting go.

Goddammit, I needed my fucking hands. I could tear

free of my makeshift shackles easily if I wanted to, but that would make her angry. What would she do to me?

"Let's play a game."

Oh, God. I wasn't sure I could take any more teasing. "Aren't we already?" I rasped.

A firm slap against my taint had stars bursting in my vision. Pain and nearly uncontrollable pleasure hit me at the same time. Fuck, a spurt of cum had to have escaped. I swear I heard it hit the floor.

"It's like you want me to punish you. Is that it, pet?"

"No, Mistress. I . . . I want to please you."

She stroked my shaft. "You do please me. Very much."

The words had me fucking preening. Even my wolf soaked in the praise.

"You are such a good mate. So strong. So virile." She took my bound hands and pressed them against her lower belly. "Such a perfect provider for us, Daddy."

My cock jerked, desperate to fill her. I'd never been so turned on in my goddamn life. Not even when she was in heat, dripping for me, presenting and begging me to take her.

"Do you need to come?"

I nodded.

"Too bad. I'm not done playing with you yet." She moved away, and I mourned her absence. I couldn't see what she was doing, and my mind raced with possibilities. Was she grabbing toys? Was she going to spank me?

Fuck . . . did I want her to?

The mindfuck of it all was that I'd started this for her, to give her something to have complete control over, and it was fast becoming all about me. My undiscovered kinks roared to the surface.

Her footsteps came closer, the unmistakable sounds of

items shifting in a box filling my ears. "You naughty boy, I found your toy box in my bedroom. There are some very interesting things in here."

She removed my blindfold, and I blinked hard against the sudden light. Sunday's cheeks were flushed with arousal, her eyes dark and hooded as she knelt at my feet again. Glancing down at the contents of my very special toy box, she raised her brows. "My, my." She reached in and pulled out a hot pink training plug. "Did you buy this for me?"

"Yes, Mistress."

"So presumptuous."

I gulped. Not because she sounded mad, but because she was so clearly into it. The thought of sliding into her tight ass, feeling her clamping down around me like a fucking vise, had my blood racing. I had to suck in a huge lungful of air.

"And what about . . . this? He looks familiar." She lifted the life-sized replica of Jake I'd had made for her. That process was weird as fuck, but the look in her eyes made every awkward moment worth it.

"In case you missed me."

"Is that the real reason, pet?"

Fuck, she knew me so well.

"I thought it could be fun to take both your holes at the same time."

Her mouth parted, and arousal turned her whole body a rosy pink, the shock of my admission causing her to drop character. "Oh."

Shaking her head to get back into the scene, she stood. "We'll save that one for later. For now, we have something else to focus on." Trailing the tip of the plug between my pecs and down over my belly, she leaned in. "Here are the rules. If you can free yourself in three minutes or less, you get to take my ass. And if you don't . . ." She slid the plug between my legs as she pressed her lips to my mark, making me moan. "I get to take yours."

Holy fucking God.

"You have to . . . lube it first."

She bit down on my mark and nearly sent me back to my knees. "Oh, that won't be a problem." She moved away before I had a chance to speak, not that I was currently capable of forming words. Then she sat down, leaning back and spreading her legs while holding my gaze. Lifting Jake 2.0, she gave me a wicked smirk. "It is very lifelike."

She slipped it down her body, over her clit.

I had to clear my throat twice before I could tell her, "It vibrates."

Her brows lifted. "Hmm. You don't do that. Maybe I like him better."

"He's an extension of me. As long as it's me making you feel good, I don't care."

"You're talking again. Now you only have ninety seconds." Then she sank the dildo deep and let out an almighty moan as her back arched and her toes curled. "Fuck, Jake. So good."

I stood transfixed, watching as she slid the toy in and out a few times. Watching that beautiful fucking pussy stretch around it. God, I could be free of this belt any second. Could claim my place between those thighs and fuck her until she forgot her name. But . . . I kind of wanted her to win. I wanted her to claim me. To own me.

All I'd ever wanted was to be hers.

"Thirty seconds," she whispered, turning on the vibe and biting her lower lip as she angled the dick upward.

My body trembled from the force of control I used to

keep myself bound. I stared hard into her eyes, willing her to understand what I was fighting for.

Her cunt pulsed around the toy, an orgasm right there, creeping across her skin in the form of a deep flush, tight nipples, panting breaths. *Please wait for me.*

Her hand paused and she sat up, looking at me. "You're not even trying to get free. You want me to take your ass, don't you, Kingston?"

I had to swallow before I could answer, my voice tight with need. "Yes, Mistress."

She pulled Jake out and set him to the side, holding my gaze as she picked up the plug and sank it into her dripping cunt, coating it completely.

Fuck. Me.

I nodded, unable to speak.

"Give me your hands," she whispered.

She unbound me, and it took everything I had not to pull her against my body.

"Turn around and bend over."

Fuck, I was entirely at her mercy as I did what she asked of me. I heard the distinct sound of a cap being popped, then her fingers, wet with her arousal and the lube I'd stashed in the box, ran across my tight pucker. When the slick tip of the plug slipped across my taint and up to my untouched hole, I shuddered.

"You can still tell me to stop, and I will. We're not playing anymore. It's just you and me, okay?"

"Don't stop, Sunshine. I want to give you this."

She reached around and laid her hand over mine where it was fisted on the chair. With the other, she applied pressure that had me gritting my teeth. I didn't have the words to describe how good it felt. The slight sting and burn of being stretched and filled. The nearly electric buzz surged underneath my skin from the countless nerve-endings I hadn't realized were there. It felt better than I'd ever imagined.

"Almost there," she whispered.

"I can take it. Keep going, baby."

She pressed it the rest of the way in, and we were both breathing hard by the time it was in place.

"You okay?"

"Fuck, yes," I growled, shifting my position a little, which caused the plug to press against something magical inside me. "Fuuuck."

"What?"

"It feels so good. God, I need to be inside you right now, Sunday. Please. I need to come."

"Sit down on the chair," she said. Her voice lacked the commanding edge she'd had earlier, but I obeyed anyway. She straddled me, her hand resting on my shoulders. "I love you, Kingston."

As she kissed me, she slid down, taking me inside her and making me moan. But when she began rocking her hips back and forth rather than bouncing on my cock, I let out a strangled cry. The plug hit me in just the right spot, sending a powerful orgasm racing up my spine.

"I'm gonna come, baby. I can't stop it."

"Yes, fuck, me too."

I gripped her hips, my fingers digging in hard enough I knew she'd be wearing bruises when we were done. I pumped into her once, twice, and I was done, my climax hitting me like a fucking freight train.

Sunday was right there with me, her warm cunt milking me of every last drop.

We were both still breathing hard when she dropped her forehead to mine. "Holy shit, that was intense."

"You're telling me."

"I didn't realize how badly I needed that. The control, I mean. It was fucking hot."

"It was."

"You liked it?"

I kissed her. "Did I not just come for days inside you? I'd say I more than liked it, Sunshine."

She smirked. "How did you know that's what I needed?"

"You're an Alpha, just like me. Control is part of who you are, and you've been floundering without it these last couple of days. So I'm prepared to give it to you even when you don't know to demand it."

Her lips ghosted over mine. "Good boy."

My cock gave a weak twitch inside her. Even after being so fully sated, my praise kink was strong. *Who fucking knew?*

"What do we do now?"

I cocked a brow. "For starters? Shower."

"And then . . ."

"And then, if you're good, maybe I'll let you do it again."

# CHAPTER
## SIX
SUNDAY

I woke gasping for breath, heart racing, unease snaking across my spine, as I had every night since Alek went away. There was no escape from that awful moment when he stepped through the portal and left me. Not while I was awake, and certainly not in my dreams where I was forced to relive it over and over. The sharp ache in my chest came to life again every time the gateway between us snapped closed in my nightmares.

Sitting straight up in the massive bed, I reached for Kingston, desperate for his warm, comforting arms. Instead I found nothing but sheets and an empty pillow. After our shower, he'd tucked me into bed and held me until I went to sleep. Where was he now?

A vague memory flitted through my mind, Kingston leaving the comfort of our little nest, pressing a tender kiss to my temple and whispering, "I'll be back by morning, baby. I'm going to run with Derek. My wolf needs to stretch his legs."

I'd mumbled something in reply and fallen back into the deep sleep of someone who'd been well loved and well used. I was safe. He had me. So whatever had me clutching my sheet to my chest and sent adrenaline coursing through my veins had to be bad . . . right? I'd learned even when it seemed good, it probably wasn't.

A soft rustling noise from the dark corner at the other end of my room had my pulse resuming its frantic pounding. I grabbed the nearest thing to me—Jake—and sent it flying in the direction of the disturbance.

"Fecking hell, Sunday. Do you regularly accost people with sex toys?"

"Caleb?"

"Well, it bloody isn't Father Christmas now, is it?"

Startled laughter left my lips, though it took my heart several seconds to return to a normal tempo. "You definitely don't have the right frame to be Santa. When you laugh, do you say *ho, ho, ho*?"

He was mostly in shadow, but I could just make out his mouth as it twitched in the ghost of a grin. "No, I do not."

"That's right. Because you don't laugh. You scold and scowl."

"I laugh."

I quirked a brow. "Sure you do. When you're torturing people in that dungeon of yours."

"The only person I torture in my *dungeon* is me."

Interesting. Was my priest a sadist *and* a masochist? As I mulled over the thought, quiet stretched between us, intruding on our playful banter and bringing reality back into harsh focus.

I shivered, my voice tight with the heartache I was trying to hide. "Why are you here, Caleb? You've been cold as ice. I figured you were done with whatever this toxic thing is between us."

"It's my nature to want things that are bad for me."

"So I *am* bad for you."

He sighed, the rustle of fabric reaching my ears as he moved. "You're my responsibility. I wasn't about to leave you unprotected while Kingston went running in the moonlight. Just because one threat has been dealt with doesn't mean there aren't others."

I needed to see him better, try to read his expression. Reaching for the bedside lamp, I had only just touched the switch when he stopped me with a firm, "Don't."

"But I can't see you."

"I can see you just fine."

I pouted and dropped the sheet, baring my breasts and provoking him.

He stood, his tall shadowed form closing the distance between the chair in the corner and the edge of my bed. It hurt a little to finally make out his heartbreakingly hand-some face. Torment was written all over him as he sat on the far end of the bed. Of course he chose to be as far from me as he could.

I was still angry with him, but honestly, his reaction to my pregnancy was predictable. Maybe it wasn't what I'd hoped for, but after some reflection and distance, it wasn't exactly a surprise either. Caleb didn't want to be with me because of his vows, his devotion to God. I couldn't hold it against him. We were only together once, and that was due to my heat, not his undeniable need to be mine. He'd helped me through it, and I'd been stupid enough to fall in love. It wasn't his fault.

Okay, maybe it was, just a little. But still, he hadn't made me any promises, not like the others. If anyone was owed an apology here, it was probably him.

"Caleb . . . I'm—"

"You should go back to sleep. It's late and you need

rest." His gaze dropped to my belly, brows furrowing and focus intense.

I curled a hand protectively over my stomach, feeling oddly defensive. "It's too early for me to start showing. It'll be months before you know anyone's growing in there."

"I was checking for a heartbeat."

My heart fluttered. There wasn't a shred of anger or disgust in his voice. It was far too gentle for that. "I don't think we'll be able to detect one for a few more weeks."

"I'm a vampire. The second it starts, I will know. Already I can sense the spark of life inside you. Do you know how rare it is for a made vampire to father a child?"

I shook my head.

"It only happens once in a blue moon."

"So why have you been so angry with me? It probably isn't yours."

He lifted his gaze, staring deep into my eyes. "Because I want it to be."

"Caleb—"

"I can never give you what the others can. There's no future for us, Sunday. Even if the babe is mine, I can't be any kind of true father. Or partner to you, for that matter. So why pretend otherwise? It will only hurt us both."

"Why can't you?"

His eyes widened as he sat there with his mouth slightly open, as though a reason was on the tip of his tongue but he couldn't force the words out. After a long moment stretched between us, he shrugged helplessly. "So many reasons, chiefly among them the fact that I am your professor. Whether you're an adult or not, I'm still abusing my position of authority."

"I don't care that you're my professor. I like it."

"I won't put your reputation and future at risk simply because I have so little control. You deserve more."

"Well, I won't be your student forever. And now that I'm pregnant, those days are seriously numbered as it is. So if that's the main reason, you won't be able to cling to it for long."

"There are more. None of which I care to discuss. I'm tired of meditating on my failings."

"So why are you here then, Caleb, if you want nothing to do with me? With us."

"Don't you understand? I want everything to do with you. If I were a man, I'd already have made you mine, and we'd be celebrating our growing family. Instead I'm worried every waking moment about what this means for you, for the future."

"Caleb," I whispered, his declaration making my heart squeeze. There was so much self-loathing in his voice. I don't think I'd ever met someone who hated themselves quite as much as Caleb. And I knew part of it was my fault. I wish he could see himself the way I did. That he would let me love him. I leaned forward, intent on crawling over to him. "Please don't shut me out of your life. I love—"

"Don't say it. I can't bear to hear the words from you if I can't say them back."

My throat tightened with tears. I hated that loving me caused him so much pain. "I understand why we can't be physical. I respect it. But it's not all about sex. Don't deny me our intimacy, Caleb. What we have is too important to me. I can't lose it. I can't lose *you*."

"I will come here and watch over what's mine. My protection is all I can offer you. I ruin everything I touch. So I will watch and guard from a distance. It's the only way I can keep you safe."

"That's fine. The chair won't move from that corner if that's what you want."

One brow rose. "Who do you think picked out that bloody chair?"

"Really?"

"Aye, *a stor*. Try as I might, I can't be apart from you, even if it hurts. I may not be able to be with you, but I am still yours."

I didn't realize how badly I needed to hear him say that out loud. Warmth curled through me, filling me, if not with happiness, at least with contentment. "You don't have to stay in that corner, you know. Lie here with me, Caleb. Just until I fall asleep."

A flicker of indecision crossed his features, sending a flurry of fear settling in my heart.

"Please take care of me, Daddy."

His only response was a tortured groan before he crawled up to where I sat and wrapped me in his arms, curling his powerful body around my back. "You'll be my damnation, Sunday Fallon."

"I'm sorry."

He pressed his lips to my temple. "Don't be. Don't ever apologize for what you are to me."

"Tell me more about what our life would be like if you'd met me when you were human."

"Are you asking me to tell you a bedtime story?"

"Isn't that what good girls get?"

"I suppose it is. What kind of story would my good girl like?"

"Tell me a fairy tale where we get a happily ever after."

We lay back together, him spooning me, his lips brushing my ear. But it was the way his palm cupped my belly and his other arm held me close that kept me feeling whole and safe.

"Once upon a time, in a faraway land filled with faeries and all manner of wee beasties . . ."

I giggled and snuggled deeper. "I think I'm going to like this story."

"Hush now, or I'll cease my telling of it."

"No, don't stop. I love your voice."

"Mmm, do you now? That's good to know. So, as I was saying before I was so rudely interrupted, there lived a carpenter's son in a small village protected by the fae who lived on the outskirts of the land. To show their gratitude, the villagers held a summer festival every year in honor of the brave fae who kept them safe. As the fair maidens of the town danced together in the square, the carpenter's son's eyes locked with the most beautiful of them all. Time stopped as they gazed into each other's souls right then and there. He had never seen her before, as until now, she'd been kept away by her cruel grandfather. But he knew, from this moment on, he'd never want to be parted from her."

My chest ached from the sweetness in his words and the honesty layered in with the fantasy. I couldn't help but join in, wanting to give him back some of the comfort he was giving to me.

"And when the maiden set eyes on the carpenter's son, she knew he was the one she'd been waiting for. The one who would save her from her sad and lonely life. The one to love her for the rest of her days."

"Aye, that he was. Now let me tell my story."

The gentle scrape of his teeth across the sensitive flesh just under my ear sent a shiver skating across my skin. "Okay. Continue."

"At the first moment he could, the carpenter's son stole

away with the maiden, taking her to a place they wouldn't be discovered. The faerie glen. He took her in his arms and kissed her under the stars, promising himself to her for all of eternity if only she'd have him."

I sighed happily, my eyelids growing heavy as he spoke. "This is my favorite story."

"Mine too, *a stor*." He pressed a kiss to my jaw.

"And then what?"

"The fae were so moved by the lovers, they blessed them with a place in their land, life eternal, and a lifetime filled with nothing but love."

"So they lived happily ever after?"

"Aye, they did. Forever. As they were meant to."

Tears misted my eyes, but I refused to let him know his tale made me cry in case he'd use it as a reason not to share it again. "Will you come back tomorrow and tell me our love story again?"

He chuckled, his chest rumbling against my back. "I'll recite it for us both as often as you'd like, darling."

"Stay until I fall asleep?"

"Of course. Now close your eyes."

I did as he told me, drifting off quickly with visions of his fairy tale dancing behind my eyelids.

# CHAPTER
## SEVEN
### ALEK

Sweat dripped down my spine, working its way toward my hairline due to my inverted position. Regular push-ups had lost their usefulness a long time ago. I preferred the challenge of doing them while in a handstand. It didn't just add extra body weight; it forced me to be completely in control of my balance and my body. And the focus was something I needed right now. Otherwise I'd start to spiral.

Again.

Out of the corner of my eye, I caught sight of a figure standing on the outside of the spelled glass barrier that kept me from breaking out of this prison. I closed my eyes and worked myself back to a standing position before facing the man who was my mirror image. I knew it was Tor before I'd even gotten a good look at him. Twins could sense these sorts of things.

"Nice ink. But I always thought the days of the week were supposed to be stitched into your underpants. What's so special about Sunday, anyway?"

I didn't want to share Sunny with him. She was mine. I

growled low in my throat, hands fisting at my sides. "Fuck off."

"Oh, he's snarly this evening. You'd think a day of being in time out would have done something about that tantrum you're throwing."

"Release me, and I'll take this *tantrum* out on your stupid face."

Tor grinned. "You mean your face?"

My brother stood there, a tray of food in his hands.

"If you're here to feed me, do it. If you're here to taunt me, shut the fuck up."

He raised one eyebrow before lifting a drumstick to his lips and taking a big bite, letting out an obscene moan. "Mother really outdid herself tonight."

"You're an arsehole."

"I'm not the one who tried to kill Father with a boulder."

"I wasn't trying to kill him . . . just maim him a little," I muttered.

"You don't maim anyone with a two-ton rock. You obliterate them." He leaned against the glass, not even looking at me as he continued to devour my meal.

"He's a berserker. He would have been fine."

"Word on the harbor is so are you."

"Jealous, brother? I finally have something you don't."

"Perhaps if you hadn't stolen my place, you wouldn't be locked up right now, and I would be the one blessed by Odin."

He thought this was a blessing? I was caged like an animal, cut off from my mate, a risk to everyone around me.

Even my own parents didn't want me near them. This was far from a blessing.

"You don't know a fucking thing," I said, disgust curling my lip.

"I know you tried to take something that didn't belong to you, and this is your punishment."

I slammed my fist into the glass between us. If it hadn't been there, I would have knocked him the fuck out.

"Temper, temper. You don't seem to be learning your lesson, twin. They won't let you out to play until you get a handle on all that anger." He stared at me, a flicker of concern dancing in his irises. "You really are one, aren't you? I see the darkness spreading in your eyes even now. What does it feel like?"

"Rage. Power. Insatiable thirst for violence and pain. Preferably yours at the moment." I knew my smile held a sharp edge.

My twin and I bickered like any siblings, more probably since we'd spent our lives trying to one-up each other. But at the end of the day, I knew he'd die for me, same as I would for him. He wasn't my enemy. No matter how much the blood thrumming through my veins told me he was.

"I wonder if I'll ever know the sensation. It seems unfair you would be the only one given this gift."

"It's not a fucking gift, you feather-headed git."

"Look at Father. He's the most powerful being I've ever known. He can defend us against any foe. You don't think it's a gift?"

I swallowed back an angry sigh. "Maybe you should ask Father what he thinks."

"Maybe I will. In the meantime, you should eat something. That's why I'm here, after all." He shoved the plate through a slot that appeared in the glass. "There's still a bit of food left."

He'd eaten all the meat, leaving a few carrots, half of a bun, and a small scoop of peas. "Great. I'm famished."

"So are you going to tell me what led to this?"

"I don't really think it's any of your business."

The truth was, I didn't actually know. How could I explain something I barely understood myself?

"Something had to have triggered it. Did someone hurt you? Did you get a bad grade on your homework?"

I glared at him. "When have I ever cared about my grades? I'm not you."

Annoyance danced in his eyes. "Tell me, brother. I'm just trying to help you. Perhaps if we understand what triggered it, we'll figure out how to help you control it. As much as I enjoy seeing you in here, I don't want you locked up forever."

Taking a deep breath, I sat on the bed and stared down at my hands. "It wasn't me who got hurt. It was *her*."

Tor leaned back against the opposite wall, arms crossed over his chest. "So it's about a girl. I should have known."

"I swore to protect her and nearly failed. She could have died because I wasn't enough. So I became more than enough. I stopped the bastard who was hurting her—crushed him into nothing more than meat. I'd do it again. I made a vow that I'd keep her safe, and when it appeared as though I'd broken it, the berserker manifested."

"What did you do, swear your vow in blood? Must have been pretty important for the gods to intervene like that."

He had no fucking idea.

"Well . . . if your berserker is tied to protecting the girl, maybe seeing her safe and whole will sate your bloodlust."

66

"Why are you so insistent on helping me? I thought you'd be glad to see me like this."

"Maybe at first, but only because you deserved it after taking my spot. But now I'd like to get my brother back."

The raw honesty cut through my anger. As much as I wanted to throttle the arse-licker, I really did love him. I gestured to my prison with a sigh. "And how do I go about visiting her when she inhabits another bloody realm?"

Tor lifted an object out of his back pocket. "With this."

He slid the thin rectangle through the same slot where he'd given me my half-eaten meal. Interest sparked inside me. A mirror. Of course.

"Might I have some privacy, brother?" I asked, holding the looking glass in my palms as though it were the most precious item in existence.

"No. Aunt Quinn doesn't know I nicked this. I'm not leaving it in here for you to tattle to her about later."

Beggars couldn't be choosers. I stepped away from the transparent barrier. He could spy on me all he liked, but that didn't mean I'd let him watch over my shoulder. My pulse pounded in my ears as adrenaline raced through my veins. I could see her. I had to see her. Make sure the others had kept her safe.

"Show me Sunny," I said as I stared at my reflection.

The smooth glass became a whirling pool of mist. I held my breath, waiting for it to clear. When it did, I nearly dropped the fucking thing.

In my wildest imaginings, I never would have pictured this. Or the way it tore me apart.

Instead of the grief-stricken mate I'd been expecting, my Sunny was curled up in bed *laughing* with that fucking priest. So much for his vows. He held her spooned against him, his lips moving as he spoke to her, a rare smile on his face.

I wasn't foolish enough to believe life would have stopped for her because I was gone. But I thought she'd at least care. That she'd miss me. But that was not the face of a woman mourning an absent lover.

She was content. Happy.

Without me.

While I was over here like some lovesick puppy, fucking dying inside, every breath without her an agony.

With a roar, I flung the mirror against the opposite wall, the sound of shattering glass welcome as fury ripped through me.

"Oh, come on! Did you really have to break it? Now we'll both never hear the end of it."

I couldn't speak. My breaths came in rapid gasps, vision blurring red at the edges.

"Odin's beard, you really have no control. I've made a huge mistake." Tor backed away from the glass as though he was afraid I'd be able to break through.

I had to get out of here. Take out anyone in my path and get back to her. Putting all my power into my stance, I shot forward shoulder first and slammed into the barrier keeping him safe from me. Nothing would stop me from getting to my mate. Not my brother, not Father, not this godsdamned cell. Over and over, I repeated the action until finally a crack spread across the clear wall.

Tor's eyes grew wide, his mouth open in shock. "I'm sorry," he whispered as I geared up to take another shot at the one thing holding me back. Then he ran.

The sight of him retreating sent my rage spiking. My target was getting away.

I screamed out my fury, tipping my face back and pouring all of my uncontrollable need for violence into it.

It wasn't enough to purge it from my system.

Spinning around, I searched for something, anything, I could use to take out my frustration. There wasn't much in the way of furniture, just a table, chair, and a bed. But they would do.

I lifted the bed, hurling it across the room with such force it cracked and broke in two. I did the same with the chair. Then the table.

And when that was done, I moved on to the pieces, not stopping until the remains resembled toothpicks.

It still wasn't enough.

So then I took my anger out on the wall, punishing it as much as I was punishing myself. Until finally, what felt like hours later, I was spent, shaking, covered in my own blood.

I curled myself into a ball, back pressed against the wall that now held numerous fist-sized craters. And in the sudden, deafening silence, I whimpered one word, infusing it with my boundless grief.

"Sunny."

# CHAPTER
# EIGHT
## SUNDAY

*One week without Alek*

The scream that tore from my throat woke me from a dead slumber. My every cell vibrated with the wrongness slithering over my skin.

"Sunday, what is it?" Caleb's concerned question helped me focus.

"Nightmare . . . I think."

"Your mother?"

"No. I haven't dreamt about her in weeks." That was odd, come to think about it. I would have much rather had one of those dreams than whatever the hell *that* had been.

Caleb's cool fingers encircled my wrist, but I jerked my arm free with a snarl.

"Don't touch me. Something is wrong. I feel . . . wrong."

"Is it the babe?" The worry in his voice cut through the unreasonable anger burning in my veins.

"No. It's . . . God, it's Alek. He's enraged."

"You can feel him?"

"I could. In my dream."

"But not now?"

"No," I forced out, the admission painful. As much as it hurt to feel him like that, it was better than not feeling him at all. "He's gone."

I closed my eyes and took a long, slow breath as I walked to the window and stared out at the moonlit sky. Wherever Alek was, he wasn't safe and happy as I'd thought. Something was threatening him.

I'd assumed he left me willingly, that he didn't want to be here. But whatever this connection had been in my sleep, the emotions roiling in him weren't those of a man at ease with his decision.

"Come here to me, darling. You're trembling." Caleb laid gentle palms on my shoulders and turned me to face him. "Saints preserve us, your eyes are black as midnight."

"What?" I pulled out of his grasp and ran for the bathroom. Flicking the switch, I blinked a few times against the blinding light that filled the space, then stared into the mirror. "Holy shit," I whispered. My irises had bled fully black, but lightning flickered in the depths, sending me reeling backward. "What's wrong with me?"

"Alek's eyes were the same. It's the berserker. How is this happening?"

"I'm not a berserker," I screeched, panic clawing at me. I already had to deal with the fact that I was probably the daughter of Satan; I really didn't want to add this to the list of Sunday is a Freakshow shit I was sorting through.

"No, I don't think you are. I think you are channeling his."

Relief cascaded over me. "What do you mean?" I asked, turning to face him.

"I noticed it the night he left."

"And you didn't think to mention it?"

"You had other matters on your mind."

Okay, fair. But still, I think berserker eyes registered as something worth discussing.

"And after?"

"We weren't exactly on speaking terms, Sunday. That doesn't mean I haven't been keeping an eye on you."

"We've been together every night for a week. Don't tell me an opportunity hasn't appeared between now and then."

"I didn't want to . . . sully things between us. We've turned a corner, you and I. Forgive me for not wanting to focus on another man while I had you near."

The unexpected sweet and surly response left me conflicted. On the one hand, I loved knowing he selfishly wanted our time together for himself. On the other, he couldn't just decide to keep important things from me.

"So I'm not turning into a berserker, but I'm still connected to him? I felt our bond weaken when that portal closed. I don't understand why this would happen."

His gaze dropped to my belly.

"You think it's his?"

"I think you have multiple mates for a reason, and there is more going on than you or I will likely ever know." He paused, seeming to weigh something before asking, "Have you ever noticed that the deeper your connection with one of your mates, the more of their strengths you take on?"

I stiffened. I had, but I didn't realize Caleb had picked up on it. "Yes, but my connection with him is broken."

"Perhaps it's not as broken as you think. Maybe it's only the distance between you making you think so."

"Am I going to start going . . . well, berserk?"

Caleb studied me for a long moment, eventually shrugging. "I can't say for sure. I'm not exactly an expert on the subject."

But we knew someone who was. Someone who'd just crossed into our realm to steal his son back.

"We need to find a way to Novasgard. I can't be left to roam around if I'm a liability. If Alek can't be trusted, I sure as hell can't. You saw what he did to Chad. I have even less control than that because I wasn't built for this."

And it gave me an excuse to go after him. One that wasn't entirely selfish. Because the second he'd stepped through that portal, all I'd wanted to do was chase after him, but he'd made his decision. He wanted to go. He *chose* to leave me. As much as it hurt, I'd tried to respect it. But now I didn't have to. I had a legitimate reason to find him.

"Am I interrupting something?" Kingston's voice covered me like a warm blanket. "You two seem like you're in the middle of solving some serious shit."

He stood in the doorway, chest bare and glistening with sweat from his nightly run with Derek. I could smell the remnants of his wolf, the wild musk of my mate. "I need to get to Alek. Something isn't right with him."

The disbelieving snort that left him had my anger bubbling under my skin. "She needs to get to the man who *left* her. You have two of us right here, one's a goddamned priest—sorry, Padre—and she still wants to find the ones who let her go." He shook his head. "Unbelievable."

"Why are you so upset? You haven't seemed mad about Alek leaving until now."

"Right, because I thought the asshole would have returned by now. I thought he'd go, handle his shit, and come back. But he hasn't. It's been a fucking week, Sunday. What the fuck is taking him so long?"

Despair replaced the rage in my heart. "I don't know. Maybe he'll never come back."

"Time moves slower in Novasgard," Caleb said as he crossed the room and positioned himself away from me. Was he afraid I'd lash out at him?

"What do you mean?" Kingston came to my side as though he sensed I needed him.

"A single day in Novasgard spans an entire week in our realm. As far as Alek is concerned, he's only been away from Sunday for one full day."

"Well, shit. Maybe he's not such a fuckup after all."

"I need to get to him. He's the only one who understands what this . . . fury feels like."

"Not to mention, he might have knocked you up."

Kingston's admission surprised me. He'd been so sure this baby was his. I cut him a glance.

"What? It's true. Frankly, I don't give a fuck who actually fathered the pup. As far as I'm concerned, it's mine."

My heart fluttered. "I haven't even thought about telling him. I was so caught up in the fact that he was gone." Turning my focus to Caleb, who was now standing in the doorway, I asked, "How do we get to Novasgard?"

"Portal."

"Where do we get one of those?"

"We don't," Kingston said.

"A witch," Caleb corrected, giving Kingston an annoyed glare. "Do you ever pay attention to your schooling?"

I rarely thought of Caleb as my hot professor, but in this moment, he absolutely was, and it was doing it for me in a big way. He was one black-framed set of glasses away from starring in a porno. Fuck, these pregnancy hormones were really getting to me.

"You should ask Moira. She's a witch."

It was almost comical, the way Kingston thought he was giving me news I didn't already know. "Is she? I hadn't heard."

"You're lucky I love you, smart-ass."

Caleb's lips twitched. "Our Sunday has a smart mouth."

"She does. I might need to find a use for it."

"I can think of several, none of which involve her reciting her nightly prayers."

"Oh, my God, what is happening right now? Am I still asleep? I can't tell you the number of times I've had a dream kick off this way."

Caleb jerked his chin toward the window, where the sky was already turning a light shade of violet. "As much as I'd love to stay and learn more about these dreams of yours, I have to get to safety before the sun rises."

"You can stay in the light-proof room Thorne included."

My chest tightened at Kingston's mention of my vampire prince and the fact that he'd taken the initiative to include a safe space for Caleb. Everyone seemed to believe we'd all end up together, even though we'd never openly talked about it.

We hadn't spoken Noah's name in a week, and he hadn't been allowed inside the house either. At this point, I wasn't sure which of us I was punishing more. Only that I needed to give my heart some space to heal before letting him back in again.

"Thank you for the offer, but you both have a long day of travel ahead of you." Caleb wasn't looking at either of us; his eyes were on the packed bags sitting under the window. He tore his gaze from the luggage and lasered it on Kingston. "Mr. Farrell, if anything happens to her over the holiday..."

"I'll take good care of our precious package, Priest.

Sunday is safer with me than anyone else. She won't be hurt on Farrell land."

"She better not, or you'll be answering to me."

I couldn't help the smile that stretched across my face at the possessive declaration. So much had changed in the last week. I never imagined it would be Caleb making such claims.

"Give me a kiss goodbye, sweetling. I won't be seeing you for a week."

A disbelieving giggle escaped me at his demand. Somehow over the last seven nights, we'd crossed a bridge from hesitant to hopeful. I was his and he was mine, even if he wouldn't allow himself to take me fully again. Even if no one else outside of our circle could know. That didn't matter. I wanted his heart more than anything else.

I closed the distance between us, leaning up on my tiptoes to lay my lips against his. It started off sweet but quickly turned into something else. I moaned into his mouth, clutching him to keep myself upright.

Pulling back slowly, I stared into his deep blue eyes. "Maybe we could close the curtains?" I asked breathlessly.

He chuckled, giving me a sharp slap on the ass. "Naughty girl, you know the rules. Now to bed with you. You have a lot of travel ahead, and it's Kingston's turn to watch over you. I'll see you when you get back."

"Bye, Daddy."

A growl rumbled from his chest as he turned away, shaking his head. "Insolent . . . and fecking perfect."

Then he was gone, his form nothing more than a blur as he left the house. Kingston immediately tugged me to him, his face nuzzling my neck, lips brushing my mark. "Does my mate need a little relief after the priest denied her all night long?"

"Yes," I breathed, melting into him.

"Do I get to be your daddy now?"

I giggled. "You can be my stand-in."

"Challenge accepted. You can have more than one, you know."

"I know. But you're my king. Do you really need to be my daddy too?"

"As long as my dick is inside you, baby, you can call me whatever you want."

"Prove it."

He scooped me into his arms before dropping me onto the center of the bed. I needed to talk to Moira, but we had a few hours before she'd be awake. Might as well use them doing something we both loved. Something that brought us together and soothed the broken parts of my heart.

"I love you, Sunshine," he said as he sank inside me, completing me.

"I love you too."

"You bitch." Moira leaned heavily against the door, her baby pink silk robe poorly tied and her sleep mask askew on her forehead.

"Good morning to you, too. Rough night?" I shoved my way past her and plopped down on my old bed.

"I didn't get off the phone with Ash until two hours ago. What even is night?"

"Sounds like you had about as much sleep as I did then."

She waggled her eyebrows. "Wouldn't you like to know?"

"I was busy with my—"

"La, la, la . . . not listening. I don't want any orgy details. At least not before I've had my coffee."

"It wasn't an orgy, for the record."

She waved a hand. "Details, shmetails. You're getting banged by four guys on the regular. You're a walking orgy."

"I wouldn't go that far. It was only the one time with—"

"Let me guess, Big Dick Number One?"

I frowned. "Which one is that?"

Rolling her eyes, she shuddered. "The fact that you even have to ask that question means you, madam, are spoiled rotten."

"You have no idea."

"Well, I have some idea."

I shook my head, laughing. "If I told you half the things . . ."

"No need to brag about the fact that your persons are within touching distance, you heartless bitch."

"Not all of them."

Guilt flashed in her expression. "See, this is why we shouldn't talk before coffee." She made her way to the kitchen and began preparing her drug of choice. "Not that I don't want to see you, but I'm surprised you're here. I thought you'd be packing or possibly already on your way to Kingston's parents' place."

"I couldn't leave without giving my best girl her Christmas present."

"Prezzies? For me?" She started eyeing me with the intensity of a German Shepherd.

I grinned. "I hid it last week. It's in my nightstand drawer."

She wrinkled her nose. "With the *toys*?"

"I cleaned it out, you jerk. I wouldn't leave those behind."

Coffee forgotten, she bolted across the room and tore open the drawer. She pulled out a small box wrapped in the sheer black scarf I'd bought to accompany her present. My favorite part was the shimmery gold embroidered constellations all throughout the fabric. "This is so pretty," she whispered. "I can't believe you got me a present."

"Open it, silly. There's more."

Her eyes, wide as a kid waking up on Christmas morning, shone with moisture. She untied the scarf to reveal the tarot deck I'd chosen while shopping with Kingston. The set was completely unique, entirely hand-painted with gilded silver edges and attention to detail I couldn't believe. They were Gothic in nature, the card imagery on the darker side with skulls and black roses decorating the back. I'd taken one look at them in the little shop and knew immediately they were meant for Moira.

"Oh," she breathed, selecting one card at random and cradling it in her palm. "These are fucking gorgeous, Sunday. You shouldn't have."

"I love you. I wanted you to have something special. Christmastime is magic, no matter what you believe in."

She blinked back tears. "This is the first actual Christmas present I've ever gotten, you know. We don't really do Solstice gifts in my coven."

"Let's make it a tradition. We can celebrate every year together in our own way. Not Christmas, not Solstice. Just us."

"I didn't get you anything."

"That's not why I got you this. You've given me so much since I got here. And, actually, I'm not done asking for your help yet."

Moira placed the cards on the small table by her bed. "Go ahead. From the tone of your voice, it's serious."

"I need to open a portal to Novasgard and go get Alek back."

She blinked. "Oh, wow. Okay. Um . . ."

It was the first time she'd seemed truly flustered by one of my requests. Usually she had a solution ready to go.

"Can you not do that?"

"Well, I *can,* it's just . . . Novasgard is a protected realm. It's not the sort of place you just pop into uninvited. The kind of magic required to even try is bigger than a one-woman coven."

Frustration seeped into my bones with every word she uttered. Defeated, I let my shoulders slump. "I don't know what to do. Something is wrong. With him. With me. I felt him last night in my dream."

"I'm sorry, Sunday. I can't open a portal to Novasgard. Not today, and definitely not by myself." I could see the wheels turning in her mind, though. She pursed her lips and stood before pacing back and forth between our beds. "Maybe I could ask my coven. There are some very old, very powerful witches. And everyone will be there to celebrate the Solstice. Someone has to know something. I'll find a way. Leave it to me."

"Thank you. I just . . . I need him."

Her gaze softened. "I know you do." She went back to her coffee, poured a cup, and then looked to me. "Want some?"

My stomach churned. "No. I'm not feeling so hot this morning. I don't think I can stomach much more than dry toast."

"Aw, is my little Abby giving you trouble already?"

I rolled my eyes. "Moira, I told you to stop naming the baby."

"What? Abby is short for abomination. Do you want me to call her Nation? Bomb?"

"I want you to—" I sighed. "I don't know."

"Fine. I'll call her Amadeus."

"Moira," I groaned.

"If it's good enough for Wolfy, it's good enough for my little god-demon."

I shook my head with a sigh because fuck, she wasn't wrong. "You're a bitch, witch."

"And you're a heathen, demon."

I stood to leave, and she met me at the door, surprising me with a fierce hug.

"Have fun meeting the fam. Don't get into trouble while you're gone."

"You too."

"Oh, sweet cheeks, I always find trouble."

The scent of home made my whole body relax as soon as we stepped out of the car. Normal. That's what we needed. Something to show her how our life could be when things finally settled down.

"You didn't tell me you live on an honest to God ranch," Sunday breathed, eyes wide as she took in our sprawling property.

"It's good to have a safe place to run. Your family has mountains and trees. We have ranch land." I loved the sound of awe and wonder in her voice. Pride settled over me that she was already so enamored.

I could already picture us building a future here. I leaned down and nuzzled her mark, enjoying the way she shivered and pressed back against me. "This could all be ours someday if you wanted. We could fill the house with our pups. Never have to see anybody if we didn't want to."

"And where would the others live?"

"With us, obviously."

"And your pack would be okay with that?"

"Our pack. And it doesn't matter what they think. I'm

their Alpha."

I said the words, but I sure as shit didn't believe them. This *arrangement* of ours was going to be a hard fucking sell to every single wolf in my pack. Hell, even *I* was still getting used to being shacked up with not one but two vampires. How could I assure the people I was supposed to protect that I was doing my job when I brought a couple of their sworn enemies into our territory to let them have their way with my mate?

Sunday let out a short laugh. "Try to tell Caleb you're his Alpha and see where that gets you."

I shuddered. "I'll let you pass that on for me."

"You want me to be your sacrificial lamb?"

"You love it."

From the flush creeping up her cheeks, I wasn't wrong. Before I could tease her further, the front door opened, revealing my father, his usually stern face filled with excitement. I held Sunday tighter, ready to deal with whatever animosity might come from their initial meeting.

"Welcome home!" he boomed, holding out his arms.

But instead of coming for me, he moved straight to Sunday and pulled her in for a . . . bear hug? My eyes widened. This . . . was *not* like my father. The last time we'd spoken about my mate, he'd cursed her name up and down. He'd nearly started a war between our packs to save face after she rejected me. Because refusing my bond meant she'd dishonored my pack. Now he was welcoming her with an embrace?

Before I had a chance to do anything, my dad started sniffing Sunday. "You're pregnant!"

"Um . . . surprise?" She went stiff in his arms, and I instinctively tugged her away from him and back against my chest.

My gaze shot over my dad's shoulder to where my mom and four sisters stood on the porch. "What happened to not saying anything?"

"I didn't," my mom said with a shrug. "He's a wolf."

"I could smell the pup a mile away," my sister, Phe, grumbled.

They all stood there staring with mixed emotions flickering in their eyes. Unease, distrust, excitement, elation. The mix was as distinct as the women wearing them. The triplets weren't going to make this easy on Sunday after her very public rejection of me. They seemed to have inherited my father's views on my mate, while my youngest sister, Trouble, looked like she was meeting her idol.

Sunday clutched my arm, and I wanted to kick myself for not immediately introducing her to them.

"Sunshine, this is my father, Ronin. My mother, Diana." Mom bounced on her toes, vibrating with the need to hug my mate. "My sisters, Ophelia"—I gestured to Phe, who stood with her arms crossed over her chest and a disapproving scowl on her face—"Olive, and Odette." Ollie and Dee were only slightly less hostile. "And, last but not least, Tessa."

Sunday's eyes were panicked as she muttered under her breath. "Dad, Mom, Sparkles, Scrunchie, Stripes . . . Tessa."

Tessa ran forward, holding out a hand for Sunday to shake. "You can call me Trouble. Everyone does."

"Everyone does not," my mom corrected.

"Everyone who knows me does."

"Tessa, I birthed you. I know you better than anyone."

Trouble cocked a brow and grinned. "That's what you think."

Sunday offered them all a weak smile. "It's nice to meet you."

"Certainly took you long enough," Phe said, her tone not amused in the slightest.

"Phe, leave it." I practically growled the words at her, but she needed to know that no matter what had happened in the past, Sunday was my mate, and she wouldn't be disrespected.

"Ronin, get out of the way. Poor thing is going to think we don't have any manners. We can't leave the pregnant woman standing outside in the snow. Come on in, sweetheart. Let's get you warmed up." My mom held out her arm, gesturing for us to come inside.

"I'm fine. I love the snow. It's really beautiful here." Sunday beamed at me as she took in the landscape again.

"Well, I want to get inside so we can unpack and rest a little. Jet lag is killer, even when you're a shifter. I need to get my baby mama off her feet."

"We wouldn't want the uppity little wolf to have to do something as difficult as standing, now would we," Phe said, making Ollie and Dee snicker approvingly.

I growled at them. "Behave."

Phe huffed and spun on her heel, sending her blonde ponytail flying as she stomped inside.

"Ignore her. Everyone else does."

"She has every reason to hate me."

Mom wrapped an arm around Sunday's shoulders, which was hilarious since she only just came up to them. My mom was the epitome of tiny but fierce. "No. A mate bond can't be forced before you're ready. I'm just glad you two found your way."

"I . . . thank you," Sunday stammered.

I pressed a kiss into her hair. "I think I need to get you to my room for a few minutes. Give you some time to settle."

My mom didn't get the thinly veiled hint, but Trouble

did, proving once again why she was my favorite sister. She tugged Mom away, and the two of us headed for the stairs.

"Thank God they aren't going to make her stay with us," Dee mumbled.

"Why would they? They're mated, and she's already knocked up. I'm just glad his room is on the other side of the house so we don't have to hear them boning all night." Ollie went inside, heading as far away as she could get from us.

Dee cackled. "Oh, you're right. I bet we won't see them for most of this visit. She looks like she spends a lot of her time on her back."

"I heard that," I called over my shoulder.

"I meant for you to!"

"Which one was that?" Sunday asked with a raised brow.

"Odette. She's technically the youngest of the three."

"Odette . . . Stripes. Which makes Scrunchie Olive."

I laughed. "Having trouble telling them apart?"

"They're freaking identical. They even sound the same."

"No, they don't."

"They do. How can anyone tell them apart? If not for their shirts, I'd be completely lost."

People said that about the triplets all the time, but for me there was nothing identical about them. She'd learn.

"They're very different. You'll figure it out."

"If they give me a chance. I'm already planning to check the shampoo bottle for Nair."

I gave her a squeeze. "They aren't that bad."

"I've seen a Farrell man scorned. Everyone knows the women are worse. I'm sleeping with one eye open, and there's nothing you can do to stop me."

I couldn't help but laugh. "My mom is the sweetest

woman in the county. So your logic is flawed, Fallon."

"She wasn't born a Farrell."

"No, but she raised us all. We're half her too."

I led her down the hall until I reached my room. My heart raced at the importance of what this moment meant. I'd be letting her into my most private space. The place I spent so much of my life, especially when I was trying to get over her.

"Speaking of your siblings. You didn't tell me you had *triplet* sisters. You just said sisters. You have multiples in your family. That's something you should disclose to the person you're having a baby with, you know."

"I did."

"You did not."

"I said I wanted twins."

"*Wanted*. Not the same thing as it runs in your freaking family. Between you and Alek, I'm practically guaranteed to pop out more than one at a time."

I bit my lower lip, desperate to get her behind closed doors so I could show her exactly what that thought did to me. "Do you have any idea how fucking hard it makes me thinking of you all full and round with my babies? Fuck, Sunshine."

Her cheeks turned a deep pink. "No. No way, Kingston. We are not doing anything under your parents' roof."

"If you think I'm sleeping in the same bed with you, the one where I jacked off every night to thoughts of you naked beside me, without making that dream a reality, you are fucking deluded, baby."

"Kingston—"

I slapped her ass, cutting off her protest and gesturing for her to go inside. "In you go."

She giggled and went in. As soon as I closed the door, I

was on her, lips tasting her, feeding on her perfect mouth.

"Kingston."

"It's okay. You can be as loud as you need. They won't hear us."

"They're shifters. Of course they're going to hear us."

"Who cares? You're my mate. This is what mates do."

"I don't know. I just met them. They'll think I'm a slut."

I pulled her hard against me. "My good little slut."

"Don't call me a slut. Not like that."

"Fine, I'll call you whatever you want as long as you're mine."

"Good girl." She flicked her gaze to the floor, but I caught her chin between my thumb and forefinger and tilted her face to look at mine.

"You were a good girl for your priest. Be a good girl for me."

"By being dirty, you mean?"

"The filthier, the better. There's nothing you could want, nothing you could do, that would make me think you were anything other than absolutely fucking perfect. You want to be bad, Sunshine. Let's be bad. Show me what a naughty girl you can be."

Sunday's lips twitched into the hint of a devilish smirk, wicked things flashing in her irises. "Do you want me on my knees?"

"Fuck, yes. Let me wrap my fingers in your hair and put those lips to good use, baby."

I groaned as she sank down, fingers tugging at my belt. She squirmed just a little, and I could see she was trying to apply friction to alleviate the building ache between her legs as those thighs of hers pressed together.

"You already wet for me, Sunshine?"

"Can't you smell me? You always say you can." She

cocked a brow. "Or was that just a lie you like to tell me?"

"Just because I know something doesn't mean I don't like to hear you say it."

She leaned forward, lifting her chin and giving me a doe-eyed stare. "Say what?"

"That I make you wet. That you want me deep in that tight cunt of yours. That you want me to make you scream."

She blushed. "Jesus, Kingston."

"Say it."

"I'm so wet for you. I'm always wet for you."

"What else?"

"I want you deep inside me."

"Try that one again."

"I want your cum inside me, or on me. Take your pick. But whatever you do, I want it now . . . please?"

"That's my good girl. Now, suck my cock like the champion you are while I figure out how I'm going to reward you."

The way she fucking preened under my praise had me threatening to burst free of my jeans on my own. My girl liked knowing how good she was, and I loved telling her.

"But I don't have anything to suck."

"Fuck yes, you do." I tore open my fly, freeing my aching cock and practically slapping her in the face with it.

She eyed my throbbing length with hunger. "Does it feel good—"

"Everything you do feels good."

She smirked. "Well, that's nice to know, but I meant specifically when I do this."

"Oh, baby, I love it when you do tha—" the word was lost on a groan when she leaned forward and licked along the ridges of my piercings, taking one of the barbells in her teeth and giving it a little tug. "Holy fucking shit balls."

She backed away and blinked innocently up at me. "Is that a yes?"

"That is a fuck yes. Do it again." I couldn't quite keep the growl out of my voice. It was all I could do to keep from thrusting to the back of her throat. "Fuck, Sunday. You make me feel so good."

She hummed and I saw stars.

"I'm gonna fucking come if you don't stop."

Those teeth found my Prince Albert and tugged, making me go cross-eyed. The orgasm was right fucking there. So close I couldn't stop myself from gripping her hair hard.

"Everything okay in there, Pooh Bear?" my mom called through the door, giving it a little knock.

I jerked, my piercing catching on Sunday's teeth. "Motherfucking shit!" I swallowed against the pain. "What is it, Mom?" My voice was strangled and a little harsher than I wanted.

"Oh . . . um . . . dinner is ready."

"We'll be right there."

"Don't make me send one of your sisters in after you. Five minutes, I mean it." Her tone changed from sweet to stern, and absolute embarrassment washed over me in response. This was worse than the time she caught me jerking off in the barn.

"Pooh Bear?" Sunday whispered.

"Shut it."

She wrapped her lips around my already softening cock and hummed.

I fisted her hair and tugged her back. "Not what I meant. The moment is gone, baby. Later, okay?"

She huffed, but I could tell it was teasing and not genuine disappointment. "Oh, all right . . . *Pooh Bear*."

# CHAPTER
# TEN
### SUNDAY

"Wrap your fingers in her hair, Viking. Show me her throat." Caleb's rough command sent sparks straight to my clit and my gaze shot to where he sat in the corner, surrounded by shadows.

I moaned as Alek obeyed, bending down to steal a kiss. His other hand snaked down my body, roughly grabbing my breast and squeezing. Something in that touch made my chest crack open a little, longing flooding through me even though he was right here.

"Oh, she likes it when you're rough," Kingston said, his voice a sensual rasp. "She's fucking dripping."

"How does she taste, Mr. Farrell? Tell me—in great detail. Don't leave out a single thing."

"How can I tell you if my face is in her cunt, Priest?"

"Fuck her with your tongue, make her come, and then report. It's a simple order of operations. I'm sure even you can understand."

"Gladly," Kingston growled.

"Yes. Gladly. Please. Now." I was all need, my words

barely making sense as I bucked my hips in search of the tongue he was denying me.

"Don't forget her tight arse. Sunday loves it when you play with her arse," Alek said.

"Does she?" Kingston's tone was playful, teasing, and a warning of what was coming. He settled between my legs and licked me from bottom to top, stopping right on my clit with the barbell piercing being the only bit of contact he allowed.

I moaned, weaving my fingers through his hair and pulling his face closer to me. "More."

"So demanding," Alek murmured, his fingers busy pulling and twisting my nipples. There was no set rhythm to it. Just sharp bursts of pain-tinged pleasure punctuating Kingston's teasing licks.

Caleb's eyes found mine as he crossed the room until he stood at my side, a bulge prominent in his slacks. But he wouldn't touch me. Goddammit.

"I want to watch you too, Daddy. Let me see you touch yourself."

"You're such a bad girl, Sunny."

Caleb shook his head. "No, she's my good girl. She knows what I need before I do." He ran his hand along his bulge, letting out a lusty groan as he palmed himself. "Is this what you want, baby girl?"

"Yes," I whimpered, closing my eyes as Alek's hands fell away from me.

"Yes, what?"

"Yes, Daddy."

The scent of bergamot overwhelmed everything else for a fraction of a second before I felt the tickle of Noah's breath at my ear. "But what about me, dove? Where do you want me?"

"Everywhere."

I expected him to groan or grunt or something. But when I opened my eyes again, he wasn't there. Neither was Alek. The room had changed. But then Kingston's mouth wrapped around my clit, and all I knew was pleasure.

"That was some dream you were having, Sunshine. Tell me it was about me."

"You were there."

"So were they. You called out for Daddy, and I know that's not me."

"Kingston—"

He dipped his tongue inside me, causing my words to cut off on a low, needy moan.

"I'm not complaining, Sunshine. I'm the one who gets to take advantage of it. Not them. What else were you dreaming about?"

"You were between my legs, Alek's hands were everywhere, and Caleb . . . He was calling the shots."

Kingston's chest rumbled, and I could feel the vibrations of his laughter run through me. "Sounds about right."

I loved hearing him laugh like that. Carefree and truly happy. I wanted to be the cause of that all the time.

"So, now that you're awake . . ." He waggled his eyebrows, pulling a giggle from me.

Reaching down, I urged him up my body. "You can wake me up like that any time you want."

He sank inside me in one smooth thrust, but it wasn't rough fucking he was after. Not with the way his forehead was pressed to mine and his eyes stared into my soul. "Happy birthday, baby."

"You already gave me my birthday present."

"Merry Christmas, then. You were born on Christmas. You'll get a present for both."

He rolled his hips, and I moaned. "It seems like I'm finally going to start appreciating my birthday with you around."

"My favorite day of the year."

"Because you get presents?"

"Because it's the day I got you."

A FEW HOURS LATER, after sharing a huge breakfast with the Farrells and opening presents, I sat by the fire, snuggled up with Kingston as we drank cocoa. It was ridiculously domestic. And I loved every single moment. This was the life I wanted. A big family, cozy home, normalcy. Well, minus the three older sisters who wanted to murder me in my sleep for hurting their baby brother. I could do without them.

"You need anything, Sunday?" Kingston's mom asked, coming back into the room with a big platter of sugar cookies.

One of the triplets—I couldn't tell them apart since they weren't in their identifiers from yesterday—rolled her eyes, making the other two laugh.

"No, I'm fine. Thank you so much, Mrs. Farrell."

"Call me Mom, or Diana if that makes you more comfortable."

"You've got to be kidding me," another of the girls grumbled.

"Ophelia, you will hold your tongue, or I'll remind you exactly what it's like when I'm angry with you. It's been a long time since I had to do it, but I can still punish you if I need to."

"Mom, I'm twenty-seven. You don't get to punish me anymore."

"Watch me."

Kingston snickered and pulled me close. "This is fun."

"Not when I'm the cause." I was uncomfortable as hell.

"Phe, let up, all right? Sunday and I worked out our shit. We're good. Happy. Totally in love."

"She broke you, Kingston. And we're just supposed to sit around and pretend nothing happened? No way. You were—"

"Ophelia, that's enough." Dad's voice boomed through the living room, stopping all conversation.

"This is bullshit. You guys want to play like everything's normal, fine, but don't expect me to." She stood with a huff, tossing her sisters an expectant look over her shoulder before storming upstairs. "Way to ruin Christmas, just like you have everything else," she snarled as she passed me.

"Hey!" Kingston shouted after her. "Not cool."

"It's fine," I said, though I'd be lying if I denied her words had cut me. Deep. I'd seen the proof of what I'd done to Kingston for myself. But coming face to face with the people that had to live with him while he was going through the worst of it? I hadn't been prepared.

The other two triplets got up and followed Phe out of the room, leaving Kingston and me with their parents and Tessa. I hated that I was the reason they were angry, that the family was torn apart just because I was here, and that we probably wouldn't fix it on this trip.

"I could always stay somewhere else," I offered.

The protests were vehement and immediate.

"No fucking way," Kingston said, tightening his grip on me.

"I won't hear of it," Diana said, resting her hand on my shoulder. "You're family, dear."

"Yeah, don't let Her Royal Bitchiness win," Tessa chimed in. "Not everyone is a megacunt. Some of us actually know how to have fun."

Kingston held up his hand for a high five, which Tessa enthusiastically provided. "That's my girl."

I didn't respond. I wasn't sure what to say.

"Come on, baby, let's take a walk." Kingston pulled the blanket off our laps and stood, holding out a hand for me. "Get your coat. It's cold."

We made our way to the stairs, intending to grab our things from the bedroom.

"Kingston," his dad called, halting our movements.

"Yeah?"

"Enjoy your walk, but don't be gone long. We need to bring the presents to the rest of the pack."

"Dad—"

"No getting out of it, son. I know your mate's with you, and you're feeling protective, but it's an Alpha's duty to celebrate with the rest of the pack and make sure everyone has what they need."

The thought of being here alone without Kingston sent ice through my veins. But I did my best not to let my reaction show. He needed me to be strong. Besides, I handled Callie Donoghue. I could deal with Sparkles, Stripes, and Scrunchie.

I hoped.

Kingston's palm on the small of my back was a comforting warmth as he ushered me into the safety of his bedroom. "They'll come around, I promise. They're just protective."

Nodding, I sighed. "I just don't want to ruin Christmas."

"You never could. Now, go look on the bed. There's something waiting for you."

"If you brought Jake 2.0, I'm going to throw him at your head."

His low chuckle sent my skin tingling. "You won't hurt him."

I narrowed my eyes. "Maybe not, but I'd definitely use him on you. Tell me he comes with a strap."

Kingston's eyes glittered, and he swallowed. "That's a conversation for another time."

Oh. Well, that was exciting.

On the bed was a bundle wrapped in a sparkling purple velvet bag. It had Moira written all over it. "Is this for me?"

Kingston practically vibrated with excitement, like a puppy ready to wag his tail hard enough he might fall over. "Open it and see."

My fingers shook as I untied the silver cord tied around the top. Inside were four gifts and a note.

*Happy birthday, babycakes!*
*The guys wouldn't let Kingston have you all to himself today. We all wanted to send you something to remind you of how special you are to all of us.*

*Love, Moira*

And then in a slightly different scrawl—still hers, but obviously added later:

*PS: I have exciting news on the Alek front!*
*Can't wait to see you.*

"Moira," I growled, annoyed that she left out the details but absolutely thrilled she might have an answer of how to get him back by the time we got home.

"Which one are you going to open first?"

Kingston was bouncing behind me. You'd think the presents were for him with the way he was acting.

I took the gift off the top and carefully unwrapped it. It was the plainest of the bunch, simple brown packing paper tied shut with twine. I knew immediately it must be from Caleb. As the paper fell open, I let out a soft gasp at what I found inside. It was a handbound leather journal with the Celtic trinity knot burned into its cover.

I set it down gently, already protective of my newest possession.

Next was a package in metallic red, the color of blood and roses. *Noah.* My heart gave a little lurch. We'd left things in a bad place, and I missed him so much.

Inside was a small black velvet box. I ran my fingers over the fabric before snapping open the lid. My breath caught at the sight of the beautiful necklace nestled into the silk padding. My name in script, but positioned vertically, the metal twisting and curving into the shape of the letters until finally forming a rose at the end.

"Will you help me put this on?" I asked, holding the delicate chain out to Kingston.

"Of course."

I held up the heavy fall of my hair so he could get it around my neck. When he let the necklace go, the pendant settled around my throat, the rose resting right above my heart. I squeezed my eyes shut, my heart aching for my vampire prince. We needed to fix things. I couldn't go on like this, with pieces of me missing.

Taking a heavy breath, I eyed the last two presents. One was wrapped in an icy blue, the other midnight black. Alek and Moira.

My hands reached for the blue bundle, desperate for anything that would help me feel closer to my Novasgardian. This package was longer and thinner than the others, but also heavier.

I tore into the paper, my heart racing as I thought of what it could be. A hinged wooden box, simple and plain. I could picture my Viking carving this by hand. Fingers trembling, I lifted the lid, a small gasp escaping at the sight of a sheathed dagger nestled in a bed of dried flower petals. Snowdrops. The blade glinted in the light, and the etched *Kærasta* down the length of the hilt brought tears to my eyes for my lost mate. He'd even included a holster so I could wear it.

I needed him.

Hope fluttered in my heart as soon as my eyes lit on Moira's gift, though. She'd said she had news. Maybe we could get him back sooner rather than later.

I caressed the blade, leaving it in its box for now, and turned my attention to the final present.

It was the smallest of the boxes, a flat square with a shimmering star on its surface. As soon as I opened the paper, glitter exploded into the room, covering Kingston's bedspread in silver sparkles.

I cackled.

"Oh, come on." Kingston protested.

"What, can't take a little glitter?"

"A little? It looks like my bed is covered in faerie jizz."

"Do they have glittery jizz?" I laughed.

"I don't know. I can imagine they do. Fucking pixies leave trails of sparkly dust everywhere they go."

I shook my head, my cheeks sore from smiling. I turned back to the box, lifting the delicate bracelet with its leather cords and flat metallic disc. There was some sort of sigil pressed into the surface, but I didn't know what it meant.

"You dropped this," Kingston said, holding out a small folded piece of paper.

*To warn you when someone who means you harm is near.*

I slid the bracelet onto my wrist and smiled. "Best. Birthday. Ever."

"Really?" Kingston asked, sliding his arms around my waist.

"Well, it wasn't much of a contest, to be honest. I spent most of them alone. I was lucky if it was acknowledged. Christmas was the big deal for everyone. It was rarely about me at all."

"That sucks."

I shrugged. "If it means I get this with you all now, I don't mind."

"You'll always have us."

"Kingston!" His dad's shout rang through the open door. "It's time to go. You wasted all your tour time doing . . . whatever you two were doing up there."

Kingston shot me an apologetic look. "Sorry. Raincheck on the tour?"

"Definitely," I said, pressing a kiss to his cheek.

"You sure you'll be okay on your own?"

I gave him a grin I knew was more wolf than woman. "Of course. I'm armed now."

"Oh shit. My sisters don't stand a chance."

"Good luck being Alpha for the day."

"Baby, I'm always the Alpha."

I raised my brows. "Except when I am."

"Fuck me. Don't get me hard before I have to go sit in a car with my dad. That's cruel."

Rising onto my tiptoes, I kissed him. "Later. I promise I'll take care of you."

"You always do."

I sighed and turned the page of the book I'd been trying to read for the last half hour. Kingston had been gone for most of the day, and I'd somehow avoided interacting with his sisters.

Thank God.

The scents of roasting turkey and herbs filled the air, making my mouth water despite the stress of knowing his sisters hated me. My phone let off a soft chime, and I couldn't seem to pull it out of my pocket fast enough. I was praying it was Kingston letting me know he was on his way back.

In the months since being at Ravenscroft, I'd forgotten how much I hated solitude. After years spent on my own, companionship was something my soul craved. Being mostly ignored for the better part of a day had brought all those old feelings of abandonment roaring back to the surface.

My heart lurched the instant I glanced at the screen.

**Noah: Come outside, dove. Please?**

**Me: Where? I'm not at Ravenscroft.**

**Noah: I know that. Come outside.**

Was he here? Noah Blackthorne could *not* be here. Any vampire, but especially a Blackthorne, would not be welcome on pack land. Crap. I had to get him out of here before someone else caught a whiff of him.

Scrambling off the couch, I let my blanket fall to the floor as I rushed to grab my boots. In my mad dash, I completely forgot about a coat or a scarf. The only thing I was focused on was getting to him.

"Sunday? Are you all right?" Diana called.

Fuck. How did I answer that? Yes? No? My vampire boyfriend was standing on their property and about to be Christmas dinner?

"Yeah, I'm fine. I'm going to take a walk. Get some fresh air."

"Okay, sweetie. Have fun, but stick close to the house. It'll be dark soon."

I stepped onto the front porch and stared down the long driveway. I couldn't see him, which was good. That meant he was farther away than I anticipated.

**Noah: Head toward the gate.**

I couldn't contain my excitement. I was mad at the handsome bastard, but I needed to see him nonetheless. Reaching up, I lightly touched the necklace he'd sent me, my belly fluttering in response. I had to work to keep my pace even. I didn't want to look suspicious or like I was running.

As I rounded the last bit of drive, the gate and Noah came into view. He looked so handsome standing there in a peacoat and wool scarf, his dark hair tousled by the wind. I'd been surrounded by flannel and denim in the Farrell household—not that I was complaining, the lumberjack look was hot—and Noah's designer clothes cut such a contrast to my rugged wolf.

"Sunday . . ." he began, but his voice faltered as we locked eyes. The hurt I'd been feeling opened up as a deep wound in the center of my chest. He didn't want us.

"What are you doing here, Noah? You weren't invited."

Pain flashed in his eyes. "I know. I don't even deserve your attention, but I had to see you on your birthday."

My heart squeezed, but the wound he'd inflicted cut deep, and I couldn't let it go that easily. "Why?"

"Why? Sunday . . ."

"Yes, Noah. *Why*. All you do is abandon me. Over and over. I can't keep doing this. My whole life has been filled with people who decided they didn't want me. Including you. As much as I love you, I won't let you keep leaving me."

His expression twisted into a snarl. It was a look I'd seen Kingston wear, but never Noah. "When the hell did I say I didn't want you? Every time I've had to walk away, it was to keep you safe, to protect you." He reached up and placed a palm over the traitor mark etched into his skin. "I branded myself for you. Nothing has changed."

"Hasn't it? I told you I was pregnant, and you all but ran in the opposite direction."

"Because it will kill you! I've killed you. I can't hardly stand the sight of myself knowing what I've done to you."

"What are you talking about? I'm fine. A little nause-ated and my boobs hurt, but I'm not dying."

"You will. Do you know how rare it is for a hybrid preg-nancy to end happily? The odds aren't good. One or both of you will die. "

The news sent chills down my spine. "Well . . . there's a chance you aren't the father. Also, technically I *am* a hybrid, so that has to count for something. Maybe my mother's demon blood will keep us both safe. Did you ever stop to think about that before jumping feet first into your panic spiral and leaving me to deal with this on my own?"

"I . . . bloody hell, Sunday. I don't know. Even if you survive, there's a fifty percent chance the baby is a vampire hybrid. The Council will come for you both."

My stomach churned. "They can try. They'll fail."

"I'm sorry my reaction hurt you. All I saw when you said you were pregnant was your inevitable suffering."

The walls I'd been trying to build between us cracked and fell. "Noah, you knobhead. Why couldn't you use your words and say that in the first place? Then we could have talked through it and avoided all of this."

He raked his hand through the thick, dark locks I loved so much. "I don't know. It all went tits up somewhere along the line. But I want this for us. If there's a way to keep you safe, I am all in. I want you to be the mother of my child and to get the chance to love you every day."

I was crying by the time he finished, my heart still tender but whole once more as I ran the rest of the way to him and threw my arms around his neck, breathing in the citrusy scent of him.

Holding me close, he inhaled deeply and murmured my name. "I called my uncle to arrange for him and Briar to take care of you and see you through safely."

"You did?"

Knowing that he'd made arrangements for me even when we hadn't been speaking had warmth unfurling in my belly. Even when I hadn't realized it, he'd been taking care of our baby and me. He never stopped caring.

"It was the first thing I did after you left the clearing."

I kissed him, telling him with my body what I couldn't express in my words. He shuddered in my arms, and I knew then he'd been feeling as hollow and broken as I had.

"I'm so sorry, dove. I never meant to hurt you. I just couldn't stand the idea of losing you."

I sighed, torn between laughter and more tears. "Next time, say that instead of the other things, okay? It's a lot easier to deal with your panic when I know the real cause of it."

He nestled me close, chuckling as his lips brushed my temple. "Done."

"I knew it. I knew you were a cheating whore." Noah stiffened as Ophelia's voice floated on the wind to us.

Turning my head, I saw her standing at the bend of the driveway, posture hostile, eyes hard and promising retribution. "Phe, you don't understand."

"Are you serious? I understand you're a fucking bitch who is *still* screwing my brother over. Is the baby even his?"

I couldn't quite control the flicker of guilt her question caused, but before I could say anything, she let out a harsh laugh.

"I knew it. I fucking knew it. You let some leech knock you up and decided to fall back on your mate bond to save your ass." She growled as her eyes flashed amber, and a ripple of her wolf ran across her skin. I could see it. If she shifted, she'd tear us apart.

"Noah, you need to go."

"I'm not leaving you to deal with this on your own."

"She won't hurt me," I said through a tight throat. I didn't believe my own words. "I'm her brother's mate."

"You're clearly not his. Not with this *vampire's* scent all over you."

Headlights came up the road, and the sound of Kingston's deep growl soon filled the air as he jumped out of the truck and ran toward us. "Phe, you need to back off."

"What? You're taking her side when you don't even know what she's done?"

"She's my mate. I will always take her side."

"You've got to be kidding me. I just watched her dry hump a vampire. She's playing you for a fool, Kingston. She's playing all of us for fools. How many times are you going to let this half-breed insult our family?"

"You don't know what you're talking about."

"Don't I?"

Ronin strode forward. "Stop speaking, Ophelia Belle. He is your Alpha. You will not disrespect him."

"I can't accept an Alpha who is a willing cuckold."

"You don't have a choice. You had your chance to claim your spot, but you failed. Kingston bested you. You submitted to him in front of the entire pack when you bared your throat. Which means you lost. This tantrum of yours proves why you will always lose. Go back to the house, and we'll talk about this when you aren't on the verge of an uncontrolled shift."

Angry tears glistened in Phe's eyes. She stared at me as though warning me she'd take me out the first chance she got.

Kingston pulled me out of Noah's arms and against his chest as Ronin went to Phe where she stood just up the drive. He passed by me, and Phe took a few steps closer, the disc on my bracelet warming and setting my nerves on edge.

"She's marked by the vampire. Look at her neck," Phe growled. "This isn't simply me being disrespectful. This is her making idiots of us all. Again."

"She has more than one mate," Kingston said. "Noah Blackthorne is hers as well. We've both given her our marks."

"Impossible," she breathed, eyes wide.

"Sunday has four mates," Ronin said, surprising all of us.

"You knew?" Kingston asked.

He gave a tight nod, gaze not shifting off his daughter. "Since she arrived at Ravenscroft."

"And you're okay with it?" Phe pressed.

"Don't get much of a choice when fate is involved. But I will say this, and I'll only say it once. She is your brother's mate. Your Alpha's mate. You will treat them both with the respect they are due, or you'll be sent to live with the pack in Juneau."

I frowned, glancing up at Kingston. "Juneau?"

"It's where the banished are sent. The ones beyond help or redemption."

Nausea made my stomach roll. "Your father would banish her over a disagreement?"

"You know how packs work, Sunshine—"

"No, actually, I don't. Ivory tower, remember?"

Kingston shot me an apologetic look. "I'll explain later."

Noah stood beside me, posture tense. "I meant no harm and didn't cross into pack land. We can end this here with no bloodshed."

Ronin and Ophelia both approached our small group

slowly and carefully. Was it just me, or was this bracelet getting warmer with every step?

"I'm not going to start a war over something as insignificant as you nearly crossing our border," Ronin said.

Noah relaxed even as Phe growled. "Insignificant? You call a vampire sneaking onto pack land insignificant?" Her eyes narrowed as she stared at her father. "I don't even recognize you right now."

"He isn't on pack land. If he'd stepped one foot over the line, we'd be having a very different conversation."

"Make a choice, Sunday. You can stay with us or leave with your leech." Phe's glare was fierce before she turned and stormed back to the house.

Noah's hand found mine. "Stay. I'll see you when you return home."

I nodded, grateful he'd made it easy on me even when part of me wanted to go with him. "Thank you for stopping by to say happy birthday," I whispered, not feeling comfortable doing more than hugging him in front of Ronin.

"Thank you for forgiving me."

"Stop doing stupid things that require forgiveness," I muttered, stepping back from him.

His lips quirked up. "I'll do my best, but no promises." He leaned forward to brush a kiss to my cheek, his mouth at my ear as he murmured, "Not when making up can be so much fun."

Then he disappeared into the trees, my gaze following him until he was gone.

"Come on, Sunshine. It's cold out here. Let's get inside and warm up. It's already been a long as fuck day." My bracelet was still warm, a steady heat on my wrist as Kingston looked at his dad. "Go on ahead. We'll walk back to the house. We need a minute to reset after Phe's hissy fit."

Ronin nodded and started up the truck again. As he drove away, I had the distinct feeling someone was watching me. But with the bracelet still warning me of danger, was it friend or foe?

# CHAPTER
## TWELVE
SUNDAY

I stared down at the seven melting marshmallows as they drifted around on the surface of my hot cocoa. God, I didn't know how to fix this with Kingston's sisters. Particularly Phe, who seemed to be the ringleader of the crew. But honestly, aside from a knock-down, drag-out fight, I didn't think anything but time would heal this wound.

And I was fine with that. Not everyone got along with their in-laws. Things didn't have to be all makeovers and slumber parties between us.

Okay, maybe I wasn't as fine with that as I wanted to be, but I was trying to talk myself into it.

As I took another sip of my rapidly cooling cocoa, I spotted the bitchy wolf in question stomping through the snow toward the house. Given the way her brows furrowed and anger sparked in those green eyes of hers when they locked on me, time to heal wasn't on the table. Knock-down, drag-out it would be. Good thing I'd opted for a

I sat my mug on the little wooden table next to my chair and stood before striding toward her. If we were going to fight, I'd rather do it in the open than on the back porch of the Farrell house.

"Phe, I—"

"Save it, slutbag. I'm not interested in a word you have to say." She tried to shoulder past me, but I caught her by the bicep and swung her back around.

"Be that as it may, you need to hear it. I think it would help with . . . this."

"You mean the part where you insulted my entire pack when you rejected my brother and absolutely destroyed him? Or the part where you continue to humiliate him when you spread your legs for other men like a fucking whore? Because excuse me, snowflake, I don't think there's anything you can say to fix that."

Hurt sliced straight through me at the truth in everything she said. In her eyes, me being with four mates was a slight against her brother, unforgivable, unfaithful. She didn't understand our relationship, and she didn't have to. But the rest was something I could apologize for.

"I know I hurt him."

"You fucking ruined him! He used to be sweet and kind, strong but still gentle. After you let him strip down and offer you his bond in front of both of our packs, then turned him down, we lost him too. I'll never get that Kingston back. But the worst part of it all wasn't that moment. It was the months, *years*, after."

"We've talked through what happened. Kingston understands why I had to say no."

"I don't fucking care. It doesn't change what you did. That you broke him. Do you have any idea how close we came to losing him for good? Did he tell you about the night we found him ready to down a bottle of liquid silver?"

Shock ripped through me. Kingston had told me it was bad, but I hadn't had a clue he'd almost taken his own life to escape the pain that I'd caused. Tears filled my eyes, and it took more than a few tries to blink them away.

"I . . . I didn't know."

"Of course you didn't. He'd never tell you, would he? No, he has to appear strong and fearless for his precious *Sunshine*." She looked me up and down, disgust on her face. "You don't deserve him."

"You're right. I don't. Maybe I never did. But it doesn't change that he's mine now. We belong to each other, Phe. I will spend the rest of my life trying to make amends for what I did, but that's my cross to bear. You don't have to like me, but I'm not going anywhere."

A deep, rumbling growl left her, filling the space between us. A warning. Her eyes flashed amber as her wolf threatened to come to the surface. Even if I hadn't felt the burn of my bracelet, I still would have known to brace for conflict.

My muscles tensed, my senses going on high alert as she lunged. She transitioned from woman to wolf in one flawless leap, knocking me into the snow as she surged past me.

I fell down in an explosion of snow flurries, too startled to immediately make sense of the fact she was racing toward the trees lining the back of their property.

"Phe? Phe, what the hell are you doing?"

I stood up, brushing the icy flakes off my now wet jeans as I stared after her. The tawny wolf ran straight for a shadowy figure at the tree line.

"Fuck," I whispered. "What now?"

Not for the first time, I resented my inability to shift. I'd found my wolf only to get knocked up and lose her again. This would be a lot easier if I had fangs and claws at my disposal. Luckily, I'd strapped Alek's gift to my wrist, wanting to keep any piece of him I could close to me. What had been a sentimental move that morning now seemed fortuitous.

Reaching for the blade, I caught a slight shifting in the trees out of my peripheral vision.

A second attacker.

Fuck, Phe was so distracted with her target she didn't even notice the new threat. I couldn't let my mate's sister get hurt. She might hate me, and I might not like her very much, but I had to help her.

"Phe, get down!" I screamed as I threw the dagger with everything I had.

Phe, to her credit, listened and dropped. The blade found purchase in the shadowy figure's thigh, causing him to stumble off the branch he was perched on. Her wide amber eyes tracked his fall, which left her open to the first man's attack. I saw the glint of his sword an instant before he sliced the back of her hind leg, her yelp of pain piercing the air.

Fury pumped through me, fueling me with its strength. I started sprinting toward them, intent on helping her. I may not have a weapon, or my wolf, but I would still tear a motherfucker apart if I had to.

Phe growled, low and menacing, leaping up onto her assailant and biting deep into his shoulder. They went down, the force of her attack combined with her weight sending them both to the ground, blood staining the newly fallen snow. The unique scent caught my nose, and I stiffened.

*Fae. What the hell are they doing here?*

All the air was knocked out of me as I fell to the ground, tackled by the man I'd hit with my dagger. He grinned down at me, his eyes cold and filled with loathing.

"Pity I have to take you back with me."

He pushed off me as I wheezed and tried to catch my breath, little stars still exploding behind my eyelids from my skull bashing into the frozen ground. Before I could do more than curl up into a ball, he cocked his leg back and kicked me straight in the ribs. There was a distinctive crack, and I cried out as pain shot through me.

"Get up," he growled.

Channeling Kingston, I gritted out, "You're sending me some mixed signals, Tamlin."

He grabbed me by the hair, completely missing that reference as he pulled me to a standing position. Nausea curled in my belly as the break in my ribs throbbed.

*Oh God, he's going to take me.*

A deep rumble radiated around us, a vibration so strong I felt it in my bones.

"Bloody fucking hell," my captor groaned. "Gods-damned wolves."

He released my hair, giving me a chance to turn my head and see the six werewolves, including Phe, as they stood in a menacing semicircle, all ready to tear these fae bastards to shreds.

"We need to go," the other fae said. "We can't face them all."

"This isn't over," he spat, dropping me and making off toward the trees.

The man Phe had taken a bite out of was right behind him, worse for wear but still alive. I thought for sure the

Farrells would go after the intruders, but all of them circled around me, even Phe.

Kingston shifted first, not caring at all that he was butt-ass naked in the snow. His eyes were wild with panic, his voice filled with tension. "Sunshine, are you all right? Is the baby hurt?" His hand trembled as he reached for me, as though he was unsure if it was safe to touch me.

I needed my mate's skin on mine. I pressed his hand to my cheek, turning my head to brush a kiss to his warm palm. "I think the bastard broke my rib."

His eyes narrowed, panic replaced by frustration. "What the fuck were you doing going after him like that?"

"I couldn't just leave Phe."

She walked toward me, back in her human form, totally nude and unbothered, the slight limp in her gait and blood streaking her leg the only indication she'd been hurt. Eyes locked on me, she held out the dagger I'd thought I'd lost to the fae.

"Here."

I took it with shaking hands. "Thank you."

Nodding, she turned away and headed into the house. It wasn't much, but that was the first time she looked at me without hostility banked in her gaze.

The searing heat of my bracelet cooled with each passing second, though it didn't diminish entirely. It probably wouldn't so long as the fae were near enough for it to register their presence. My eyes scanned the trees, trying to seek out any sign of them lying in wait.

The smallest wolf let out a soft whimper.

"It's okay, Trouble. I don't think Sunday will mind if you come check her out for yourself." Kingston's tone was gentle and sweet. I loved the way he was with his little sister.

Tessa slunk over, making wolfy noises of concern as she sniffed at me and then nuzzled into my hip. She offered me one wet lick on the hand Kingston wasn't holding before she hurried back to her mother's side.

"I called Doc. He's on his way." Phe's voice boomed across the yard. She stood on the porch wrapped up in a blanket with a phone in her hand.

"Come on, Sunshine. They're going to patrol the grounds while I take care of you." He scooped me into his arms as gently as he could, but he still jostled my ribs, and I cried out. "Sorry, shit. I'm so fucking sorry. Fuck, Caleb is going to have my balls for this. I promised him nothing would happen to you, and then the goddamn ranch gets attacked."

"I'll deal with Caleb. This wasn't your fault."

He brushed his lips over my cheek, a slight tremor in his words as he said, "You don't know what it means to me . . ."

"What?"

"That you'd defend her after the way she treated you. Thank you."

"Of course I did. She's your family, Kingston. And you're mine. We always protect our family."

A soft sniff on the porch told me Phe had caught my words. I lifted my gaze to hers as she started to speak.

"Family first. And that means in-laws too."

I blinked at her retreating form as she went back inside the house.

Well shit . . . I guess that knock-down, drag-out *did* fix things after all. I just expected the fight to be between the two of us rather than a couple of fae assassins. Because that must have been what they were . . . and clearly, they'd been here for me.

Crap.

~

"WELL, EVERYTHING LOOKS JUST FINE," Doc said in his soft Southern twang as he wiped the blue jelly off my skin and took me by the hand, helping me to sit up. "Now let's get your arm stitched up. You'll have to take off that bracelet so I can get you all cleaned up."

The disc had been cool since we entered the house, so I nodded and let Doc unfasten the clasp.

"So . . . the baby's okay, Doc? Are you sure?" Kingston's voice had a wobble to it that hit me straight in the heart.

Doc smiled with a kindness reserved for kindergarten teachers and grandparents. "Yes, Alpha. The baby is perfect. Heartbeat is strong, and the little one is exactly the right size. I'm seeing everything I expect to see at this stage." He patted my knee as he turned that comforting smile in my direction. Then he focused on my arm, giving his full attention to the few stitches I needed. I hadn't even realized I'd cut open my forearm. It must've happened when I fell, but there was no denying the three-inch gash in my skin.

"What the hell is Doc doing here?" Ronin asked as he burst into the room. "Who's hurt?"

Kingston tensed from the spot where he'd been hovering like a . . . well, expectant father. "There was an attack. Two fae tried to take down Phe and abduct Sunday."

"On our land?" he said, a snarl slipping into the words.

Kingston nodded.

"I'm only sorry I wasn't here to see to them myself. Wait until the—" Ronin blinked, pink tinging his cheeks as he looked away and stopped himself from whatever he'd been about to say. "Never you mind. How's the pup?"

"Fine. Just fine." Doc stood, finished with my sutures, his posture tense. "Sunday too. Shifter mamas are strong.

They may not be able to call on the change, but they heal just as quick as ever. And they aren't prone to the usual ailments of human women, which makes the pregnancy itself the easy part. It's the births that get tricky."

Kingston stiffened. "Do you think she's going to have a hard time? Should we stay here?"

What? Oh, hell no. I could not stay at the Farrell house for seven more months. "I have to go back and finish school, Kingston. I can't just stay here."

"You should stay. I'll have a word with the head-mistress, get your courses set up for correspondence. Make sure you come through this safely. My grandchild and daughter-in-law are in danger of more than complications from birth. You were attacked."

I wanted to point out to Ronin that it was his land I was attacked on and Ravenscroft was probably the safest place for me, but that didn't seem prudent at the moment. "Um . . ."

"I don't think that's necessary," Doc said, coming to my rescue. "Truly. Until the birth is closer, there's very little to worry about. And that high falutin' school of hers is as fancy as they come. They can handle anything that comes up between now and then."

I could have kissed the handsome older man.

"Well, if you're sure," Ronin said, not convinced.

"I am. I wouldn't play fast and loose with our future Alpha's life."

"So it's a boy?" Kingston asked, hope brightening his voice.

"Hey, girls can be Alphas too. Remember?" I said, poking him hard in the ribs.

"Ouch," Kingston winced, playfully rubbing his side.

Doc used that moment as an opportunity to get out

from under Ronin's disapproving stare. "I'd better see to that daughter of yours. She's not letting me stitch up her wound. Stubborn as her mama."

Diana sighed. "She was waiting for Sunday to be in the clear before letting you help her. Go on, she's in the kitchen with her sisters. Tessa is dutifully putting pressure on the gash."

"Good girl. At least someone here has their head on straight."

As soon as Doc and Diana left, the mood changed, and Ronin leveled his gaze on Kingston and me.

"Tell me about the fae," he ordered, pinning me with a hard stare.

"They came out of the trees. Two of them. They didn't say much, but it was clear they meant to take me."

He growled. "The absolute fucking nerve. Coming onto our land. Stealing what's ours."

Kingston threaded our fingers as he took the seat next to me on the couch. "Dad, how did they even get here?"

"I don't know, but I intend to find out. I have a call to make. Excuse me."

Ronin left as quickly as he'd come in. Kingston and I exchanged wary but amused glances.

"Is he always like that?"

Still staring in the direction his father had gone, Kingston shook his head. "No. Not even a little."

"Well, we leave tomorrow. Maybe this has been stressful for him. I know it has been for me."

That got Kingston's attention. He squeezed my hand tight. "I'm sorry about that, Sunshine. This was supposed to be a break from all that bullshit. A little bit of happy after all the crap you've been dealing with."

I cupped his cheek, giving him a soft kiss. "It was.

Honestly. Even the Phe stuff wasn't so bad. I think we cleared the air, and if we're not exactly friends now, we're at least on speaking terms, so that's a win, right?"

He leaned down and kissed my forehead. "Right."

I hesitated, the other things she said to me echoing in my mind. I looked away, biting my lip.

"I know that look. What's on your mind, baby?"

Taking a steadying breath, I steeled myself to broach the subject. "She told me how bad it was right after I said no."

His gaze went hard. "She shouldn't have told you that."

"No, she shouldn't have. *You* should have."

"It doesn't matter now. I'm past it. We're together."

"But you were so—"

"Drop it, Sunday."

That shut me up. But knowing the truth made every single moment we had together more precious. I'd never take him for granted again.

"Fine, but if you ever want to talk about it, I'll listen."

He looked at me, an odd sort of anxious energy radiating out of him and making his eyes burn bright.

"What is it?"

"Don't tell the guys, okay? I don't want them to know ... about all that."

"Of course not. That's not my secret to share. And I don't tell them everything, you know. Some stuff is just between us."

He nodded, looking relieved. Then his signature smirk curled his lips.

"What's that look for?"

"Wait until I tell them I got to see the baby before they did. Thorne's gonna lose his shit."

"It's always a competition between you two," I said with a snort.

"There's no competition, baby. I always win."

# CHAPTER
# THIRTEEN
### ALEK

I sat amidst the rubble of my room. After repairing my cell for the third time in as many days, my parents finally gave up trying to undo the destruction I'd caused. They promised that time would help soothe the creature seething inside of me, but they lied. Time had done nothing to temper the storm. If anything, it made it worse. Especially since every time I closed my eyes, I saw *her*.

Sunday was there in each breath, each pump of my heart, each thought. But she was real in my dreams, which only added to my heartache when I woke. That was when the berserker was at its worst. When I opened my eyes to find her lost once again.

Footsteps sounded down the hall, but I didn't bother looking up. I didn't want visitors. Tor and my parents would stop by at least once a day, but I was through talking to them. Unless they were going to let me leave, I wasn't interested in anything they had to say.

Rage coursed through my veins even now, the beast pushing at the periphery. If I got out of here, I'd hurt someone. I knew that. It didn't stop me from searching for every opportunity to escape.

They thought keeping me here would teach me control, but I was coming to realize that the only way I'd ever feel in control again was to be by my mate's side.

"Oh, Tiny. It's worse than I thought."

I didn't move from my position on the floor. I'd been seated with my knees bent, arms draped over them, gaze locked on the same patch of tile for hours. At my aunt's words, I lifted my eyes, but nothing else.

"Come to see the freak in his cage?"

"Don't be like that. We're all trying to help you. You've never seen an uncontrolled berserker."

"Haven't I?" I asked with a mocking grin.

"Tiny, this is child's play compared to the real thing. Trust me, I've seen it. It's not pretty. You'd never forgive yourself if you hurt one of them."

Frustration burned in my throat, constricting the muscles against my will. "Why are you here, Quinn? If you're not going to let me out, then leave me be."

"That's exactly why I'm here, actually."

I snapped my head up, giving her my full attention. "What?"

"I have a solution that will allow us to release you. Would you like that?"

"Yes. I need to get back to her."

"Then come here where I can get a good look at you."

I unfolded myself from the floor, muscles groaning in protest at the rapid shift after being unused for so long. "What do you need me to do?" I asked once I stood directly in front of her.

She lifted one of her hands, pressing it against the glass between us. Instinctively, I matched the motion until we were both standing with our hands pressed together.

"All I need you to do is think about her."

That was easy. Sunday existed in my every thought since the moment I first saw her.

Floating to the surface of my mind like it had been summoned was the memory of the first time Sunday's lips touched mine and the soul-deep connection I'd felt as I healed her.

"That's it," my aunt whispered, her dark purple eyes seeming to ripple like water as she held my gaze.

The recollection lost its color, taking on a wine-colored hue as it faded away to be replaced by another memory. This time, it was when the runes of my name flared to life on her arm, marking her as mine. But just as fast as the moment appeared in my mind, it was cast in purple, becoming a mist and disappearing into nothing.

Panic clutched my heart. No. She was taking my Sunny from me. Quinn, the memory weaver, was using her powers on me but not to help me, to steal my mate. My berserker roared to the surface, trying to fight to keep what little I still had of Sunny, but it was no use. Memory after memory flashed in my head, unbidden, unprotected, and at Quinn's mercy.

"Stop!" I shouted, hitting the glass with my free hand. I tried to tear my gaze from hers, but she held me in the thrall of her eyes.

"Don't fight, Alek. It'll be over soon."

"How could you do this? You have no right."

"I have every right. You are my godson. I swore the day you were born I would never let any harm come to you. That includes harm you cause to yourself."

"My parents would never agree to this."

"It's a good thing you won't remember, so you can't tell them."

"Aunt Quinn, please. Don't do this. I love her. Don't take her from me." My words were a frantic plea as my berserker rattled at his chains, desperate to break us free of her mental chokehold.

"She will be your downfall, Alek. I can't let that happen when there's something I can do to stop it. I'm sorry."

"I will never forgive you for this."

"When I'm done, there will be nothing for you to forgive."

I was helpless against her as one by one, my nights and days with Sunny vanished into oblivion. And then, there was nothing. No pain. No heartache. No happiness. I was a void. Empty. Calm. In perfect control.

I blinked, feeling like I was coming out of a deep sleep. Confusion settled over me. "Quinn, what am I doing in here?"

A tear rolled down her cheek. "You were sick, sweet boy. But you're better now. Come on, let's get you out of here."

# CHAPTER
# FOURTEEN
## SUNDAY

*Two weeks without Alek*

The hairs on the back of my neck prickled as I sat in the headmistress's office. Again.

"I haven't even been back a full day, and already I'm in trouble? What did I do now?" I muttered.

"Well, you got pregnant and were involved in a fae attack on Farrell land."

The woman appeared from the shadows like she had melted into them to hide from my sight. Tricky.

My throat went tight. She knew? "How did you find out?"

"About the baby or the fae?"

"Both."

She smirked. "You should know by now there's not a thing that happens on this campus of which I'm not aware. As for the fae *situation,* Ronin called me personally as soon

*So that's who he'd run off to call.*

"He wanted my personal assurances that I would do everything in my power to keep you and his future grandchild safe while you were here. I thought you'd be happy to know we're taking this threat to you seriously and have hired additional staff to join us and lend their considerable strength to our own. The last of them will arrive by next week." She quirked a brow. "Did you know your father-in-law was trying to insist on you marrying his son so he could send Farrell guards here as well?"

My mouth dropped open in shock. "We're already mated."

"But a marriage, one where you take his name and pledge to be loyal to him in front of the old gods and new ones . . ." Her eyes twinkled with mischief. "Well, that would be a strong move in the game of mates and packs."

"The game of mates and packs," I repeated, confused by her reference. "You make it all sound so political."

"Of course it is. Everything is about politics and power when the Families are involved. Please don't tell me you are foolish enough to believe that something as whimsical as *love* bears any weight on these sorts of things."

Swallowing past the lump in my throat, I forced myself not to pick at my cuticles as nerves wreaked havoc on my blood pressure. "I can't do that."

I couldn't choose one of them over the other. Noah would be gutted. Not to mention Alek . . . once I got him back. As for Caleb . . . well, who even knew what the hell he was thinking, but I didn't see him signing up to be the officiant.

"Oh, I know. What a mess that would be. There'd be bloodshed, sure as the night is falling." She arched an inquisitive brow. "Does that mean Mr. Farrell isn't the father, then?"

"I'm . . . not sure." I hated feeling so helpless, but right on the heels of my admission came a surge of righteous anger. "By the way, I took your stupid suppressants, so how the hell did I get pregnant anyway?"

She shrugged. She *fucking* shrugged. "Must've been a bad batch. Or, how do you say it? Fate? One never knows what's in store when fate is involved."

"Convenient excuse."

She lifted her palms and held them out. "It's the truth."

"Easy for the person who didn't get knocked up to say."

"About that . . . you should keep it quiet for as long as you can. Especially since you're unsure of the paternity. No need to get the gossip mill going. We don't need any territorial pissing matches to break out."

"They already know."

"I don't doubt it. But they aren't the only ones affected by your condition. As a rule, Ravenscroft does not allow pregnant students to continue their studies."

"What kind of backward puritanical bullshit is that?"

"It has nothing to do with chastity. It all goes back to politics. Children tip the scale, especially in powerful families. Not just between natural enemies such as the wolves and vampires, but amongst allies. Everyone here is a target, Mademoiselle Fallon. But if it becomes public knowledge that you are carrying *Kingston's* child, those who want to take down the Farrell pack will have him at a disadvantage. You know he would risk anything to protect his child, even his life."

"But it might not be Kin–"

She held up a hand and pinned me with her glare. "For

139

the sake of everything that hangs in the balance until you leave Ravenscroft, this child belongs to Mr. Farrell. It cannot be anyone else's. Do you understand? From now on, if you don't take the step of publicly solidifying your bond through marriage, then you must act as though Kingston is your sun and moon or you will bring down far worse things upon yourself than a couple of fae."

My back stiffened. "What are you talking about?"

"You don't want to know, Sunday. Trust me. Do this and protect not only yourself but that child you're carrying. Your mates will understand. It's all part of the game, *non*?"

A shiver raced up my spine, and I placed a palm over my lower belly.

"Take this advice. I know you don't like to listen to anyone, but hear me now. If you are discovered to be pregnant, let Kingston take the lead. Let your heart guide you. Reflect on the consequences. Then make your choice."

MARRY KINGSTON? The headmistress's suggestion rolled around in my mind as my feet carried me to the church. I'd let my heart guide me and it had brought me here. To my confessor. Who better to help me sort through the complicated tangle of my thoughts?

The sky was a deep pink blended with purples, clouds reflecting the setting sun and reminding me of Caleb's limitations. He wouldn't be here. But this was the place I felt closest to him. This was where he sought solace and comfort.

As I walked down the aisle, my shoes noisy on the stone floor, I let the comforting scents of my priest wash over me.

It may not be a true church anymore, but Caleb always left candles burning so anyone who needed a quiet place for reflection would feel welcome. I appreciated the small kindness as I made my way to the front pew and took a seat, staring up at the crucifix behind the altar.

No one had ever taught me how to pray. I wasn't even sure there was a God up there listening to me. Instead I imagined I was talking to *him* as I closed my eyes and bowed my head.

"I don't know what to do. Everything is such a mess." My voice shook with emotion I couldn't hold back any longer. "It's too much. Things I never considered are at my feet, and I don't have a plan. How can I choose to marry Kingston without destroying everyone else who matters to me? I didn't want to choose between them then, and I definitely don't want to now. But I don't want to put this baby in danger either. How do I keep everyone safe?"

I felt him before he spoke, but I kept my head bowed, my eyes trained on the tile floor.

"Maybe you *should* marry him."

My muscles tensed, and my head snapped up. "You can't mean that."

Caleb stood a few feet away from me just beside the altar, his figure cast mostly in shadow. I could only just make out the dark glitter of his eyes from here, but there was no missing the harsh cast of his expression.

Apparently absence did not, in fact, make the heart grow fonder. This was not a man filled with joy now that the woman he secretly loved had returned home. He didn't look happy to see me at all.

I'd hoped things would be unchanged between us after I came back from my visit to the Farrells, but it seemed like my time away had just allowed Caleb to rebuild that stupid fucking wall of his. He was as closed off from me now as he'd ever been.

I hated it.

"Can't I? You have spent the last few months doing what you want with who you want. Now perhaps is the time for you to stop being selfish and do what you should."

I flinched. I wasn't sure what was worse, being called selfish—one of my own personal worst fears—or him pushing me away again.

"If I'm not mistaken, you participated too. How can you call me selfish when you were just as much a part of what we did?"

His jaw tensed, and he took two steps closer, stopping in a pool of candlelight. My chest ached as I looked at him. He was so fucking beautiful. How could someone so angelic be so cruel?

"At least I tried to resist."

"Why are you acting like this? When I left—"

"Your time away has helped me regain my perspective. There is so much more at stake than my wicked desire for you."

"Love isn't wicked."

"Who said anything about love?"

Angry tears sprung to my eyes. "'She knew he was the one she'd been waiting for. The one who would save her from her sad and lonely life. The one to love her for the rest of her days.'" The words trembled as I forced them through my tight throat. "And you said . . ."

"'Aye, that he did.' But that was a faerie story for a stubborn child who wouldn't sleep."

I rose from the pew, my legs shaking as I closed the distance between us. "You can lie to yourself all you want,

Caleb, but please, don't lie to me. Not here. Not after everything we've been through."

"Leave me, Miss Fallon. The sanctuary is closed to students. Don't make me send you to my office."

"You always leave the church open."

"Not to you."

"You're a real asshole, Father Gallagher."

"I know. Now go. Tell your fiancé the happy news."

That stopped me. I stared hard at him, searching his endlessly blue eyes. "Is that what this is about? Jealousy?"

A muscle fluttered in his jaw, but he didn't answer me. He didn't need to. I knew I had him figured out.

"You don't need to be jealous, Daddy. You know how much you mean to me."

Taking a chance, I lifted onto my toes and pressed my lips to his. He stood still as a statue for a full heartbeat before his breath washed over me and he clutched me to him, returning my kiss with a vigor I could only describe as desperate.

"Caleb," I moaned, threading my fingers through the thickness of his hair.

His hands tightened on my arms as he pushed me away with a groan. "Enough. We have to stop this, Sunday. I can't be your secret. It hurts too much."

"I don't want you to be a secret."

"Being yours requires me to give up my post here, and I can't do that. So I cannot be yours. Not the way I want to be. Not the way you deserve. Please, stop torturing me and let me go."

The pain in his voice was the thing that broke us apart. It was the ache, the plea for mercy. I was ruining this man as surely as he had ruined me.

If I really loved him, I needed to give him space so he could see how our bond wasn't just lust. It was fate.

Before I walked away from him, I looked into his eyes and whispered, "All right, Caleb. I'll stay away—for now. But I'm never going to be able to let you go."

# CHAPTER
# FIFTEEN
## SUNDAY

*Three weeks without Alek*

"Ugh, why are these Novasgardians so tricky?" I shoved the book away from me, frowning at it as though the thing had done something personally offensive to me.

"I don't know what you expect from a group of people who fled to protect themselves. Isn't secrecy the name of the game?" Noah asked with a laugh.

"Look, if I wanted logic, I would have invited Caleb."

His brow quirked. "Well, unlike your priest, I don't combust in sunlight."

I glared at him, but there was no heat to it. Glancing up at the clock, I sighed. "Where is that witch? She was supposed to meet us here ten minutes ago."

As if the question summoned her, Moira burst through the library door, a flurry of snow flying in behind her.

followed by a decidedly rumpled-looking Ash. My little witch was also waving around a catcher's mitt.

"Sorry we're late! We got a little sidetracked. Happy New Year, you two. I see you've made up." Moira flopped into the chair opposite me and waggled her eyebrows.

"What the hell is that for?"

"Oh, this? I did a little studying up on break. I'm no midwife by any means, but my aunt is. I'm ready to catch whatever you want to throw at me. Aunt Millie is on standby to project over whenever you're ready to talk through things or if you have any questions."

I laughed, both touched and amused. "I take it this means you're planning on being in the room during the birth?"

Moira gave me a look. "Duh. Where else would I be?"

Great. Four hulky, broody men—assuming everyone was back where they were supposed to be by then—and a tiny powerhouse witch. I might as well just have the baby in the middle of this library so the rest of England gets a good look at my hoo-ha too.

Moira booped me on the nose. "Missed you, roomie."

"You're cheerful today. What's wrong with you?" I asked, narrowing my eyes suspiciously.

"Nothing's wrong. My girl is on the right side of the pond, and she's staying, but the part you should be interested in is that we come bearing gifts for you."

"So you found it? A way to help me go to Novasgard?"

"Not quite," Moira said, deflating a bit. "But it's the next best thing. I found a spell that will bring him back to you."

I jumped up, knocking my chair over. Noah righted it for me, chuckling under his breath.

"Great. Let's go. What are we waiting for?"

"Not so fast, sweet cheeks. I already warned you this

kind of magic requires beaucoup power. It's not a whenever we want kind of deal. It requires a *celestial event*."

I frowned, dropping back into my seat. "What the hell does that mean?"

Ash shifted in her chair next to Moira. "It means this spell is connected to the moon and stars. It needs something to open the portal that's beyond our realm. A comet, meteor shower, eclipse. Something like that."

"Great. Where are we going to get one of those?"

Noah's palm rested gently on my knee. "Calm down, dove. Your heart is hammering so loud it's echoing."

"I can't just calm down. Alek is gone, he's hurting, and I can't do a damn thing to help him."

Ash's warm brown eyes were apologetic. "Well, you can. It's just going to take a bit longer than you'd hoped. There's a lunar eclipse in five weeks."

"A month! You want me to wait an entire month—more than a month—just sitting here on my ass?"

"Would you rather wait for the next comet to pass by? That's five years from now. If we want one powerful enough." Moira narrowed her gaze at me and frowned. "Be grateful we don't have to do that, Sunday. You've waited this long for him. You can wait five more weeks."

I knew she was right. I was acting like a spoiled brat. My emotions were on a hair trigger these days. The connection I had to Alek and his berserker, combined with all the ridiculous pregnancy hormones raging through me, made my every reaction more intense than it should be.

"I'm sorry. I just . . . it's a lot."

Noah nuzzled my neck and pressed a kiss at the base of my jaw. "It's all right. We will get him back, but in this, you have to be patient. Besides, you heard Caleb, it'll be like five days have passed for Alek, not five weeks. Torture for us, the blink of an eye for him."

His words were meant to be reassuring, and they were to an extent, but something in my gut told me things weren't going that well for Alek back home. I didn't know why exactly, but the connection between us had kept me on edge ever since he left. If things were all sunshine and rainbows, wouldn't I know it?

"There's one more thing I need before we can start getting this spell ready," Moira said, almost hesitantly.

"What? I'll give you anything you need."

"A piece of him."

I stared at her like she had lobsters crawling out of her ears. "Excuse me? In case you haven't noticed, there are literally no pieces of him on this plane."

"It's like you've never watched an episode of CSI in your life."

"I haven't."

"Well, have you ever heard of DNA, cupcake?"

I wrinkled my nose. "You need his blood? Where are we supposed to find that?"

Moira rolled her eyes like I was a lost cause. "His hair, woman. We need a single strand of that long glorious mane of his. He didn't exactly pack before he took off. I'm willing to bet he left behind a hairbrush filled with it."

"Oh, that's definitely likely."

Noah cleared his throat. "We've already moved all his belongings to the shared house. You have free rein to search his room whenever you wish."

"I knew I liked you best," Moira said, winking. "I'm glad you pulled your head out of your ass and put on your daddy pants."

"Daddy pants? No."

"Hat?"

"Have you ever seen me wear a hat?"

"Mustache?"

"How about a button?"

I didn't miss the twinkle in her eye. "Done. Babe?" She looked at Ash, who grinned.

A soft glow lit between her hands, and before I could fully comprehend what just happened, she held out a circular button that said *Daddy?*.

"Very funny," Noah grumbled, but he took it and immediately pinned it to his coat.

"Why the question mark?" I asked, still laughing at the hot pink button with its turquoise font.

"Because unless you make the guys take paternity tests, there are four possible fathers out there."

Moira's words were teasing, but I couldn't help my flinch. *Would it always be this way? Did they need to know? Did I?*

"I'm this child's father. No matter what."

His words made me gasp before I could stop myself. "Really?"

"Yes. I love you. This baby is part of you. So I love this baby. It's simple maths."

"Aw, see? He's my favorite." Moira glanced at Ash.

"Speaking of taking care of you two, you skipped breakfast. I won't allow you to skip lunch. You both need your strength."

I was hungry. Most mornings went by with my head in the toilet these days, so by lunchtime, I was ravenous. Today was no exception. "I accept."

"Bye, babycakes. Have a good lunch. I'll come by before dinner, and we can go Viking hunting."

I waved as we left the two of them chatting softly with

each other, heads close together, fingers intertwined. Unexpected tears pricked my eyes.

"What is it? What's wrong, love?"

Noah's worried voice made me laugh as I caught the teardrop before it could fall from the corner of my eye. "She just looks so happy."

He blinked at me. "And that made you want to cry?"

"Don't question the pregnant woman."

He lifted his hands in surrender. "My apologies." Twining our fingers, he lifted my knuckles to his lips and pressed a sweet kiss to them.

"You said something about food?" I asked.

"I did. Let's go."

We walked out of the library and into the courtyard, stopping to stare up at the lightly falling snow. My thoughts drifted to life without him. How detached I'd forced myself to become from him while things between us had been tense. Even now, he was here, but we hadn't *been* together.

"Go on, say it," Noah said.

"Say what?"

"Whatever you're trying to block out. You promised, no hiding behind your walls."

"I just . . . I thought you would've come to me after Kingston and I got home."

"I thought you would need to rest after your travels. I didn't want to keep you up if you needed to sleep."

I rolled my eyes. "It's been a week. That excuse might cover the first night, but what about the rest of them? Why are you staying away?"

"You haven't invited me back."

I jolted. "I hadn't realized you needed an invitation."

"Vampire . . . invitation, they do sort of go hand in hand."

I snickered. "You don't need an invitation into your own house, Noah."

"Perhaps not, but I still needed you to ask me to come back. Not just to the house, but to your bed. I needed you to tell me I had a place there again. That I was wanted."

My body went hot and cold, a little shiver racing down my spine. "Oh, you're wanted."

His steps faltered, his smile falling a bit at the edges. "Do you think it's . . . safe?"

"Safe?"

"With the baby . . ."

His concern both warmed me and annoyed me. Not because he cared—I loved the proof that we were important to him. But I didn't want everyone to treat me like a breakable doll just because I was pregnant.

"Listen to me right now, Noah Blackthorne."

He stopped, turning to face me fully, expression expectant.

"Do not start acting differently around me or treating me like some precious, fragile thing."

"But you are precious."

"You know what I mean. Stop being swoony while I'm annoyed with you."

He smirked. "I can't help it."

"Women have been having babies since the dawn of time. I'm no different. If you start holding back in any way, I'm going to resent you for it."

He wove his hands through my hair, kissing me deeply. "No holding back, I promise."

"Good. Now . . . I want you to move in—to the house, to

my bed, all of it. Officially. Right now. But first, feed me, good sir."

Forehead pressed against mine, he closed his eyes and breathed in long and slow. "Fuck, you smell amazing."

"So do you. I missed you."

"And I you, dove. But we are on a mission to get you fed. Shall we?"

Nodding, I let him pull me in the direction of the house . . . our house.

We walked along together, talking about nothing important, but this moment was everything. It was right and normal. The only thing keeping me from being bliss-fully happy was my missing Novasgardian.

Noah froze, posture going tense.

"What is it?" After everything we'd been through, I could only imagine what kind of threat loomed in the distance.

"Your heartbeat sounds so strange. Like there's an echo." His brows furrowed. "Are you feeling okay? Any lightheadedness or weakness? Have you been drinking enough water? Maybe we should get you to a doctor. Ensure things are progressing the way they are supposed to be."

"Noah," I said with a laugh. "I saw a doctor when I was at Kingston's, and everything is fine. I think maybe you're just picking up on the baby's heartbeat."

"What?" He dropped to his knees right there in the snow, laying his ear against my lower belly. "Bloody hell, you're right. It's so fast. Is it meant to be so fast?"

The panic in his voice made my heart swell. I glanced around, making sure no one was nearby as I threaded my fingers through his hair. "Yes. I think they're like little hummingbird heartbeats until they're older."

154

His expression cleared, and his body visibly relaxed. "Thank fuck."

"Come on, Daddy Question Mark. You look like you're in need of a warm fire and a stiff drink. Let's get you inside."

"I'm the one meant to be taking care of you. Not the other way round."

"We can take care of each other. That's what mates are for, right?"

He rose back up and took my face in his hands, his eyes shining with affection. "Have I told you lately that I love you, Sunday Fallon?"

I pursed my lips and pretended to consider the question. "Hmm, not that I can remember."

His lips feathered over mine. "Then allow me to remedy the situation. I am desperately in love with you, dove."

"Good, because I'm desperately in love with you too."

We walked up the path to our house, and I smiled to myself. Kingston came out of the front door, cocky grin already firmly in place. Until his gaze zeroed in on the button on Noah's coat.

"Daddy? He gets to be called Daddy now?"

"Don't we all?" Noah looked between us with a small frown.

"Not the way I want her to."

Noah looked at me, silently asking me to explain.

My lips twitched. "Kingston wants to be my daddy. He's jealous of Caleb."

"I'm just saying, I'm the Alpha. If anyone gets a status title, it should be me."

"And like I said last time, tell Caleb that and see what happens."

Noah leaned in and whispered, "I don't need to be your

daddy to know you're mine. Call me whatever you want. I'll still fuck you senseless no matter what."

"Suddenly I'm hungry for something other than lunch," I murmured.

"Me too, dove." Noah looked up at Kingston. "You joining us?"

"I could eat."

## CHAPTER

# SIXTEEN

### THORNE

The bedroom smelled of fresh cut roses, which sent a wash of pride through me because I knew that flower made Sunday think of me. There was also a strong echo of wolf and incense, reminding me how easily my absence had been filled by her other mates.

"Stop that," she said, reaching up and touching my cheek. "I can hear you."

I tried for a reassuring smile but could tell I'd missed the mark when her expression softened.

"You might not have been here, Noah," she said, gesturing toward the room, "but you were always here." She rested her hand above her heart. "No one replaced you. Even as upset as I was, I still missed you. I still wanted you to be here."

"Stop it, you two. You've already made up, and someone promised me a snack."

Kingston lifted Sunday and tossed her onto the bed. On instinct, I flinched. He shouldn't throw her around like that. What if something happened?

I stopped myself from saying anything. He wouldn't put

her or the baby at risk. If anything, he was the most vocal about how invested he was in this pregnancy. But I couldn't help it. My nature was to protect and worry over the person I was bonded to. If she was gone, I'd never be okay again.

She held out her hand and locked eyes with me, her perfect cherry red lips begging for me to kiss them again. "You're so far away. Come on."

Kingston tugged her pants down, no finesse, no seduction, just pure need on his face. It was such a sharp contrast to how I would have done it, but seeing the heat bloom in Sunday's cheeks and the way she squirmed eagerly as she worked to help him with his task told me she enjoyed his rough treatment as much as she did my methods.

She really was perfect for both—all—of us. I had to assume the reverse was true as well. Instead of making me feel redundant, the realization comforted me. Because if Sunday needed all of us, it meant *I* brought something to the table no one else could for her.

"I love you, Noah. I want to touch you." She arched her back and reached for me.

"Kingston, help her sit up. I want to savor her before we make her come."

The wolf cocked a brow from where he had already positioned himself between her bare thighs. "I was just about to dive in."

"I know. But before she goes boneless, I need her naked."

"Then get over here and do something about it. I'm busy."

I rolled my eyes. The man had no care for seduction techniques. Unbuttoning my shirt, I let it drop to the floor as I joined Sunday on the bed.

"Arms up, dove."

She was biting down hard on her lip as Kingston licked up her seam, but her eyes were hot on me. I moved behind her, lifting her body so she rested against my chest. I needed as much of her as I could get. In one fluid motion, I pulled the shirt she wore over her head, baring that velvet-soft skin and the hint of a swell in her lower belly. No one else would know if they saw her, but I did. *We* did.

Cupping her breasts, I kneaded the tender flesh. "No bra?"

"They don't fit. I need to get new ones."

"Don't. I like this new development," I murmured, lifting a hand to brush her hair to one side so that I could nuzzle and kiss her mark.

Kingston looked up at us from where he'd been making her writhe. "Pregnancy perks."

"Are there others?" I asked, genuinely curious.

Kingston shot me a wolfish grin. "Oh yeah. She's going to be fucking insatiable in the next few months. Not quite like her heat, but close. And right now, she tastes like the most delicious thing you've ever had."

"I'll have to put your statement to the test."

Kingston surprised me by moving. "Be my guest."

"Don't trouble yourself. Sunday will help me, won't you, dove?"

She moaned as Kingston slid his fingers deep inside her. "How?"

"Reach down and finger yourself. Bring me some of your honey to taste."

Sunday whimpered at the command, her skin turning a rosy pink as arousal swept through her. She might claim to be a good girl, but she loved it when we were naughty.

"Fuck," Kingston groaned as she slid her hand between

her legs and dipped two fingers inside her core along with his. "Why is this so hot?"

"Don't question it. Now let her get me my snack."

She dragged her hand up her body until her fingers found my lips. I sucked every last bit of her arousal from the digits, and bloody hell, he was right. She tasted even better than before.

"I can't stop thinking how this would feel if it was both of us inside her. She's already tight. Fuck, my dick is so hard, and I haven't even gotten it wet yet."

"Both of you?" she asked, voice trembling. "At the same time? Where?"

She shuddered as Kingston pulled his fingers free and toyed with her clit. "Here, in your perfect cunt. Or here . . ." From the way she jerked, he'd found her tight little arse. "Both holes at the same time, maybe? Oh . . . she loves the sound of that. She's fucking gushing."

"Is that right, love? Do you want both of us inside you at the same time? Filling you up?"

"I don't . . . I don't know if I can."

"We'll work up to it. Next time, if you're ready."

Kingston's deep, rumbled laugh filled the room. "That's what the plug is for, baby."

Goosebumps broke out over her skin at the suggestion. Her nipples, now hard and deep red, beckoned me. Fuck, I wanted to suck on them and make her come just from that.

"Do you want me to go get it?" he asked.

Sunday's gaze shot to mine, as if she was afraid to answer.

I stroked her cheek, pressing my lips to her ear. "You can have anything you want, sweetheart. You simply have to ask for it. Neither of us will deny you your pleasure."

"I want it," she whispered, cheeks flaming, voice dark with need.

Kingston moved away from the bed, heading off toward the closet to pull out a chest. Taking advantage of the time alone, I tipped her face up so I could kiss her more thoroughly while my other hand drew lazy circles over her clit. I kept my pressure light and teasing, just enough to drive her wild without actually giving her what she wanted.

The way her pulse raced, I knew she was already close, but I didn't want to rush this. It had been so long since I'd had her. So long since I'd watched her fall apart. I wanted to draw it out. Savor it as long as I could.

"On all fours, Sunshine. This is going to work a lot better if you give me full access." Kingston stood at the foot of the bed, a little pink plug held between his fingers, a bottle of lube in the other hand.

I shifted out from behind her, reclining against the pillows and watching as she got on her hands and knees. She braced herself over me, her face now teasingly close to my aching cock.

"Noah, take off your pants." Her gaze was hot on mine as she told me exactly what she needed.

I reached for my belt and made quick work of unfastening it as Kingston settled his weight behind her. His knees brushed my legs, but I didn't care. I just wanted Sunday crying out for both of us.

I wasn't able to pull my trousers down past my thighs with the way Sunday was holding herself above me, but she didn't seem to mind, her gaze hungry as my heavy length sprang free.

Her lips parted as a gasp left her, and my focus flicked to Kingston, who, by the determined expression on his face, was slowly inserting the plug.

"Oh, God," she whimpered.

"Look at me, dove. Let me watch you take it."

"You're so fucking wet, Sunshine. I can see it dripping down your thighs."

Those blue eyes of hers locked onto mine. Panic and pleasure raced across her features. "Noah."

I reached up and ran my thumb over her lips, their softness almost unreal. Then she sucked my thumb into her mouth, and all my restraint flew out the bloody window.

"Fucking hell, I can feel that all the way in my cock," I groaned. "Put your mouth to better use, sweetheart. Suck me off."

She bent down, wrapping her lips around me, but the change in her position must have adjusted the plug because she let out a deep moan, and the vibration sent tingles racing through me.

I fisted her hair, pulling the dark curtain out of her face so I could watch her cheeks hollow out. "Fuck, yes. Just like that. You know what I like."

The slight scrape of her teeth over my crown had me bucking up, searching for more.

"Our girl sucks cock like a champ. Look at how deep she's taking you. Fuck."

From the rhythmic motion of his arm, he was wanking himself off rather than pleasuring her, and that just wouldn't do.

"Christ, Kingston, give our girl what she wants. Fuck her so she can come. I'm not going to last, and I'll be damned if I come before she does."

Sunday's gaze found mine, and I shuddered with pleasure as she took as much of me as she could.

At the same time, Kingston slid in hard and deep, jostling her and sending me sliding down her throat, all the way to the root. She swallowed instinctively, and I damn near went cross-eyed at the sensation. "Jesus wept, dove. Don't do that, or I'm going to blow inside you right bloody now."

She hummed, and I had to pull my hips back as my balls tightened and the orgasm I'd been fighting built at the base of my spine.

"Make her come, wolf." If I'd been in my right mind, I would've berated myself for begging, but I needed this release more than anything.

Kingston's hand slipped around her hip and between her legs as he started pumping into her faster. With each hard thrust, her tits grazed the tops of my thighs, the brush of her nipples over my skin featherlight and sending tingles racing through me.

"She's gripping my cock like a fucking vise. Are you ready to come all over my dick, Sunshine?"

In response, she drove her hips back until she let out a strangled groan. Then, with one hand, she cupped my balls and squeezed as she sucked me hard and deep.

I could tell she wanted me to come with her, but I didn't want her mouth. Gently, I pushed her off me and up into Kingston's arms. Once again the shift in position must have felt amazing because her eyes rolled back and she moaned.

Kingston wrapped one hand around her throat as he continued to work the other between her legs. From this vantage point, I could see the glistening arousal dripping down her thighs and Kingston's cock driving up inside her. The barbells of his piercings glinted in the light as he moved. She must like that. She seemed to.

Fuck, I was going to lose it without any more stimulation if I kept watching them. I reached down and squeezed the base of my cock to fend off the climax racing to the finish.

Kingston brought his lips to her ear and whispered, "Come for me, baby." It wasn't a command, but a plea. "Oh, God . . . please."

Sunday's eyes caught mine as she came with a loud cry. Kingston fell apart right behind her.

"Fuck," he shouted, pumping into her three more times before going still aside from a few involuntary twitches as he held her in his arms.

I gave them two seconds at most before I was pulling her on top of me. I needed to be inside her. I didn't care about anything else. "Bring me off inside you," I growled.

Breathing heavily as she was still coming down from her high, she nodded and sank down on my rock-hard length. I could feel Kingston's cum coating my shaft, easing my passage, opening her to me.

She rocked her hips, once, twice, a third time, and when she whispered, "Come for me, Noah," in that husky voice of hers, I did. I came with the force of a freight train, my fingers digging into her hips as I held her in place.

"Fuck, that's hot."

My eyes flew open, finding Kingston standing behind Sunday, watching us. Our eyes locked, and there was a spark of appreciation for what we'd done for her. He grinned at me.

"Our cum is leaking out of her. Looks fucking amazing. Too bad you can't see it."

"I can feel it. That's even better."

Interest flickered in his gaze. "Next time, we swap. You blow first."

She sighed happily and leaned forward until she rested on my chest. "Stop plotting and start snuggling."

"Let's clean you up first," Kingston said.

"No. I want to keep you both inside me."

As though on command, my dick perked right up, already sheathed inside her. "I'll stay inside you for as long as you want me."

"I always want you. Both."

Kingston reached forward, his hand disappearing behind her. It only took a second before I could feel what he was doing as he twisted the plug inside her. I felt the roll of it against my cock and rocked up involuntarily. "Christ, give a guy some warning."

"What about this, Sunshine? Do you want to keep this inside you?"

Cheeks rosy with pleasure, she groaned. "Maybe just a little longer. I think I might still be . . . hungry."

He slapped her arse and crawled up on the bed, sandwiching her between us. "Anything you want, baby. Always."

# CHAPTER
# SEVENTEEN

CALEB

"Fecking hell."

I looked up from my book as the clock chimed, signaling the start of a new hour and reminding me I was now running late for a meeting with the headmistress. She'd been even cooler toward me than usual since everyone returned from the holiday break, her icy demeanor now resembling that of a glacier rather than a blizzard.

But tonight was our first official staff meeting of the new year. The five new professors who'd arrived to replace those we lost during the demon attacks needed to settle in, and what better way to do that than an awkward as arse mixer in the headmistress' office?

Slamming my book closed, I hurried out of my office, not keen on eliciting more of Antoinette's wrath than necessary. She'd already been on the warpath; no need to draw her attention my way if it could be avoided.

My footsteps were silent as I rushed through the halls, but I came to an unexpected stop as the heady scent of lilacs washed over me.

*Sunday.*

I waited in the shadows, like the skulking monster she teased me about being, until she rounded the corner. Her skin was damn near glowing, radiant and healthy, and a part of me couldn't be prouder that she was doing so well. The other part resented that she was thriving without me. Even though our separation was due to my request and not her own preference.

*'I'm never going to be able to let you go.'* She was the one who said it, but they were the exact words lingering in my heart. The ones I could never voice. They opened up the gnawing pit in my stomach, a reminder that this separation between us was unnatural. A wound of my own making, no matter how necessary.

I knew she was staying away because I asked her to. Still, it would have been nice to know she felt the effects of my absence as much as I felt hers.

As Thorne and Kingston came into view, it was easy to see why she hadn't noticed me. One played with the ends of her hair, tickling her neck and making her laugh, while the other held her hand and casually ran his thumb along the back. Their easy affection made me ache for the same.

I'd had seven blissful nights with her before she left. Each one filled with the intimacy she craved and the promise of a future I couldn't give her. It should've been enough. But it wasn't. Not when I'd had a taste of the thing I wanted more than anything. Even my godforsaken soul. Playing house with her was dangerous. It was why I hadn't seen her alone again since that night in the church. I couldn't face her. The temptation to give in to her was impossible to resist. The only way I could keep my resolve strong was to stay away altogether.

It should have been easier, perhaps, knowing she was well taken care of by the others. The proof of their care was staring me in the face. She was happy. Loved.

She didn't need me.

So why couldn't I let her go?

As she passed, her head turned toward me, eyes finding mine even in the darkness. My fecking heart stuttered. It throbbed painfully, the pulse I hadn't had as a vampire until I met her racing unsteadily. But I couldn't stay, not when the headmistress was already waiting on me. I shook my head as I stepped into the hall and tore my gaze from Sunday's.

But not before seeing the flicker of pain my leaving caused. So she wasn't as unaffected as she appeared.

My foolish heart clung to the knowledge.

*Fool.*

We'd only hurt each other in the end. No, that wasn't right. *I'd* only hurt *her*.

"Father Gallagher, I was just starting to think you weren't coming."

I snapped to attention at Antoinette's dry tone. "You know how needy our students can be. It's not always easy to extract myself from their clutches."

She raised a mocking brow, not buying my excuse for a second. "Ah yes, and you are so good about tending to your flock."

The back of my neck prickled with unease at her pointed statement. "Can we get on with this, then? I am a very busy man and am afraid I don't have time for parties."

"What could possibly be more important than meeting your new colleagues?"

*Anything else.*

Stepping past the statuesque woman, I entered her domain, an office disguised as a fecking faerie land. It reminded me of the story I told Sunday, but that was a fairy tale. This place was laced with an air of darkness. Everyone knew not to trust the fae.

She breezed past me, the door shutting behind her with a small wave of her hand. "Now that we're all here, we can begin the festivities. As you may have noticed, there are some new faces among our ranks. Before the term gets fully underway, I thought it best to give you this chance to mingle and get to know one another. Our greatest allies are here in this room. We need them now more than ever. It appears the world is ending. At least, if the demons and the fae are to be believed." She smiled slightly, making the words seem as though they were a joke.

But knowing that she was also part of the Society, I was perhaps the only other person in the room to realize she was telling the truth.

My gaze swept the space, catching sight of many familiar faces and a few new ones. But my breath caught when there in the corner stood the Seer. The bloody fecking *Seer*. What was she doing here?

Antoinette continued with her speech, but I couldn't make out the words over the roar of blood in my ears. My focus was locked on the prophet standing in the shadows.

Was this some kind of joke? Or worse, a test? Surely it had to be. Why else would she be here?

Glancing around, it didn't appear that anyone had noticed her. And then she stepped forward, and the head-mistress's words crystalized once more.

"And last but not least, the esteemed Trelawney Sinis-tra, who will be taking over for our beloved Sanderson."

I jerked. Who the bloody hell were they trying to fool

with that load of shite? It wasn't even a good pseudonym. I may be little more than a stodgy professor, but I was up to date on my pop culture references, and that wasn't even an attempt at discretion.

How was she going to teach anyone anything? The Seer only had a voice when the visions spoke through her.

"It's my esteemed pleasure to join you. Though under tragic circumstances."

My mouth fell open at the sound of her voice. Sweet and light, like bells. What in God's name was happening?

"Please, mingle and get to know one another. As I said, you are each other's allies, and we need to be a united front if we're to successfully navigate the remaining months of this term. We have a long way to go."

Voices broke out in cheerful conversation all around me, but I ignored everyone and beelined straight for the robed impostor.

"What are you doing here?" I snarled.

She blinked at me, something like panic flickering briefly in her eyes before she offered me a cool smile. "My dear Caleb, how nice to see you again. Did you enjoy your holidays?"

"Who are you? The Seer only talks to share her visions."

She lifted one shoulder in a careless shrug. "Perhaps I simply had nothing interesting to say."

"This is a blatant falsehood. You are not her. I've been in her presence enough times to know. If you think I'll allow you to get away with stealing her identity, you're wrong."

Her eyes fogged over, arms going slack. "Once upon a time, in a faraway land filled with faeries and all manner of wee beasties . . ." I stiffened, ice water flooding my veins as she continued her intonation, "The Irish house is calling you, Caleb Gallagher. Your heart is at home where you worship Sunday."

*Sweet Christ, it really is her.* No one else could possibly know about the bedtime story I told Sunday, much less the Irish house. I had to get out of here.

Leaving her side, I made for the door, but Antoinette's palm on my chest stopped me.

"Not so fast, Caleb. We have one more topic which must be discussed before anyone leaves."

Finding her hard stare with my own, I worked to rein in my frustration. "Get on with it then. I have work to do."

She turned to address the room at large once more, clearing her throat to silence the bubbling conversations. "Apologies for the interruption, but . . . well, to be perfectly frank, we all must clear the air on one rule I have been too preoccupied to enforce of late. There will be no fraternization with students. Although they are all adults and well beyond impressionable ages, we are still their guides through this challenging time in their lives. No matter how much we may feel we connect with them, please do well to remember this. Immediate expulsion from Ravenscroft will result for any student or faculty member caught breaking the rule. No exceptions."

Her eyes landed on me as she spoke these last words. There was no doubt who they were intended for.

My gut churned, but I tamped down the nerves and held myself together. "Is that all?"

"Yes. Enjoy your night, Caleb."

I grabbed the handle and began opening the heavy door as Antoinette whispered in my ear, "From now on, you will no longer hold private sessions with Mademoiselle Fallon, and any punishments will come from me. Are we clear?"

I bared my teeth in a feral smile. "Crystal."

My heart thundered in my chest as I raced back to my office, fury and fear creating a potent cocktail in my gut. It wasn't until I sat back at my desk, hands shaking as they cradled my head, that I finally allowed myself to acknowledge the panic clawing inside me.

*She knows.*

# EIGHTEEN

ALEK

“I knew I'd find you here.” My brother's voice rolled over me, catching me off guard and tearing me from my lost thoughts.

This wasn't like me. I was always alert, aware of my surroundings, but lately my mind drifted, searching for . . . something.

For the last week, there'd been an inexplicable gnawing at the fringes of my awareness. As if I'd lost something important but had absolutely no idea what. It was irritating, to say the least. An itch I could not scratch, even if I wanted to.

“What are you doing here?”

“Looking for you, obviously.”

“Well, you found me. Bravo. Now fuck off.”

“One would think you don't like me, brother.”

“One would be smart.”

Tor didn't leave, though. The cocky arsehole laughed and sat down next to me on the bench I'd claimed. “This has always been your thinking spot. Ever since we were old enough to be trusted to go out alone.”

"Even before. Mother was always so angry with me when I'd go missing."

"You've always had a fondness for wandering off where you shouldn't. They used to think you'd grow out of it, but then you proved them wrong when you snuck off to Ravenscroft, didn't you?"

"Still pissed about that, are you?"

"Seeing as some girl set off your berserker while you were there, definitely. I'm itching for a fight."

*Girl? What girl?* A flash of memory—demons, brimstone, and blood—sent rage tickling the edges of my mind. "Well, it wasn't technically stealing your spot when Cora was the reason I went in your stead."

Tor's expression tightened. The shift wouldn't have been noticeable to anyone else, but he was my twin; I recognized the frustration as well as if it was bubbling up in my gut. "Ah yes. Technicalities. Your favorite."

"Don't make me turn you into an otter again."

"You wouldn't dare. Not after the last time."

I smirked. "Try me. You were so cute. Especially when that female found you and decided you were her mate."

"Oh, piss off. I swear you grow even more annoying the older we get."

"Perhaps that stick you like to keep implanted firmly up your arse has simply gotten bigger."

We exchanged glares and then grinned in mirror images. These barbed exchanges have been going on since we were children. We communicated best when we were taking the piss out of each other, but if anyone else ever dared fuck with my brother the way I did, I'd be the first to stand up for him. Likely by throwing my fist in the offender's face. You didn't fuck with one twin without calling down the wrath of the other.

Tor let out a hearty chuckle. "Perhaps. But in all serious-ness, you seem haunted by something. Not like yourself."

I shrugged, annoyance scratching beneath my skin. "Ever since returning, things have felt . . . off. I can't put my finger on it. Maybe it's simply the presence of the berserker."

Tor frowned at the mention of my new gift. Jealousy always had been his downfall. "Do you like it now that you have it under control?"

"The berserker?"

He nodded jerkily.

I looked out at the harbor, watching a few fishing vessels come back in from their morning expeditions. "Hard to say. It's intense. Unsettling. A complete loss of control combined with absolute focus. I've never really experienced anything like it."

"I'd think it would be quite handy to have a superpower hiding inside you that you can pull out whenever you need."

"It's not that easy to turn on and off. Not yet anyway. He just sort of takes over and doesn't go away until the rage runs its course. I'm pretty sure you'd hate it. You despise being out of control."

"I don't know. It sounds pretty great to me."

I shrugged, looking away from the boats and back to my brother. "Then perhaps you should be the one to return to Ravenscroft and see the year to its end."

His brow furrowed. "What would that accomplish?"

"The attacks on the school awakened my berserker. It stands to reason my twin would react the same when threatened. No one would know the difference."

His eyes, so like mine, glittered with interest. "You would be okay staying behind?"

179

I shrugged again, even as something tightened in my gut at the thought of not returning. "I don't see why not. There wasn't anything special for me there. Maybe Cora's insights were pointing toward the berserker coming out. What else is left for me?"

"If I can convince Finley to open a portal . . ."

I shook my head. "Fin's not here."

Disappointment filled his face. He really wanted his chance to leave Novasgard.

"I suppose you could always use the gateway . . ."

He sat up a little straighter. "It would be a challenge to travel by mortal means, but if you think it's important that you not go missing and finish out the terms of your assignment, that's a sacrifice I'm willing to make on your behalf."

"Oh, you are so noble. On my behalf?" The sarcasm dripped from my words.

"I'm nothing if not noble."

I snorted. "I'm glad you buy into your own bullshit. Someone has to."

He grinned. "If you can't be your own number one fan . . ."

I laughed. "Your ego is truly limitless. How do you manage to walk through doorways?"

"The same way you do. Dick first."

"I guess it does tend to lead the way."

Standing, the two of us began the trek back home, but I really didn't feel any lighter.

"So, brother, are there any girls at this school worth taking for a tumble? What about the one you pledged yourself to protect?"

I thought of Moira, but Tor didn't have the right equipment to give her what she needed. And the only other one who came to mind was the valkyrie. Honestly, I hadn't paid much attention to any of the females at Ravenscroft. I frowned. That wasn't like me at all.

"Not really, but there is a club made for mischief. I'm sure even you could manage to have a good time there."

"Oh, really?"

"Yes, *Iniquity*. It's run by a succubus. Dark corners, private rooms, and creatures of all kinds looking for trouble."

"Intriguing." He tossed his beefy arm over my shoulder. "Sounds like you enjoyed your time there more than you're letting on."

My frown deepened. It sounded like exactly the kind of thing I would revel in, but I couldn't recall taking part in anything more than the alcohol. What the hell had gotten into me? I wasn't some celibate priest. I was born for mischief. It was my sacred domain. How had I forgotten that?

"Maybe that's why you lost it. Your berserker was sexually frustrated."

I didn't feel like I'd gone without. In fact, that was the last thing on my mind. "I'm not sure. Perhaps I was just preoccupied with all the demon attacks."

"*Demon* attacks? This is the first time you've mentioned any demons."

"Well, if you're going to go in my stead, I suppose I should share what I know so you're prepared for what you might be walking into."

Tor's eyes sparked with excitement. "In that case, brother, let's take the long way home."

# CHAPTER

# NINETEEN

## SUNDAY

*Five weeks without Alek*

I winced as the sound of Alek's dresser drawer shutting filled the empty room. Kingston and Noah had been fast asleep when I'd slipped out from our bed, but I just couldn't sleep. So many things were missing; too many people were gone.

I couldn't do anything about Alek, not for a few more weeks, and I didn't know how to get Caleb to change his mind.

Lifting the pilfered hoodie to my nose, I breathed in the scent of my missing mate, filling my lungs with the smell of ice and pine. I'd taken to wearing his T-shirts or jackets whenever I could, replacing them with a fresh one when the essence of Alek faded. I dreaded the day I ran out of options. Hopefully he returned before then.

"What are you doing in here, Sunshine?" Kingston's voice was low and warm, with no trace of jealousy.

I turned, offering a weak smile as I stared at him, leaning against the doorframe, brows pinched, shirtless torso on full display.

"Couldn't sleep. I have a lot on my mind."

"Do you need me to fuck you to sleep, baby? I wouldn't complain."

The offer sent heat cascading down to pool low in my belly, but as tempting as it was, it wasn't what I wanted.

He read the answer in my eyes.

"Missing him?"

I hid the sweatshirt behind my back. "What gave me away?"

He grinned. "It's not just that, though, is it? You're missing the other one too."

My chest squeezed at the thought of Caleb. "He's not mine. Not really. Not like you three are."

"Fuck that. Yes, he is. There's just as much chance that baby you're carrying is his as it could be the rest of ours."

"Playing 'just the tip' doesn't make him mine, Kingston."

A flash of amber glowed in his gaze before he stalked toward me. "When are you going to remember what you are, Sunshine?"

"A demon with a thing for butt stuff?" I tried and failed to make the joke, but his lips twitched anyway.

"A wolf. An Alpha. My mate, which means you're my equal. And I also like the butt stuff."

"I'm aware," I murmured, heat warming my cheeks.

He winked. "Alphas take what they want, Sunshine. So do it. Make him yours. Stop waiting around for him to come to you."

"That's not how relationships work."

"Isn't it?"

"Maybe if you're a caveman."

One brow lifted. "I think I've proven the value of my caveman qualities more than once."

"But this isn't about you."

"I know. It's about you and what you need. You need the priest, and even if he won't admit it, he needs you. We can all sense it."

"You can?"

"He's miserable without you. Haven't you noticed? He's even more of a fucking asshole than usual."

"I couldn't tell. He's been too busy icing me out."

"Stop allowing him to get away with this half-in, half-out bullshit."

"I'm not allowing him—"

"By not confronting him, that's exactly what you're doing, and you know it. You're just too scared to force the issue."

The wolf made an excellent point. I was scared. Avoiding the conversation meant I could go on pretending everything was fine, that I wasn't losing him.

With Alek missing and everything going tits up with Noah, my heart couldn't take another blow. Even if things with Noah were mended, Kingston had been my only constant lately. Who the hell would have thunk it?

"You know what? You're right. He needs to make a choice. Me or . . . whatever the fuck he thinks he's protecting."

"That's my girl. Did I mention it makes me hard when you let your badass come out to play?"

I should have taken a moment to let his willingness to share wash over me. After all, this was Kingston. Possessive, protective, Lord of the Assholes Kingston. But his actions were proof positive our group wasn't complete without Caleb.

Kingston gripped the nape of my neck and tugged me hard against him. "Now go get your wayward priest, but I expect you to get back in bed after. I woke up spooning Thorne and never want to do that again. You're the middle of the sandwich."

I snorted at the mental image. "Tell me you were the little spoon."

He growled at me. "When am I ever the little spoon?"

I lifted on my tiptoes, licking him as I whispered. "When I command it, pet."

"Jesus, are you trying to kill me? Get out of here before I take you up against this wall, Sunshine. Can't send you off to another man with my cum dripping down your . . . wait . . . that's not a bad idea."

I backed away slowly, knowing if he made good on his promise, there was no way I'd make it to Caleb before the sun came up. "Save that thought, wolf. I have to see my priest about my impure thoughts."

THE CHURCH SMELLED of frankincense and beeswax, lit only by the multitude of candles placed in sconces along every wall. I found Caleb immediately. He was standing behind the altar, his head bowed low over the holy objects spread out across it. His lips moved in softly murmured words I couldn't make out, and when he finished, his entire body stiffened, nostrils flaring, eyes snapping open.

He pinned me with a hard stare, burning straight through me without saying a single word. I knew what he wanted as soon as his focus shifted to the pews.

*Sit. Be still*, he seemed to command.

"Okay, Daddy," I mouthed, mostly to myself, but Caleb's sharp inhale told me he caught it anyway.

Knowing I'd probably already pushed my luck by coming here again and intruding on his sacred moment, I moved as quietly as possible as I slipped into the pew he'd indicated.

Not being Catholic, I had absolutely no idea what he was doing when he raised a flat white disc and mouthed something in Latin. There was a certain drama to his performance as he moved seamlessly from one part to the next, almost as if he was dancing. It was oddly intimate, watching him this way. He looked both peaceful and tortured. Like it hurt him to participate in this rite, but it hurt more not to.

When he knelt and bowed his head, I had to fight the urge to suck in a breath at the beauty of him giving himself over to his God. I had ruined this for him. I shouldn't be here.

Standing, I turned to leave him alone with his principles.

"Where do you think you're going, Ms. Fallon?" he breathed, his mouth at my ear, one hand wrapped around my throat, holding me in place. Despite the strength of his hold, I couldn't help but notice the slight tremor in his grip.

A shiver raced down my spine. God, I was such a romance novel cliché. "I'm leaving."

"The hell you are. You interrupted my Mass. You don't get to leave now that I'm done."

I swallowed, loving the way his hand tightened and exerted just a bit more pressure.

"I can feel your pulse fluttering. Erratic and frantic. Are you afraid of me now? After everything?"

"I'm lots of things when it comes to you, but afraid isn't one of them."

"Oh? Then what are you, Ms. Fallon?"

*Horny. Needy. Desperate.*

"Angry. Sad. Disappointed."

"Then we are of the same mind, you and I."

"What do you have to be angry about?"

"You." His lips trailed over the line of my throat, teeth lightly grazing my skin. "The things you make me crave."

My breaths came in sharp gasps as his other hand slid around my front, resting between my breasts. He had me bound to him, my body pressed tight to his. I could feel his heavy length against my ass, and it took everything in me not to roll my hips.

"What do you crave, Father? What can I give you?"

A low groan left him. "I'm so hungry. It's been so long."

"How long?"

"Since I've fed from a living source? You were the last."

*How can he go so long? Noah needs to feed every few nights.*

"Why?"

"Because it is a temptation I cannot give into."

"But you have to eat."

"I do. Bagged blood is easy enough to come by."

"But it isn't satisfying?"

"No. It's a bit like drinking water when all you want is the meal right in front of you." That tremor rattled his hand again.

"And I'm the meal?"

He sighed, then pressed his lips to my ear. "You're a fecking feast."

"Then feast on me. Take what you need," I said, reaching back to pull my hair over my shoulder and bare my neck.

188

"Sunday," he groaned, my name shuddering from his chest.

"I'm giving consent, Caleb. I noticed you didn't participate in your sacrament, so let me be your communion."

He tightened his grip, a growl rolling through him as he tipped my head further to the side. "Heathen."

But then his teeth pierced my skin, hands holding me fast. I gasped and whispered his name as he fed from me, a wash of arousal chasing away any hint of pain. He rolled his hips into me, and I had never wanted us to be naked more than I did right then. I *was* a heathen, desperate for a priest to defile me on the same altar where he'd just performed a sacred rite.

"This is my blood, given for you," I whispered.

His body trembled, his grasp so tight it was hard to draw in a full breath, but then he pulled away, his lips feathering over my skin as he responded, "Amen."

I wanted to melt into him, to let him take me in his arms and hold me close. But he stepped back, and I turned around to face him. The expression he met me with was stormy, my blood tinting his lips red.

"I shouldn't have done that," he murmured.

"Why?"

His gaze held mine, strong and steady. "You know why."

"I want to hear you say it."

"Because it's been forbidden. I'm your professor."

"You never cared about that before."

"Yes, I have. You just refuse to listen to me, and I've let it slide. But things have changed. We can't keep doing this without risking being caught."

"Isn't that what makes it fun?"

A dark laugh left him. "There are many things that

make this fun. But I won't be able to keep an eye on you if I'm sacked and sent away because I can't keep my fucking hands to myself." He sighed, eyes focused on the place he'd bitten me. "Or my fangs. Feck, you taste so good."

Hunger and need deepened his voice, making my clit throb in response. Something had happened when he fed, a connection, a deepening of the bond we hadn't yet finalized. I recognized it for what it was now. Just like Noah, Caleb needed to claim me.

"You know, if you would just give in to the bond between us, you could drink from me whenever you want."

"I can't."

"You won't. There's a difference."

"Saints preserve us, Sunday, you don't understand what's at stake."

"Because you won't tell me. All you ever say is you can't. What am I supposed to do with that, Caleb? How am I supposed to take it as anything but a rejection? You obviously want me." I emphasized my assertion by reaching forward and giving the erection tenting his black robe a squeeze.

He hissed out a breath. "Of course I bloody do. You're the most tempting creature on God's green earth. That doesn't mean I can let myself have you. Not when so much is on the line."

"What is on the line? Tell me."

"Your safety, your eternal soul."

"I'm probably the devil's daughter. I don't think my soul is going anywhere but down."

His sapphire eyes darkened until they were practically black. "That's not true, *a stor*. Your soul shines so brightly I can see it even now. You're pure."

"Pure?" I snorted. "I think that ship has sailed."

"Purity isn't just about chastity. Your heart is good. Mine is black and empty."

The despair in his voice cut me apart. "No, it's not, Caleb. You wouldn't care about me the way you do if that was the case. You wouldn't care about anything."

"You're right. Now leave me be, Miss Fallon. It's because I care that I'm rejecting you now. Nothing good can come from the two of us sharing stolen moments, I swear to you."

I didn't quite manage to hide my flinch as I rested my hands over the slight swell of my belly. "Nothing good, huh?"

Pain burned in the backs of his eyes. "You heard me."

"You're a coward, Caleb Gallagher. And a fool."

"Better a coward and a fool than the instrument of your damnation."

"Maybe I'm already damned."

"I hope to God that's not the case. There is redemption for everyone who asks for it."

"Even you?"

He gritted his teeth, a muscle ticking in his jaw. "Miracles do happen."

I held his stare, frustration and anger making my voice hard. "Your God is a real dick. Why bring us together, why make us fall in love, only to keep us apart? You speak of compassion and forgiveness, but all I see is pain and heartbreak. Is that really the kind of divine entity you want to serve?"

"I don't have a choice. This isn't something I can pick. I was called to serve Him."

"There's always a choice, Caleb. I may not know a lot about your religion, but I do know it's based on free will. You said you don't want to be my secret, but you are the one who's hiding me. You can make any choice you want. You just don't *want* to choose me."

"It's the only thing I want. But it's also the only thing I can never have. Leave me, Sunday." Despite the harsh bite of his words, there was also an undercurrent that sounded a lot like a plea.

I didn't have a response for that. My shoulders slumped in defeat.

"Finally, she gets it."

I glared at him. "What about the promises you made me? To always take care of us?"

"I made my promise to Him first."

And that was it. With one sharp retort, he cut the fragile bond between us and crushed my still-beating heart. I let out a strangled noise, a combination of a cry and a scream. Tears swimming in my eyes, I turned away from him and walked toward the doors. I had to get out of here. I would not let him see me cry over him.

Before I left, I allowed myself one final glance at the man who well and truly broke me. He knelt in the middle of the aisle, palms up, face turned heavenward, eyes closed and expression tortured.

"Are you happy now?" he asked, and I knew the question wasn't for me.

The pain in his voice was the only thing that kept me from shattering completely. If it hurt him this much to send me away, then there was still a chance for us. No one could deny their heart forever.

I had to believe it. Because the alternative was unbearable.

# CHAPTER
# TWENTY
## SUNDAY

*Eight weeks without Alek*

"Are you sure about this?" Noah asked, his voice pitched low as we watched Moira and Ash set out seven crystal pillars to create the circle we would need for our spell.

"Sure about bringing Alek home? Uh . . . yeah. Why wouldn't I be?"

"Is it really fair to ask them to perform such powerful and potentially dangerous magic just so you can get what you want?"

Guilt instantly wormed its way through me. "Moira promised me it was safe."

"Would she tell you anything different knowing how badly you want this?"

My gaze traveled from his face to Moira's. "No . . ."

"Just remember, he chose to go back to Novasgard. He can choose to return on his own."

I hated how right he was, but I grabbed his hand and slid his palm over the small belly I had just recently noticed. "Wouldn't you want me to find you and tell you?"

His expression softened.

"Don't forget the dreams," Kingston interjected.

"Dreams?" Noah asked.

"The berserker is getting more insistent. She wakes up a few nights a week, coated in sweat, eyes fully black. It's scary as fuck. She needs to talk to someone who understands what she's going through. If only to learn how to control it."

"Why didn't I know about this? I've been with you every night too."

I pushed back the anxious trembling in my gut. "It always seems to happen while you're hunting."

"And you're sure it's Alek?"

Kingston snorted. "Of course it's Alek. He's the one who hulks out and goes literally berserk. You didn't see his eyes, Thorne. They looked exactly like hers do."

Noah's frown deepened. "Just what we need. Something else to worry about."

"Stop making her feel like shit, and let's get the Viking back so we can help her. She's better with all of us. You and I both know it."

"If that's the case, why isn't the priest here? He's been noticeably absent lately. Are we just letting him off the hook?"

"Who says I'm not here, Mr. Blackthorne? I'm never far. It's my job to keep an eye on errant students, and you five are as errant as they come." Caleb appeared out of the shadows, climbing the steps of the observatory to join us on the rooftop. My stupid heart fluttered.

I hadn't seen him again since that night in the church.

My neck tingled with the memory of his fangs sinking into my flesh. Before realizing what I was doing, I reached up to feather my fingers over the small raised scars where his teeth pierced me. My pulse raced, nipples tightening to painful points, and when he caught my eye and I saw the answering heat in his, desire pooled low in my belly.

He noticed. There was no way he didn't. And the slight flaring of his nostrils, the shift in his posture, that adjustment he made to his stance—crossing his hands in front of his crotch—all spoke of unwanted arousal.

Unconsciously, I bit down on my lower lip, swaying toward him, my body eager to go to its mate. But no sooner had I taken a step to do just that than Caleb's eyes hardened, his expression cold and detached as he looked away.

It would have gutted me if not for the sweet message I'd discovered in the journal he'd given me for my birthday.

*Even if we are apart, you're never far from my thoughts.*

The meaning behind those words hit harder after he'd fed from me. I could only assume his callousness was his attempt at keeping up appearances. Only last week, an announcement was made reiterating the no fraternization policy after a student and professor were dismissed for breaking it. It made me wonder how much of his speech the other night was true and how much a performance to protect me.

I was nothing to him because I had to be—for both our sakes.

"Come to dole out a punishment, Priest?" Kingston taunted. "We all know you enjoy that a little too much."

"Only if punishment is warranted. Miss Fallon, have you and your compatriots been up to something you shouldn't?"

This was the first he'd spoken directly to me since

ordering me to leave him and not to come back. I didn't know what to say. Swallowing past the lump in my throat, I pulled up my big girl panties. "That depends on what you think I shouldn't do."

Challenge sparked in his eyes. "There are many things that fit the bill."

"Does bringing back a lost student count?"

His brows lifted. "That would depend on whether it was against his will, I suppose."

"Well, last I checked, witchcraft was encouraged at Ravenscroft, so regardless of the particulars, I'm confident we haven't broken any rules."

"Yet."

"Come on, Daddy Gallagher, let her be. We're going to bring back her Viking and set the world on fire. What could possibly go wrong?"

Caleb shot Kingston a death glare that could have turned him to stone if my priest had been a warlock. "No. It's Father Gallagher to you."

Kingston smirked.

"Just get on with it, but the moment things get out of hand, I'll be putting a stop to it. Do you understand?" Caleb set his firm gaze on me.

I nodded, saved from having to say anything else by Moira's announcement.

"Okay, we're ready. We should start as soon as the eclipse is at its peak, which will be any minute now. Sunday, take your place in the center of the circle."

Caleb snatched my wrist. "You're not setting foot in that circle."

I may not be able to shift, but my wolf was close to the surface as I snarled and tugged my arm free. "Try and stop me."

"God, it makes me hard when she goes all Alpha like that," Kingston said to Noah, making no effort to hide the fact that he was adjusting himself.

I couldn't lie; the sight sent a zing of arousal through me, but I didn't say a word as I stepped into the circle, Caleb seething as he watched.

Moira and Ash were wearing matching T-shirts that said 'Witch, please.' The sight made me smile just like it had the first time I'd noticed. Those two were adorable. Moira might pretend to be prickly, but seeing her with the person she loved proved how much of a softy she was.

"Is this going to hurt?" I asked, unable to keep the fear from my voice.

Ash shrugged. "I don't know."

"Maybe." Moira's forehead had that little worry line she worked so hard to glamour away all the time.

Shit.

"Just make sure not to cross the boundary once we start the spell," Ash warned. "You're the anchor. Everything hinges on you."

"Why am I the anchor again?"

Moira tickled me, running her fingers along the runes proclaiming Alek's name. "Because of this, sweet cheeks. You're magically tied to him. It's the strongest connection we have between our two realms."

"I thought his hair was?"

"His hair was the conduit. You are the thing that will pull him back."

It all sounded like a bunch of witchy nonsense to me, but they were the experts. "Okay then."

"Sunday, I don't think this is—" Caleb began, coming toward me, but Noah stopped him with a palm across his chest.

"Stay back, or I'll make you."

Caleb sneered at him. "As if you could, Blackthorne."

"Now, now, if it's a dick measuring contest you want, you should both know Jake and I have you beat by several inches. Stop wasting her fucking time."

I wanted to volley something about Alek and how he had them all beat, but the clouds parted, revealing a moon so full and bright I had to blink against the glow.

"It's time." Moira's voice was reverent and serious.

"Don't we need to wait until it reaches totality?"

"Nope. Just for it to turn red. Now get into place, or you're going to miss your chance."

I scurried to obey, not keen on the idea of waiting another couple of years to get a second chance. A baby bump was one thing; a full-fledged toddler would be far more complicated to explain. Especially if he ended up a blond-haired, blue-eyed demigod.

"Okay. I'm ready."

Ash and Moira linked hands, and my eyes bounced between them to the three men standing shoulder to shoulder a few feet away. They couldn't look more different. Kingston seemed like he wanted a bucket of popcorn, Noah appeared seconds away from vomiting, and from the apprehension in Caleb's eyes, it was obvious he wanted to throw me over his shoulder and run for the hills.

Soft female voices began murmuring in unison, their words barely discernible over the immediate hum that took up residence in my head. It was unsettling, reminding me of a cat when you rubbed its fur the wrong way. Then the hum built and spread across my skin, lifting the hairs on the back of my neck as the air seemed to sizzle.

I had to blink as the air rippled and swayed in front of me. Faint lights shimmered, almost invisible to the naked eye, and it was as if I was witnessing my very own Aurora show as the colors blossomed in the sky.

My arm burned where the runes were magically inked into my skin, and the tightness in my chest intensified as my connection to Alek pulled taut, feeling like a string just about to break. Since I hadn't felt anything from Alek outside my dreams, the return of our bond flooded me with hope.

*It's working.*

I wasn't sure if I was imagining it or not, but I swore I saw his ice-blue eyes glowing in the mist.

"Alek." I whispered his name, hope taking flight after being caged for so long.

Voices echoed in my mind, sounding like they were speaking directly to me.

"Now's your chance, brother."

"Are you sure?"

"Go. You need to finish the mission."

"Holy shit, there really are *two* of them," Kingston whispered.

"Sunday, he needs to hurry. I can't hold it open much longer." Ash's voice was strained, but I didn't dare look away from the growing doorway between realms.

Alek and Tor—it *had* to be Tor—stood together in the snow. They were identical aside from one having his mane flowing free and the other's was pulled up and away from his startlingly handsome face.

But everything else, the icy gaze, the well-groomed beards—even the chiseled cheekbones and sculpted brows were the same. Beautiful. Deadly. Powerful.

My gaze was pulled to the twin with the bun, but it was the one with his golden hair spilling down his back that stepped forward, his image clarifying and sharpening with each step.

My lungs seized as adrenaline sent my pulse skyrocketing.

And then he was right there, standing in front of me. Whole. Safe. Real.

"Alek!"

I sprang forward, jumping up and wrapping my legs around his waist and kissing him without giving him a chance to do or say anything else.

He caught me in his arms, his hands grasping me by my ass and giving an appreciative squeeze. It took a second for his lips to move beneath mine, but I assumed that was only because I'd caught him off guard.

"No one exceptional, my arse."

His voice was unfamiliar. Deeper perhaps, more gravelly. I let that thought flicker in my mind but pushed it away the moment his lips claimed mine again.

The change of pressure in the air was my only sign something had shifted behind us. I glanced to where the portal had been, only to find it back to normal. All that was left to remind us of what we'd done was the remnants of the circle Moira and Ash had set.

"Bloody fucking hell, Moira," Noah ground out, his voice tight with worry.

It was enough to tear my attention away from the Viking in my arms. I turned Noah's way, my eyes widening when I spotted Moira on the ground, blood dripping from her nose. Ash was faring little better, her skin chalky and tinged almost gray.

"I'm fine. Leave me alone, bloodsucker. The buffet is closed."

"As if that's what I'm interested in."

"I see you eyeing me." She tried to get to her feet but stumbled, Noah rushing to her side in an instant. "No sampling the goods, Blackthorne."

He rolled his eyes as he righted her. "Witches taste like shite."

"Tell that to your ancestors."

"I have a more discerning palette."

She laughed, but it was a rough, grating sound. Like she was having trouble breathing.

"Moira, are you okay?" I asked, loathe to leave the protective circle of Alek's arms but genuinely concerned for my best friend.

"Fine. Fine. Just don't ask me to do that again for another decade or so. I think it might kill me."

My stomach twisted at the pain in her voice. She'd hurt herself to get me what I wanted. Alek's hands gripped my waist, holding me close as though he sensed I was going to leave.

"I can see the worry on your face, babycakes. I'm stronger than I look."

"Don't worry, Sunday. I'll take care of her. You have other things to see to," Ash said, taking Noah's place beside her girlfriend.

As she and Ash came closer, holding each other tight, something inside me eased. They had each other. They'd be okay. I had to trust them.

"You good, Viking?" Kingston's question held a note of tension.

"Of course."

"You smell weird."

"And you smell like a wet dog who hasn't had a bath in a fortnight."

Kingston's eyes narrowed. "You're just lucky our girl is

in your arms. After the shit you pulled last time I saw you, you should be grateful I'm not welcoming you home with a fist to the face."

Alek's expression turned thunderous. I would have sworn I heard an answering rumble rolling in the distance. "I dare you to try, wolf."

"Sunday, take a step back," Caleb growled.

"What?"

"Take a step back right bloody now, you insolent girl. Do as you're told."

Now there was a mixture of anger and fear in his voice, and I couldn't bring myself to question him further. I extricated myself from Alek's arms. It wasn't easy with the way they tightened as soon as I tried, but his attention shifted as Caleb approached. My priest had me behind him in a flash.

"You're a danger to her."

"Caleb, stop it."

"He's a berserker. He can't be trusted."

I shoved Caleb out of the way. "Yes, he can. Alek would never hurt me. He's my mate."

Alek stiffened, his back going straight as an arrow.

"I don't know, Sunshine. His scent has something new in it. Less snow, more storm. And . . . ozone?"

Alek's brows rose as he crossed his arms over his broad chest. "There's a simple explanation for all of this."

"Enlighten us," Noah said, his voice a dangerous snarl as he joined the others.

"I've been away. It's only natural the time spent in my homeland has left a mark. Things will go back to normal soon. You didn't know me when I first arrived. Novasgard clings to you for a while. The same goes for this plane. You should have seen the looks my father got when he'd come back from a trip to Manna-Heim."

"Manna-Heim?" Kingston asked.

"Earth, the home of man. Also called Midgard." Caleb's tone held the weight of a put-upon professor.

"Oh, like from the Marvel movies."

Alek groaned. "Leave those out of this."

The suspicious glances my mates cast Alek's way abated, but only just. There was a definite hardness lingering in Caleb's dark eyes. And Kingston seemed like he was about to fight it out first and ask questions later. Noah was tense too, his body tight and ready to pounce at the first sign of trouble.

I needed to put a stop to this.

"I'm not in the mood for another dick swinging contest."

"Come on, dove. Let's get you home. It's the middle of the night, and you're fucking exhausted. I can sense it," Noah said, shifting into his caretaker role.

"You guys go ahead. Alek hasn't seen the new place yet. I'll give him the tour. It will give us some time to catch up."

I silently pleaded with them all to understand. It had been *months*. My body craved him. My soul was starved for him. I needed a little time where it was just the two of us.

"I don't know if that's—"

The stare I gave Kingston could have turned him into ashes on the spot if I had it my way. "We will be fine. Alek isn't a threat."

"I would never hurt a woman." Alek's gaze traveled down my body. It wasn't a possessive look, but it was appreciative.

Warmth unfurled low in my belly as I took Alek's large hand in mine. "Come on, there's a big bed with your name on it back at the house. We brought all your things from the dorm there."

"My things?"

"Is that a problem? Would you rather go back to a dorm with a single bed you barely fit on?"

He gave me another one of those sweeping glances, his lips curling up with familiar mischief. "I think I'd rather stay with you."

"That can be arranged."

He let me lead him back toward the house, his palm somehow not fitting quite right with mine. We'd get through this little bump in the road. Back to the Sunday and Alek we'd been. We had to . . . I still had my little secret to share, but not until we were comfortable with each other again.

It would just take a little time, and now that he was back, we had some. At least . . . a few weeks until there would be no more hiding my condition even if I wanted to.

The house came into view, and I gave Alek a big smile, drawing him toward the door. "Welcome home, *elskan mín*. We—I—missed you."

His shoulders stiffened as he stepped over the threshold. Then he took a deep breath and looked around. "Ah, it's good to be home."

"And here's your room." I opened the door, forcing myself not to look over my shoulder at the hulking Viking male behind me as I entered his space.

My heart was in my throat as I strode to the corner and ran my fingers over the leather wingback chair I'd asked Kingston to steal from the library. A memento from Alek's special quiet place, something to make his room feel more like home. And, of course, remind him of the same spot we'd first truly come together.

"I thought you might like this," I said, sitting on the supple leather and bringing my focus to his.

His brows rose. "A chair? Yes, it's very nice."

That was it. Not a flicker of recognition in his gaze. My heart dropped. Maybe I'd misread its importance to him, accidentally projecting my own sentimental views onto it.

Clearing my throat, I stood and gestured to the rest of the room. "Well, what do you think?"

He glanced around, the room dwarfed by his size. I'd forgotten how *big* he was. There was no hiding from him here. Nowhere I could stand where I wasn't within an arm's length of him. But even so, I still felt an entire world away.

"Do we not share a bed?"

"We can."

"But you're my mate. You should never be without me. Always within reach." His features twisted with absolute confusion. "Why would we have separate rooms?"

"Well, it's just that it can get a bit crowded. And I thought you might appreciate having a place that was just yours. In case you needed space."

"Why would I want space?"

His words sounded off, as though he was leading me into a trap. I stepped closer to him. "Things are changing for us. So many things." I swallowed.

Now was the time. I needed to tell him.

"Alek . . . *elskan mín* . . ."

I waited for his response. For him to reassure me and call me his beloved. He didn't—hadn't since he'd returned. The lack of his endearment for me hadn't registered until now, but its absence was all I could think about. It felt significant.

"What is it?"

I stared into his eyes, eyes that seemed different from my memories, but I steeled myself against the unease raging inside me. Grabbing his hand, I pressed his palm to my slightly swollen middle. "I'm pregnant."

All color drained from his face. His hand twitched once before he sucked in a sharp gasp and backed away as though I'd bitten him. "No. This cannot be."

*Not him too.* Alek was supposed to be Team Pro-Baby, like Kingston. I blinked, feeling as though he'd slapped me. "Trust me, it is."

He spun away, raking his hands through his long mane

as he started pacing back and forth, muttering to himself. "What the fuck game is he playing? *Heimdall's shriveled dick*, he's always been irresponsible, but a mate? A child? I cannot keep up this charade. I won't. This is beyond mischief. This is insanity. Toying with her emotions like this? She's an innocent. She doesn't deserve to be played with."

As the tirade continued, his voice grew louder until he was practically bellowing with rage. The longer he spoke, the harder it was to deny the voice in the back of my mind screaming at me that something was very wrong.

"Take off your shirt," I demanded, my voice strong even though my heart was broken.

"Pardon?"

"You heard me. Take off your shirt. Right now."

Panic flickered in his eyes. "Why? Are you that desperate for it?"

My body hummed as anger took over for the heart-break. I needed the truth, and I needed it right the fuck then.

"Take. It. Off."

"No," he said mulishly, crossing his arms over his chest like that would stop me.

Clearly he wasn't familiar with hormonally charged pregnant women. That shirt was coming off, and I was getting my answers.

I stepped forward, gripping a piece of the cotton and yanking it back, tearing the garment in two.

He gaped, looking down at his exposed torso. His exposed, *unmarked* torso.

The Norse runes were nowhere to be found.

"Tor," I whispered, his name little more than a growl.

"I see my reputation precedes me."

The rage I'd been barely controlling took over, and I wrapped my hand around his throat, strength I shouldn't possess coursing through me. "What did you do to Alek?"

His eyes widened, hands lifting to peel my fingers back, his strength easily matching my own as he pulled free. "I didn't do anything. It was his idea."

"What?" That one word was nothing more than a shattered sound. Barely intelligible.

"I wouldn't have agreed had I known what he'd left behind. He told me there was nothing here for him. No one of importance."

That was it. I was done. I collapsed to the floor, my body trembling with the aftershocks of what he'd revealed. I'd never known pain like this. Not even when Noah had left me. This was worse. So much worse.

I was spiraling out of control, my pain bleeding into fury.

Tor reached for me, looking conflicted. I slapped his hand away with bone-snapping force, and he grunted in pain.

"Get away from me."

His eyes met mine, and they went wide with shock at whatever he found there. "Berserker," he whispered. "It can't be."

Reaching behind me, I grasped the leg of the chair I'd so lovingly arranged for his twin and hurled it at Tor's head, hating this impostor with every fiber of my being. The chair crashed into the wall, splintering and breaking as Tor dropped to avoid impact.

"Get out!"

It was the last I could manage as my vision turned red and my rage consumed me.

# TWENTY-TWO

Sunday's scent filled the shower stall as I rinsed the shampoo from my hair. So sue me, I liked smelling like my mate. Especially when she was alone with another of her men. The hot water hit my back, easing muscles that had been holding tension all night. Watching her put herself in harm's way to get Alek back had been one of the hardest things I'd done lately. But now the last of our group had returned, and all should have been right in Sunday's world. She finally had us all in one place again.

As if wanting to prove to me what a fucking naive fool I was, fate chose that moment to slap me upside the head.

Sunday's sudden grief cut through me like a knife, making me cry out in surprise and throw my palms against the tiles to keep from falling to my knees. Suds continued to trickle down my neck and shoulders as the steamy water sprayed over me, but I couldn't feel its heat, only her mounting fury.

Something was wrong. Already.

"Motherfucker," I muttered, stepping out of the shower

and snagging a towel as I made a mad dash for the woman I treasured more than anything.

I burst through the door, not wasting time on stupid things like manners. "Sunshine!" She was curled up on the floor, hair in her face, tears streaming down her cheeks, her lips curled back in a savage snarl.

"What the fuck did you do?" I asked, grasping the Novasgardian by his collar and slamming him back against the wall.

He shoved me away. "Nothing. She's gone mad."

I got in his face, growling low in my throat. "Say that again, and I'll make sure you never utter another word."

"He took Alek's place," Sunday said, her voice low and menacing.

"So you're the twin. I knew you smelled different."

"He didn't tell me he had someone waiting for him."

Sunday growled, pushing herself to her feet, and flinging herself at Tor.

I spun, intercepting her in the air and pulling her away from him. With the rage she was pumping out, I couldn't be sure she'd leave the guy standing, let alone alive. She was pissed now, but she'd regret killing her mate's brother once she calmed down. I couldn't let her do something she'd regret.

"Let go of me!" she screeched, her unnatural strength causing her to nearly break free of my hold.

"Stop, mate. You will listen to your Alpha." My voice was hard and cool, immovable.

She continued to squirm, but I could feel the resistance seeping out of her. Her wolf couldn't help the instinctive need to submit, even though the part of her that was berserker fought against it.

"He's keeping Alek from me."

"Alek sent me in his place. I've done nothing."

"He wouldn't do that," she shot back, but I could hear the doubt in her voice and see the slight quiver of her lip. Once again a tidal wave of her pain washed through me.

"Quiet your thoughts, Sunshine. Look at me." She met my gaze, and I pressed our foreheads together. Softly, I hummed the melody of the song I'd come to associate with her. The sound caught her ear if the slight relaxation of her muscles told me anything.

She was coming back to me. With each note the black bled from her eyes until they were a sparkling ocean blue once more.

"Kingston," she whispered, her voice broken. "Why would he do this? Why would he leave me?"

"He doesn't know about the child," Tor said, his words soft. "He'd never stay away if he knew."

"So let's go tell him," I said, ignoring the implication that if there wasn't a child, Alek would still have stayed away from Sunday. If you had told me I would be the one championing the mission to hunt down the other men my mate loved, I'd have laughed my ass off. But here I was, trying to keep the rest of these fuckers in line. I was a regular Mary fucking Poppins. Chim-chim-cher-ee, motherfuckers.

"It's not that easy."

"You managed to worm your way in even though it was supposed to be Alek. Seemed easy enough for you. That spell was supposed to be a one-way ticket on the Sunshine express. Non-transferable. Seems to me like you can make it happen. How about you give it the old college try before I make good on my offer to tear out your vocal cords?"

Tor narrowed his eyes, looking like he wanted nothing more than to pull my spine out through my asshole. I really hope he tried. I was itching for a fight after finding Sunday distraught on the floor. Even now, her tears slid down my chest.

"There is one way . . ."

"Ah, so he can see reason. Good. Keep talking, you Marvel knockoff. I'm not convinced I shouldn't eviscerate you yet."

"I would rip your heart out before you landed your first blow, you ill-mannered mutt."

"It takes one to know one."

"Next you're probably going to insult my mother. I should warn you, one more foul word about my family, and I'll be wearing your balls as a necklace."

"Sexy. You'd probably like having them that close to your face. Remind you what a real man looks like."

"Kingston, stop," Sunday's soft command and the hand she rested over my heart were the only things that could have stopped me in that moment. I wanted blood, but I'd settle for anything that took that haunted look out of her eyes.

"How can we get him back, Viking?" I scooped Sunday into my arms, cradling her shivering form close. "She needs him. Her connection to him is what's causing this berserker rage. It needs to be controlled."

Tor's nostrils flared as he released a heavy breath. "I have a device in my possession which will open up a portal to Novasgard. It's only good for one use and supposed to be my ticket home, but given the state of things here, it might be wise to use it early. If she's carrying my brother's child . . . if she's his mate, neither of them will survive being separated long without going mad."

"It gets worse?" I asked.

"You don't want to know how much worse, wolf."

"Get on with the portaling, then."

"We should get the others," Sunday said. "They have to come with us."

"Thorne is out hunting. He won't be back till sunup. Can you wait until morning?"

I glanced down at Sunday's tear-stained face. Her expression told me everything I needed to know. This one thing meant the world to her. I wasn't the only man in her life. I knew that. And now that I'd finally accepted she wanted all of us, I'd be damned if I'd let some long-haired, bearded lumbersexual get in the way of what she needed.

"Okay, new plan. I'll go track down your vampires."

"How will you find them?"

I shrugged. "Easy. Follow the scent of self-loathing and despair."

"I know where Caleb is. I can get him. You handle Noah."

"Are you sure? You look like you could use a nap."

She glared at me. "You were doing so good right up until the end."

I grinned before jutting my chin in Tor's direction. "What are we going to do with this asshole?"

"I'll call Moira. She and Ash can babysit him and make sure he doesn't get into any more trouble."

"I don't require a sitter."

"Tough shit," I said. "My woman says you do."

"I thought she was my brother's mate?"

I understood his confusion but didn't have the energy, let alone the time, to take on that explanation. What was I going to say? She has a magic pussy, and we all get to dick her down real good? Didn't see that going over well. Or worse, he might try to join the party. Fuck that. Four sausages were enough. There was already an excess. Too many hot dogs, not enough hot dog buns. Story of my life.

"It's a long story, one I don't have time to explain to someone whose brain is as puny as yours. Let's just leave it at there are four of us and call it a day."

"Four of you—"

"I said leave it."

He snapped his mouth closed, but disapproval radiated from every line of his body.

"Come on, baby. Let's get you cleaned up, and then we'll both go on hunts of our own."

I set her on her feet, and she smirked as her gaze raked my form. "You might want to put some clothes on first."

Shrugging, I dropped the towel. "Debatable. I run better when I'm naked."

"You do a lot of things better when you're naked."

"Damn right I do."

# TWENTY-THREE

Moriarty's voice grated on my last nerve as we finished our final circuit of the witch's garden. Night-blooming jasmine filled the air, at once cloying and delectable, the only thing that had been able to overpower the memory of the scent of lilacs that haunted me. Even when she wasn't with me, I smelled her. I could taste her honey on my tongue.

Bloody fecking hell, I could *not* have an erection right now. Not with this arse standing next to me telling me about some variation of spores, mold, and fungus.

"That reminds me, have I told you the one about the mushroom?"

I was going to murder him.

"No," I gritted out.

"Well, you see, it's really quite punny. A mushroom walks into a pub, and when the bartender tries to shoo him away, he says, 'but I'm a fun guy.' Get it? A mushroom is a fungi."

His obnoxious wheezing laugh floated on the air. The fool had no clue he was a single breath away from death.

I didn't respond. If I was honest, from one moment to the next, I forgot he was there because I felt *her*. Sunday was near. Her heartbeat matching my own. The lilacs I had tried so hard to forget permeated my senses.

As we came around the final bend, she was there, marching our way with a single-minded determination I knew spelled trouble for me. She was too damned stubborn for her own good.

"Father Gallagher, I need to speak with you."

"It's a little late for a chat, isn't it?" Moriarity asked.

"Away with you, you toady fool. Miss Fallon is clearly in a state. As her adviser, it's my job to hear her out. You wouldn't want to keep me from my duty now, would you?"

Moriarty gave me a lascivious wink. "Of course not, Father Gallagher. I'll leave you to it."

*What the hell was that about?*

Unease built in my gut, but I couldn't let it keep me from seeing to Sunday.

"What's all this, then?" I asked, forcing myself to keep my distance even though I wanted nothing more than to hold her tight and feel her curves against my hardness.

"The man we brought through the portal was Tor, Alek's twin. I'm going to Novasgard to bring my mate back."

"Why can't you simply heed the headmistress's advice and let us go? Marry the wolf and be done with it."

She scowled at me. "You know I'd never put any of you above the others that way. Marrying Kingston was never an option unless I could marry all of you."

My heart lurched at that.

"I want you to come to Novasgard with me."

"Sunday, I can't let you do that."

"You don't have a say. You stopped having a say when you decided I wasn't worth risking your precious job for."

I glared at her, even as her blow landed. She had no idea how much it pained me to deny her—to deny myself. But everything I did, I did to keep her safe. If I had to make her believe I didn't love her, I would. I could bear her hatred, but not her death. Just the thought of it sent a chill down my spine, reminding me that what I wanted didn't matter. Only the greater good.

"You're not." Fuck, those words burned on my tongue like acid. Still I kept going. "You're insolent, stubborn, spoiled rotten, and nothing more than a child."

"Everyone's a child to you, *grandpa*."

"There you go, proving me right once again."

"What are you going to do, spank me? Is that what you need, Caleb? You always feel better after punishing me. Do you need to bend me over your knee so you can get your mind right?"

I balled my hands into fists, willing away the hunger that visual caused. "You will die in Novasgard if you go. They aren't welcoming to strangers."

"I'm not a stranger. I'm their prince's mate."

"You can't go alone."

"I won't. And that's why I asked you to come with me."

"I couldn't go even if I wanted to. I have obligations here."

"More important than me?"

"Yes, Miss Fallon. More important than you. How many times are you going to make me say it? Do you enjoy rejection as much as I enjoy punishment? You and your childish whims do not make the list of my priorities."

Hurt flashed in her irises, but she was quick to school her expression. "You don't mean that."

"Don't I?"

She stared into my eyes, her gaze intent and searching for a glimmer of fallacy within me. "Fine. Lie to yourself if you need to. I'm going. When I come back, we'll continue this conversation."

"We won't. Our time is over."

For the first time, her expression hardened with genuine anger. "You know, I was in that room too, Caleb. I felt the way your hands shook when you touched me. How hot you burned for me. I felt your cock weeping with your cum as you came inside me."

"Enough! Throwing my indiscretions in my face will not get you what you want. I'm a man. I have the same weaknesses as the rest of them. You can't blame me for giving in when you spread your thighs so willingly."

"Maybe not, but I can sure as hell blame you for acting like it never happened."

"Because I should have been better! I should never have let myself touch you. Watch you. Want you."

"You can't help who you love any more than you can deny what you are."

"Watch me."

Her lips pressed into a tight line. "That's your job."

Turning on my heels, I blurred back to my quarters. I should have felt relief at my departure, but my body was still burning with need when I entered my private space.

I leaned against the door, not entirely sure what to do with myself. I was too on edge, brimming with emotions I had no right to feel. I was in no state of mind for atonement, too restless to trust myself not to go too far.

Needing to quiet my mind, I knelt at the small altar in the corner of my modest living space, desperate for some focus, some way to ground myself.

"Give me the strength to resist temptation, to remain steadfastly loyal to my goal. Remind me of why I am doing this in the first place. My eternal soul hangs in the balance, but I am weak. The sins of the flesh torture me. *She* torments me. Please guide me on the correct path. Help me remain virtuous. Give me what I—"

As if mocking my plea, the door flew open, and Sunday swept into the room with the full force of a tempest.

"What do you think—"

"No. You will not deny what's between us again."

She began stripping off her clothes, flinging them on the floor without a word. Fuck me, I couldn't have her naked in my chambers for a multitude of reasons. Chief among them that I was a breath away from shoving her against the wall and sinking inside her here and now. Was she a sign from God? Had He sent her to me?

I chuckled darkly. No. That would be far too easy. She was sent by the devil himself to tempt me.

"Stop this, right now."

She met my gaze and peeled her knickers down her legs before sinking to the floor and assuming the most sensually submissive pose I'd ever seen.

"I need to be punished, Daddy."

My knees nearly buckled as all the blood in my body rushed straight to my hardening dick. As happened every time she used that name, I became helpless to do anything but shift into the role. And if I was honest with myself, I didn't try to stop it. "Why can't you simply be a good girl?"

"I tried that, but all you do is ignore me. Being bad is the only way to get your attention."

"Your behavior disappoints me."

"You disappointed me first. You're not a very good daddy."

A growl slipped free as her accusation sliced through me. She wasn't wrong, but it still hurt. "My palm will be raw by the time I'm through giving you what you deserve."

"Do it. Give it to me. I need it."

Unable to stop myself, I gripped her by the hair and forced her to look up from where she'd trained her gaze on the floor. "Insolent."

"Yes."

"Spoiled."

"Yes."

"Stubborn."

"Yes."

"*Mine.*"

"Yes, Daddy. Yours."

A groan ripped from my throat as I bent down and stole a kiss. There was nothing kind or gentle about it. It was a claiming. A message. This woman belonged to me. I would own her. Body. Heart. Soul.

Everything stopped as my ears picked up the distinct sound of a rapid heartbeat in the room with us. Not hers. Not mine. I released her, backing away. There it was, clear and strong. A reminder of exactly how I'd failed her already.

A message from God the second I needed it most. A reminder of why I needed to stay away from her. Of my true purpose. My redemption.

"Put your fecking clothes on and get out."

Her eyes widened at my tone, and her resolve cracked. "Caleb . . . this is what we need. It will help put everything back into perspective. Make me yours. Remind me who owns my body." She reached for me, but I took three more rapid steps back.

"What I *need* is for you to leave me. The fuck. Alone."

Tears pooled in her eyes and my heart splintered. If she

228

didn't leave right now, I'd break. I'd pull her into my arms and make love to her until the sun rose. She could drag me straight to hell, and I'd have a smile on my face while we went.

"Now!" I thundered, desperation lending my voice a strength I didn't remotely feel.

I needed her to be the one to walk away. I wasn't strong enough to do it myself. It had to be her. It was the only way.

Her body trembled as she gathered her discarded clothes and slowly dressed. She wouldn't look at me. It was the least I deserved.

As she left my quarters, she glanced over her shoulder, heartbreak written on her face. "I love you, Caleb. Even when you make me hate you."

She walked out, shutting the door so gently it was almost worse than if she'd slammed it. Hating myself for how low I'd sunk, I picked up my coffee table and hurled it at the wall. I watched it break and shatter like the pathetic pieces of my heart.

What was the point of trying to regain my soul when I wouldn't have her to complete it in the end?

# TWENTY-FOUR

I sat on the back porch, a mug of cocoa in my hands keeping me warm as I stared blankly at the falling snow. I hadn't trusted my instincts when Tor had walked through the portal. I should have. There'd been something off about him from moment one. And Alek had been right there. So close. Within reach. Why didn't he want to come back?

"You don't look very happy for someone who's about to go get her mate back," Tor said, joining me.

It hurt to look at him now that I knew the truth. For all that he was a mirror image, it was easy to spot the subtle differences in their appearance. Tor raised his left eyebrow instead of his right. And there was a golden freckle in his eye that Alek didn't have. He also had a small scar right along his cheekbone. All small things, but when taken together they couldn't be ignored.

"I can't believe I didn't see you weren't him."

He shrugged; the slight movement from such a large frame made the bench wobble. "We spent our lives pretending to be one another. Even our parents had trouble

231

telling us apart most days. Father used to threaten us with tattoos just so he'd know which of us needed punishment."

"Well, I guess that makes me feel a little better."

He offered me a smile. "That was the point."

"How'd you get that scar?" I pointed to his cheek, trying to distract myself from the guilt I couldn't escape.

"Alek. We were no more than seven at the time. Our baby sister Astrid had just been born, and the two of us had been acting out. He threw a rock at my face."

"Why would he do that?"

Tor's lips twitched. "Because I called him Alistair. He hates his middle name, even though he was named for a famous mage."

I snorted. "Ah, so he was having one of his temper tantrums. That sounds like something he would do. Your mother is a healer, right? So why didn't she fix it?"

Tor settled back, his hands folded over his flat stomach. "My father told her scars add character. And it would be a good reminder that I needed to be more vigilant. Though, truth be told, I think he just wanted a way to tell us apart."

"Your father seems a little . . . intense."

"That's the berserker. He's not so bad once you get to know him. You'll see once you meet him. He's firm but fair. He'll do right by you and the babe."

The mention of the baby, of doing right by us, had fear creeping up and taking over. Things I hadn't given voice to finally took center stage. "I'm not sure I should go."

"Why? You're carrying my brother's child. Of course you should go. He needs to know."

"Alek chose to stay in Novasgard. If our bond was as strong as I thought, why wouldn't he jump at the chance to come back to me? I don't understand what happened to keep him there."

Tor's jaw tensed, a small muscle jumping in his cheek. "I don't know. It's not like him. He's a mischievous fucker on his best day, but he's not the kind of man who would leave his mate behind. That kind of bond means everything to us—to him. Something must have happened—" He broke off, shaking his head and releasing a frustrated growl. "I just can't think of anything that explains it."

"So something is wrong. That's your explanation?"

"He told me he hadn't met anyone. That no one important was waiting for him." He must've seen the hurt in my eyes because he took my hand and squeezed. "I can see now that wasn't true. My brother would never have given you his name to etch on your skin if you weren't important."

"He called me Kærasta."

Tor went still, his eyes sweeping over my face. "No wonder he couldn't control his berserker. There's no way he would use that word, knowing what it means, and leave you here."

"But that's exactly what he did."

"Maybe he thought sending me in his place would give you some kind of connection to him while he works on learning control? That having me here to protect you was better than nothing at all?"

"Really? My tongue was down your throat. That seems like an unnecessary connection."

"Well, that's not new either. There are perks to being identical." He waggled his eyebrows. "Mirror images in every way."

"My dance card is full."

"I noticed. I can't understand how my brother would willingly share you with two—"

"Three."

Brows lifted, he let that sink in, then continued. "Three other men. Berserkers are notoriously possessive. Some might say irrationally, even. If a single man, let alone three, tried to come between my father and mother, he would have ripped their balls off and served them for breakfast."

"That's the difference. They don't come between each other. They all love me, and I love them equally. Sharing is caring, you know."

He shook his head. "I can't picture willingly sharing my woman. How can she service me if she's busy with someone else?"

I laughed despite my aching heart. "Do you need me to draw you a diagram?"

"Perhaps. I'm much better with visual aids."

"Too bad I left my Barbies back home. You'll just have to take my word for it. No one is left *unserviced*."

"We're coming back to this conversation, *svigerinne*."

"What did you just call me?"

"My sister-in-law."

Something eased inside me when he called me that. As though he put up a block between us. I was thankful because as much as he resembled my mate, he didn't *feel* like him. I didn't want to touch him the way I wanted Alek, misplaced kisses aside. Those didn't count anyway. I'd thought I was welcoming my mate home. No one could hold that against me.

"I'm not anything-in-law just yet. Alek doesn't even want to be here."

"Which is why you need to get up off your pretty little arse and come with me. We need to get you to him, and if I need to, I'll knock some sense into him."

"Thank you, Tor."

"Don't mention it." He took my hand again and helped me to my feet. "Now when we arrive in Novasgard, let me do the talking. We are very private and protective of our own. You'll be a stranger. Instant suspicion will cloud everyone's minds. We'll take you to the jarl and get his blessing first."

"Isn't that . . . your dad?"

"Yes."

"Okay, so after I talk to him and he gives me the guest pass, then I'll get to see Alek?"

Tor nodded. "I can't imagine he'll stay away once he finds out you're there."

At least one of us seemed confident about it.

"And then how do we get back here?"

"My uncle, Fin. He should be home from his assignment soon. He'll open the portal. But if he's not, there's a gateway between our two realms. It will require additional travel once you cross over, but that can always be arranged."

"Where does it open?"

"Norway."

"Norway?"

Tor grinned. "It *is* the homeland of my ancestors."

I shook my head. "Fucking Vikings."

The back door opened, revealing Moira, today with a very aggressive electric blue hairstyle. She had it braided tightly at the sides while the bulk of it was pulled up into a series of complicated twists that created a badass semi-mohawk.

"Don't you love it?" she said, patting the back of her head. "I wanted to look the part for Vikingland. Doesn't this just *scream* shieldmaiden?"

Tor raised his brows. "Sure."

Neither of us believed him. I could see it in her face. "You look like a bad bitch, Mo."

"Want me to do yours before we go?"

"No. I'm good. Thanks." The last time she did my hair, I had so many bobby pins stabbing my scalp the resulting migraine lasted two days.

"Suit yourself. I'm sure Alek will appreciate my effort to look the part."

"Alek won't have eyes for you at all," Tor said with so much conviction my heart stumbled a little.

I wish I was as certain of that as he was.

"Whatever. We're ready. The bags are packed and everyone is waiting." Moira jutted her chin toward the inside of the house.

"You ready?" I asked, looking up at Tor.

"I was born ready."

"Now you sound like your brother."

"I'm the oldest. Alek sounds like me."

I rolled my eyes. Men. Always competing. "I'm sure he'd love to hear that."

Winking, he waited for me to enter the house before following me inside. Even Vikings could be gentlemen.

I found Noah, Kingston, Moira, and Ash standing in the living room, all of them softly chatting in front of the fireplace. They went quiet as soon as I entered.

Noah was the first to approach me, his expression twisted with concern. He cupped my cheek in his palm. "Dove, you're practically frozen. You should stay here, warm and safe. We can go through and bring him back for you."

I smiled and pointed out his obvious flaw. "And leave me here all alone?"

"Technically your priest is here." Kingston's teasing

tone wasn't appreciated at all. I told him what happened with Caleb. Not all the gory details, but enough for him to know better.

The glare I leveled on him had his jaw ticking as he tried to keep from smirking. "Too soon, Kingston."

"What? It's true. He's here."

Noah pulled me closer. "Consider yourself uninvited the next time Sunday needs a midnight snack, wolf."

"Hey," he protested.

Their friendly posturing accomplished what Kingston's teasing had failed to do. I was feeling much more relaxed as I snuggled into Noah's arms.

"This is beyond comprehension. Two Alphas in the same space sharing her. How are any of you still alive?" Tor ran a palm over his beard as he shook his head.

Kingston clapped him on the shoulder with a low laugh. "Trust me, man. You have no idea how good it can be until you feel your mate come on your cock because you fucked her raw, then before you can even pull out, she does it all over again while he's playing with her—"

"Earmuffs!" Moira barked, slapping her hands over Ash's ears.

"That's enough detail," Noah said, stopping Kingston before he could say anything else.

But from the interest in Tor's gaze, it had been enough. He finally looked like he understood the appeal.

My cheeks were on fire.

"Anyway . . ." I started, unable to look at Tor.

"Right. It's time. I'll open the portal, and we'll all go through. Together."

Tor pulled a stone the size of his palm out from his pocket. It was flat and wide, one surface covered in runes.

"The portal will open as soon as I activate the sigils. Stand ready."

We huddled closer together, not sure what to expect when Tor set the stone on the ground and then pulled a small pocket knife out and sliced through his palm. Curling his hand into a fist, he let his blood dribble onto the carved surface.

Much like when Moira and Ash had opened the doorway between our realms, the air shimmered and moved, rippling like water as the spell took hold.

"Hurry. It won't stay open long."

Noah, Kingston, and I rushed ahead, Kingston shouldering our bags while Noah kept my hand firmly grasped in his.

I was halfway through when a soft grunt pulled my focus from my goal. I spun around to find Moira on the floor and Tor curled over her, helping her stand. His eyes found mine, panic in them.

"Go! It's closing."

Noah gave my hand a sharp tug, and together we tumbled into a snowbank as the magic passage from one realm to the next sealed shut. Our Novasgardian guide was trapped on the other side.

# TWENTY-FIVE

"That bastard betrayed us," Noah growled, eyes scanning the horizon.

"You don't know that," I said, pushing myself up.

Kingston gestured to the veritable forest stretching out in every direction. "Don't we? Where the fuck even are we?"

"Novasgard?" I shrugged as he brushed snow out of my hair.

Noah wrapped his arms around me and pulled me into his chest. "Yes, but *where* in Novasgard? All I see are bloody trees and stars. I can't get the scent of anything other than snow. We may be supernatural beings, but we're still made of flesh and blood. We can freeze."

"Probably exactly what he wanted. Send us out here to die." Kingston stroked his palm over my mark, the contact warming me despite the bitter cold.

Panic had my heart thundering, but I refused to allow myself to believe Tor had set us up. He'd been way too earnest about Alek needing to know what was going on. His intentions had been pure. Getting left behind had been an accident. I was sure of it . . . mostly.

"Stop it. You know that isn't what happened. Things went sideways, but the plan is the same. We need to find the town and speak to Nord. We can't be that far away."

"Okay, but are we just supposed to spin in a circle and walk in a random direction? I'm not picking up the trace of anything either. Not even a fucking bear."

"They hibernate, so you probably wouldn't," Noah pointed out.

Kingston glared at him, clearly unamused. "Helpful."

"I do try."

"Well you're failing, so stop it."

"Okay, boys, as much as I love listening to the two of you argue, we need to move. There could be any kind of creature out here. Not just bears. We're not in Kansas anymore."

"Kansas? Dove, we weren't—"

"How sheltered were you as a child?" Kingston cocked a brow as he assessed Noah. "The Wizard of Oz is a classic."

"I had better things to do with my time than waste it on idle pursuits."

"Culture is not an idle pursuit."

Noah raised a mocking brow, mimicking Kingston's pose. "Well what good is that movie of yours right now, hm? Did it teach you any useful survival skills?"

"Well, I wouldn't turn down a yellow brick road right now. Even some flying monkeys would be nice."

"Too bad I don't have any ruby slippers."

Kingston smirked. "I'd like to see you in pigtails, baby. I can imagine it now. Two handlebars for me to tug on."

"What the bloody hell are you two going on about?"

Noah asked, frowning. He looked thoroughly put out, hating that he didn't understand our references.

"We'll have a movie night when we get home," I promised. "It'll all make sense."

"Especially the pigtails," Kingston said, tossing him a wink. "I have a feeling you'll be way into some Dorothy-Scarecrow role play."

"What?" Noah muttered.

I shook my head at Kingston, picking up on his unspoken insult that Noah was the brainless one. He just grinned at me.

"Tell me I'm wrong. Clearly Alek would be the lion, and I'm the tin man."

"Why is Alek the lion?" I asked. "You're the shifter."

"Because I'm not a fucking coward who tucked tail and ran. Alek, however, did exactly that. And besides, Sunshine. I don't have a heart because you stole it a long time ago." He leaned in and kissed my mark, growling low in his throat. "If we weren't lost in the fucking woods right now, I'd totally take you up against a tree and prove it."

Heat bloomed between my thighs, even in this freezing cold air, and Kingston noticed. He inhaled deeply.

"Oh, I smell *that*. Someone needs some attention. Don't worry, baby. I'll take care of you as soon as I can."

"*We* will. I can smell her too."

The hunger in both of their voices had my nipples tight and painful. Fuck. I could not let them spit-roast me in the middle of the Novasgardian wilderness. Frostbite notwithstanding, we had a job to do.

"Channel that lust, boys. No one's fucking anything until we find somewhere safe to bunk down for the night."

Kingston laughed but nodded his agreement. "Talk

MEG ANNE & K. LORAINE

about a solid pep talk. I find myself incredibly motivated all of a sudden."

"You weren't before?" I asked.

"Well, I mean . . . now there's a prize."

"Staying alive wasn't enough?"

"Eh."

The three of us began a slow trek through the thick snow, following the glow of lights in the distance. It wasn't a yellow brick road exactly, but it was the only thing we had to go on. Where there was light, there was likely a city.

"My thighs are numb. I did not dress for a hike in the snow," I grumbled as we pressed on for what felt like hours, but could have been only minutes. I had no way of knowing.

"We must be going in the wrong direction," Noah said. "If this wasn't a trap, Tor would have mentioned something before we left so we'd be better prepared for the elements."

*Crap.*

"Kingston, where's our stuff?"

His eyes widened. "Fuck. I must've dropped it back where we fell through. The goddamned snow is so deep I didn't even see it."

"You had one job . . ."

"Fuck you. I didn't see you offering to carry anything, asshole."

"I had Sunday. She made it through just fine."

"She's a popsicle."

"We all are. And now we're stuck in the middle of God knows where without supplies."

"Oh, my God. Stop. Fighting about this isn't going to fix it." I stared at the sky, my anxiety getting the better of me as the lights glowed in the distance, seeming farther away than they had when we started walking toward them. "It doesn't make sense. They should be closer."

"Aurora," Noah whispered.

"You did not just call me some other woman's name."

His lips twitched. "No, dove. Look, it's *the* Aurora." He pointed up between two towering conifers where neon lights were dancing across the inky sky.

My breath caught in my throat. Magic was the only way to describe what I was seeing. No wonder people stayed up all night to see this. I'd seen photos of this phenomenon, but here, in Novasgard, it was infinitely more striking, the colors vibrant and jewel-like. I'd only ever known them to be shades of blue and green, but here they ranged all the way to violet and electric pink. It was incredible.

The three of us stood beneath the majestic sight, just taking in the rare and unearthly beauty when a shadow streaked across the night sky.

My whole body froze as my brain tried to assign a name to the unfamiliar shape.

"Is . . . was that a . . . dragon?" Noah asked, his voice strangled.

"Not a dragon," I whispered as Alek's description came back to me. "Wyvern."

We were rigid with shock, not one of us remotely prepared to deal with the threat looming above us. Beside me, Kingston started to strip.

"What the hell are you doing?" I whispered, terrified of moving and drawing any attention in our direction. If that beast saw us, we were dead.

"I'm getting us the fuck out of here. None of us are going to be able to fight that thing. Our only defense is to get away from it."

"Agreed," Noah said, wrapping his palms around my

245

biceps and holding me to him. He knew me so well. If given the chance, I would've run to Kingston and tried to stop him from shifting. "Dove, the speed that wyvern was flying at has already put it out of range, but it could return. Now is our chance to find the right path. Let him do this."

I sighed, frustrated but resigned.

Fully naked, standing in the snow, Kingston gave me a wink. "Look at that, not even a little shrinkage."

I couldn't stop my laugh. "Of course not."

"I'll shift, catch the scent of the village, and lead us there. Do me a favor?"

Lifting my brows in an expression that clearly said continue, I waited for him to ask his question. Honestly, I think he just wanted me to stare at his dick a little longer.

"Bring my clothes?"

"Of course—" My assurance was cut off as soon as my gaze swept across the ground. "Uh . . . Kingston. Where'd you put them?"

"What do you mean? You just watched me take them off." His brows veed down in confusion. "What the fuck? They were right here."

A soft, childlike giggle caught on the wind in the distance. "What the devil . . ." Noah's eyes narrowed. "Sprites."

"You can see them?"

"Only just. They've taken your clothes, Kingston. It's likely what happened to ours as well. It seems you gave them quite a show."

Kingston smirked. "Fuck yeah, I did. It's a good thing I don't mind being naked. Novasgard is going to write stories about the handsome wolf shifter who waltzed into town and put all their men to shame."

I bit my cheek. It took everything in me not to remind

him that Alek more than had him beat in that department, but I couldn't bear to take the wind out of his sails. He was just so damn proud of himself. The cocky ass.

"If you're going to shift, then bloody do it. Sunday might not mind looking at your cock, but it's not my favorite sight in the world."

"Jealous?"

"Not remotely. I don't need any extra hardware to get the job done."

"You're missing the point." Kingston scowled as he looked down at himself. "Don't listen to him, Jake. You're perfect."

Before I could tell him to stop talking to his dick and get on with it, Kingston shifted.

An explosion of pine needles and snow accompanied his transformation, a shadow once again streaking across the sky. I was prepared to stop, drop, and roll for cover, but it didn't take more than half a second for my brain to catch up. It wasn't the wyvern. The shadow was much too small for that. Just a bird. An enormous bird.

"Ravens," Noah whispered. "Of course."

Kingston dropped his nose to the snow, then raised his snout into the air. His ears pricked forward, his posture going tense before he let out a howl. Then he began stalking in the opposite direction of where we'd been headed.

He didn't make it far, twelve feet at most, before a figure dropped from the trees.

My breath left me in a gasp. This guy was *huge*. And scary. Like . . . find me in a dark alley and violently murder me scary. His hair was black as night and wild about his face. A scar bisected one of his eyes, which was a milky white. The other was a piercing green that seemed to glow with fury. His upper lip curled back in a snarl.

"Trespassers."

Kingston growled, crouching low and ready to pounce while Noah put himself directly in front of me, his posture tensed for a fight.

"We're not—"

"Sunday, don't speak. They mean to kill us." Noah turned to face me, and I barely recognized the man before my eyes. Fangs fully extended, eyes blazing an eerie amber, skin pale as death. He looked every bit the vicious vampire I'd learned about. "I'll kill them all if they touch a hair on your head."

"You can try, vampire. You will fail." The scary Viking aimed his crossbow at Noah, and my heart nearly stopped.

Kingston padded backward, placing his wolfy body between the man with the weapon and me. Things were spiraling out of control quickly. I needed to diffuse this situation and fast before one or all of us got hurt.

Tor's words echoed in my mind.

"Nord!" I shouted.

Those dual-colored eyes landed on me, and I knew my breaths were numbered if I didn't play this right.

"I demand—"

"You demand? You make no demands on our land, trespasser."

Facing down a demon was less terrifying than this. Swallowing, I raised my chin and tried again. "I demand to be taken to your jarl, Nord."

"Is that so, hóra?"

Kingston let out a low growl, his hackles raising. I placed my hand on his back, silently begging him to stand down.

"You dare insult my mate?" Noah said, his fury permeating the air. He was about a second away from losing his shit.

"You speak the old tongue?" the Viking asked, head canting to the side as he studied Noah with more interest.

"I don't need to understand Norse to know you just called my woman a whore."

That had my spine stiffening. Why did men always toss that word around when they were threatened by a woman? Apparently not even Vikings had imagination when it came to insults. How disappointing.

Rustling in the trees had my eyes darting from side to side as several more armed men and women came out of hiding.

The scary fucker lifted his weapon, this time leveling it on me. "It's time for you to tell me why you're here. And I should warn you, if I don't like your answer, I *will* kill you."

I swallowed, my body going both hot and cold as a tinny ringing started up in my ears.

"Alek." His eyes narrowed, so I repeated myself. "I'm here for Aleksandr Alistair Nordson. My true mate."

Shucking my coat, I pulled up my sleeve and bared the runes tattooed into my arm. The group of Vikings gasped and shuffled, their expressions laced with suspicion and curiosity.

"Bind them. We will take them to the jarl." He trained his terrifying gaze on me. "Your wolf can either return to human form, or we will muzzle him and string him up by his feet. His choice."

# CHAPTER
# TWENTY-SIX
### SUNDAY

"Get in there," the intimidating Viking said as he shoved a fully nude Kingston over the threshold.

"You could at least buy me dinner before you get handsy."

I stumbled in behind them, Noah on my heels as we left the chilly outdoors and entered what could only be described as a throne room. The first thing I noticed was how it smelled. The scent of *Alek* filled my nose, and I froze, my heart seizing. But a quick sweep around the room revealed he wasn't there.

High arched ceilings, dark as night, glittered with the echoes of candlelight from a multitude of chandeliers. The glow gave the space a much less sinister feel, but I knew this could easily go badly for all of us. The monstrous fossil hanging in the middle of the room was testament enough to that.

"Ah, there are the lights we were searching for," Noah said, his focus trained on the bank of windows, which showcased the horizon as perfectly as if we were staring at a picture.

The Aurora was on full display, lighting up the night sky as well as the entirety of the harbor as its reflection danced on the ocean below.

"Seen it. I'm much more interested in getting what we came for so we can go back home." Kingston's low grumble as he took my hand almost made me smile . . . almost.

"You'll only get home if you prove yourself to be harmless." The Viking who'd taken us hostage gave Kingston another shove.

"Keep shoving me, and I'll show you how harmless I am, *One-eyed Willie*."

Noah snorted. It seemed like even my vampire prince knew about *The Goonies*.

The Viking's low growl was cut off by the sound of a door opening.

"Søren, you've never returned from a hunt empty-handed, but this is new fare, even for you. What happened to the boy's clothes, or was the fool really roaming around the forest armed with nothing but his cock and a smile?" The deep voice boomed from the end of the hall, one I'd heard before as he entered and stalked toward the massive throne.

"Nord," I whispered, finally finding my voice.

He sat, his legs splayed wide, arms draped on each of the armrests. "That is my name, little one. But the question is, why do you know it?"

"We've met before, although I don't think we've ever been properly introduced. I'm Sunday," I said, stepping closer so I was surrounded by the golden candlelight.

He narrowed his gaze, and Søren tensed as I approached

the jarl. "Sunday. What a strange name. You do look familiar. Ah, yes, the crying girl in the woods."

*Great first impression, Sunday. Way to be memorable.*

"In my defense, things were a little . . . tense."

He lifted a brow. "You'll find no argument from me on that front. But what brings you here? And more to the point, *how* did you find your way to Novasgard?"

"Funny story, actually."

His lips twitched. "Is that so? Indulge us." He waved a hand, the gesture reminding me of a king at court. I couldn't afford to forget how this man held my fate in his hands. As charming as he was, he was also dangerous.

"You took my mate from me. I came to get him." Was it a tactful approach? No. But in cases like these, where a literal Viking stood between me and my mate, the only way through was direct.

His brows rose, the expression so similar to one I'd seen on Alek it made me ache. "You came to . . . get him?"

"Yeah."

"I am sorry to be the one to tell you this, but Alek stayed of his own choosing."

"Only because he didn't have all the facts. At least, that's what Tor said when he opened the portal for us."

An indistinct murmur rose from the few people in the throne room. I'd hit a nerve.

"What do you mean, he opened the portal? He'd never let outsiders into Novasgard unaccompanied."

"Well, he was supposed to come with us, but he tripped or some shit," Kingston added.

"Will someone get this fool some clothes?" Nord called out.

"Or perhaps a muzzle," Søren muttered, making Noah snicker and Kingston glower.

The woman standing closest to the throne stepped forward. "I'm sure I can find some clothing that will suit him. Though he is quite scrawny."

"Scrawny? Who the hell you calling scrawny, Brunhilda?"

Nord's pleasant expression vanished, and he rose slowly from his throne, face thunderous. "You will hold your tongue. Strega is a fierce warrior who will have your balls for breakfast if given half the chance."

"Say the word, and I'll slit his throat and bathe in his blood."

Kingston swallowed. "Maybe I was a bit hasty."

"Don't kill him, but take him with you. Perhaps some time in your presence will school his attitude."

Strega pulled a dagger from the sheath at her thigh. "Follow me, puppy. But if you try anything, I'll stab first and apologize later."

Kingston shot me a wary glance, but I nodded. "Go with her. You need clothes, and I need to be able to talk without you getting us all killed on principle."

He smirked. "That's fair. I'll be back, Sunshine."

"Do I have to bring him back? I could take him to the docks and toss him in."

"We do need to feed the kraken . . ." Nord mused, a smile playing on his lips.

"Excuse me, a kraken? No one said shit about a kraken," Kingston said, panic making his voice high and tight.

"Is it my birthday? I'm rather enjoying Novasgard."

I leveled a glare at Noah. "Well, *I'm* rather attached to him, so let's make sure they bring him back, please."

"Your wolf will remain intact, little one. As long as he behaves. As for the vampire . . ." Nord started, "I guess that remains to be seen."

I cleared my throat, not wanting Noah to start in on the alpha male posturing too. "I think we've gotten a little off-topic."

"That happens quite often," Nord said. "Especially when dealing with humans."

Søren grunted his agreement. "Mouthy fuckers."

"So are Vikings," I ground out.

Nord's laughter boomed around the chamber. He sat back down, leaning forward with his elbows resting on his knees. "This kitten has balls."

"That's not how the expression . . ." Noah began, but shut his mouth almost as soon as he started. "Never mind. That one suits just as well."

"Thanks for that," Nord said dryly before turning his attention back to me. "Now, why did you come all this way to see my son? You can't have been close. He would have mentioned you."

Pain sliced my heart, but I stood tall. "He's my mate."

Nord's posture stiffened. "What?"

"And I'm pregnant."

"Frigg's fucking foreskin," Søren gasped.

Something lit up inside Nord. "Strega!" His bellow rang out so loud I felt the vibration in my chest, and the wyvern skeleton suspended above us shook. "Get my son and my wife."

"I live to serve you, oh, jarl." Strega's annoyance was thinly veiled as she grabbed Kingston by the ear and tugged.

He gave a yip of annoyance, but all that got him was her low murmured, "Bad dog."

"Sunshine, you better make this up to me." His words were muttered as he trailed after her out of the room, but I caught them all the same.

The silence following their departure was awkward and absolute. Nord stared at us from his throne, his gaze clearly assessing. Noah shifted restlessly behind me, moving until his breath fanned over my neck and his hand was pressed against my lower back. I knew it was a statement; I just didn't know if it was for my benefit or Nord's.

The door opened, and hurried footsteps came from the corridor as a woman I recognized entered the room.

"Nord, what the ever-loving he . . . llo?" Lina stared at us, eyes wide. "Sunday? What are you doing here?"

Nord grumbled. "This girl says she is Alek's mate. That she's carrying his child."

Lina's eyes flew wide, her mouth falling open. "Oh . . ." She looked at Nord, then back at me, her other hand pressing to her chest. "Oh."

Nord reached out and wrapped a hand around her waist, tugging her closer until she sat gracelessly in his lap.

"We're going to be grandparents?" she whispered, eyes shining.

"So you know this girl? She's truly Alek's mate?"

"Yes. She is."

"Strega! Where the bloody hell is Alek? Get him in here."

Lina beamed. "He'll be so happy to see you."

My heart nearly burst with hope and relief. I hadn't made it all up. Our connection was real. Lina knew it, and so did I.

Seconds later, Alek stumbled in, Strega smirking as she and Kingston followed, muttering as he adjusted the leather pants he was now wearing. But my eyes were only for my Viking, looking absolutely edible in his low-slung sweatpants with my name on full display down his side.

His hair was disheveled, his eyes hooded with sleep. "Has someone died?"

"Why do you assume the worst?" Lina asked.

"Why else would you wake me in the middle of the bloody night?"

"You have company," Lina said, her smile huge as she gestured to where Noah and I were standing.

"Thorne? What are you and Kingston doing here?" His gaze lasered onto me, and he gave me an appreciative once-over. "And who is this exquisite creature?"

"Not the time for a joke. They came with me to bring you back." My throat was so fucking tight. I wanted to fling myself into his arms, but something stopped me.

"Who's joking?"

"Alek . . . stop it," Lina said. "Is that any way to treat poor Sunday after she's come so far to be with you?"

Confusion clouded his face, his brows scrunching low. "Sunday?"

"Yes, Sunday. You have my name tattooed down your side." Frustration burned like acid.

"Oh, that? I lost a bet. Had to get it."

What was he talking about? We'd shared a beautiful moment. He'd used such care when he sent the magic through us both. "No. That's not what happened. I was there."

He laughed. "No. You weren't. I have never seen you before, and trust me, sweetheart, there's no way I'd forget you if I had."

Now I was just angry. I'd come all this way. Frozen my tits off. Cried for him. And *this* was how he reacted? "Oh, really? Then how do you explain this?" I tore my coat off and showed him the runes trailing down my inner arm, the perfect lines now marred by a scar from Chad's handiwork.

He glanced at his parents and then back at me. "I

cannot, except to say that clearly you are obsessed with me."

"What is wrong with you?" Noah asked, his hand slipping around my waist, holding me up even as my knees wobbled.

"Nothing. I feel better than I have in ages."

Alek and Nord exchanged a loaded glance. The jarl of Novasgard looked conflicted, like he wasn't sure who to trust. His son about not knowing me, or his wife who'd just whole-heartedly vouched for me.

"He doesn't remember. Why doesn't he remember me?" I whispered, tears clogging my throat and making my voice come out strained.

Lina's face twisted with horror. "Oh, Quinn, you didn't."

"Satori!" Nord's expression turned savage as he grasped the edges of the chair. He cut his gaze to Strega and in a low, even tone, demanded, "Take them to the house and provide them with rooms while we get to the bottom of this. They're not to leave until we get our answers."

"It will be as you say," Strega replied, with a slight bow of her head. "You three, with me."

Sunday's pain was a hook in my heart, tugging me forward and pulling me from my room. The tether might be invisible, but there was no ignoring the connection as I followed it down the hall and toward the source. I shut the door to my assigned quarters behind me, the heavy wood sealing closed with a loud click, echoing down the hallway. I didn't care if anyone heard me. Sunday needed me. That was all that mattered.

I'd heard Alek's father, I think Sunday called him Nord, say that guards were to stay outside our rooms, but there was no one as I padded down the corridor, mostly ignoring the antique furniture and statues, except to note them as landmarks so I could find my way back. Sunday was two doors down from me, a massive taxidermy bear the halfway mark between us.

Kingston stood in front of said bear. He stared up at the creature, arms crossed, eyes narrowed. "Hey there, Yogi. Can you tell me where Sunshine's picnic basket is hiding?

"Weren't you paying any attention when they led us to our rooms?" I asked with a sigh.

"I was too busy trying not to get shanked by the stab-happy Viking."

"Which one? The woman?"

"Yes. She was handsy and scary as fuck. I'm not ashamed to admit it."

"You should be, *Alpha*."

"Fuck you, asshole. I'd like to see how you hold up when you're the one at knifepoint. She threatened Jake. There's nothing you wouldn't do to protect little Noah."

I cocked a brow and smirked. "There's nothing little about him. You've seen what I'm working with. Sunday never complains."

"Not to you."

"Piss off, wanker."

"I have no interest in the toothpicks the two of you are sporting under your trousers, I promise you. Now, what the hell are you doing wandering around unattended?"

Strega leaned against the wall next to Sunday's door, her frame at once intimidating and striking.

"We're coming to help our mate. She's upset. I can feel it."

"Yeah. She called us."

Strega's perfectly arched brow lifted. "Is she? *Your* mate? I thought she was Alek's?"

"It's a long story, and frankly none of your business."

She lifted her hands. "My orders were to watch, not to interfere. Go in, if you must, but from the sounds of it, she's not going to make great company. Poor girl hasn't stopped crying since she went inside."

Kingston and I exchanged looks. That was the exact

reason we were both here. We'd felt her pain and been helpless to ignore it.

"You heard her. Let's go." Kingston shoved past me and reached for the door.

"Don't try anything shifty, puppy. I'll tame you if I have to."

He growled low in his throat. "Only one woman has that power, and as scary as you are, it's not you. This may be your realm, but I will do whatever's required to protect what's mine. You'd do well to remember that."

"And you'd do well to remember that I have cum stains in my sheets older than you, puppy."

"Maybe you should try washing them."

She bared her teeth in a terrifying imitation of a smile.

"Care to demonstrate the proper way to remove said stains from linens? You look like you have a lot of experience."

Kingston's mouth hung open as he searched for a rebuttal, so I opened the door and walked into Sunday's room. If they wanted to have a battle of wits, more power to them, but I was only interested in the woman behind the door.

The spray of water grew louder as I crossed over the threshold, leaving little doubt where my mate was hiding. I took in the four-poster bed, roaring fireplace, and the mantle filled with fat pillar candles, but mostly ignored them as I followed the sound of the shower to Sunday.

"Bloody hell, Sunday," I murmured the moment I saw her curled into a ball as she sat under the spray of water, rocking back and forth. "Why didn't you call me?"

She rested her cheek on her knee, her eyes bloodshot as she looked up at me, not even a little surprised to find me in her bathroom. "What was I supposed to say?"

"That you needed me, dove. That's more than enough."

"I need you," she whispered, her voice broken.

"As you wish," I whispered back, stepping under the water, fighting a shiver at the cold as I scooped her into my arms.

"You're supposed to take off your clothes when you get into the shower, Thorne. Didn't your vampire dad teach you anything? Oh, shit . . . " Kingston's voice filled the bathroom, his teasing tone dying as I turned to face him with Sunday in my arms.

"Shit is right, you dolt. She needs us, and you're making fucking jokes."

"That's what I do, asshole. It's how I deal with stress."

"How about you try manning the fuck up for once?"

"What do you need me to do?" he asked, surprising the hell out of me by taking my words to heart instead of fighting me.

"She's damn near frozen. Get a towel, a robe, something to warm her."

Without another word, he tore off his shirt. "Hand her to me."

"I beg your pardon?"

"Now's not the time for you to be so British. Hand. Her. To. Me. I'm a wolf. Naturally warm."

I was loath to part with her, but the dog had a point. He could warm her with his body heat far better than a cold-blooded creature like me. My human half didn't hold a candle to his animalistic warmth.

I handed her to him, careful not to jostle her too much during the transfer. Her violent shivering had her teeth chattering dramatically as the air hit her nearly frozen skin.

"There it is, Sunshine. Just wrap yourself around me. I've got you. It's okay."

Kingston's low murmurs were so genuine. His words

were stronger evidence of his love than anything else he'd shown me. He might have been a cocky arsehole, but he truly was devoted to Sunday. Same as me.

Her expression crumpled under his tender regard. "He doesn't remember me," she said, pressing her face against his neck as she sobbed.

"Something happened to him. There's no other explanation." I wrapped a towel around her shoulders and kissed the place I'd marked her.

"How do you know?"

"Because he loves you just as fiercely as I do."

Kingston coughed.

"As *we* do," I corrected. "The only way I'd forget you is if someone—"

"If someone stole you from us." Kingston finished the sentence without letting me take a breath.

"Is that even possible?"

"You've roomed with a Belladonna for nearly a year and can still ask that question with a straight face?"

"She's never stolen my memories."

"That you know of." I offered.

"Fuck." Kingston's low oath sent a chill down my spine. "We can't trust a single goddamned person, can we?"

"Save each other," I replied, running my hand up and down Sunday's back.

Kingston tossed me a look. "Who'd have figured you and I would end up on the same team, bloodsucker?"

"Me."

Her voice was so small it broke my heart. "You should get some rest, sweetheart. You and the babe need it."

"I'm not tired."

"I don't care. You need to have a lie down because I'm trying to be strong here, and you're breaking me into pieces with every passing moment. Please, dove, for me, lie down and let us care for you."

Her tear-stained face lifted, and she held my gaze for a long moment before giving me a slight nod. "Will you lay down with me? Both of you? I don't want to be alone."

"Of fucking course we will." Kingston kissed her cheek. "Sunday sandwiches are my favorite."

I snickered. "Why does everything go back to food with you?"

"Because I'm a growing boy," he said, winking over his shoulder as he turned to carry her to the fur-covered bed. "I have a voracious appetite."

"Down, boy," I muttered.

Depositing her in the center of the large mattress, Kingston crawled in beside her as I peeled wet clothes from my body.

"Looks like you're the one who needs to get it under control, Thorne," Kingston teased, one brow cocked as he took in my obvious erection.

"Just because I want her doesn't mean I'll expect anything of her."

The side of his lip twitched higher. "That's not what little Noah is saying."

"Call him little again, pup. I dare you."

Sunday gave a weak smile and held out her arms for me. I slid in beside her, turning so I was facing her and able to gaze into those beautiful, haunted eyes.

Kingston shifted so he spooned her from behind, his large palm resting on her hip while he pressed kisses against her mark. It wasn't long before Sunday's eyelids grew heavy, and she drifted off into slumber.

When I was sure she was fast asleep, I caught Kingston's eye.

"What?" he grumbled.

"We need to talk about this."

"Sharing her? I thought we were past that."

"No, you idiot. Something isn't right here. We need a plan before it all goes tits up."

His eyes moved to focus on something behind me. "I don't want to wake her. Should we take this somewhere else?"

I followed his gaze, finding a candlelit balcony. "Are you trying to seduce me? Boundaries, Kingston. They're important."

"You'd be lucky to have me trying to seduce you. Come on. We need to talk, and I don't want her to hear. She's been through enough for one day."

I glanced back at her sleeping face, easily spotting the tear tracks and deep purple smudges beneath the thick fringe of her lashes. "Balcony it is."

The bracing chill in the air hit us the instant we stepped outside, making me thankful I'd stopped to put on a robe I'd found hanging on the bathroom door. I couldn't help my smirk as Kingston tugged at the tight leather pants the Viking woman had found for him. He glared at the fur wrap, leaving it where he'd tossed it on the floor, and followed me outside.

"Fucking sprites. If I catch those little dicks, I'll kill them for stealing our clothes."

My low laugh escaped before I could stop it. "Uncomfortable? Those trousers do seem a bit tight."

"Leather isn't all it's cracked up to be. The chafing." He made a face and tugged at the crotch of his pants again. "And my piercings keep catching on the laces."

"Sounds like a personal problem."

"Fuck you, you're the one who asked."

As fun as it was to poke at him, I had frost forming on my eyelashes as we stood there. Before long, I'd be of no use to Sunday until I thawed. "Get to talking, wolf. I'm freezing my bollocks off out here."

"Okay, listen." He lowered his voice and leaned in closer. "Alek clearly had someone messing around with his head."

"What do you mean?"

"Don't act stupid. You were in there with me. The guy didn't even recognize her. I don't think these people can be trusted."

"You think they did it?" My gut turned to a cold pit at his observation. So much about this didn't track. Tor showing up, Alek's indifference, the great bloody warrior taking us into custody.

"Yes. They wiped his brain, scrambled him up, and locked him into a life he doesn't want. Then, to make matters worse, they sent Tor to replace him. The fucker already broke, but he was prepared to pretend to be Alek for the long haul. That doesn't scream *trustworthy* to me."

"What do you suggest we do about it? We're sitting ducks here. We don't even have clothes, let alone a way to fight back."

"We need to find that gateway and get our asses home. The longer we stay here, the worse off I think we'll be. This place is no good for Sunday. She barely got through a couple hours. What's she going to be like after a few days of that mind fuckery?"

As someone who had firsthand experience being parted from her, able to see her but not be with her, I knew it wouldn't be pretty. And she hadn't forgotten me when we'd been separated. But the thought of her looking straight through me, the way Alek had her, sent a chill seeping into my bones that had nothing to do with the weather.

I opened my mouth, but a scream from inside the room had us both bolting back inside. Each of us rushed to the bed.

"Sunshine!"

"What's wrong, dove?"

Sunday thrashed on the mattress, her hair a tangled mess around her shoulders as she battled whatever demons haunted her dreams.

"Hold her. Don't let her fall."

Kingston shot me a glare. "What the fuck do you think I'm doing? She's strong."

I cupped her face between my hands and pressed my forehead to hers. "Open your eyes, dove. I'm here. We're here. We have you."

Her eyes flew open, pupils blown, as she wildly searched the room. It was like she didn't even see us at first. Not until after she blinked a few times and bolted upright.

"Noah? Kingston?"

"That's right, sweetheart, we're right here. We won't let anything happen to you." I brushed my lips over her damp forehead, pulling her to a kneeling position so I could wrap my arms around her and cuddle her close.

"It was just a dream, baby," Kingston said from the position he'd taken behind her.

"God, it felt so real." Her voice wobbled as Kingston pressed his mouth to the mark at her throat.

"Let us make it go away. Let us love you." He slipped his arms around her waist as I threaded my fingers in her hair and held her gaze.

"Yes," she whispered against my lips. "Make it all go away."

She reached back, lifting her arm to curl around Kingston's neck and hold him in place as she kissed me.

We were ready to give her what she needed. I was desperate for it if I was being honest. It had been too long since we'd been like this. My fangs descended, another type of hunger rearing its head, and I groaned.

"Take what you want, Noah. I don't mind."

Fucking hell, I didn't have the control I needed after such an ordeal. I gave in and sank my fangs into her throat, the blood I craved more than any other hitting my tongue in a burst of flavor unlike anything I'd ever known.

Knuckles brushed against the silk of my robe, running up my torso and making me shiver. It took me a second to place the sensation as Kingston moving his hands to cup Sunday's breasts. As I fed, a frenzy started to build. She tasted fucking amazing. The same, but enhanced somehow. The flavor bolder. More enticing. Every pull of blood sent me spiraling deeper.

"Thorne, stop. You're taking too much." Kingston's low warning hit my ears at the same time Sunday cried out in pain, her fingers digging into my shoulder, pushing me away.

She whimpered as I tore my fangs from her neck, panting. "Fuck, Sunday. Are you all right?"

Before she could answer, the door splintered inward, a hulking beast of a man looming in the opening, his eyes black as pitch, muscles bulging and death in his stare.

Kingston stiffened and made eye contact with me. "Oh, shit."

# TWENTY-EIGHT

## ALEK

I couldn't get the dark-haired beauty out of my thoughts. The pain in her eyes, the hope written on her face, and the undeniable love threading through her voice when she'd said my name all rattled around in my brain without end. I had no escape from the strange ache in my head. Everything was clouded with her. Who the hell was she? Why couldn't I remember her? Even my mother knew who she was.

The lack of answers had my temper riding a razor's edge. Never a good thing for a berserker, but far worse for one newly turned. I was liable to bite someone's head off if they breathed too loudly in my general direction. Guard duty sounded worse with each step I took toward the door to the room she'd been assigned. The closer I got, the tenser I became.

"Ah, the lost prince at last. I thought you might show up here," Strega said from her position at the door. "If you meant to show up for duty, you could have tried being on time for your shift. Or has your time away spoiled you and made you forget about things like punctuality and codes of conduct?"

"Piss off, Strega."

She laughed. "Oh, my little mischief maker's found his balls. Well done, you."

A pained cry caught my ear from behind the door, the sound feminine and somehow absolutely terrible. I turned away from Strega and reached for the doorknob, but she shook her head.

"They're in there with her. She's not alone."

"She's hurting."

The sound of the wolf's voice filtered to me, a low warning of something dangerous.

Strega's eyes flashed, and she made a disgusted sound in the back of her throat. "Fucking hell, I should have known better than to let a hungry bloodsucker in there with her. She's ripe for the picking."

"What?" Rage coursed through me. Untamed. Familiar. This time, I greeted it like an old friend.

Something in my voice must have sounded off because Strega blinked and lifted her gaze back to my face. "Fuck. Not again."

"Get out of my way."

"No. You can't go in there—"

"Get the fuck out of my way or so help me, Strega, I will throw you on your arse."

She bared her teeth in a snarl and took off down the hall. I didn't need her to say a word to know she was on her way to get my father. In my current state, he was the only one who could stop me.

A soft whimper from inside the room was the final straw. I broke down the door rather than knock and stared at the three figures on the bed.

"Oh, shit," Kingston said, his hands cupping Sunday's breasts. Blood trickled from a wound in her throat, a matching crimson trail running down Thorne's chin. "This is, uh, exactly what it looks like."

But my eyes shifted to the line of black runes running across her pale skin.

"Mine," I growled. That word escaped before I knew what I was saying, and when she locked gazes with me, I stalked forward, berserker in full control.

"Alek," she breathed, her voice caressing my name, making me throb with want.

"Move!" Kingston shouted.

"Where am I supposed to go?" Thorne countered. "I'm not letting him come near her like that."

I could hear the words, understand them even, but the only thing that fully registered was the bone-deep fury at seeing my woman in someone else's arms. My cock swelled with need for her. I had to claim her, to shove those other two distractions out of the way and make her mine.

Prowling forward, I readied my hands to rend their heads from their bodies if they fought me. Somewhere in the back of my mind, I knew we were friends, sort of, but Sunday was my goal. Which meant right now, they were in my way. Insects to be crushed beneath my boot.

Kingston was the first to move, shoving Sunday behind him as he jumped off the bed to place himself between us. Thorne was only a second later, standing so that the two men were shoulder to shoulder in a poor imitation of a wall. As if they could ever stop me.

"So you chose death?" I barely recognized my voice.

"Don't do this, man. You'll never forgive yourself." Kingston reached back and held Sunday in place even though she fought to get free.

"Alek, stop. Don't hurt them." She peered over Kingston's shoulder, but all I saw was someone who needed me to take her. I wanted to hear her scream my name. To feel her nails clawing down my back as I drove inside her.

Reaching for Kingston's shoulder, I snarled deep in warning. "I can make it quick."

Fire raced through my scalp as something gripped my hair hard enough to pull it out. "No, son. You'll do no such thing."

I twisted around, finding my fury mirrored in my father's eyes. "She is mine."

His brows lifted. "I'm glad you finally seem to realize that. Does this mean you remember her?"

I couldn't answer the question. Not only because I was in a full-blown berserker's rage, but because I didn't. Not even a little. I wasn't sure of anything except that I needed to be inside her more than I needed my next breath, and I was prepared to kill anyone that tried to stop me.

I struggled in his hold, the shackles he'd clamped around my wrists without my knowledge stronger than they should have been. "Release me."

"No."

I lunged forward, and I noted the resignation in my father's eyes as he grasped my face in his hands.

"Why do you always insist on making me hurt you?"

"You couldn't hurt me, old man. You traded in your balls long ago."

Fury burned in the back of his ice-blue irises as he snarled. "Thank you, son. That makes this so much easier."

Then he snapped his head forward, and the last thing I remembered was an explosion of pain.

~

"Do not make me ask you again, Satori."

My mother's voice was the first thing I heard as I slowly regained consciousness. I blinked a few times to clear my vision. Glass walls. A plain, nearly empty space. Imprisoned again, then.

"Oh, it's Satori now, *Cuska*?" Aunt Quinn stood with my father, uncle, and mother, her posture defensive.

"Answer the fucking question, or you'll have another berserker to deal with," my mother spat, the anger pouring off her surpassing that of my father's.

My uncle wrapped his hand around the back of Quinn's neck, pulling the choker she always wore a little tighter. "They deserve the truth, princess."

"Fine. Yes. I took them."

*Took them? What did she take?*

"Quinn," Uncle Finley said, the disappointment in his voice unmistakable. "How could you? After everything we went through, you'd really do that to someone else?"

She spun out of his hold, her eyes filled with lavender fire. "I did what I had to do. When those boys were born, I swore I'd do anything to keep them safe. I kept my vow when no one else wanted to step up to the plate."

My mother took a step closer to her. "Quinn, no. Not like that. You promised never to interfere with our memories again."

Her finger shook as she leveled it at my mother. "I never made you that promise. Only him." She pointed to my uncle. "The boys were never part of the arrangement."

"You took Alek's memories?" Father asked. "She is his mate, Satori. No wonder he slipped into the bloodlust. A berserker deprived of their mate is more dangerous than anything else in existence."

So that's what this emptiness inside me was. She'd taken away my memories of Sunday. My mate. Anger and grief clashed within me. How could she do that to me?

Quinn snorted. "You haven't seen Finley's reaction to a scratched hood on one of his precious cars, then."

"Not the time for jokes, sweetheart," Finley said, his expression grim. "Have you already forgotten what it did to me when you took away my memory of you?"

Her shoulders sagged, but her expression remained fierce. "You know I can't forget anything."

"Then you, better than anyone, know that coming between mates is the worst thing you could ever do. Death would be kinder than ripping out a man's soul. Give them back, Quinn. Right now."

I got to my feet on shaky legs and stumbled to the glass wall, pressing my palms to the cool window. "Give her back to me. Please? I feel . . . wrong without her. Broken."

Her bravado fled when her eyes met mine. "Oh, Tiny. I didn't do it to hurt you. I was saving your life."

"You didn't save it. You ruined it."

"Alek . . ."

"You know he's telling you the truth," Finley said, ducking his head so he was speaking directly in her ear. "A man cannot live without his soul. It is a half-life at best, you said so yourself. Would you really condemn your own godson to such a miserable existence?"

She lifted her chin, but there was no missing its quiver. "To save his life, there's nothing I wouldn't do. She's going to get him killed."

"Please," I begged. "It's my life. I should be the one who gets to decide what I can and cannot endure."

My mother reached out a hand and rested it on her best friend's shoulder. "Quinn, I'm begging you. Don't make my son suffer like this. I know your heart, that your intentions were pure. You never intended for things to turn out this way, but look at what it's doing to him. We will find another way. We always do."

She looked between all of us, utterly defeated. "Okay. Fine."

Relief and something that felt a hell of a lot like hope swelled inside me as she stepped forward and placed her palms on the glass.

"Look at me, Alek."

I mimicked her, the thick barrier between us not stopping the energy from transferring through her and into me.

"Stare into my eyes and let me weave the threads back together."

So I did. I fell into that purple gaze and waited for my life with Sunday to come back to me.

And I waited.

And waited.

My aunt pulled back, her hands shaking and her expression tinged with terror.

"What is it?" Father demanded.

"It's . . . it's not working," she said, shaking her head. "I keep weaving the strands, but they wither and die before taking root. I don't . . . I don't know what's going on. This has never happened before."

No.

Dear gods, no.

"What are you saying?" I asked, voice tight with fear. I needed my memories back. I needed to know the woman responsible for setting off the beast inside me. I needed to remember my mate.

"I'm so sorry, Alek. There's nothing I can do. She's lost to you."

CHAPTER

# TWENTY-NINE

### SUNDAY

"Well, this can't be good." Kingston gripped my waist tighter than necessary as the three of us entered the throne room once again, the same eerie shadows cast on the walls greeting us.

"Keep moving," Strega said from her place holding open the massive metal doors.

She'd been our constant guard since the night before. Well, technically it had been this morning. It was a little hard to keep track of the passing hours, but it had been the middle of the night when we'd arrived, and the sun had just started to sink back into the horizon when we'd been summoned. Somewhere between Alek bursting in my room and now, I'd managed to fall asleep and get a little rest. It was that or continue pacing like a caged lion.

Nord had called us his guests, but with the way we'd been confined to my room after what happened with Alek, I was feeling more like a prisoner. Especially since no one had seen fit to speak to us except to order us dressed and ready for this meeting. To say I was nervous about what was about to happen was a serious understatement.

"Don't be afraid, Sunday. Come forward." Lina's warm voice eased something inside me, but only a little.

Alek stood with his parents, the three of them a unit, flanked by a younger woman who resembled Alek so much I could only assume she was his sister Astrid. All they were missing was Tor, and we'd have a perfect family portrait.

My mate's eyes locked on me the second I crossed the threshold. My heart clenched. It was such a different reaction than the last time. There was an intensity in his gaze that had been missing before. Perhaps not recognition, exactly. But it was certainly more than curiosity. The difference was enough to give me the courage I needed to take the next step.

Noah, Kingston, and I moved into the room. They'd sandwiched me between them, neither one wanting to leave my side after Alek's earlier rampage. I couldn't blame them. I would do the same thing, and I definitely appreciated the show of support. Especially once my focus landed on the other trio in the room.

We were joined by a handsome man I recognized from the night Alek was taken and two women I'd never seen before but were clearly related. Their purple eyes were trained unblinkingly on me, and frankly, freaking me the fuck out.

Who were they, and why were they here?

We walked forward until the three of us stood mere feet from the Vikings who held our fates in their hands.

"You summoned?" I tried for strong, confident badassery, but was pretty sure the question came out weak and wobbly.

"We did. We need to explain what's happened," Lina said, threading her fingers with Nord's. "And offer you an apology."

I blinked. Well, that wasn't what I'd expected to hear. I was expecting something more along the lines of us getting thrown out on our asses.

"An explanation would be nice," I said, hoping this time my voice passed for something more even.

"His memories were taken in a misguided attempt to control his berserker. I don't know how much you know about berserkers, but when separated from their mates, they often go mad. That's where Alek was headed."

"So you stole me from him? How is that better?"

The younger of the two unfamiliar women cleared her throat. "I can't help but notice you're only concerned about how this affected you."

"Quinn," Lina murmured, a warning in her tone.

"What? It's true. What you are all failing to mention was that taking away the memories saved his life."

"What do you mean?" I asked.

"He was on the verge of never coming back to us. He'd have gone into a rage spiral, destroying everything in his path, even himself, if we'd have let it go."

"It doesn't look like he's got that much more control now. A few hours ago, Nord had to stop him from tearing us apart with his bare hands for no good reason." Noah's words were strong and self-assured.

"That's because you were hurting her. You dared take what's mine. She's been given to me by Odin himself, and you spilled her blood." Alek stared Noah down, a threat in his tone.

"You make it sound like I was brutalizing her. She gave me her permission, berserker. Any bloodletting was consensual, I assure you."

Alek glared at Noah, the distinction not swaying him in the least. "I don't see your name etched into her flesh. If she was your true mate, you'd defend her against any others trying to mark her."

Kingston snorted. "Seeing as how you were the *third* to claim her, I'd back up that high horse of yours. Those are *our* marks on her neck."

"It's my child in her belly," Alek protested.

"Are you sure about that?"

God, I was going to kill Kingston if he didn't shut up. Now was not the time.

Every eye in the room was trained on me.

"You said you were with child," Nord accused.

"I am."

"You made us believe it was our son's."

"It could be."

"You mean to tell me you are my son's mate and still you took others into your bed? That you bear their marks as well as his? This is absurd."

I couldn't help it. I laughed and held out my arms. "Welcome to my fucking life, Your Majesty. I don't know what to tell you. Fate saw fit to give me more than one. I didn't go looking for them. They found me."

"She speaks the truth."

I glanced to my left as the older of the two strangers took a step forward.

"How can that be, Cora?" Lina asked.

"Multiple mates are not all that uncommon," she said with a shrug.

"It is for us."

Lina tossed her husband an annoyed look. "You were the one who told me our souls are made of multiple parts. Why couldn't Sunday find hers in more than just our son? Don't be so stuffy, old man."

"Careful, wife. I may be old, but I can still best you."

"We'll see about that."

The obvious love they had for each other made me smile. I hoped one day Alek and I would be just like them. Assuming, of course, we ever settled the matter of these missing memories.

"How can we get his memories back?" I was done pussyfooting around the issue. Alek needed to know me again. If anything was ever going to be normal for us, that much I knew was true.

"You can't," Quinn said. "They're gone. Every single memory he had of you was destroyed when I took them."

"What? You destroyed them?"

"It was an accident. But I'd erase you again if it meant saving him." She raised her chin in a defiant gesture, and my vision went red. I took a running step forward, only to be brought up short by an arm around my waist.

"Let me go," I snarled, thrashing in Kingston's arms.

His mouth was at my ear, his voice pitched low and just for me. "Not gonna happen, Sunshine. You're outnumbered and carrying my pup. I'm doing this for your own good."

Nord's sharp intake of breath filled the room. "Berserker. It's not possible."

"Oh, eslkan mín, how quickly you forget your mate," Lina murmured.

"You becoming a berserker was a miracle. The odds of it happening again are . . ."

Lina's eyes narrowed as if a thought had just occurred to her. "How did the two of you manage to perform the Transference?"

"What's that?" Alek spoke, his voice calming the fury in my blood.

"Well that answers my question. Nord, this has to mean

more. She's bound to him. She's taken on echoes of his berserker..."

Nord stepped forward and rested his palm on the top of my head, closing his eyes and focusing. I felt it the moment he found the berserker inside me. It was as if a string had been plucked, and the vibrations of my endless fury rang out, filling me.

"Alek," he whispered, his eyes opening and boring into mine. "It's true. The berserker lives in her, but it's not her own beast. She shares Alek's."

"That's what we've been trying to tell you," Kingston said, annoyance in his tone. "Jesus, these people."

Nord speared Kingston with a pointed glance. "You do not know me or what I can do, so allow me to educate you, wolf. I am a berserker. My first language is violence. I thrive on chaos and pain, blessed by the Allfather himself to ensure there is no enemy I cannot defeat. Insult me or a member of my family again, and I will personally rip your dick off and make you choke on it. If you would like to test me, please, keep talking."

Kingston didn't back down, but I didn't miss him bringing his hand down to cover his package protectively. "I'm here to bring Alek back. He belongs with Sunday, just like the rest of us do."

"Nord," Cora said, pulling his attention back to her. "The boy is telling you the truth. I have a feeling none of us will be safe if Sunday is separated from her mates. It is not only our world that hangs in the balance, but all worlds." She flicked her gaze to Alek, and the way he squirmed under her attention sent unease curling in my belly. This woman had power, and the way everyone stiffened the moment she said *'I have a feeling'* made it clear what came next should not be ignored. "Your son has to return with her. He must be at her side to help her face what's on the horizon."

"What's on the horizon?" Alek asked.

She looked me dead in the eyes, sending a chill down my spine. "War."

"You'd think portal dude would have been able to at least drop us off at home instead of the middle of the woods," Kingston muttered as we walked up the few steps leading to the front door of our house.

"Portal dude, as you call him, can only open the fabric of space in a location he's been previously. Count us lucky we were able to step out on Ravenscroft land at all." Alek waited for me to go first, his intense stare never leaving me.

I hadn't been able to bring myself to look at him directly, but I could feel his eyes on me. He hadn't looked away for more than a second. Perhaps it should have reassured me, that sign of his devotion, but I was afraid to trust it.

He still didn't remember me, Sunday Fallon. He was only interested in me because he'd learned I was his mate. Some people may not care about such a distinction, but I did. I didn't want him to feel like he *had* to want me. I wanted him to choose me . . . if that made sense.

"You coming, Sunshine?" Kingston held out a hand as

he used his free one to palm the doorknob. "You look a little lost."

"Just soaking it all in. I finally have everyone back on the right plane of existence. It's kind of a big deal."

"You really missed me that much?" Alek asked, his voice filled with wonder. As though there was no way I could genuinely feel deeply for him.

"Yeah. I did."

The front door opened, revealing Noah, an amused grin on his face. "What's taking you lot so long? Come on, then. You're going to want to see this."

He hadn't been away from us for long. He'd run ahead to make sure the heat in the house was on and things were ready for our return, but that twinkle in his eye spoke of mischief. What the hell could he have gotten up to already?

"What did you do?"

"It wasn't me."

We exchanged curious glances and went inside. I only made it a few steps before I stopped dead in my tracks, giggles bubbling up in my chest.

"Loki's enormous cock, what have you done to my brother?" Alek's words were colored with laughter.

I couldn't blame him, not when there was a 6'5" demigod sitting in a chair with sparkly pink goop on his face and curlers in his hair.

"Don't criticize my work. This is important," Moira said from behind him as she secured the final roller in his hair.

"I can see that," Kingston said.

Moira glanced up, her mouth falling into a little o of surprise before she let out an unladylike snort. "What the hell are you wearing? You look like a stripper I once saw at *Iniquity*." She glanced at Tor and winked.

He rolled his eyes at her, but there was no missing the upward curl of his lips.

*What kind of mischief did those two make while we'd been away? And do I really want to know?*

Kingston looked down his body, a smirk twisting his lips. "Like what you see, huh? I'm thinking of making a permanent change. Viking chic."

Tor snickered. "You may wear the clothes, but that doesn't make you a Viking. For one thing, you don't have what it takes to properly fill out the leathers."

"I haven't had any complaints. Besides, I'm not the one getting a perm."

"Ah, so he's insecure in his masculinity. Noted." Tor gave his head a little shake, then locked his gaze on Alek. "I see they were successful in returning you, brother."

Alek crossed his arms, still amused as he stared at his twin. "So . . . did you lose a bet?"

The offhanded comment stung, bringing back the memory of the moment he called the tattoo of my name something he'd had to get due to a lost wager. I pushed it aside, not letting myself fall into the spiral of emotion.

It was hard to tell under the face mask, but I was pretty sure Tor blushed. "What gave it away?"

Alek lifted a hand to tug on his own beard. "Can't imagine another reason for you to rid yourself of your manhood."

Moira's laughter tinkled like bells. "How do you think I talked him into any of this? Tor knows now never to go up against a Belladonna."

"It'll grow back," Tor grumbled.

"At least now we have a way to tell the two of you apart," Noah said.

"The way I see it, I'm doing the women of Ravenscroft a

favor. I don't think they could handle two of these guys walking around all rugged and Viking-y," Moira said.

"Are you staying, then?" Noah asked, his palm gently resting on the small of my back as he came up behind me. It was like he knew I needed something to help ground me with all the feelings coming to a head inside me.

"Yes, I think I'd like to. Ravenscroft has grown on me, and Alek will be too busy making up for lost time with his mate to focus on much else."

My cheeks burned with embarrassment, and suddenly all this was too much. "Excuse me," I said, spinning around and racing up the stairs, not stopping until I was safely hidden in my bedroom.

I felt like such a fool. All I'd wanted was for Alek to be here with me, and now that I had him, I couldn't even bring myself to talk to him. Even though I wasn't the one who lost my memories, he was a stranger.

Curling up on the forest green velvet chaise lounge Kingston had given me as a housewarming present, I stared out the window at the gray sky and rain falling in a fine mist. How had this gone so wrong?

Oh, that's right, Quinn Satori. The memory weaver. She'd woven me right out of his mind, making it as if all the moments I remembered so fondly had never happened. And in doing so, she'd taken Alek from me just as completely as she'd stripped me away from him.

My berserker woke, melding with the wild spirit of my wolf. The woman was lucky I'd been kept at bay in Novasgard. With the amount of fury pumping through my veins, I'm not sure she'd still be breathing if I'd gotten my claws in her.

A soft knock on the door was the only warning I got before it opened, revealing Alek. He stood in the doorway, a slightly bewildered expression on his face as he filled the frame.

My heart gave a pathetic flop in my chest. He looked as confused as I felt. Like his instinct was telling him to do something, but he didn't trust it.

"Are you all right?" he asked, his voice low and hesitant.

I tore my gaze from him and resumed watching the rain. "No."

"I'm sorry."

A bitter laugh escaped before I could stop it. "Why are you apologizing? None of this is your fault."

"Because I forgot you." He raked a hand through his hair, frustration in his heavy sigh. "I don't know how to do this."

His admission did what nothing else could. It pushed me out of my own grief and back onto my feet, the need to comfort him outshining everything else. I crossed the room and closed the distance between us until he was within my reach. "It's okay. I don't either."

His lip hooked up in a lopsided grin. "Shall we figure it out together, then?"

"I don't suppose we have any other choice."

"Where should we start?"

"How do people usually start when they're getting to know each other?"

He considered the question, and then his smile changed, becoming achingly familiar. It was an invitation to play, and I was unable to resist it. "I believe they refer to it as dating."

"Are you asking me out on a date, Alek Nordson?"

"Yes, Sunday Fallon. I believe I am."

My heart fluttered, cheeks warming at the gesture. "Then . . . yes. Take me on a date."

He closed the distance between us, reaching out to grasp my hand in his much larger one. Then holding my gaze, he dipped his head down and brushed his lips over my knuckles.

The gesture was so damn charming little butterflies took flight in my belly.

"I'll pick you up at sundown."

"Pick me up?" I laughed. "Alek, we live in the same house."

"I'll come to collect you from your room. Be ready."

I nodded, my smile uncontrollable. "Okay."

"We will find each other again. I promise."

My throat constricted as tears pricked my eyes. "I'll hold you to that, Viking."

With a wink, he left me. My heart was lighter, my tears no longer sad, but hopeful. He'd promised. Alek never broke his promises.

"Ugh, nothing fits." I glanced down at the small swell of my belly and ran a palm over the bump. "This is your fault. You'd better be cute."

I knew the baby would be. There wasn't a possibility otherwise, not with how handsome my men were. Would she have Kingston's wavy locks? Noah's intense amber eyes, or maybe Alek's blues? Caleb's perfect mouth? Would it be obvious who her father was once she was born? I didn't want that. I liked the idea of never knowing. That way I could pretend she belonged to all of us equally.

I tugged on the hem of the too-tight dress and scrunched my nose. "Nope."

I pulled off my eighth choice of the night and selected

something a bit looser. The floral maxi dress was more appropriate for warmer weather, but at least it would be comfortable.

A sharp knock on the door had my heart lurching with the thrill of possibility.

"Come in," I called as I selected a leather jacket from my closet.

Alek opened the door and peered inside, his expression filled with the same excitement I'd been trying and failing to tamp down myself.

"I'm almost ready," I said, smiling as I pulled the jacket on and tugged my hair free from the collar.

"You're . . . perfect."

My cheeks burned under his attention. "So are you."

He looked like he'd just stepped out of the pages of a men's magazine or maybe a romance novel. He'd dressed up for the occasion too, with a fitted black button-up, nice trousers, and a belt. He'd even taken care with his beard and pulled his long hair back into a low knot at the nape of his neck.

The smirk that twisted one side of his mouth made me wish we were past this awkward stage already. Even when we'd first met, it had never felt this forced between us. Being with him had always been so natural; I just wanted to go back to the way we were.

"So, Viking, where are we going?"

He crooked his elbow and offered me his arm. "Come with me."

I felt almost giddy as I wove my arm through his and let him lead me out of the bedroom. We'd only taken a few steps when I noticed how quiet the house was.

"Where is everybody?"

"Thorne mentioned something about giving us space."

"Oh . . . that was nice of him."

Alek's brow furrowed, and then he let out a low laugh. "I must admit, I'm still trying to wrap my head around how to navigate a relationship with a woman who has other men. Do we need to ask permission if we want time alone with you, or . . ."

"No. Never. You all have me, and I have you. Whenever we want. This only works if that's the arrangement. As much as they play at being jealous, none of them really are." I frowned as we walked down the stairs. "At least, I don't think they are. I don't really know. This has just happened so organically. They've never made me choose."

He hummed low in his throat. "Perhaps you're not the person I should be asking."

I chuckled. "Maybe not."

He shook his head, still smiling. "That's going to be a fun conversation."

"I'm glad I'm not the one who has to have it."

"I'll bet you are." His eyes sparkled as he smirked down at me. "So do you share . . . *everything*?"

The way his lips curled around the word left little doubt what he was referring to. He wasn't asking me about G.I. Joes or the OJ in the fridge. My Viking wanted to know about our bedroom games.

"Sometimes. Others are more, um, intimate. It just depends on who's around when things start to head in that direction. If it feels right to add in more participants, that's what happens." Butterflies fluttered in my stomach. "Is that a problem?"

We'd just reached the front door when he stopped and turned to face me, lifting his free hand to cup my cheek. "I won't lie to you and say it comes naturally to me to share you. But I also won't lie and say the idea doesn't hold appeal either. I'm a big man with large appetites. I'm interested in anything that brings you pleasure. All I know for sure is that when we were parted, a piece of me felt like it was missing, and now that I know that piece was you, I am willing to try anything if it means never losing you again."

There he was. My Alek. The swoony, sexy Norseman.

Something lifted from my shoulders, the invisible weight of tension between us. "Okay."

Was it poetic? No. Did it get to the point? Yep.

"Now come along. We're going to be late."

"I didn't realize there was a timeline."

He cocked a brow. "We have many lost hours to make up for."

"Well let's get going then."

I was surprised when Alek started leading me toward the forest path, walking with no hint of hesitation, and then I remembered. It wasn't the school he'd forgotten, just me. There was a momentary pang at the reminder. But when he led me to a part of the grounds I hadn't been to before, it was hard to be upset.

The greenhouse's doors stood open wide, twinkle lights visible through the glass panes. Soft music permeated the air, and a small table filled with all kinds of treats was positioned inside. He'd obviously put a lot of thought into our date and gone out of his way to make it special for me.

"This is so pretty," I whispered as we stepped through the entrance and into the warmth of the structure. "You did all of this?"

"I might've had a little help."

As if on cue, Moira popped out from behind a table of orchids, giving me a little wink and a wave as she and her periwinkle bob made a hasty exit, closing the doors behind her. Of course, she knew exactly what I'd need in this moment.

"Do you like it?" The raw vulnerability in his question made my heart ache.

"I love it. I really do."

He reached out a hesitant hand, and I leaned in, needing his touch as he brushed a lock of hair behind my ear.

I sucked in a sharp breath as tingles raced down my body at the contact, igniting a fire I knew he would not be able to extinguish. His touch was so innocent, but I wasn't the one without the memories of all the other times his hands had been on me. My mind knew we needed to go slow. My body didn't care.

He locked eyes with me, uncertainty in the depths of his blues. "I'm sorry, is it too soon?"

"No, of course not. It's not like you kissed me or anything." I felt so stupid for reacting to his small gesture.

"So is that off the table then?" he teased, his lips hitching up.

"Not if you play your cards right."

His eyes dropped to the soft swell of my belly. "I feel good about my odds."

A slight giggle escaped me. "You're not wrong. It's so easy to forget that you . . . well, forgot everything."

We were standing close enough that I couldn't miss the flare of anger in the back of his eyes, but I knew it wasn't aimed at me. "I do feel like I'm at a bit of a disadvantage. You know everything about me, and I know so little about you. But maybe we can remedy that."

"I like the sound of that."

Resting his large palm on my lower back, Alek ushered me over to the table, helping me take a seat in the wrought iron chair. Then he popped the cork on a bottle of sparkling cider and filled a champagne flute for each of us. "Pretend this is the real deal, yeah?"

"You thought of everything." I brought the glass to my lips, smiling as the bubbles tickled my nose.

"I wanted you to have a proper date. From what I've gathered, none of us have come into this in a traditional way."

"What do you mean?"

"Well, you fell into Ravenscroft and found each of us. At least, that's what Thorne shared with me. You deserve to be properly wooed."

"Is that what you're doing?"

"That depends. Is it working?"

Heat unfurled in my belly. "Maybe."

He winked at me. "Then I guess I am." Alek made us each a plate, putting a little bit of everything onto it before setting it in front of me. "So, Sunday Fallon. Tell me about you."

I had no idea which way to go. Did he really want to be bored with my whole history? My time spent isolated? How did you tell your mate who you were without overwhelming him?

"CliffsNotes version? I was abandoned on my dad's doorstep when I was a newborn, a shame to my pack because I couldn't shift. I didn't know anything about the world until I came here and learned from you four. Oh . . . and I'm pretty sure my mom's the devil."

He snorted. "I'm sure we all feel that way about our parents from time to time."

"Oh no," I said, taking a sip of my cider. "I don't mean metaphorically. I think she could be the literal devil."

His smile faded as he held my stare. After a beat, he

301

scratched his cheek and shrugged. "Well, I guess it's a good thing you're mated to a demigod blessed by Odin himself. I'm pretty indestructible."

"It's always the indestructible ones who take the biggest risks."

"Is it? You're the most breakable of us all, and you crossed realms to find me."

"It was only one realm." I ducked my head as a blush crept up my neck into my face. "You would have done the same for me."

"I don't think you're giving yourself enough credit."

I lifted a shoulder. "Stepping through a portal didn't seem all that scary after facing off with demons and almost being sacrificed during some douchey dude-bro's ritual."

"Dude-bro?"

I waved the question away, sneering at the thought of *Chad*. "Don't worry about it."

"So you gave me your basic stats, but what made me fall for you?"

The question caught me off guard. "I . . . um . . . I don't actually know. It never really came up."

His expression went from tender interest to disbelief. His brows dropped low, and his smile faded. "Then I failed as your mate."

"What?"

"If you don't know everything I love about you, I wasn't doing my job as your mate. It's simple. I should've made you aware of exactly how wonderful you are."

Emotion constricted my throat, and it took me a few tries before I could respond. "You always made me feel like I was the only woman in the world."

"Because you are."

I waved a hand at my face, lifting my drink with a nervous giggle. "Is it warm in here?"

His smile was doing things to my insides. "Since I genuinely don't know, tell me what your favorite thing is about me."

I laughed at the question, which was equal parts cocky male charm and boyish innocence. "Your hair."

Mirth sparkled in his blue eyes. "My hair?"

"Yes. It's this massive golden mane. Like a lion, but it's so soft. I love running my fingers through it. Tangling my hands in it . . ." *Okay, Sunday, rein it in.* "If you ever cut it, I think I'd cry."

He reached up and pulled the end of the leather cord holding his hair back. Then he held my gaze, and he shook all that glorious hair free, looking like he belonged in a sexy shampoo commercial.

"Better?"

"Much," I agreed, leaning forward to take a section in my hand and brush my fingers through it.

"Is it as good as you remember?" His voice was a husky whisper, and I was surprised to find how close our faces were.

I had to swallow before I could speak. "Yes."

He caught my hand in his and got to his feet, pulling me with him until I was against his chest, looking up at the face I loved with all my soul.

"I'm going to kiss you now."

My heart flipped over as he trailed the tips of his fingers along my jaw.

"Yes, please."

My breath caught as he lowered his mouth to mine, the hesitance between us lasting for one fraction of a second before it disappeared and he finally claimed my lips.

It was sweet, sexy, and filled with a passion I knew he was keeping on a tight leash. I could feel it in the way he held me. Like I was something precious, and he didn't want to scare me off. It was a perfect first kiss, and it promised many others.

"Sunday," he whispered against my lips.

Everything stopped as he said it. My name sounded wrong coming from him like that, in a sweet, intimate moment. I was his Sunny. Never Sunday.

"What's wrong?" he asked as I stepped out of his embrace.

I cleared my throat, not meeting his gaze. "Nothing's wrong."

"You're lying to me." His voice was flat, just a hint of temper giving it a sharp edge.

"No, I'm not."

He took my chin between his thumb and forefinger and tilted my head up so I was forced to look into his eyes. "Yes, you are. One second you're melting against me like you can't bear to be apart. The next, you can't get far enough away. What did I do?"

"You didn't do anything."

The words sounded false even to my ears. Even though they were technically true. But somehow it just didn't feel right or fair to tell him the thoughts whispering around the back of my mind.

*You don't remember me.*

It wasn't his fault, so how could I hold it against him?

"Why do you want me?" I asked, avoiding the question and turning it back around on him.

His brow furrowed. "What?"

"Why me when you could have anybody?"

"You're my mate. Destined to be mine."

"And that's why I pulled away."

"I don't understand."

I rested my palm on his broad chest, loving the warmth radiating there. "I don't want you to want me just because you're supposed to."

"But I don't. That's not how mate bonds work. How could I possibly be interested in anybody else when I've just rediscovered the missing part of my soul? I can guarantee you this was how it started the first time too. When you find the one you are meant for, no one else exists. They couldn't hold a candle to the things I feel when I look at you."

Alek pressed his hand over mine, where his heart thumped steady and true beneath my palm. If I wasn't already head over heels in love with this man, his impassioned speech would have done it, but then he went and sealed the deal, ensuring I was an absolute goner.

"I may not remember you, Sunny, but I want to. More than anything. And if that's not possible, then I want to learn you now."

With that one utterance of my nickname, he'd just given me everything I wanted without even knowing it. I should have trusted him. He promised me we would find our way back to each other, and I knew he was right.

One way or another, Alek would keep his promise.

# CHAPTER
# THIRTY-ONE

### ALEK

My abs burned as I completed yet another set of curls using the tree branch I was suspended from to offer a bigger challenge. I needed to hurt. To distract myself from the emptiness in my brain where memories of Sunday should live.

I'd already been out here for hours, taking my frustration out on my body, punishing myself in the only way I knew how. I'd seen the disappointment in her eyes last night. She hadn't wanted to voice it, but there'd been a moment right before we kissed when I knew I had her. She was mine. And then she sealed herself away, as if she needed to protect herself from getting hurt.

From me.

It was absurd. Hurting her was the last thing I'd ever want to do, yet somehow I had.

Because I couldn't remember.

"The ground wasn't good enough for you? You had to assault this poor tree with your bulk?" Tor's voice pulled my eyes open, and I saw him, the view of his frame distorted from my upside-down vantage point.

Swinging myself, I launched off the branch and curled into a ball as I spun, landing in a crouch in front of him. "Jealous?" I cocked a brow.

"Of what? Your fat arse?" He ran a hand down his flat abs and grinned. "We both know I'm the good-looking one."

"I wonder if you understand what identical truly means? I suppose it must be hard for you after you allowed Moira to shear you like a sheep."

He rubbed his palm over his jaw, the stubble already growing back. "I'm a fan of my chiseled jaw. And the ladies love the dimples you're hiding under all that hair."

I rolled my eyes. "As if you'd know anything about getting ladies. You're perpetually single, you fucking monk."

"As if you know anything about my bedroom habits."

"I've lived in the room beside yours since we were teenagers, and before that we shared one. I think I'm privy to all your secrets, brother."

"Do you now?" He began stretching, reaching his arm across his body. "So why are we punishing ourselves tonight? You already worked out this morning."

"I'm missing so much, and I can't get it back. You don't know how that feels."

Tor grabbed a log, lifting it high in the air and tossing it to me. "Don't be such a pussy. You knew that when you agreed to go back."

I threw the wood back at him with more force, but he caught it with no issue. "Knowing something in theory and living the reality are two very different things."

He studied me, his expression not softening in the slightest. "Quinn told you the memories are gone. It's past time you wrap your head around the fact you will never get them back."

"You make it sound so easy. How am I just supposed to be okay not remembering so many moments with my mate? I feel like an outsider in my own fucking relationship. I don't even remember possibly getting her pregnant. Who would be okay forgetting that?"

"Then make new memories, you idiot. Replace the void with something you can hold on to."

"I did take her on a date last night."

"See? There it is. You know how to do this. You've just been a lazy sod and never had to work for it before."

"I'm not lazy. You're the one who had to be dragged kicking and screaming to every morning session with Father."

He chucked the log at me one final time, this one hard enough catching it made my teeth rattle. "You're lazy where it counts. If she was mine . . . if I lost her like you did, I'd be a man possessed. I'd do everything I could to fall for her again. To prove to her that even without my memories, she meant the world to me."

"I will. I am."

"Are you? Looks to me like you're out here licking your wounds instead of in there putting the work in."

"I'm not her only mate, arsehole. I can't monopolize her time."

"Sure you can. You're just too scared she'll turn you away to fight for it."

I hurled the wood at a nearby tree, the log splintering and branches falling around us. "I'm not afraid of anything."

"Prove it."

I glared at him. "What? Right now? I'm not winning anyone back smelling like this."

Tor rolled his eyes. "Then take a fucking shower first. Odin's hairy arse, Alek, it's like you're a fucking virgin."

I laughed at his ire, appreciating my twin's specific brand of tough love. It was exactly what I needed.

"All right, fuck face. Let's head back to the house."

"Already on my way, twatwaffle."

"Twatwaffle?"

"Like that one, did you? The witch taught it to me."

"Taught it to you? Or called you one?"

Tor grinned. "Same difference, really."

The tension between us faded into our more typical brotherly jabs and digs as we walked through the woods at the back of the house. I saw her in the window, curled up with a blanket and staring out at the night sky. For a moment I simply stood there, taking her in, memorizing the lines of her profile, the curve of her shoulder, the things that made up Sunday.

Thorne appeared next to her, his pale fingers running along her collarbone and tearing her gaze from the stars so she could look at him.

"I still don't understand it." Tor shook his head before clapping me on the back and jogging toward the house. Something stopped him halfway across the grass. His posture tightened, body on the defensive, and that one small action had my berserker rattling its chains.

The shadows shifted, a figuring emerging from the darkness. I was across the lawn in three long strides.

"Take another step, and I'll rip your fucking throat out," I snarled.

The threat to my mate froze, his neck craning back so he

could peer up at me. "I was just about to say the same to you, Mr. Nordson."

The priest. His fangs were fully extended, brow furrowed, eyes filled with violence.

Confusion sent my berserker back. Not far, rage was still simmering in my veins, but the unexpected reveal allowed some of the fog to dissipate.

"I always knew you were a dirty bastard. But I didn't expect spying on your students would be your kink of choice."

He leveled a hard stare at me. "You know perfectly well what I'm about. You've lived it after all."

What the fuck was he talking about?

The crunch of grass pulled me out of my musing as my brother joined us, keeping me from giving voice to the question.

"Why are you out here?" I asked instead.

"To ensure all is well."

"Why wouldn't it be? Is something going on?"

He tutted. "Aye, Mr. Nordson, there's always some mischief being made. You should know that better than most."

"Aye, but that's no reason for skulking about where you're not welcome. What game are you playing, priest?"

Pain flashed in the back of his eyes, but the good father didn't answer my question. His gaze flicked from me, back to the now empty window. And that was when I knew. He'd been stalking her. Father Gallagher was after what was mine, and if he wasn't in the house, that meant he wasn't wanted.

Without thinking, I encircled his throat with my palm and shoved him into the nearest tree trunk. "Stay away from my mate and my child."

"You fecking bastard. You know as well as I that the bairn could just as easily be mine."

"Plot twist," Tor murmured, letting out a low whistle behind me.

I faltered, loosening my grip ever so slightly. It was enough. Father Gallagher snarled and shoved me back hard enough I stumbled.

"Keep your hands off me, lad. I may not look it, but I could snap you in two as easily as a communion wafer."

My inner monster shifted back to the surface, and I knew Caleb could tell because he stiffened. "Oh, please do try. I've been itching for a fight, Father. I would love a reason to rip your spine out through your asshole."

Tor winced. "I've heard about that technique. One of our father's favorites. I'd love to see it in person."

"You won't keep me away from her. I have a duty." Caleb stood there, casual and relaxed. As though I hadn't just threatened to turn him into a spineless sack of bones.

"Seems to me you're already *away*. You have no place with her. It can't be because you've chosen it. No one is that stupid. Which means Sunday doesn't want you. You're not welcome here. We've got it covered."

He sneered. "She's not the one who made the choice."

I shook my head, disgusted with him. "Then you're a fool, and you don't deserve her. She was taken from me against my will, and yet here I am, desperate to find a way to get her back while you stand there with her in your reach and choose to remain in the shadows. What a pathetic creature you are, Father Gallagher. No wonder your God has forsaken you."

I pushed past him and made my way to the door, knowing my brother was right on my heels.

I would not be like Caleb. I would not let this miracle slip through my fingers.

Sunday was my mate. It was time for me to claim what was mine.

# THIRTY-TWO

"Thank you so much for mentioning this. I didn't realize how badly I needed to get out and have some fun."

Moira did a little shimmy, showing off her sexy silver dress. The fringed gown hit her right at the knees and went perfectly with the matching silver T-strap shoes and 1920s hairdo. "Please, you're doing me the favor. I was dying for a girl's night."

I glanced back at Kingston, Noah, Alek, and Tor leaning against the bar ordering our drinks. "Sorry about the brute squad."

"I feel like there's a *Princess Bride* quote coming at any moment."

Alek turned to face us, elbows braced on the bar top as he murmured. "Inconceivable."

Moira snickered and booped Alek on the nose, looking more like she was shooting a free throw than reaching up to touch him. "Impressive. I'm surprised you even understood the reference."

He smirked. "We don't live in the Dark Ages, häxa."

"Coulda fooled me."

"Mo, play nice. He's still fragile. Even if he pretends he's fine." Ash smiled at my bestie and threaded their fingers together. "Come on. Let's go. I want to dance."

Alek's gaze followed them as they wove their way into the center of the dance floor.

"Want to dance?" I asked, my throat a little tight as he handed me a club soda with a twist of lime.

He frowned at the writhing bodies. "Not really my scene."

Disappointment lanced through me, though I tried to shrug it off. "Oh. Okay, no problem."

Tor slapped his brother upside the head. "Idiot. Come on, Hellraiser. Let's show him how it's done."

"Hellraiser?" I asked as he led me to the dance floor.

"You're a cute little thing, but something tells me you can rain down unholy hellfire when necessary."

The hairs on my body stood on end, something like premonition running through my veins. The Norseman wasn't wrong, but I wondered if he had any idea just how *right* he was.

"Hmm . . . I'll allow it."

The laugh he released was rich and booming, audible even over the thumping bass so loud it radiated through my chest. "A queen in the making. My brother chose well."

"I don't think he really chose me. It was out of our hands."

Tor winked as he tugged me with him into the crowd. Then, leaning close, he slid his palm over the small of my back, and we began dancing as he said, "That's called fate. A very different situation."

"How do you figure? That sounds like exactly the same thing. Fate threw us together. He had no say in the matter."

"Didn't he? He's here now, by choice. He's made a point to do something every day to try and win back your love by choice. How is he *not* choosing you?"

Well, shit. When the big lug put it that way . . .

"He never lost my love," I muttered eventually, surprised he could actually hear me over the music.

"He's trying so hard to show you that even without memories of what you had, you are the single most important thing in his world."

I thought about everything Alek had done in the two weeks since our date. The hand-carved wolf figurine was the first thing that flashed in my mind. He'd even gone to such detail as to include the crescent moon marking between the wolf's eyes. Did he remember the day when I'd shifted in front of him, or was it just a coincidence?

"I know."

"So why are you keeping him at a distance?"

The question caught me off guard. I hadn't realized Tor had been watching his brother and me so closely, but maybe I should have. They were twins, after all. He was obviously invested in how things played out between us.

"I'm not. Not really. I just don't want him to feel pressured. He deserves to be in control of something, considering what happened to him. It might as well be how things progress between us."

"Maybe he's waiting on a sign from you before taking the next steps."

"Maybe."

We danced for a few more minutes before Kingston stalked through the crowd, laser-focused on where Tor was touching me. His eyes blazed with jealousy, and for a moment, I worried if Tor didn't remove his hand from me, Kingston would do it for him.

"My turn," Kingston growled as the music changed to a slow, sexy beat.

Tor released me without argument, giving me the patented Nordson smirk. "Think about what I said, Hellraiser. I know my brother. He's taking his cues from you. If you want more, you need only let him know."

All I could do was nod. Then my gaze was commandeered by my wolf mate.

"I couldn't take it anymore."

"What?" I asked teasingly.

"Watching you dance with that tool. Knowing you could be moving against me but were doing it with him instead. Take your pick, baby." He yanked me closer, grinding his already hardening cock against my thigh.

"Is my King feeling jealous?"

"Fuck yes. Always, when it comes to you."

"Really? You seem more than happy sharing these days."

"Only when they're one of yours, Sunshine. Knobhead over there doesn't count. He might be related to Alek, but he's not part of our pack. Not in the ways that would make me okay seeing his body crowding yours."

"Knobhead? Noah is rubbing off on you, I see."

He chuckled and leaned his head closer, dipping his chin and giving my mark a little nip. "I think he needs to rub off on you, sweetheart."

I sucked in a sharp breath at the hunger in his tone. "Does he?"

"Someone needs to."

Arousal rolled through me, hot and fast—as was the way these days. It didn't take more than a lingering glance to get my panties damp lately. And with these three, there were a lot of fucking glances.

"Are you volunteering?"

He leaned back just enough to catch my eye. "Always."

"Volunteering for what?" Noah asked, sliding behind me and curling his arm around my hip so his hand could rest on the swell of my belly.

"Our girl is in need. Can't you tell?" Kingston inhaled deeply, his pupils dilating. "Fucking delicious."

"Is it the heat again? That doesn't make sense."

"Not the heat. The pregnancy. I hear the hormones can make a woman's libido ravenous."

"Stop talking about me like I'm not right the fuck here," I groused.

"Am I wrong?" Kingston teased, grazing the underside of my breast and making me let out a soft moan.

"No, you fucker, but you didn't have to point it out either."

"Why not?"

"Everyone knows it's impolite to discuss a lady's appetites," Noah said smoothly, his thumbs brushing the vee of my inner thighs as we continued to sway to the hypnotic beat.

"It's not like I'm telling everyone about how she ate half a damn turkey on her own. It's just sex."

I blushed at the mention of my afternoon snack. "It's still rude."

I leaned back into Noah as Kingston continued to search my body with his palms. We pretended this seduction was dancing, but we all knew better. Rolling my gaze upward, I nearly stopped what I was doing as Caleb's form came into view. He stood on the balcony, palms clenched around the metal railing, burning eyes pinned on me.

Why was he torturing us both?

"I need a break," I said, stepping out of their holds.

Kingston's eyes followed mine up to where Caleb continued to stare at us from the shadows. "We'll be here when you're ready."

I nodded, smiling a little despite the ache in my heart when I caught Ash and Moira doing a slow version of the Charleston. Ash pulled Moira in close and then dipped her low, following up the move by leaning down and stealing a kiss.

Continuing toward the table where I saw Moira's ostentatious feather jacket waiting for her, I forced myself to focus on that one goal. I would have made it, too, except for the massive hand that encircled my wrist.

*Not Caleb again.*

But no . . . there was no incense in the air. The voice gave my captor away a second later.

"Do you have any idea what it was doing to me watching you out there?"

His voice was a low rasp, and the pure need threaded through it sent a shiver straight down my spine. Alek reeled me in until I was standing between his spread thighs.

"Why don't you tell me, Viking?"

Gripping me by the hips, he pulled me even closer, forcing me to straddle his muscular legs, my skirt riding up with the motion.

"How about I show you?"

God, the heat in his voice made things tighten low in my belly as an answering wave of lust hit me hard.

"I've been trying to go slow with you. Ensure you know it's your heart I want before asking to have your body too."

That intense blue stare of his made my breath catch.

"But you called to me like a siren out there while you were dancing. I'm aching, Sunny."

"Me too."

I wrapped my arms around his neck as I rocked my hips into him, aided by his large palms grasping my ass. I expected to feel the delicious friction of our clothing and his rock-hard length rubbing up against my throbbing core. But it was so much better. A moan left me when my slippery folds found the leather of his pants.

Wait a second . . . I was wearing underwear before coming over here. I know it. I picked them out special.

"Alek," I whispered, bringing my lips to his ear.

"Yes?"

"I had panties on earlier."

"Did you?"

"I did."

"Wonder where they went."

"So do I."

He reached between us, hand disappearing beneath my skirt as he dragged one finger over my slick lower lips, causing a shudder to ripple through me.

"I'm not complaining. You smell fucking delicious."

"If you keep doing that, I'm going to ruin your pants."

His answering laugh was low and sensual as he took his fingers away from the place I wanted them most. His knuckles grazed my center as he slowly unzipped his pants. Excitement unfurled inside me, and I cast a furtive look around. People were everywhere, but no one was paying any attention to the two of us.

"Here?"

A wolfish grin was my answer. Then, with a ragged groan, he moved me forward so my pussy slid along his thick length. "I'm tired of fucking waiting. I'll die if I don't sink inside you right now."

I continued the slow rocking motion until the wet heat of my arousal had made us both slick. Hands on my waist,

Alek shifted his hips, notching the tip of his cock at my entrance. Jesus, I'd forgotten how *big* he was.

Blazing blue irises locked on mine as we sat there together, both of us breathing heavily, not moving, suspended in the torture of the moment stretching between us.

"Alek," I moaned.

"Say the word and I'll stop."

"Don't you dare. But people can see us."

"Isn't that what makes it fun?"

I bit down on my lower lip and nodded. "But we need to be quiet and slow."

He pulled me down on him, impaling me in one smooth movement, catching my scream of pleasure with a hungry kiss. My heart was still thundering when he pulled away, my lip caught between his teeth. He released me with a sweet nip.

"What happened to slow and quiet?"

He shifted, pulling out of me and then slowly gliding back in. "Better?"

"Oh, so you can follow directions."

"Sometimes. When it suits me. Better not get used to it."

Somewhere between him sinking inside me and kissing me senseless, the rest of the world faded away. It was just the two of us now. Here. In this moment. Finding our way back to each other.

It was perfect.

"I may not know our past, but I know you're my future, Sunny." He ran his palm up my spine before canting his hips in rhythm with mine. "I can't be parted from you. Fate won't allow it, and neither will I."

My heart tumbled. This is what I'd needed. The assurance that he was all in, regardless of whatever mystical forces brought us together. Like when he'd given me his name. A turning point. A moment of claiming.

"Alek, I—"

I swallowed back my confession as his fingers slipped back between my legs, his pressure perfect and setting off tiny sparks of pleasure in my body.

"You what?"

"Need you. I need you."

"I'm right here, Sunny. I'm not going anywhere."

"God, I'm coming," I said on a harsh whisper. My thighs shook as the orgasm ripped through me.

"Make as much noise as you want. No one can hear you."

That couldn't be true, but I really didn't care. I threw my head back and brought him deeper into me as I rode out the pleasure around his cock.

Alek's grip on me bordered on painful as he drove his hips up into me, stretching me wide as he chased his own release. And then he was right there, spilling himself inside of me.

Our eyes were locked onto each other as he came, his darkened with desire as a single word was torn from his throat.

"*Kærasta.*"

Emotion flooded me, and tears pricked my eyes. I hadn't realized how badly I'd needed to hear him say it. How much the endearment had come to mean to me.

"Elskan mín."

He banded his arms around me, pressing me against his chest as he cradled me with his body. Then he threaded the fingers of one hand through my hair, kissing me so tenderly I felt as if I was dying and having life breathed back into me all at the same time. He may not have given me the words, but there was no doubting his feelings. Or mine.

A slow clap from behind us had me stiffening against him, his softening cock still inside me. He made no move to pull out as he broke the kiss and glanced over my shoulder.

"Wow, dancing *and* a show. All for a five quid cover charge. This place is a bargain." Kingston's voice had goose-bumps rising on my skin. Not because I was embarrassed, but because I wanted him too.

Then it hit me, and actual mortification washed over me. "Alek, you said they couldn't hear us."

"They couldn't hear you, but they could sure as shit see you."

"Don't worry, dove. No one knows what the two of you were up to. We were right here the entire time. Blocking their view."

Alek lifted me off him carefully, his cum already drip-ping down my thighs.

"God, I'm a mess."

Noah reached into his pocket and pulled out a handker-chief, offering it to me. "Here you are, love."

Alek snatched it out of his hand and gave me a slow shake of his head. "Leave it."

*Okay, then. Don't argue with the big bad Viking.* Especially when his voice sounded like sex and domination. I adjusted my dress and clenched my thighs together. I wanted more. I wanted all of them.

Kingston's nostrils flared as he locked eyes with me. "Our mate is insatiable when she's carrying."

"She's always insatiable," Noah corrected.

"Well, let's take care of her then, boys." Alek stood and wrapped one arm around me. "Let it never be said a Novas-gardian male left his woman wanting."

Heat crept into my cheeks as thoughts of the night ahead danced through my mind. "Hurry."

As a unit, we made our way out of *Iniquity*. I stumbled slightly when my eyes raised back to the small balcony where Caleb had been watching me. He was still there, although he was no longer alone. Lilith was at his side, a noticeable smirk on her red-stained lips.

She winked at me, mouthing, "Well done."

# THIRTY-THREE

Their hands were everywhere as we entered the house, Kingston kissing my mark, Noah caressing my breasts, aching and tender, as Alek watched with a devious gleam in his eyes. I was so turned on I could barely get words out to tell them I needed to shower before we went further. But eventually, I managed.

"Let me clean up a little," I said, my voice breathless.

"Why bother? We're just going to get you dirty again," Kingston breathed in my ear before biting down on the lobe and sending a shock of need straight to my clit.

"Because it's hard to feel sexy when you're a sticky mess."

"Perhaps I could help you with that, dove," Noah said, sinking to his knees and sliding the material of my dress up my thighs.

Before he touched me, the energy in the room changed from charged with lust to ice cold. "What's wrong, Noah?"

"There's blood. Sunday, you're bleeding." He stood and, in a blur of motion, had Alek pinned against the wall as he snarled, "You hurt her, you animal."

Alek's outrage at being manhandled morphed into horror. "But I was so careful. You saw. You were both right there."

Slipping my fingers between my thighs, I frowned down at the pink-tinged cum. "Noah, I'm fine."

"You think I don't know blood when I see it? When I fucking smell it?"

Kingston scooped me into his hold, cradling me like a baby.

"What are you doing? I can walk. Put me down."

"You need to be off your feet. I won't risk you or our pup."

Sighing, I rolled my eyes. "Fine. Carry me to the bathroom, will ya? These shoes make my feet hurt anyway."

"Why aren't you taking this more seriously?" Noah asked.

"Why should I, when you three are overreacting enough for all of us? It's just a little blood. I'm fine. Spotting after sex is perfectly normal."

"How do you know?"

"Because I've done my research. I do have a midwife I can call with any questions, remember? Everything is more tender, but that doesn't mean I can't have sex. This is probably going to happen again, especially since I've been blessed with three big-dicked mates to satisfy me."

As always, my heart gave a little pang at the number. *Four*, I silently corrected as the memory of Caleb's desire-stricken face swam back up.

I'd hoped that would have relaxed them all a little, but they looked at me with worry in their eyes.

Kingston pressed his lips into a thin line as he carried me up the stairs. "If you say so. I just don't want anything to happen to either of you."

POSSESSION

"I say so. I'll tell all of you if it's too much. But women have been having babies since the dawn of time. I'm not special."

"You're incredibly special."

I blew out a breath, knowing there was no way to win this argument. Not right now. The mood was gone anyway, so there was no need to force the issue.

Noah and Alek stayed back as Kingston carried me into the bathroom. But I put my foot down at his climbing into the shower with me.

"No. Nuh-uh. Out."

"But—"

"Fuck off, Kingston. I don't need you to wash my ass. I've got this." I couldn't help but think he looked like a sad puppy as he left the room, so I called, "Good boy."

"Maybe you'll give me a treat later?"

That made a grin spread across my face. "Maybe."

"Love you, Sunshine."

Well, shit. Now I couldn't be annoyed. "Love you too."

He shut the door and left me alone with a mess to clean up.

As frustrated as I was at the unexpected turn of events, I couldn't really be mad at them for being worried about me. This was unfamiliar territory for all of us, and Noah, more than any of them, had been jumpy from the start. I was just going to have to prove to my men that I wasn't suddenly made of glass because I was pregnant. It would take some convincing, I was sure, but as I rinsed the almond-scented suds from my body, I was confident I could make them see reason.

The rag slipped from my fingers as I felt it. A little flutter, like bubbles. My heart raced, my thoughts following suit. Was this what I thought it was? I was four months pregnant, seventeen weeks to be exact. It *could* be.

I waited in silence with my palm pressed over the spot where the tickle had happened.

"Are you there?"

I held my breath, and just when I was about to give up and chalk the sensation up to something a lot less exciting, like gas bubbles, it happened again. Movement inside me. Tears swam in my vision.

The bathroom door swung open, slamming into the wall hard enough to leave a dent in the plaster as Noah stormed straight for me, stepping into the shower fully clothed in a pair of cotton pajama pants and a white T-shirt I'd never seen before. I didn't even know he owned PJs.

"What are you doing, you crazy vampire?"

He cupped my face and stared into my eyes. "What is going through your mind? I felt you. You're crying."

Kingston and Alek shuffled into the bathroom, all but stepping into the shower with us. I shook my head with a wordless laugh and took Noah's hand, pressing it to my belly. "I felt the baby move."

"You . . . what? You did?" Noah dropped to his knees and pressed his ear to the gentle swell of my stomach. "I never tire of that sound. The heart beating like a hummingbird."

Alek's expression was broken. "I wish I could hear it. I might be Odin blessed, but superhuman hearing is a gift he left out."

I threaded my fingers in his hair. "I can't wait until I can hear it again too."

"It wasn't real to me until just now. Knowing I might've missed it all..."

"You and me both," Noah said, holding me tight.

"Okay, drama queen. Now that we know she's not

dying, can you two get out of the shower? Or do you enjoy being a one-man wet T-shirt contest all the damn time?" Kingston asked, making me laugh with his put-upon expression. I'd never out him, but I think he was jealous that Noah could hear the baby's heartbeat and he couldn't.

Noah got to his feet and stripped out of his clothes then and there. "I'm going to wash up. We'll meet you in the bedroom."

I laughed and shook my head. "I'm already clean. Sorry to disappoint."

"Dove, you never disappoint me." He turned off the water and snagged a towel for each of us as Kingston and Alek left the room.

Tying his towel around his waist, Noah got to work drying me off. He was thorough in his ministrations, taking his time as he worked the soft terry cloth over my wet skin. I recognized the act for what it was. An apology, even though one wasn't needed.

Finished, he kissed my cheek. "I'm going to go get you something to sleep in. Be right back."

Once he left, I took a few minutes to pull myself together. The baby fluttered again, as though she wanted to remind me she was there and all I could do was stand there with a dopey grin on my face.

I finally left the bathroom, towel secured around me, to find pajamas draped across the chaise lounge by the window and three pairs of devoted eyes on me. They didn't want anything other than to be near me now. No expectations. No demands. Just comfort.

Which was perfect, because it's exactly what I needed.

"I call middle spoon," I said, pulling on the stretchy shirt and loose pants.

Alek came over to me and scooped me up. "Then I'll be the big spoon."

"Can I be the fork?" Noah asked.

"Fork?" I asked with a snort.

"Yeah, so I can see your face and tangle my legs with yours. You know, like two forks facing each other?"

"Real romantic, man. You're a regular Shakespeare," Kingston said.

"I love it. Yes, Noah, you can fork me whenever you want to."

Kingston rolled his eyes. "Oh, come on. That was so fucking lame, Sunshine. Besides, where am I supposed to sleep?"

"At the foot of the bed like every good dog?" Alek offered.

"Nope." Kingston jumped onto the bed, positioning himself right in the center. "I'm the motherfucking silverware organizer. Come on, baby, settle yourself on top of me, and they can fork and spoon us to their heart's content."

"I didn't sign up for your arse nestled in my crotch," Alek grumbled, climbing onto the bed.

Kingston glared at him. "My ass is planted on the mattress, so don't go and get handsy, berserker. And by the way, if I wake up getting stabbed by your boner, I'm shoving you off the bed. That goes for both of you," he said, pointing his finger at both Noah and Alek. "No swordplay."

Noah snickered while I tried to hide my smile behind my hand.

"You, however, can be as handsy as you want," Kingston said, sitting up to grasp my hips and pull me on top of him. "In fact, I think I'm going to demand it."

"Do I get to push you off the bed if you stab me with your boner?" I asked as I snuggled into his chest.

"Nope. You get to take care of it."

"How is that fair? I thought you were the ones who were supposed to take care of me?"

"We'll always take care of you. Forever." Kingston's promise turned my insides to mush.

Noah's hand slid over my hip, Alek's on my waist, and Kingston held me against him. My cheek was pressed to Kingston's chest, right over his heart, the steady pulse soothing.

"When will we be able to feel the baby?" he asked, his words a resonant rumble as he spoke.

"A few more weeks," Alek said, surprising me.

"How did you know that?"

"You're not the only one who does research."

I smiled, already dozing off as Kingston began threading his fingers through my hair, combing from scalp to tip over and over. If I could have purred, I would've.

The door flew open, popping the contented little bubble we were floating in. Alek was the first off the bed, Noah right on his heels. Underneath me as he was, Kingston couldn't do more than tighten his arms around me as he sat us up.

"What the fecking hell are you three gobshites doing? The goddamn house is on fire, and you're laying up in here in a fucking puppy pile while your mate's life is in danger?"

I'd never seen Caleb so upset. A vein was pulsing wildly in his forehead, his sapphire eyes nearly black, an angry flush high in his cheeks.

"Fire? What the hell are you talking about?" Kingston snarled, sniffing the air. "I don't smell any smoke."

Caleb sent the door crashing into the wall. "What do you call that?" he roared, pointing to the smoke billowing in the hall illuminated by the angry glow of flames.

We were frozen in shock for a single heartbeat before all of us were moving.

"How did this happen?" Alek asked.

"Now's not the time, Viking." Caleb lunged toward the bed, pulling me out of Kingston's arms and holding me tight to him. "Hold on to me, *a stor*. Close your eyes." The way his voice caressed my skin had me desperate for us to reconcile.

Flames engulfed the hall and staircase, the wood banister crackling and the paint on the walls bubbling from the heat.

"Feck me," he muttered. "The window it is."

He ran back into the room and, with one hand, tore open the window, kicking out the screen and leaping to the ground like it was nothing. He barely jostled me at all as he ran us away from the burning building.

Tears blurred my eyes as I watched Noah's beautiful gift to us disappear beneath the inferno.

"I don't understand. How?"

"You have more enemies than you could ever know, *a stor*. I've tried to protect you the best I can. I failed."

Before I could ask Caleb what he was talking about, Noah, Kingston, and Alek sprinted toward us. I squinted and blinked, doubting my eyes for a second when other figures moved in the darkness.

Caleb's breath was in my ear as he inhaled deeply, taking in my scent. "Sunday, I've mis—" his words cut off with a pained grunt, and his hands fell away.

I dropped to the ground, landing on my feet, senses on high alert, the bracelet on my wrist burning hot. I'd noticed it was warm earlier, but I'd been so distracted by everything else, not to mention how inaccurate it had seemed to be in the past, so I dismissed it. *Idiot.*

"Caleb?"

My priest stumbled, brows furrowed as he reached behind him and yanked on something before pulling a bloodied arrow out of his lower back. Then he fell, the silver arrowhead glinting in the moonlight.

"Fae," he grunted.

I rushed to him, desperate to help, when a pair of unfamiliar arms wrapped around me.

"Caleb!"

My shocked cry must've triggered Alek's berserker because he bellowed with rage before I even finished saying Caleb's name.

Suddenly the moving shadows made sense. We were under attack. The fire was a distraction to lure us out.

"Watch out," I cried as two of the figures angled toward Kingston while several more headed for Noah and Alek.

Noah bared his fangs, his eyes going dark and wild as he took on the warrior rushing him. Kingston shifted, his wolf ready to tear out every one of their throats. But it was Alek who held my gaze. He barreled through the men in his path, knocking them down like a bowling ball meeting pins.

The arms around me tightened, and the sharp pinch of a cool blade against my lower belly as it sliced through my shirt had absolute terror lancing my heart.

"I'm sorry about this, little one." The fae man's voice was smooth and probably would've been appealing if he wasn't trying to kill me.

"You'd really hurt an unarmed pregnant woman?" I taunted, preparing to snatch the blade out of his hand.

"For the good of the many . . ." he murmured, bringing the blade back, then slashing forward.

Before I could make a grab for it, the fae's arm was

just . . . gone. I blinked, my eyes trying to make sense of the bloody appendage in Alek's hand. He just ripped the guy's arm right off like it was nothing.

I stumbled backward, barely catching myself before I fell. I hated not being able to shift. I could still defend myself, but that didn't make me any less of a liability.

Alek had never looked more like one of his ancestors with the spray of red covering his face and the moonlight falling on him like he was some kind of avenging, albeit terrifying, angel.

The fae fell to his knees, and I thought for sure he'd bleed out and die right there, but then he stood, determination shining in eyes that said he was serving a greater purpose than his own life. He pulled another dagger from the sheath around his left thigh and ran forward, screaming a battle cry that rivaled Alek's.

"He's fae, Alek!" I shouted.

Alek locked eyes with me and nodded. Then as I watched, a broadsword manifested in his hand. "Iron."

One word in that deep growl of his, but I knew it spelled death for the man trying to kill me.

There was little I could do but watch as the fae launched himself at my warrior mate. Alek was unfazed as the man aimed his blade straight for his heart. In one easy move, he swung the sword down, cutting the fae in two.

My stomach churned as the pieces fell to the ground, but there was another part that reveled in the bloodshed.

Berserker. Perhaps not my birthright, but every bit a part of me as my wolf.

Shocked cries rang out from the rest of the fae. They hadn't expected us to take down one of their own.

"Get behind me," Alek growled as he put himself in my way.

All my men stood ready to attack, even Caleb, his eyes ringed in dark circles and pain evident on his face. But the fae fell back, slinking into the shadows. They might be retreating, but I was smart enough to know by now this wasn't the last we'd see of them.

We'd just killed one of their brothers. There was no way we wouldn't pay.

# CHAPTER
# THIRTY-FOUR

## CALEB

I knew it was only a matter of time before I'd be called to stand before the Society and answer for the death of a fae warrior. That it had taken two full weeks was a special exercise in patience. My nerves were shot, knowing Sunday was back in her old dorm room with Moira, separated from Blackthorne, Farrell, and the Viking now that their home had been destroyed.

Only a fool would believe that hadn't been part of the plan—separating Sunday from her mates. She was stronger with them, drawing her strength from theirs. Getting everyone alone only made for easier pickings if they failed in their initial attempt to harm her. The wound in my lower back gave a dull ache as a reminder.

It had been close. Far too close.

I'd been a careless fool, too caught up in having her near me again to notice the archer in the brush. And I'd paid dearly. Sunday will never know how close to death I'd been. A few inches higher and I'd have bled out in minutes, the silver arrowhead piercing my heart, effectively staking me.

As I rounded the corner from my tunnel that led to the

bottom level of *Iniquity,* I spotted the succubus owner herself. Lilith was deep in conversation with a fae male I didn't recognize. The presence of any fae right now had my hackles rising.

It wasn't until I caught his bitten-off words I realized this man was neither friend nor foe.

"It was a fae, but not of the Night Court. We wouldn't waste our time on something as trivial as a mortal realm prophecy."

Lilith laughed, but it was a low and scathing thing, utterly devoid of humor. "How arrogant you fae are, pretending our worlds are not interlocked."

"If I had my power right now, I'd show you just how little time and space mean."

She yawned loudly and dramatically, a golden chain around her wrist going taut and pulling him closer. "So you keep reminding me, poppet."

"Call me that again, succubus, and see where I take you in your nightmares tonight. You won't enjoy it."

Her eyes flashed. "You know nothing of the monsters that come to me in the night, prince. If you believe you are the worst I've come across, you grossly underestimate my past. But allow me to remind you, I defeated *them,* and if you come for me, I will show no mercy doing the same to *you.* You've met your match, poppet. Don't forget it lest you want this little arrangement of ours to become a permanent one."

I stared at them openly, the exchange fascinating. What had transpired between them to cause such loathing?

"We aren't alone, Lil"—she tugged on the chain, making him wince—"Mistress."

Her perfectly stained lips turned up in a smile as she

made eye contact with me. "It's okay. Father Gallagher likes to watch, don't you, love?"

I ignored the taunt as I memorized the midnight hair and silver eyes of the man staring daggers at me. He was trouble. Danger was written in every annoyed line of his body.

"You know your secrets are safe with me, Lilith."

"A priest safekeeping the sins of a demon? Whatever is this world coming to?"

"You tell me, poppet. You're the one in the thick of it, aren't you?"

The man in her keeping sneered but didn't say another word.

"Should you be inside terrorizing a certain archangel?" I asked, looking pointedly at the door to our meeting room.

"Oh yes, that's right. I heard there was a bit of an accident the other night. Here to get on your knees and beg for absolution, Priest?"

"Oh lovely, your brand of hospitality is the same across the board. Here I thought I was special." The fae man settled in a chair, and Lilith immediately yanked on his chain until he moved to kneel at her feet.

I raised a brow. "Does your new pet have a name, Lilith?"

"Oh, he's gone by many names over the years, but my prince currently answers to the name Crombie. Don't you, poppet?"

"Fuck you," he spat. "This is a disgusting abuse of our arrangement, and you know it."

"Is it? Hmm. Feel free to take it up with me during our weekly business meeting, love. I'll be sure to listen to all of your grievances very attentively."

"Crombie . . ." I let the name roll around in my brain,

recognizing it vaguely. None of the feelings I got about the man were pleasant.

The doors creaked open, and Blaire Belladonna hit us with a hard stare. "Are you coming, or do we need to continue aging while you yammer on? Some of us don't have the luxury of eternal youth."

"Come along, poppet. Your mistress is required elsewhere."

"You're not my mistress," he hissed.

"Who's the one holding the chain, love?"

I shook my head as they continued to bicker behind me, even though my heart was lodged solidly in my throat. I already knew nothing about the meeting to come would be pleasant.

Then again, who better than a masochist to walk head-long into torture and punishment?

The Society members were all seated as I walked into the center of the room.

"So good of you to join us, Caleb." Gabriel's voice was the most annoyed I'd ever heard it.

"I'm hardly the last in attendance." I gestured to the empty seats where Finbar and Lilith both should be.

"Settle down. I'm here and you know it, Daddy Caleb." Lilith's voice had my hackles rising before I could stop them.

"Don't call me that," I snapped.

"Oh, that's right, there's only one person who gets that privilege."

"Are we all just going to ignore the fact that Lilith has brought an outsider to our meeting?" I asked, still internally seething.

Lilith chose that moment to run her free palm over Crombie's head. He snarled at her, baring his teeth and jerking his head away, causing her to laugh softly and lean down to whisper in his ear. I only caught the change in his expression because I was looking at him as it shifted from outrage to blatant arousal.

Gabriel arched a brow. "Do you really think I would risk the secrecy of our cause without putting some measures in place? Due to the nature of the contract between them, Crombie cannot do anything that would harm Lilith. Speaking of the things that happen here would mean death to her, and subsequently, death for him."

"I'm nothing if not crafty," Lilith murmured.

"That's not what I'd call it." After Crombie spoke, Lilith jerked the chain, and he winced but shut his mouth.

"You should consider a different kind of collar, Priest." Lilith's eyes sparked. "We could even engrave your name on it for her."

Gabriel's attention shot to me, but I took my seat, and he blessedly didn't press the issue. "Finbar will be here shortly. That leads me to the topic of our meeting. The Shadow Court."

I knew then the fae attackers had been Shadow Court warriors. Alek had committed a grave sin against them, and I was going to be the one to pay the price. As the only member of the Society not in any kind of social standing, I was the only one who could be legitimately blamed.

Deservedly so. The reason I'd been indoctrinated into the Society was that I'd be useful. My soul on the line meant I'd have to do their bidding. I may not be in chains, but I was as much a prisoner as the man in Lilith's control. Especially when the angel Gabriel was the one enslaving me.

"I don't see what all the fuss is about. The Shadow Court attacked her. They defended their mate, as any true mate would. So what is the problem?" Antoinette le Blanc asked as she inspected her nails. "This all seems like a lot of needless drama."

"The problem," Finbar spat, striding into the room, "is that a member of our court has been murdered."

"You mean the assassin you sent to murder Sunday?" I asked, the need to defend her rising hot and fierce inside me.

Finbar raised a brow. "Murder was not the intended goal. They were charged with bringing her to the queen."

"That's not what it looked like. From the arrow in my back to the blade held to her belly, these fae meant to kill."

"Be careful what allegations you lay at my feet, Priest. You know who I serve."

Gabriel shot Finbar a withering glance. "We'll deal with your insubordination later."

"How is what my court has done any different from the goals of the Farrells? We sought to isolate her until the time to act comes."

Crombie snickered. "Sounds *exactly* like something your court would do. Because reason and altruism are core values of the Shadow Court."

Finbar tossed him a disgusted look. "Your opinion means nothing to me. You are a disgrace to your court and the rest of the fae."

"Better a disgrace than a mindless slave."

Finbar cocked a brow. "It looks to me as though you are the only one in this room on his knees, at the mercy of a demon."

"Clearly you don't understand how much power comes from submission," Lilith said, surprising everyone in the room by coming to her new pet's defense.

"I'm not interested in your bedroom habits, Lilith."

344

Gabriel stood in the center of the room and stared at me. "Nor am I interested in yours, Caleb. I just want to know about the events that led to the death of a Shadow Court warrior."

"The Viking brutally killed Seamus. There wasn't enough of him to bring back home to his wife for burial." Finbar's voice shook with anger.

"If Alek killed him, there was a reason. My son would never harm someone without cause." Nord, jarl of Novasgard, stood from his chair, having replaced his previous ambassador. Not surprising after I'd learned how she'd meddled.

"He was protecting Sunday," I offered.

Blaire Belladonna scoffed. "I still don't understand why you won't let me brew her one of my special tonics. Women have been coming to my family since the dawn of time to help with her specific affliction."

"She's pregnant, not diseased." Lilith rolled her eyes.

The elder witch shrugged. "Same difference, really. Not everyone views childbirth as the miracle it's proclaimed to be."

"Don't forget, this isn't a child. It's a demon. The harbinger of the apocalypse." Ronin Farrell stood from his chair. "Whether my son sired the blight or not, it needs to be snuffed out or, at the very least, kept contained."

Antoinette raised a single finger and cut a glance at Ronin. "There will be no snuffing on my watch."

"I already tried to get her to stay at my compound in order to take care of matters myself. She's a headstrong little bitch, just like her grandfather."

Niall Fallon snarled from his seat, but Antoinette continued speaking before he could respond to the verbal dig.

"Sunday Fallon is my responsibility, and I will not allow her to be harmed."

"You seem to be rather shit at your job," Cashel Blackthorne said, his knuckles white as he gripped the armrests of his chair.

Antoinette gave him an icy stare. "I assure you, Blackthorne, you have no idea how determined I am to see my job completed successfully."

"My son could have died."

"And he didn't."

Cashel huffed. "Are we all going to ignore the fact that our children are at risk because of this girl? This child?"

Gabriel cleared his throat. "Now, now, don't be overly dramatic."

"The end of the world seems like the right time to be dramatic, angel." Ronin's tone was a strange kind of sarcastic.

I quietly seethed, the indignation of the wolf patriarch not quite ringing true. He was enjoying this far too much.

"So what are we going to do about the girl? The priest clearly cannot be trusted to play his part in keeping my granddaughter out of trouble." Niall leveled me with a pointed glare.

"It's not simply fae after her. Demons, hunters, and more will come for her once news of the child gets out." Blaire shook her head. "This has gotten out of control. I still don't see why you won't let me take care of it. One drop in her morning smoothie, and the baby is gone."

"These things must be handled with more finesse, witch. Certain rites must be performed now that the harbinger is on the way. There are seals to be closed. Blood sacrifices . . . it's all very biblical." Gabriel sighed and pinched the bridge of his nose. "Father, give me strength."

My chest tightened. I didn't know what the right choice was now. Where did I go from here?

"Then we bring her to Blackthorne Manor and hide her until the time comes. Somewhere she'll be safe from prying eyes and where we can watch her." Cashel's eyes bounced between Ronin and Antoinette. "Since you two managed to do the exact opposite."

"Is no one going to address the fact that the Shadow Court was sending their warriors after this girl? Or do they get a free pass since they're in this merry band of perverts too?" Crombie's cultured drawl was cut off as Lilith gave his chain a tug.

"Hush, poppet. The grown-ups are speaking."

I looked to the fae ambassador staring daggers at me. "Lilith's plaything does raise an excellent point."

A muscle in his jaw ticked. "I'm not here to debate whether this child means the end of the world or who should take care of her. I'm here to demand retribution for my dead clansman. One of yours killed one of mine. That debt must be repaid."

"My son did the killing. Take your wrath out on me," Nord said.

"No," Finbar said. "The priest was there. He should have stopped it."

The fae's hard stare landed on me, followed by the focus of every creature in the room.

Gabriel stepped in front of me, a long-suffering expression written on his face. "Rise, Caleb. Retribution has been demanded. Justice must be served. Yadda, yadda, yadda."

"And what price could you place on the life of a fae warrior?" Finbar asked.

"I'm sure a life for a life would suffice." The archangel was rife with intention as he turned toward me.

Finbar snorted. "As if the life of a vampire could ever be equal to one of a fae."

"Twice then," Gabriel offered. "Two deaths for one."

"More. Make it hurt."

Before I could move back, God's own messenger had my head gripped between his palms. "Immortality has its perks, Caleb."

Then the angel snapped my neck, and I died.

Again.

# CHAPTER
# THIRTY-FIVE
### SUNDAY

I knew I was dreaming the second the taste of ash hit my tongue. It was all around me, like swirling gray snowflakes that burned when they got in my eyes. This was my mother's handiwork. She hadn't come to me in a dream since the night she held my unborn daughter in her arms. I'd thought I was finally rid of her. I should have known better.

I glanced around the barren wasteland, looking for her. She had to be here. She'd never pass up an opportunity to take credit for terrorizing me. Dread sat thick in the air, so palpable it seemed to have a life of its own.

Whatever my mother wanted me to find wasn't going to be pretty. Death walked here. But who had she come to claim?

With no landscape to guide me, I picked a direction and started walking. There was little change in the cracked, gray dirt and not so much as a mountainscape in the distance. But on the horizon, I saw a gnarled tree, its empty branches reaching for the heavens as though desperate to be saved.

Unease skittered down my spine, but there was no

escaping it. This is what I was here for, and the only way out was to get it over with.

I rushed to the tree, an invisible breeze sending a dark piece of fabric floating backward on the other side of the thick trunk. I squinted but couldn't make out anything more than that from this distance. Quicker than should've been possible, I was in front of the massive elm, my chest fluttering as everything in me screamed something was wrong.

As I rounded the trunk, my gaze locked on the reason for my anxiety. Confirmation.

"Oh, Caleb," I whispered, horrified at the sight of my confessor.

He hung limply, a noose around his neck, eyes open and glassy, mouth slack. Dark bruises colored his throat, and there was no denying he was dead.

"You can't be dead. You're a vampire."

I had no way to get him down, and from the glow in the distance, the sun was rising. If I didn't get him out of here, he'd burn. I staggered forward, grasping his legs and trying in vain to pull him down from the branch. Pleas fell mindlessly from my lips as I struggled with his weight.

"Wake up. Wake up." My voice was barely a whisper stolen by the now howling wind.

Persistent shaking and an urgent male voice pulled me from the dream.

"Wake up, dove. You're dreaming."

"Noah?"

"I'm right here. You're safe."

I bolted up. "Caleb's not. Something's wrong."

Noah stopped me with a palm on the shoulder as I swung my legs over the side of his bed in his old flat in Blackthorne Hall.

"Sunday, it was just a dream. I'm sure he's fine."

"No," I insisted. "You weren't there. You know my dreams always mean something."

He frowned, looking torn. "What happened?"

"Caleb was hanged, and the sun was about to rise. I think it was a warning. I need to get to him."

"I'll come with you." He was already grabbing one of the hoodies I stole from Alek, tossing the fabric at me.

I slipped the soft sweatshirt over my head, then pulled on a pair of leggings. "No. You have to get the others. Bring them to Caleb's place. If there's something seriously wrong, he'll need all of us." He wanted to argue with me. I could see it in his eyes. "Please, Noah. Trust me."

"Fine. I'll meet up with you as soon as I sound the alarm."

Rising to my tiptoes, I brushed a chaste kiss on his lips, inhaling his spicy scent on reflex. "I'm probably wrong, and he's fine. I just . . . this is something I can't shake."

The journey to Caleb's room was a blur as I sprinted toward his door. Heart hammering, limbs trembling with the onslaught of adrenaline, I pounded on it. When he didn't answer, I tried the knob, but it was locked.

I slammed my flattened palm on the wood, letting out a frustrated growl. The overwhelming grief I'd felt since waking up hadn't lessened. Closing my eyes, I took a deep breath in an effort to calm down, focus, think.

"Where are you, Caleb? Where would you be?"

My heart lurched. I knew there was only one other place he'd go. The chapel.

As soon as the answer came to me, I was off again. I missed my wolf. Running with four legs instead of two would have made this so much faster. As it was, each step felt like I was running through mud. Painfully slow.

When I finally reached the church, my breath caught at the wide-open doors. He never left the doors open.

"Caleb?" I called, rushing into the sanctuary, my voice echoing off the domed stone ceiling. "Caleb, where are you?"

I ran down the aisle all the way to the altar and then back into the sacristy, but he wasn't there either.

"Caleb?" I tried again when my eyes landed on the confessional. The little booth was ajar, not quite flush with the wall behind it.

He must have gone down into the catacombs.

I pressed my palms to the confessional, shoving it with everything I had, determination giving me a boost. "Come on. Move."

The wood creaked before it finally slid across the tiles, revealing the entrance to the underground tunnels and rooms. He had to be there. The urgency building in my chest had to mean something.

I didn't waste time searching the little rooms. I knew if he was down here, there was only one room he'd have gone to. The same one he offered me while I was riding out my heat.

When I found him, a part of me wished I hadn't.

"Oh my God, Caleb. Who did this to you?"

He was on the ground, clad in only a pair of dark boxer briefs. His silky hair was dull, the curls obscuring his face. But my eyes were locked on the markings ringing his neck. They were an angry, swollen red.

I dropped to my knees next to him, unsure of what to do. Reaching out, I brushed back the hair that had fallen across his face. From this vantage point, I could see the severity of the wounds. Blood streaked down his throat where the skin had been burned raw. Blisters and sores that looked so painful I shuddered accompanied the deep bruising.

I was afraid to touch him; wounds like that on a vampire must have been left with silver. He would have healed by now otherwise.

"No," he groaned softly. "No more. Please."

My entire body relaxed when I heard his voice. He wasn't dead.

"Caleb, you're okay. I'm here. No one is going to hurt you."

"Blood," he whispered, his eyelids waxy and bruised as he tried to open them.

Without stopping to think, I offered him my wrist. "Here. Take what you need."

There was zero hesitation as he latched onto me, the bite clumsy but sure. I scooted myself closer until his head was resting in my lap as he fed. The pleasure that accompanied a vampire's bite was there, but not as strong. An edge of pain came with this one. He was too out of it to worry about making it feel good for me.

Caleb grunted, his hand gripping my forearm and holding me tight to him. When he sucked harder, his eyes opened, locking onto mine. There wasn't a shred of recognition there. All I saw was a feral, hungry vampire staring back at me.

A low trill of fear raced through me, but before I could do anything, Caleb released my wrist and jerked upright. He blinked a few times, his color already returning as the wounds on his neck began healing.

"Caleb?" I whispered.

A chilling smile stretched his lips, now coated with my blood, right before he lunged and tore into my throat.

**B**lood. Rich, warm, heady. Everything I needed and always denied myself. Drinking straight from the vein always sent a rush of arousal through me, which is why it was an act I refused. Except for my moments of weakness.

She would always be my weakness.

Clarity returned to me in stages as her blood healed me, my broken body knitting back together with the precious life she was giving me.

Gabriel killed me more times than I could count. Each time more painful than the last, until I thought I'd go mad from it. Only then had Finbar said the debt had been paid, and Gabriel brought me back here to nurse my wounds in peace.

I never expected *her* to come for me.

Sunday's soft mewl of pleasure had my cock threatening to punch through my shorts. My lust for her was intense, but my hunger eclipsed all else.

"Caleb," she whispered.

The sound of my name on her sweet lips had me pulling

her body closer to mine so I could drink deeper. She was such a good girl when she wasn't being naughty.

"It hurts."

*It hurts me too. Not being with you.*

*I'll make us both feel better.*

The taste of her on my tongue healed more than just my body. It eased the endless ache that being apart had caused.

Her pulse, which had beat sure and strong, weakened, giving her words new meaning. She pushed against me, struggling in my hold. "Caleb, stop."

Those two words hit me like a whip's lash. I tore myself away from her. The lack of my support sent her crumpling to the ground. She lifted her still bleeding wrist to the gaping wound at her throat, blood running steadily down her body. Hunger roared inside me as the scent of what I wanted most permeated the room. But it was the look on her face that knocked back the thirst. I'd hurt her.

Put her in danger.

I wore the evidence of my guilt as even more of the crimson dripped down my chin and chest.

In her eyes, I knew what she saw. Not the priest she loved, but a monster. But Sunday Fallon was loved by the monsters humans feared. And being what I was meant I could fix what I broke.

"*A stor*, come here to me. Let me heal you."

Bless her foolish little heart, she didn't even hesitate to obey. Her trust in me was unfounded. I'd done nothing to earn it and far more to prove myself unworthy.

I took her in my arms and lifted her, carrying her over to the bed. I rested her in my lap, selfishly needing to feel her body against mine. Slicing open a vein, I offered her my neck.

"Drink."

Her mouth sealed around the wound, and the first pull was utter bliss. I sucked in a sharp breath, fighting the tidal wave of desire her lips on my flesh always released. It was all I could do not to free my cock and drive deep inside her here and now.

"That's a good girl. Drink deep. I took too much. You were so good to me."

I ran my hand down her hair and along her spine, loving the way we fit together. Like a puzzle that had finally found its missing piece.

The foreign feel of my heartbeat racing distracted me from the sensations she evoked. It was as if a drummer had taken up residence inside my head, and I could hear it as clearly as hers. Which was why I knew the very second their rhythms synced up, becoming one perfect melody.

"Take me into you, Sunday. Let me heal you and make you new."

She moaned against me as she shifted positions until her knees were planted on either side of my hips, and I could feel the heat of her tight cunt pressing along the throbbing length of my cock.

"You'll make a sinner out of me yet."

She responded by tightening her grip on my hair and rolling her hips over me, sending ripples of pleasure flowing through me. Pleasure so intense and multi-faceted, I knew I wasn't only experiencing my own.

Fucking hell, the bond. I'd allowed us to complete it by performing our blood exchange. Why had I resisted her so long when I could feel whole by joining with her?

A smile spread across my face as the understanding of what having a mate felt like washed over me. At least, it did until searing pain shot through my chest in a circular pattern.

*No. Not another one.* A seal. I'd opened a fecking seal.

The time to turn back had long since passed. There was no undoing this.

Sunday Fallon belonged to me as surely as I did to her. And if I was already going to hell, I might as well enjoy the trip.

"That's enough, my lovely one. Don't take it all." I stroked her hair and gently detached her from my throat, her eyes glazed with euphoria, lips red with my blood.

"Caleb, you gave me your blood," she whispered, awe in her words. "You bonded with me."

"Aye, and I'd do it all over again if it means I get to keep you."

"But your vows. The rules."

"Fuck the rules. It's you I want to devote myself to. You are the reason I exist. I've just been too bloody stubborn to let myself admit it."

She swallowed, her eyes bright with unshed tears. "I love you, Caleb."

I didn't have the strength to keep from kissing her then. Those perfectly innocent and equally powerful words stabbed straight through me in a way she'd never understand. I crushed my mouth to hers, tongue delving between her lips.

Grasping her beneath her thighs, I stood and turned us around, laying her back onto the bed. She stared up at me, her chest rising and falling in time with my own as I spread her legs wide. Her eyes ran over my body, lingering on the circular markings on my chest.

"I didn't know you had a tattoo. What does it mean?"

There was no way in hell I was about to have that talk with her. I had other plans. "Penance."

Her lips twitched. "That seems appropriate for you."

*If you only knew.*

She sat up, her hand outstretched as if to trace the circles with her fingers. I caught her hand and kissed her fingertips. Then kneeling down, I gripped her knees and tugged her forward.

"Look at me, darling."

Wide blue eyes found mine. "I'm looking."

"And what do you see?"

"My mate."

"Fecking right."

Leaning close, I ran my nose along her inner thigh before I buried my face in between her legs, inhaling the scent of her arousal. It was the most perfect thing I'd ever smelled, a perfume composed of honey and musk, a bouquet I wanted to explore further with my mouth. She wriggled her hips, a little whine coming from her as she begged for more friction.

"Stay still, or I'll have to take you over my knee, and that would ruin my plans."

"Yes, Daddy."

Jesus and all the saints. My cock pulsed, a rush of pleasure building in my balls. She'd bring me off with her words alone if I let her. Using my fangs, I tore the pleasure-damp fabric of her thin leggings open, then my fingers ripped the poor excuse for clothing straight down the middle until she was bared to me.

"No knickers? Naughty girl."

"I was in a hurry."

"I never want you to wear any when you're with me."

"You don't?"

"I require complete access to this perfect cunt."

She batted her eyelashes at me, pure lust in those fathomless depths. "It's yours."

With one swift flick of my wrist, I slapped the glistening lips of her pussy with my fingers, making her jolt and cry out.

"What was that for?"

"Just to remind you of the first time you tempted me."

She smirked. "Do it again."

"You don't get to make the demands, sweetling. I'm the one in charge. In fact, I think you need a reminder." Leaning forward, I licked up her seam, a growl of primal satisfaction rumbling in my chest and vibrating directly onto that sweet bundle of nerves. "You don't get to come until I say." And then I nipped her clit with my fangs.

She cried out, her fingers finding my hair and gripping tightly, the strength afforded her by my blood sending pain across my scalp. "That's right, my darling, hurt me if you must, but know it won't get you closer to your peak. Not until I say so."

"But you've already made us wait so long."

*The absolute cheek of this one.*

I rubbed my grin along the inside of her thigh, giving her another little bite. "Behave, or I'll not let you come at all."

She didn't utter another word, so I slipped a finger inside her and dragged a moan from her instead.

"So fecking hot and tight. You're ready for me, aren't you, sweetling?"

"I've been ready for you. Make me yours, Daddy."

I stood, staring her down as I shoved my boxers to the floor, letting my weeping cock spring free.

She licked her lips, eyeing me hungrily. "Caleb, let me choke on your dick. I want it so bad."

God in heaven. My length twitched, a pearly drop of cum sitting on the tip. "Later. Now it's time I had what I've been denying myself. Scoot back on the bed, little one. Spread your thighs and get ready. I'm going to fuck you now."

She tore her shirt over her head, tossing it aside. I almost scolded her for doing that without permission, but then she rubbed her thighs together as she scooted up and made room for me to join her on the mattress. When she spread them for me, they were sticky and shining with her arousal.

I couldn't contain my grin of dark amusement.

"What's so funny?"

"Just a passing thought."

"You going to share with the class, Father?"

"I was just thinking you look damn good wearing only your Sunday best."

She quirked a brow, clearly not understanding my joke, so I slid my fingers up the inside of her thigh, coating the digits in her slick. Her eyes burned with desire as I lifted them to my mouth and sucked them clean.

"Shouldn't it be you wearing it?"

"Thanks for the idea, darling." I dropped my gaze back to her glistening center. "Wider."

She obeyed with a soft whimper.

"Such a good girl. You like to make me happy, don't you?"

She nodded, her breaths coming in little pants, nipples pert little buds begging for my mouth. I played at being calm and in control, but everything in me was wound tighter than a piano string.

Climbing onto the bed, I knelt between her thighs. I'd imagined this so many times. The first true claiming. My moment with her that had nothing to do with her heat or my shame.

Reaching for her, I lifted her hips, bringing her level with my aching cock.

"Fuck me, Caleb. I want to feel you inside me."

"Gladly."

I watched with my pulse pounding in my ears as we joined. My dick slowly spread her open, filling her, making her mine. It was better than I ever could have imagined. The heat. The pressure. The grip of her around me like she was made for me. A ragged moan was all I could give her as I sank to the hilt.

"Are you okay?" she asked, her voice soft and tender.

"I haven't felt this whole since the day my soul was stolen from me."

I stared at our bodies, connected in more than just the physical sense. But then my little minx moved. She rolled her hips, making me slide out a little and then taking me in again. Feck me, but it felt so good. I knew now why so few priests truly went without committing the carnal sins.

"Christ, you'll never be rid of me now. I think I'll chain you to this bed, so we never have to stop."

"Sounds good to me."

I almost forgot my wicked plan to deny her an orgasm as I began a slow rhythm of deep thrusts in and out of her. The way her skin flushed, our blood staining her lips and some of her throat, the moans and little cries escaping her, all made me chase one singular goal. Pleasure. For me. For her. For us.

"Fuck me, Caleb. I can't stand it."

"You can and you will. I'm savoring this. Burning you into my memory, and I won't be rushed."

But little did she know, I was already on the precipice of my own release. I couldn't hold it back much longer, not with her looking the way she did, feeling so perfect, giving me everything I'd been missing.

I slid my hands along her thighs, my thumbs gliding over her swollen petals and up to the soft mound of her belly. I hesitated, but Sunday's husky question brought me straight back.

"Do you like seeing what you did to me?"

Hips jerking involuntarily at the question, I had to wait a beat to let the gravity of what she'd asked me settle. "More than I ever thought possible."

She laid one of her hands atop mine. "Me too. I hope she has curls as dark as her father. And if she looks like me, we'll just have to try again . . . and again."

Jesus wept. I lost it. I drove in to the hilt, some primal urge inside me taking hold as I fucked her long and hard, making her scream my name to the heavens. Her cunt pulsed around my shaft as she came, the tightening of her walls doing nothing to stop my own climax. But I didn't have to stop it any longer. I'd broken every last vow in favor of new ones. Sunday was my religion. The goddess I worshiped with my body. The only mistress I served.

I filled her with my seed, giving her everything I had.

"Thank you, Daddy," she whispered in the quiet as we came down from our shared euphoria.

"For what?"

"Letting me come."

"Oh, my naughty girl, that I didn't do. Now you need to be punished."

Footsteps raced down the hall. I glanced over my shoulder in time to find three familiar faces peering in from the doorway, their expressions ranging from panic to confusion and mirth.

"Fuck, Thorne. You made it sound like someone was

dying. Did you really bring us all the way down here just to watch the priest nut on our girl? Unless . . . was this a group invitation?" Kingston smirked, his taunt obviously aimed at me.

I looked back down at my mate, dark satisfaction making me smile.

Lust flared to life in her eyes, an answering ripple tightening around my cock.

"I know exactly how I'm going to punish you."

# THIRTY-SEVEN

A punishment? That made my dick go from six to midnight instantly. The priest pulled out of Sunday, his cock still half-hard and covered in her. She laid there looking dreamy-eyed and sated, her tits swollen, belly gently rounded, those full hips of hers just accenting exactly how perfectly she'd been made. She was the picture of everything I needed, laid out like a feast.

Minus the blood. They were both covered in it. Since neither one of them was dead, I wasn't worried, and since he was a vampire, blood sort of came with the territory. I sniffed deep, the answer for their state coming to me as the scent of her newest bond layered through her arousal.

"You two bonded. Fucking finally."

"Does it always look like a fucking murder scene when a vampire claims their mate?" Alek asked.

"Not when I did it," Thorne said.

"Shut the fuck up. You're ruining this. I think an orgy is on the table. Can we help?" I blurted, hoping I didn't sound like an eager fucking kid, but God, I was dying for a taste

"Only if you are willing to follow my orders and act as the implements of her punishment."

"What do you have in mind?" Alek asked, his eyes fever-bright as he leaned against the door frame.

"Sunday broke the rules and came without permission. So now our little wolf isn't allowed to come until everybody else gets their turn."

Sunday's mouth rounded in a silent 'o.'

"As this is my punishment to oversee, you three must do as I say to deliver the blows."

"I'm not going to hit her," Thorne ground out.

"I'm not asking you to. These blows will be more carnal in nature."

"That I can handle," Thorne said, unbuttoning his shirt.

I looked back to Sunday, needing to make sure this was something she wanted. I lifted my brow in a silent question she had no trouble interpreting. She nodded eagerly, her tongue darting out to wet her lips.

"I'm ready. Sunshine, it looks like you've been a bad girl. You just can't help yourself, can you?"

"No. I can't."

Caleb stood next to the bed, his gaze hard and intense.

"What do you want from me, Padre?" I asked.

"Clean up the mess I made."

Sunday pressed her legs together and moaned my name. The desire in her voice went straight to my balls.

"You don't have to tell me twice."

Caleb moved over, making room for me as I tugged my shirt over my head and whipped off my pants. I was already popping out of my boxers as I climbed up her body and gave her an open-mouthed kiss.

"Roll over and present."

Sunday bit her bottom lip and nodded, twisting

beneath me as she moved to obey. I sat back on my heels, kneading her ass as she raised it for me. Then with both hands, I spread her cheeks before leaning in and licking the seam from taint to tailbone. She cried out and arched her back, trying to get away from me, but failing.

"I said, clean her up." Caleb's words were harsh and firm. I didn't give one single fuck.

I backed away, inspecting that perfectly juicy ass before I slapped one cheek. "Arch that back, baby. I want to see every single inch of your cunt."

Sunday did so immediately, a little whimper of need escaping her.

"We're only just getting started, darling. Don't go begging yet. You're the one who broke the rules."

As Caleb spoke, I leaned down and started eating her like a starving man. She squirmed against me, her body chasing my tongue even as she tried to get away and fight off her orgasm.

"Look at you. Such a good girl, trying so hard not to come. You can't stay away from him, though. He's your punishment."

I pulled away and shifted so that I was lying between her legs.

"Sit on my face, Sunshine."

Her cheeks were flushed, hair a wild halo around her head and shoulders. "But what if I smother you?"

"If I can breathe, I'm not doing it right."

Alek snickered, clearly agreeing with me.

"He gave you an order, little one. You'd better listen," Caleb said, his voice still holding the sharp edge of a disciplinarian.

She brought her hips down, bringing her sweet pussy to my lips, and I took that moment to reach up, grab her hips, and pull her fully onto my face. If this was what punishing my Sunshine was, I hope she broke the rules more often. I wanted to do this every fucking night.

Her thighs were quivering, the desperate moans and whispered pleas slipping from her throat conveying her approaching climax.

"Enough," Caleb softly ordered. "Stand up, Kingston."

I wasn't sure how I felt about taking the priest's orders, but I'd been enjoying myself so far, so I figured I'd go with it a little while longer.

Caleb tipped Sunday's chin up. "You wanted to choke on my cock, darling. How about you choke on his while I watch?"

*Jesus. Fuck.*

Maybe I was a fan of his orders after all.

Sunday's legs trembled as she crawled across the bed toward me, her eyes locked on mine. "Take it out, Kingston. You heard the man."

I pulled my boxers down my thighs, freeing Jake and adjusting my position on the bed to make it easier for her to take me into her mouth.

"All the way to the root," Caleb ordered from somewhere behind me.

I honestly had no idea what the other guys were doing. I was too focused on the woman currently licking her lips and staring my dick down like he was her favorite flavor of ice cream.

She glanced behind me, likely at Caleb, and whispered, "Yes, Daddy."

My cock fucking throbbed, and she wasn't even talking to me. Fisting her hair, I brought those plump lips to my weeping tip.

"Suck me, Sunshine."

Flattening her tongue, she got to work, teasing me by licking the bottom of my shaft before finally taking the tip of me into her mouth and sucking it hard.

"Fuck. You were born to take my cock, baby."

"She's good at everything, but the way she takes me is better than anything," Alek agreed.

"Well, not *anything*." Noah's words were light and teasing.

"Her mouth is a close second to her pussy."

"Can you two shut the fuck up? I'm trying to concentrate." I really didn't want to come while those two peckerheads chatted like the goddamn Muppets at the opera.

Sunday chose that moment to take me all the way. Jake bottomed out deep in her throat. Suddenly it was no trouble at all to focus on her.

She glanced up at me, tears shimmering in her eyes.

"You okay, beautiful?"

She hummed, the vibrations more stimulating than I could comprehend. My fingers tightened in her hair, and my hips gave an involuntary jerk.

"Shit, you're gonna make me come," I gritted out.

"On her, not in her mouth."

The fuck did this man think he was doing? I wouldn't be told by anyone where I could blow my load. Least of all a priest with a daddy kink.

But . . . coming on her perfect tits was hot. I liked how she looked painted in my spend. Claimed by me.

The convulsions of her throat as she sucked me, along with the image of me spurting all over her, had me ready to blow.

"Stop, Sunshine. Fuck. I'm close."

She backed away, and I immediately replaced her mouth with my fist, flying over my cock as the orgasm barreled through me. Jet after jet of my seed landed on her and fuck me, male pride washed over me at the sight.

When the aftershocks of pleasure died down, I leaned close and kissed her, whispering, "Good girl," before backing away.

"You don't get to call her that, Kingston." Caleb's voice was low and even. "Now go sit down. Blackthorne, you're up."

# THIRTY-EIGHT

THORNE

"Where do you want me, dove?" I approached the bed where my wanton beauty lay panting, on edge, and dripping with desire.

"No one has taken her ass yet." Kingston took me by surprise by offering that.

"I'd have thought you would be the first one to try."

He shrugged. "She needs someone less girthy. That Slim Jim of yours will do just fine."

I would have tossed an insult right back in his face if Sunday hadn't run her palm up my torso.

"It's long and thick and exactly what I need, Noah. Don't listen to him."

Wrapping my fingers around her wrist, I bent down and kissed her palm. "I'll give you whatever you want, love. Whenever you want. All you ever need do is ask."

She flicked her eyes over my shoulder, seeking permission from our little choir director.

"Is that what you desire?"

"Yes, Daddy."

"Then take that cum dripping down your perfect tits and prepare him."

"Ah, now I see why you didn't want me to blow in her mouth."

My balls ached as I watched her do precisely as she was told.

"She'll need access, Blackthorne."

I frowned, my brain too muddled with lust to make sense of his words.

Kingston chuckled. "That means you need to get your cock out."

I was on board before the wolf finished his sentence. My trousers were open, cock ready and waiting.

Sunday pouted. "Noah, I need all of you. Take off your clothes."

She didn't need to ask me twice. I stripped and approached her once more, this time fully naked and straining, desperate for her touch.

"Much better."

Wiping her palm across her torso to gather more cum, she then worked it over my shaft until I was slick with it.

"Fuck, does anyone else think that's hot?" Kingston asked.

"Quiet, Farrell, or I'll make you leave," Caleb said.

Under his breath, Kingston muttered, "You could fucking try."

My knees shook as she continued stroking me. "Get me ready, Noah? I want to be able to take your cock without pain."

I inhaled sharply but gave her a jerky nod. "Turn around and spread wide for me. I'll take care of you."

There was more of Kingston's cum to go around; the bastard had damn near painted her with it. But that didn't stop me from leaning closer to her arse and spitting right where my cock needed to go.

"*That* was hot," Alek rumbled.

Then with one careful digit, I pressed inside the tight channel. She tensed, then moaned as I began moving.

"More," she urged.

Never one to deny her, I did as she asked, sliding a second finger in and scissoring them back and forth to help stretch her out.

I was dying from wanting her, and as though he knew, Caleb said, "Lie on the bed, Noah. We are going to try something new. She needs to be the one driving for this."

I nodded, moving so I was on my back with Sunday kneeling beside me.

"Face the door, sweet girl. You're the one in control. Take things as fast or as slow as you need. And if it's too much, we will stop. Do you understand?"

Sunday nodded eagerly, facing away from me as she climbed up over my hips.

"Noah?" She glanced over her shoulder, vulnerability shining in her eyes.

"Yes, dove?"

"Will it hurt?"

I couldn't lie to her. "It may burn a little, but if it's more painful than that, we'll stop and try again another time."

Biting her lower lip, she nodded. I held my cock, ready for her, and waited as she slowly sank down, her arse exactly as I'd hoped.

Hot. Tight. Sexy as fuck.

Goosebumps raced down her skin, and she shivered as she adapted to the invasion. "It feels so much better than I ever imagined. Why did we wait so long to try this?"

"I don't bloody know. Can you take more? God, I'm not even halfway in."

She squirmed and sank lower, her breath catching in her throat as I stretched her further. "Help me?" she begged.

Taking her hips in my hands, I slowly rolled my pelvis up until I was fully seated inside her. By the time it was done, we were both trembling with pent-up need.

"I'm so full," she whispered.

"You're about to be more full. Alek, are you ready?" Caleb's question caught me off guard.

"I'm not finished."

"No, you're not. You're just getting started. Lie back, Sunday. Let Noah hold you. Aleksandr needs space for what I have in mind."

"You want me to . . . at the same time he's . . . is that wise?"

"Oh, look, the big bad Viking's flustered. It's like you've never seen porn, bro." I ignored Kingston's unwanted commentary. It was the easiest way to deal with the mouthy arse.

I stared at Sunday, speared on Thorne's dick, dripping and needy. "But she's so small."

"I can take it, Alek. I promise."

Her breathless assurance, coupled with the heated look she leveled on me, made my beast roar with the need to be inside her.

"Tell me if it's too much. I don't give a damn what *he* wants. This is about you." I climbed onto the bed, my knees between Thorne's spread legs as I slid my palms over her thighs and up to her breasts.

She reached for me, lifting her hands up in a silent plea I had no trouble translating. I leaned down so she could curl her fingers into my hair and press her mouth to mine.

Thorne chose that moment to roll his hips, and I swallowed her cries as pleasure racked her body.

"You're still dressed, Alek. How are you going to fuck me with all those clothes on?" she asked, her lips swollen from my kiss.

"Easily remedied." With a snap of my fingers, my clothes vanished, and my cock made itself known, pressing up against the treasure between her legs, already begging entrance.

"Fuck, I'm hard again. Sunshine, I think you might be part witch."

"She's busy. Take care of it yourself, and shut up," Caleb barked.

"How do we do this?" I asked, my question as much for Thorne as it was Sunday.

"Slowly," Thorne gritted out, his voice thick with tension. "Once you're inside her, we'll take turns moving and make sure to follow her lead."

"Go on, Viking. Fill her. But don't make her come. Not yet."

Pleading blue eyes found mine as Sunday lay back into the cradle of Thorne's body. "Please, Alek. I need you."

I was aware the legs pressed against mine weren't hers, but it was easy to tune everything else out as I trailed the tip of my cock along her slick folds, making her whimper as I lined myself up with her entrance. My size already made it a snug fit, but even as ready as she was for me, I knew this would be damn near impossible.

"Gently," Thorne said.

Part of me didn't want his help. The other part welcomed the reminder. She needed me to take extra care. I nodded and pressed forward, her cunt hot and slippery, easing the way . . . at least initially. I noticed the difference instantly, the way she stretched around me, the tension in her, the change in her breathing.

"Are you okay?" I looked straight into her eyes.

She squirmed, taking me deeper. "Keep going."

"Fuuuuuck." Thorne's hissed curse filled the room as I sank in deeper. "I can feel that."

I couldn't help it; I looked at him. His face was etched in a kind of pained pleasure I was familiar with. The man was holding on by a thread.

"Alek," Sunday whimpered, drawing my attention back to her. "Don't stop."

The way her pussy gripped my cock had me ready to drive deep, but I knew none of us would survive without coming. So with control I didn't know I possessed, I continued my slow glide.

"Jesus. I've never felt anything like this," Thorne said on a groan. "I need to move."

"Yes. God. Move." Sunday tilted her face toward him, kissing his jaw as he palmed one breast.

His hips shifted, a slow, rolling motion that caused the strangest fucking sensation to run along my length. It was him. Moving in her arse. Now I understood what he'd meant earlier. The added pressure and the unexpected caress had my balls tightening in preparation.

There was no way this was lasting long. It felt like I was going to detonate at any second. I'd be embarrassed, but from the sounds the other two were making, they were in the same situation.

A low grunt came from Kingston, who was openly stroking himself as he watched the show with rapt attention. Caleb stood with intense focus in his eyes, but from the straining fabric of his boxers, he was just as affected as the rest of us.

"Get what you want, gentlemen. If she's good, she can have her orgasm too," the priest said.

Thorne and I began moving in a careful sort of dance. He pulled back, I sank in, over and over, until Sunday was practically weeping with the need to climax, and I couldn't take it anymore.

"Please, Daddy, I need to come," she whimpered.

"Not yet, my darling one."

Noah tipped his face to Sunday's ear. "You love it when he calls you his good girl, but you and I both know just how dirty you really are. You love to be naughty, don't you?"

"Yes," she panted.

"Would a good girl let herself be impaled by two men at the same time?"

"N-no."

Noah's dark chuckle filled the room. "Then why are you listening to him right now?"

He nipped her throat where the mark he'd given her still appeared as a raised scar. "Come for me, dove. Don't worry about the priest. Take what you want. Give me what I need."

Indecision warred on her face. She wanted to please both of them. I wouldn't make her choose. Reaching down, I pinched that slick bundle of nerves, making all three of us cry out as she arched her back.

The shift in position set off Noah's climax, and the tight clamp of her contracting walls took me over the edge right behind him.

"Come for me, sweetling. You've been my good girl. Now you may take your reward."

I was pretty sure from the way she was clenching me that she was already coming, but the whispered command gave her permission to let go. Sunday screamed out her release, grinding down on both of us as we pumped her full of our seed.

Noah claimed Sunday's mouth while I rained kisses along the side of her neck. All of us were still working on coming back down from the high of our joint orgasms. The only sounds in the room were our breaths and hammering heartbeats.

Until Kingston spoke. "Hey, uh . . . does anyone have a towel? I made a mess over here."

**S**oft tickles across my belly pulled me from the haze of sleep. The sound of a deep baritone filling the room had me blinking my eyes open. Alek's fingers trailed along the exposed skin of my bump, his lips close to the swell as he sang.

"'*My mother told me, Someday I will buy, Galleys with good oars, Sail to distant shores . . .*'"

I combed my fingers through his long hair, and he stopped, backing away just a little.

"Don't stop. It's beautiful."

He gave me a bashful grin. "My father sang it to us as babes. It was the same lullaby his mother sang to him. Some old Norse poem she loved, written by a berserker war poet."

The contradictions of such a person existing made me snicker. "How fitting."

"Right?" His lips twitched with mirth, and then his soft smile faded, his eyes narrowing as he searched my face. "Why do you look like you're about to cry?"

"I'm so glad you came back to us, Alek," I said, my

throat suddenly constricting as a swell of emotion hit me out of nowhere.

He reached up and brushed his knuckles across my cheek. "As am I, *Kærasta*." His expression darkened. "Even if I never remember our past, I have fallen in love with the woman meant to be mine all over again. How many people get to say they've been blessed twice?"

The tears I'd been fighting spilled free. "Alek . . ."

"I mean it, Sunny. I love you. Not because I *have* to, but because I couldn't stop it if I tried. You are mine."

"I love you so much. Now keep singing. She likes it."

"Already our little one has me wrapped around her finger." He grinned and palmed my belly before beginning the song again. The baby shifted, moving in response to his resonant timbre, and his voice faltered, focus steady on his palm. "Sunny? Did I . . ."

"You felt that? So far I've been the only one who could."

Wonder transformed his handsome face, making him appear more boy than man. "Good morning, my beautiful girl. I can't wait to meet you and teach you the proper way to destroy your foes."

"Uh . . . Alek. We need to work on your baby talk. Maybe we save the slaughter and revenge stuff for when she's older. Like . . . way older."

"Why? I had a blade in my hand before I could walk."

"That's mildly terrifying."

"But look at me now."

I shook my head. "She has us to protect her for now. No need to worry about her taking care of herself."

Alek gave me an exasperated but still affectionate look. "Sunny, teaching her to protect herself *is* how we take care of her. No child of ours will walk the realms free of enemies. The earlier we start, the safer she will be."

As if in answer, she gave a solid kick to his hand, and he snickered.

"See? She agrees with her father."

Rolling my eyes, I sat up and stretched. I felt good. Like . . . really fucking good. Better than I had in months. Was it because of the blood Caleb had given me? Maybe. But part of me thought it had something to do with the fact that all four of my mates were *finally* where they belonged. Bonded to me.

"Where are the others?" I asked, looking around the room and finding no evidence of them.

"Caleb returned home before the sun fully rose. The others went hunting for food and showers. I volunteered to stay behind and keep watch over you while you slept."

My stomach rumbled. "What time is it?"

"Nearly sunset. You slept most of the day away."

"You four exhausted me."

He glanced up at me. "How are you feeling? Were we too rough?"

I was sore, deliciously so, but not in any sort of pain. "Just the right amount of rough," I promised, leaning over to kiss him.

"So we'll be doing that again then?" he murmured against my lips.

"Oh yes. Often, I think."

I could feel his smile as he kissed me. His beard brushed my mouth, making me giggle.

"What?" He pulled away and stared into my eyes.

"Just thinking about Tor."

"You're thinking about my brother while I'm kissing you?"

I laughed. "Not like that. Just that he's beardless. Poor bastard."

Alek's laughter joined mine, washing over me and cocooning me in his joy. "When my family learns of it, he'll never live it down. Facial hair is a point of pride for us."

I gave his well-groomed beard a little tug. "You don't say."

"I'm glad you like it. If there's anyone in this world I'd shave it for, it's you."

"Don't you dare."

He grinned and captured my lips with his once more, pushing me back with his body as the kiss turned from a sweet tease to something hotter. I shouldn't have been ready for more after last night, but my body said yes.

"Bloody hell, Viking. Haven't you had enough?" Noah stood in the doorway, a takeout bag in his hand and a packed duffel bag in the other.

"Never. And I'm not in the mood to share, so fuck off."

"Sorry to burst your bubble, but plans have changed. We've been summoned, dove. We have to leave right now. It's not safe here."

My gaze landed on the luggage. "What's in there?"

"My clothes, yours, anything I thought we might need."

Moira had been a godsend after the fire. It was thanks to her that any of us had clothes to speak of at all. She and Ash had conjured up as many replacement items as they could, going so far as to make replicas of our personal favorites. Some days it really paid off to have a tiny witch as a bestie.

Alek stood, his body tense.

I sighed. "Well, fuck."

"Perfectly said." Noah handed me the takeout bag, and my mouth watered at the scent of my favorite sandwich. "Eat up. We have a long evening ahead of us."

"Where should I meet you? I'll go pack a bag," Alek asked.

"There's a car waiting. Then we'll pop off to the airport."

Alek nodded, leaving me with a kiss and a wink. "See you soon, Sunny."

After I finished my sandwich, I changed into some of the clothes Noah brought for me. Warm fleece-lined leggings and a cozy cable-knit sweater. If you didn't know I was knocked up, you'd have no clue in this getup. Probably the point, but I sure as hell was comfortable.

Noah and I walked hand in hand out of the church after I was dressed. Tension rolled off him in waves as we navigated the cobblestone path. He was on high alert. Something serious was going on.

"What the bleeding hell do you think you're doing, Blackthorne? Where are you taking her?" Caleb stormed down the path, his face twisted in anger.

Not stopping our forward motion, Noah continued marching us toward the waiting car. "She's no longer safe here. I'm bringing her home with me. You better than most understand how well protected she'll be under Blackthorne care."

Caleb sneered and grasped my hand once we'd pulled alongside him, finally stalling us. I felt a bit like I was trapped in the middle of a vampire tug of war. If I was a human, I might be at risk of losing a limb.

"Yes, take a delicious-smelling woman into a den of vampires and see how well that works out for you."

"My father would never allow harm to a single hair on my mate's head."

"Clearly you don't know your father very well."

I caught sight of Alek and Kingston, accompanied by

Moira and Ash, standing next to an obsidian Range Rover with windows so dark you couldn't see anything. With one pleading look from me, Caleb released my hand. I saw the resignation flicker through him. He knew we had to go.

"Priest, you can stand here and pick a fight with me, or you can come with us. But I'm taking her away from this place." Noah dragged a hand through his hair and sighed. "My father wouldn't summon us if the threat wasn't imminent."

Caleb took a long, slow breath, pinning me with his stony glare. "My place is with her."

"OH MY GOD, it's like a mini-Ravenscroft," I whispered as the car approached the gates of Blackthorne Manor.

"Your family has a real hard-on for wrought iron, huh? You really lean into the Gothic hero bit."

Noah smirked at Kingston. "All the better to stab you with, wolf boy."

"Better watch out, bloodsucker. Big bad wolf play gets me hard."

Alek snorted, wrapping his arm around me and tucking me into his side. "Everything gets you hard."

"Children," Caleb said with a drawn-out sigh. "All of you."

The car pulled to a stop in the circular driveway, the house looming, lights in the window making it appear sinister and alive.

"Oh, good, the Addams family is here to greet us," Kingston muttered.

Noah didn't respond, but he stiffened at my side.

"It's okay, Noah. I had to meet them sometime."

"I would have preferred we do this without the hecklers."

"Sorry, fangface, you can't get rid of me." Kingston spread his legs wide, his arms splayed out over the bench seat running the length of the limousine that had picked us up at the airport.

Caleb sat across from him, his expression pure loathing.

"Like a rash," Moira whispered, making Ash giggle.

"More like a sexy as fuck tattoo," Kingston corrected.

The car door opened, and the driver held out a white-gloved hand.

"Oh, he's trained. Does he wipe your ass for you too?"

Noah ignored Kingston but batted the driver away. "I've got a handle on this, thank you."

"As you wish, Mr. Blackthorne. Your father awaits."

"Yes, I can see that."

The driver nodded and moved away as Noah turned to help me out of the car. Before I got out, I looked over my shoulder, giving Kingston the sternest expression I could manage. "Behave. This is stressful enough without your bullshit."

He blinked. "Yes, Mistress."

We approached as a group, the entire Blackthorne family staring at us with eyes the same disarming amber hue as Noah's. Well, except for the woman I assumed was his mother, who was clearly human.

"Mother, Father, I'd like you to meet Sunday Fallon. My bonded mate." Noah's voice was strong, but I felt a tremor of fear from him.

The human I'd clocked as his mom smiled in welcome as Noah introduced me. Then the tall, devastatingly handsome man who looked so much like Noah I had to do a double take stepped forward and extended a hand. "Cashel

Blackthorne. You are welcome to take sanctuary in our home as long as you need, Sunday." He cocked a brow at the ragtag crew I brought with me. His gaze lingered on Caleb, a fraction of a second too long and my priest's jaw ticked in discomfort.

"You and your ... friends."

I blushed. "Thank you. I wish we were meeting under more pleasant circumstances."

His eyes dropped to my stomach, his expression impassive as he said, "Nonsense. Please, come in."

I started up the steps, Noah's arm tightly banded around me as he escorted me inside. I was well ahead of her, but there was no missing Ash's trembling whisper.

"This is not a good place. The dead are restless. So many have died here."

"Yes. That's true. Countless lives have been lost in Blackthorne Manor," Cashel said, his words draining the color from Ash and Moira's cheeks. "But don't worry. We have changed our ways. Mostly."

We walked through the halls, the eyes of every single Blackthorne heavy on us. "Noah, why does it feel like they don't want us here?"

"They do. They're just . . . wary. Shifters and vampires typically don't mix, remember?"

"Neither do vampires and witches," Moira said, her voice sullen.

"You're the one who hitched a ride," Noah reminded her. "Don't act like you're here against your will, Belladonna."

"Someone has to keep their eye on you," she snapped back.

It was so easy to forget that while Moira didn't have fangs, her bite was every bit as painful as ours could be.

"Brother, how could you be so rude as to pass by me without introducing us?" A striking woman with pure alabaster skin and wide amber eyes approached us. She looked exactly like a porcelain doll I'd once played with as a child—long dark hair falling to her waist, a beauty mark on her right cheek, perfect cupid's bow mouth, and a thick fringe of lashes framing those Blackthorne eyes.

Noah's whole attitude changed when she came into the room. "Rosie, I'm sorry, love. I just needed to get Sunday into the safety of the house."

She rolled her eyes at him and shoved him out of the way so she could stand in front of me. "So this is the mate I've heard so much about. I guess I can forgive my big brother for leaving me with his mess to clean up now that I see the reason for him breaking his betrothal."

"And saddling you with an unwanted fiancé." Noah had the grace to look abashed.

"That too. Ugh, Gavin is insufferable."

"That's not what you were saying a few years ago."

"Just because I used to fancy him when I was a child doesn't mean he's worthy of my affection now." She dropped her gaze and her cheeks reddened before she jabbed him with her elbow.

"And neither are you."

"I love you already," I told her. "I'm Sunday."

"Roslyn, though you may as well call me Rosie. Everyone else does."

"It's nice to meet you, Rosie."

Her smile was genuine, and not a hint of fang. She looped our arms together and began pulling me toward the massive staircase. "Come along, everyone. I'll show you to your rooms."

I glanced back over my shoulder, giving him the *is she*

*going to eat me?* stare. He smirked and shook his head. Before I turned back, I caught Noah's father stopping him with a hand on the shoulder.

"A word, Noah. If you will."

"But I—"

"You'll be returned to your mate soon enough. We have prepared a late meal for you all and will eat together in the dining room shortly."

"Is that safe?" Kingston stage whispered.

"Doubtful," Moira said, linking her arm more tightly through Ash's. "Stay close, sweet cheeks. I'd hate to burn this place down in a jealous rage."

"I think that's more my style," Alek joked.

"You've never crossed paths with an angry witch before, have you?"

"Not that I recall."

"Touch wood you never do, erm . . . I'm sorry. What was your name?" Rosie gave my Viking an appraising glance.

"Alek," he supplied.

"Right. As capable as you look, I doubt you'd survive the encounter."

"I like her," Moira said.

"They all seem to," Rosie murmured, tossing a look over her shoulder. "Until they get to know me."

With that cryptic warning, we followed her up the grand staircase to the second floor. She led us down the hallway decorated with paintings of Blackthornes past and present. I stopped at one which was clearly a portrait of Cashel and Olivia, her seated in a chair and holding a raven-haired newborn while Cashel looked on from his place standing behind her.

"Is that Noah?"

"Oh, yes. Apple of our father's eye. The most like him of all of us as well."

I shuddered at the thought. Cashel seemed so cold and callous. "I don't see it."

"You will. If Noah has to fight for you, you will recognize it, I promise."

"Let us hope it never comes to that," I said, chuckling uncomfortably.

Caleb's eyes met mine, and the promise shining in them shook me to the core.

*It will.*

She opened a door, and before I even stepped inside, I knew it was Noah's room. It just . . . felt like him.

"This is where you and my brother will stay. It's the easternmost point in the house, so it gets the most sunlight. He's always been a fan of the sunshine."

"So have I," Kingston murmured.

I blushed and shook my head. "Behave," I mouthed, charmed despite myself. Bastard.

"All right, then. That's you sorted. The rest of you, follow me."

"Wait, wait, hold on now, Vampirina. The boys and I stay where Sunday stays." Kingston crossed his arms over his chest.

"No. You stay where I put you, or you can sleep in the dungeon."

Something must've flashed in her eyes because Kingston blanched, Alek placed a palm on his shoulder, and Caleb let out a long-suffering sigh.

"My mistake. Those rooms sound great."

Even my Alpha wolf recognized when he'd met his match, and slight though she was, Roslyn Blackthorne was a powerful woman. Definitely not someone any of us wanted to trifle with.

Alek grinned. "Give you a couple of hand axes, a few braids, you'd fit right in back home in Novasgard."

Rosie's answering smirk reminded me of Noah when he was up to something. "Well, you're spoken for, but is stealing brides from their beds still a Viking pastime?"

"I think it is, actually."

"I'll leave my window open."

"No one is stealing anyone from anywhere." Kingston turned his gaze to me. "Keep your window shut."

Sighing, I stepped closer and kissed him. "I'll see you at dinner. Don't worry. We're safe here."

Kingston frowned. "I'm just down the hall, right, cupcake?"

Rosie rolled her eyes at the nickname. "Yes. You won't be far from each other."

My Viking's gaze was hot on mine as he gripped my nape and pulled me close. "If anyone is stealing you, it's me, Kærasta." Then he kissed me deeply, the passion behind it weakening my knees and leaving me lightheaded.

"Oh, my, if that's how they do it in Novasgard, perhaps I *will* leave my window unlocked." Rosie fanned her face before heading away from my room and calling over her shoulder, "Come along, chaps. Before you set the tapestries ablaze."

That seemed to appease my men as they wandered down the hall after her, Caleb trailing just a little behind. When he reached me, he paused just for a moment, brushing the backs of his fingers against mine.

"If you need anything, just call out my name. I'll hear you."

Why did that make a curl of excitement form in my belly? Oh, I knew why. The heat in his eyes confirmed it.

I closed the door after he left and leaned against the wood, letting out a heavy breath as I stood alone in a house full of vampires. Noah assured me they'd keep me safe, but why then did I feel like I'd just jumped out of the frying pan and into the fire?

My father sat in his favorite wingback chair in the library, his expression stern, eyes stormy.

"What is this about?" I asked.

"The danger you're in is far greater than you realize."

"Isn't that always the case?" I drawled, frustration seeping into my tone. My father knew better than anyone how much Sunday's pregnancy worried me. For him to toy with me like this by withholding information didn't sit well. I knew he had my best interest at heart, but he was acting guarded in a way I wasn't used to. At least not in his dealings with me.

"Watch your tongue."

"Perhaps if you would be honest with me, I wouldn't be so on edge."

"Some things aren't able to be shared."

I raised a brow. "It's always secrets with the Blackthornes."

"Secrets keep us safe."

"Do they? Because from where I'm standing, things

"Noah, I need you to trust me. I can't say much, but what I can say is that in addition to the fae, Sunday is being hunted by humans, demons, and vampires alike."

"Why? What do they want with her?"

He shook his head. "There are things I am unable to tell you even now."

"So you brought us here."

"Can you think of a better place? Blackthorne Manor is a veritable fortress."

"So you mean to keep her prisoner?"

"It's only a prison if you give it that name. She will want for nothing, be with her mate, be happy, and well cared for. As long as she doesn't leave."

"How can she be happy locked within the walls of our estate?"

"She is going to be a mother. Knowing she will receive the best care and that her child will be taken care of will keep her content enough she won't even realize."

I snorted. "You don't know her at all."

"Maybe not, but here's one thing I do know. If that child growing in her belly is an abomination *you* created, we will all pay the price. There is nothing more important to me than the well-being of you, your mother, and your siblings."

"And what about your grandchild?"

He clenched his teeth, his eyes going hard, but he didn't say a word.

"I see. Your silence speaks volumes, Father."

"If we can confirm the child is a Blackthorne, it'll be a different matter, but from the looks of it, there could be two other fathers. I won't risk you for a bastard who isn't yours."

"Three."

"What did you say?" His focus narrowed as he shoved to his feet.

"Sunday has four mates. Any one of us could be the father."

"Priest," he sneered. "Self-righteous, loathsome snake."

The venom in his voice surprised me. I hadn't realized my father knew the man well enough for that kind of reaction. What else wasn't he telling me?

His cell phone rang, the jarring sound cutting through the tension in the room with all the subtlety of a chainsaw. I took that as my opportunity to leave him. I had the sudden and desperate urge to hold my mate close and make sure she was whole.

As I left the room, the unmistakable sound of the headmistress's voice caught my ears. Tinny and thin through the phone, but definitely her. I stopped just outside, eavesdropping without shame.

"Do you have them?"

"Yes. They're all here. Safe and sound. You didn't tell me the priest was coming."

"Ah, so that's where he ran off to. Good. Keep them there. Tell no one else where they are. Moriarity is dead. His corpse was found just this morning. Our enemies grow bolder the closer we get to our goal. Keep me apprised. I need to know when the girl goes into labor. She and the child are my responsibility, and I will not fail because of your incompetence."

What the fucking hell was this? My father and Madame le Blanc working together? To what end? I wasn't sure I wanted to know.

My heart was racing as I tore up the stairs in search of Sunday. I needed to hold her close, listen to the baby's heartbeat, remind myself they were my purpose. I'd never doubted my father before, but something wasn't right.

She was curled up on the bed, eyes closed as she napped after such a long day of travel. I didn't have the heart to wake her, so I slipped off my shoes and climbed into bed with her, nestling her into the curve of my body as I pulled her close.

Before I could do more than kiss her forehead, the door to our room flew open, and Kingston stalked toward us. Sunday woke, blinking in confusion.

"What the hell do you want?" I barked.

"I'm not staying in that room. Your sister put me up in the one where the king was executed. Message received, loud and clear. No way will I be the next king on the chopping block. Scoot over and make a spot for me. I'm the big spoon this time."

I sighed and acquiesced, bringing Sunday with me as I moved. She smiled and welcomed him with open arms. Kingston had no sooner crawled up beside her when the door swung open a second time, this time revealing the Norseman.

"Bloody hell, not again. I suppose you found issue with your room as well?"

"There was a ghost in my shower. I don't fuck with ghosts, not after the stories my mother told me."

Kingston sat up. "Really, bro? You're afraid of a little leftover energy?"

"Yeah, she was scary."

Oh, for fuck's sake.

"Aunt Callie, can you come here, please?"

My aunt manifested beside the bed, her transparent body bobbing as she floated in the air. "Yes, Noah, sweetie?"

Alek, the giant oaf who could rip apart a demon with

his bare hands, screamed bloody murder and jumped up, pointing a shaking finger at her. "See? There. Tell me that's not terrifying."

Sunday giggled. "She's not scary. She's just a little see-through."

"Did you need something, Noah? I was just haunting the halls before heading down to my laboratory for a little light research."

"Alek, you've seen a ghost before."

"Not one that popped into the shower with me. There I was, washing my hair, eyes closed as I rinsed the shampoo out, and then . . ."

"Boo," Callie said, her form appearing inches from Alek's face.

He screamed. "See?"

The door swung open for the third time, revealing a wild-eyed Caleb. "What the bleeding hell is going on in here?"

Alek pointed to Callie. "You're a priest. Exorcise her."

Callie glared at Alek, hands on her hips. "I was just having a little fun with you. I was going to leave you alone, but now I'm going to haunt you until your time here is through. And maybe after that too."

"What?" The bewilderment in Alek's voice was more entertaining than I expected.

"Watch your back, Viking. I'm not linked to this house. I can go where I want." Then Callie faded away, leaving us without another word.

"You really put your foot in it, mate. She's vindictive."

Alek's brows furrowed. "She can't really do that, can she? Follow me?"

Sunday patted the mattress. "Come here. I won't let the mean ghostie get you."

Alek crawled up the bed, pushing me out of the way as he took my place.

"You've got to be fucking kidding me. Where am I supposed to go?"

"I could name a few places," Kingston offered.

I flipped him the bird. "That's my bed you're in, you tosser."

"Not from where I'm laying."

"Right then. I'll just return to my room and let you finish this pissing contest of yours, shall I?" Caleb said, his tone exasperated.

"Why bother? Everyone else and their bloody mother is here. Make yourself at home."

Sunday laughed. "I think you mean aunt."

Alek gave a dramatic shudder and burrowed into her side. "Don't remind me."

Even Caleb cracked a smile at that. That's when I realized the tension that had sent me racing up here was gone, replaced with a contentment I hadn't expected. This, these people crowding into my room and my life, was exactly what I'd needed. Family had always come first to me, but I was learning that it may not always be the one whose blood ran through my veins.

Sometimes family was made of the most unlikely creatures.

Over the last week, we'd reached a sort of easy routine at Blackthorne Manor. All of us settled into the flow of the family, rising in the latter part of the afternoon, exploring the house, then avoiding the grumpy vampires when the sun went down. While Cashel was terrifying, Noah's human mother, Olivia, welcomed me like I was her own daughter. She made me feel like I belonged, just like Kingston and Alek's mothers had done.

Moira had declared today a girl's day, and she'd brought Ash and me down to Callie's lab to test out her witchy face masks. We invited Olivia and Rosie to join us, but they had other engagements in town.

"Callie, what did you do down here before . . ." Moira started, but trailed off when Ash shot her a deadly glare.

"Before I died horribly? It's fine. I'm not precious about it." The lovely little specter waved a hand. "I spent most of my nights trying to find a cure for sun sickness."

Ash gasped. "I've heard of that. It was terrible."

"Yes. Awful way to go. Speaking from experience," She

flitted from shelf to shelf, not touching anything but examining each organized notebook closely. "Ah, here it is. My final journal. If you want a good read, check that out. So much drama. Until I died, of course."

Ash accepted the leather-bound book with a wide smile. "I look forward to it, thank you."

I was pretty sure she meant it too. Ash had zero poker face.

"Mo, what did you put in this one again?" I asked, poking at the baby pink goop on my face.

"Rosehips and charcoal to pull out the impurities because pregnancy is tearing up your skin."

I took a small handful of the concoction and flung it at her. "Thanks for pointing it out, witch."

Moira blew me a kiss. "At least it smells better than the one I made for Ash. I know she needed it, but phew, she smells like a bottle of furniture polish with all that lemon and citrus."

"It's supposed to help me reawaken my third eye."

"Was it closed?" Callie asked.

"Not until I arrived here. This place obfuscates everything. The energy is . . . challenging. It's hard to get a read on anyone here."

"I've been feeling that way myself," Callie said, bobbing her head. "Just these last couple of weeks. Feels like a veil of death is shrouding everything."

"Yes, that's exactly it. A heavy gray fog clinging to everything and everyone. It's unnatural. I'd leave here if I had a choice."

My stomach churned at the knowledge my friend wasn't comfortable here. "You don't have to stay, Ash. Really. If you want to go, it's okay."

"I know. I think that's more reason for me to be part of this. Something isn't right. Maybe I can help."

Moira took her hand. "We can help."

Ash smiled at her, looking beautiful despite the layer of thick yellow pudding she had smeared on her face. "I love you."

"Same."

Callie giggled. "You two are the best. I wish I'd had you before I died. It would've been nice to have some friends to talk to about . . . well, who I am."

"You can talk to us now." Moira turned her attention to the ghost.

"Thanks. I had a ghoulfriend for a brief spell a few decades ago, but that didn't work out. She crossed over and I stayed behind."

"It must be hard finding someone special to spend your afterlife with," Moira said.

Callie nodded. "I try not to dwell on that which cannot be changed and focus instead on what I can."

A soft rap of knuckles on the door had me turning, dripping pink slop onto my shirt. Noah popped his head inside the lab and promptly burst into peals of laughter.

"What in God's name is on your face?"

"Moira."

He cocked a brow. "That's . . . not what I expected to hear."

"It's a face mask, Blackthorne. Have you never heard of self-care? Probably not since you seem to think the only thing Sunday needs is dick."

Noah blinked at her, taken aback by the waspish reply. "I don't think you're doing it right if your 'self-care' has left you in a worse mood than the one you started with. Try it again. Maybe you'll actually learn how to smile."

"Did he just tell me to smile?" Moira asked, her tiny hand balling into a fist.

I grabbed a towel and began wiping off the gelatinous muck. I didn't stop until it was all gone, and I had to admit, my skin felt amazing.

"Better?" I asked.

Noah grinned. "There you are."

"What's going on?"

Moira, Ash, and Callie were deep in conversation as Noah closed the distance between us.

"I know this is your time with the girls, but I was hoping once you'd finished up I could take you somewhere."

"Of course, let me just tell Mo—"

"It's okay, babycakes," she called out, cutting me off and proving that once again, she was an eavesdropping multi-tasker. "Unlike *some people,* I can be understanding and accommodating. Have fun, lovebirds."

Noah shook his head. "Sometimes I think she despises me more now than she did before we were mated."

"Not possible. She only sasses the people she loves."

"So what did she do to me before?"

"Terrorized? Traumatized? Take your pick."

"All of the above. Come on, let's go." He took my hand and led me up a series of stairs to a room I hadn't seen yet.

"What is this?"

"My observatory."

"Yours?"

He nodded, his lips spread in a proud smile. "My father built it for me when I was five. I've always had an affinity for the stars. He taught me about the constellations, the planets, the universe. Anytime I needed to be alone, this was where I'd hide."

"You don't seem like the hiding kind."

"Before I learned to control it, the noise of all those voices ringing in my head was too much to bear. I needed someplace I could be alone with my own thoughts."

The way he stared up at the domed ceiling made me want to touch him and tell him just how special he was to me, how special him sharing this was. "I love it here. You're right. It's perfectly still. Peaceful."

He turned that amber gaze to me, his expression open and filled with adoration.

"Now it's you who makes me feel that way. I don't need this place like I used to."

I wrapped my arms around him and leaned in to steal a kiss. "You make me feel that way too."

Being alone with him like this made me realize how essential private time with my men was. I'd connected with Alek recently, but not the rest of them. I needed to rectify that—soon. These stolen moments were essential to helping us feel connected and whole.

Not one of them had mentioned it, but I was sure they wanted time when they didn't have to share me. I had to do better about giving them what they needed since they all made such a point of doing it for me.

He reached for a small remote control mounted on the wall and pressed a button, a panel in the dome instantly sliding up with a mechanical whirring sound. Stars came twinkling into view as I watched.

Wrapping an arm around me, he pulled me close so I could rest my head on his shoulder. Contentment washed through me as we stood in silence staring at the stars. I'd seen these same ones from my home, but this was the first time the sight of them didn't make me feel lonely.

At the reminder that both Noah and I called the Pacific

Northwest home, a thought came roaring to life. Like an itch I couldn't scratch.

"What is it?" he asked.

"I didn't say anything."

"No, but your thoughts are loud. You're curious about something. What is it?"

"Well. . .I was just wondering."

"Yes?"

"Your family lives here. . ."

"Is that a question?"

"In America. . ."

"Obviously."

"But your accent is British."

He laughed. "Oh, that. Well, we have homes scattered across the continents. I've spent as much time in London as I have here. And besides my mother, everyone else in my family *is* British. The accent's authentic, I promise."

I let out a theatrical sigh, pretending to wipe my brow. "Well, that's a relief. I was prepared to write its obituary so I could mourn it properly."

"Minx," he growled playfully, tipping my chin up to steal a kiss.

Breathless, flushed, and hearts pounding in unison, we pulled apart to resume our star-gazing positions.


LOOKING UP AS I WAS, I didn't see exactly what he did next, but soft romantic music filled the space around us.

"Dance with me?" he asked, sweeping me into his arms.

I recognized the song instantly, laughing as Adele's lyrics registered. "A little on the nose, isn't it?"

"So what if I'm crazy for you? Love is the sweetest madness." He spun me away, then pulled me back in, dipping me low and kissing me. When our lips parted, he whispered, "You're the only thing I need, Sunday. The wonder of my world."

"You're more than I ever hoped for. Before I met you, my world wasn't just small—it was microscopic. Your love has given me an entire universe of new experiences. You bring me to life."

We danced until the song ended, then kept going in the silence, not caring that there wasn't music.

I rested my cheek against his chest as we swayed together, watching the stars until my eyelids drooped and I began fading.

"Come on then. Bedtime for the human."

"I'm not human."

"You are. Until you can shift again, you're the most human of us all."

"Fine. Take me to bed, Mr. Blackthorne, you stodgy vampire."

He let out an affronted noise. "Oi, who are you calling stodgy?"

"Oh, did I say stodgy? I meant stuffy."

He slapped my ass, the sting sending me skittering toward the door. "I'll show you stuffy."

"You did not just spank me."

"I did, and I'll do it again if you keep it up, dove. I know what it does to you, so pretend all you like, sweetheart."

"Is that a promise?"

"You know it is."

"I wouldn't have teased you if I knew you were so . . . fussy."

He let out a warning growl, then said, "You'd better run, little wolf. When I catch you, you won't think I'm so fussy."

I grinned at him, taking off down the stairs and through

the hallways back to his room. As I made the last turn, there was a flash of heat licking up my wrist that made me stumble into a wall. But by the time I glanced up, the only one nearby was Noah, hot on my heels.

I paused as I brushed my fingertips over the bracelet, but it was cool, as usual. That one moment of hesitation was my biggest mistake. Noah caught me in his arms, giving my mark a nip before he kissed my neck and breathed in my ear, "I have you now. You're never going to escape."

I wrapped my legs around his waist, clinging to him. "Good. The only place I want to be is in your arms, Noah Blackthorne."

"Mmm, Noah, you know what I really want? A fried chicken sandwich with dill pickles. Oh, and some fresh from the oven honey-butter biscuits." I rolled over in bed, eyes still closed as I reached for him. My palm met cool sheets. "Noah?"

Sitting up, I opened my eyes to find him gone, a note resting on his pillow.

*Went for a midnight hunt with my father and brother. If you wake while I'm gone, just know I love you, and I'll return soon.*

*N*

"While the vampire is away . . ." I murmured, swinging my legs over the edge of the bed.

After my impromptu date with Noah last week, I'd made it a point to alternate between group sleepovers and solo nights with my guys in addition to stealing an hour alone with them here and there. Honestly, the change was good for all of us. No one was left out, and I didn't feel guilty about who got to be the big spoon.

Wrapping myself in a soft robe that smelled like Noah, I crept out of the bedroom, careful to stay quiet. These guys were like watchdogs. If they heard me, one of them would come running, worried something was wrong. Luckily they seemed to be sleeping heavily tonight, and I made it down the hallway unnoticed. Not even Caleb peeked his head out.

The lights in the manor were still on, which made sense since most of the inhabitants were nocturnal. As I reached the kitchen, I was still surprised to find so many people milling about.

The cook, a couple of her helpers, Martin the butler, and Olivia. My bracelet gave a warning flash of heat, and I looked down at it in confusion.

I must have seemed to be in some kind of distress because Martin hurried over to help me.

"Are you well, Ms. Fallon?"

Rubbing my wrist, I gave him a distracted nod. The heat was still there, but it wasn't searing me like it would if I was in imminent danger. Then it hit me, I was in a house full of creatures who couldn't help but have urges to actually eat me. That had to be the reason my bracelet kept going haywire.

"I came down to make myself a snack."

"Me too," Olivia said, offering me a bright smile. "Cravings?"

I nodded.

"I always woke up wanting french fries and ice cream. What got you out of bed tonight?"

"Fried chicken and biscuits." I grinned. "Oh, and dill pickles so I can make a sandwich."

"Excellent choice. I'm sure we can take care of that for

you." This was directed at the cook, who nodded and got to work pulling ingredients out of the fridge. Turning back to me, Olivia asked, "How are you feeling? You must be close to halfway through now."

I ran my palm over my belly, looking down at the swell. "Twenty-one weeks. She's so strong. They can already feel her from the outside." As if she knew I was talking about her, the baby moved, making me laugh. "There she goes."

Olivia's eyes brightened. "It's the strangest feeling, isn't it?"

Nodding, I took a deep breath and decided now was as good a time as any to bridge the gap between Noah's mother and me. "Would you like to feel?"

She smiled, the joy in her eyes telling me everything I needed to know. That was the right decision. Her gentle hand settled right where the baby had been kicking, and within a few moments, she did it again.

"Oh, she is strong. Noah was like that. He never stopped dancing in my belly. Kept me up all night kicking me in the ribs."

My wrist heated in warning, and I backed away, nearly bumping into Martin as I tried to separate myself from Olivia.

"Are you all right?" she asked.

"Oh, yeah, I'm fine. Just tired. My feet hurt all the time now."

"I have just the thing. Martin, will you get me the bath salts?"

"Right away, ma'am." The butler left but returned almost immediately, a small container of white powder with dried flower petals in his hands.

"Thank you."

He nodded once and moved back to the other side of the kitchen to grab some spices off the top shelf for the cook.

Olivia held the jar out to me. "I want you to go upstairs and run yourself a nice warm bath. Your chicken will take a bit to prepare, and this way you can be cozy and relaxed while you enjoy your treat. Martin will bring it up and leave it in your room as soon as it's ready."

My bracelet still stung, and every moment in the company of all these vampires made me more uncomfortable. Someone was here with the intent to harm me, but who?

As quickly as the pain came, it vanished, but the same people were in the room. Weren't they? Maybe this thing was defective.

I took the bath salts and thanked Noah's mom, heading back to my room with a pounding heart. Everything we'd been dealing with made me suspicious of any new person in my life. Perhaps the bracelet was picking up my anxiety. Blackthorne mate or not, I was trapped in a house with vampires who hated my kind, and I was pretty sure all of them would feed on me if they had no other blood supply around.

With that happy thought in mind, I started the water, pouring in a liberal amount of the fragrant salts. I undressed and removed both the necklace Noah had given me and Moira's bracelet, setting them on top of my folded clothes. Then I sank into the water, letting the claw-foot tub fill up to my chin.

The soothing scents of lavender and vanilla filled the air, mixed with a hint of chamomile. God, Olivia was right, this was the tits. Exactly what I needed to help me reset after the incident downstairs.

Closing my eyes, I draped my hair over the back of the

tub, keeping it from getting wet. It would take me forever to dry it otherwise. The heat seeped into my aching muscles as I gently ran my hand over my belly, feeling the baby chase the warmth of the water. I guess my little one enjoyed a good soak as much as I did.

Head lolling as I crooned the Norse lullaby Alek taught me, I came dangerously close to falling asleep in the bath. Thankfully, the sound of the bedroom door opening brought me back to consciousness.

"Thank you, Martin," I called, dipping a washcloth into the water before placing it over my face and breathing in the relaxing aroma of the salts. "I'll be out in a minute!"

My stomach growled, hunger gnawing, reminding me of the entire reason I'd gone downstairs in the first place. But I could wait five more minutes. This was the kind of pampering I didn't want to rush.

Sharp pain in my scalp tore a yelp from my throat before I was shoved down into the bath. Water filled my mouth as I twisted and fought against the hand holding me down. Even with the berserker inside me rising to the surface, lending me its strength and desperate to fight back, I couldn't shake them. They'd timed their strike well.

My attacker's vicious use of force sent terror through me, panic making me gasp for air that wasn't available, letting even more liquid into my oxygen-starved lungs. I choked and thrashed, clawing at their arm, but it was no use. I was drowning.

I should've listened to the bracelet's warning. Instead, I'd left myself entirely at the mercy of the Blackthorne vampires. The last thought I had before my vision went dark was the pack I'd created. My four loves and the child we'd made.

The child I would never meet.

CHAPTER

# FORTY-FOUR

CALEB

Night-blooming jasmine filled my senses as I turned yet another corner of the Blackthornes' garden maze. This spot. So reckless. So dangerous a thing to have when security was of concern. Fecking royalty.

"What are you doing skulking about in my maze, Priest?"

"I thought you were hunting, Cashel."

"And I thought you were celibate."

What response could I make to that? I would own my sins, if nothing else.

"It's only been an hour since you all left your charge unsupervised."

Cashel stood at the mouth of the path I'd turned down, looking at me like something he scraped off the bottom of his boot. "She's not unsupervised. She's exactly where she's supposed to be. Out of my hair and unable to make trouble

The disdain with which he spat the word *mates* had my lips twitching. "Can't handle your son being a cuckold?"

"That would make one of you as well, wouldn't it? Does Gabriel know you are so . . . involved with her?"

I shoved my hands in my pockets so he wouldn't be able to make out my balled-up fists. "I have to assume so. He's God's Messenger, after all. I don't imagine there's much he isn't privy to."

"How cavalier. You claim to serve your God, but you are in bed with the devil. Whose side are you on?"

"Sunday is not the devil."

"Isn't she? The harbinger of the apocalypse is hardly one of the good guys."

"That's either a matter of semantics or philosophy, neither of which I'm inclined to debate with you, Cashel. As for my loyalties, I will keep my vow."

Cashel let out a derisive snort. "Because you are *so* good at that, *Priest*."

I bit down on the inside of my cheek to keep from lashing out and doing something that would get me sent away from here. The metallic taste of my blood filled my mouth as I fought for control of my emotions.

"Struck a nerve, did I?"

"Sunday is my purpose, same as she's always been."

"So you'll do your duty when the time comes."

I stared hard into his eyes. "Aye."

"Then she's not your mate. I burned down my world to keep Olivia once I bonded with her."

"Who says I won't?"

"You can't have it both ways. It's her, or your soul."

"Don't you think I fecking know that?"

"And yet you fucked her anyway. Hardly the actions of a pious man."

The words cut deep. I gave up everything I'd ever wanted to belong to Sunday. *Fucking* was something reserved for sordid encounters. It didn't come close to expressing what had happened between us. It was a communion of souls. A way to touch the divine. To express the most perfect love two people could share. She was the closest I'd ever come to knowing God again.

"Fuck you, Blackthorne."

He smirked. "Such a temper for a holy man."

"I haven't been a holy man for decades."

His mocking laughter cut through the night, making me nearly convulse with rage. "No. You haven't. Which is why I can't trust you to follow through on your vows now."

"And you always do everything you've sworn to do?"

"When it comes to protecting my family? Yes."

I took a step toward him, then blurred across the distance, grabbing him by his collar. "Your family is *your* priority. She is mine."

His eyes widened. "Fuck me, you really love her, don't you?"

I didn't answer. Instead I released him and turned to walk away. "Stay out of my way, Cashel. Let me do my job."

I stormed away from him, not paying attention to the path I was taking as my body quaked with fury. Whose idea was it to create damned mazes out of a hedge? Every turn put me at a dead end.

*"You're not where you're needed, Caleb."*

The Seer's voice sounded in my head, stopping me in my tracks. I spun in a circle, searching for the speaker. But I was alone.

*"Go to her. She's dying."*

One thought solidified in my mind. Sunday.

That was enough to send me running. I tore through the

MEG ANNE & K. LORAINE

hedge, worming my way through thorns and bramble without care. Fuck the Blackthornes and their fucking labyrinth. I wasn't going to waste time when she was in danger. They were lucky I didn't burn the fecking thing down.

It took far too long for me to get to her, precious seconds wasted. Where were the others? Why was no one protecting her?

The door to her room was wide open. Splashing came from the bathroom, and as I approached, all I saw was the next death I'd have on my hands.

"The abomination must not survive," the hooded figure muttered, hate seeping from every word.

"That's not for you to decide," I snarled, gripping him by the head and twisting until I felt flesh tear and tendons snap. The bones in his neck separated, and his hold on Sunday went lax.

His body crumbled like a house of cards, blood pooling on the white tile floor. But I only had eyes for the woman lying so still under the water. I dropped the attacker's head with a thunk and pulled Sunday from the bath, her skin still warm but her face deathly pale.

Setting her on the tile, I started counting out the compressions on her chest and then tipped her head back to breathe into her mouth. I was on my second set when the footsteps sounded behind me.

"What happened?" Alek asked, fear making his voice tight.

"Sunshine?"

I ignored both of them, too focused on breathing life back into her. She couldn't die. I leaned down to bring my lips to hers again, whispering, "Come back to me, *a stor*."

"Where the fuck is Noah? He's supposed to be with her," Kingston snarled, his wolf slipping into the question.

"I'm right here," Noah said, sounding as worried as the rest of us as he raced into the room with more Blackthornes on his heels. "I was already on my way back when I felt her fear. Is she going to be all right?"

A deep gurgle followed by coughing came from Sunday, and my heart started beating again. Rolling her onto her side, I stroked her back as she choked up the water that had nearly been her end.

She dragged in a ragged gasp of air and looked around from person to person, fear and mistrust in her eyes.

"Somebody get her a fecking towel," I snapped, shielding her with my body.

Alek was the first to reach us, holding out his shirt. "Here, use this."

I draped the fabric over her as I cradled her to my chest.

"I'm assuming this is the culprit?" Cashel asked, toe kicking the attacker's severed head. "Or what's left of him?"

"This was the assassin, aye. But who hired him, I don't know. He was on a mission to kill the *abomination*."

"That's a Council term," Noah said, looking ashen. "They must have found out she was pregnant and sent someone to dispatch her. But how were they able to get inside?"

"Yes, that is the question, isn't it?" I asked.

"I found a guard dead by the tunnels as I returned from the hunt." Cashel pulled Olivia tight against him. "I'm sorry I wasn't here sooner."

"Convenient." The word was soft, but I knew everyone heard it.

"If you're implying *I* had anything to do with my son's mate being attacked, I assure you, you're wrong."

Noah's eyes flicked to his father, but before he could say anything, Kingston reached for Sunday.

Possessive anger took hold as his fingers brushed her arm, and I snapped, "Don't touch her. I've got her."

Kingston assessed me and then stepped back with his hands raised. "All right, Padre. That's fine, but can we get her out of here? She's shaking and clearly in shock. She doesn't need to see the aftermath right now."

I flinched, rising immediately and baring my fangs at the bodies standing between me and the door. "Out of my way."

In the blink of an eye, I had her on the bed, a heavy blanket covering us both as I clung to her. I couldn't let her go. Not yet. I needed to hear her heart beating strong and steady, see the color returning to her cheeks. I closed my eyes and pressed my lips to her forehead, homing in on the rapid thrum of the baby's pulse as well.

They were safe. I hadn't lost them. Thanks to the Seer's warning, I'd reached her in time. But what if I hadn't? What if I was too late next time? Because surely there'd be a next time. The Vampire Council wouldn't give up that easily.

"Um, is this guy okay?" Roslyn's wary voice rang out as she slowly backed away from Alek, whose eyes had bled black. Even from my place on the bed I could see the lightning flashing in the inky depths.

"No. Rosie, get away from him right now. He's a berserker, and his mate was just threatened." Noah put himself between his sister and Alek. "Nordson, she's all right. Look there. Sunday is breathing and safe."

Alek let out a menacing snarl and grasped Noah by his throat, shoving him up against the wall. "You brought us to *your* house, under *your* roof, guarded by *your* family. Give me one reason I shouldn't kill you right now."

"Because I would never forgive you if you did, Alek," Sunday said, her words raspy but strong all the same.

"You almost died on his watch. He left you. How is that acceptable behavior for a mate? You have three others. You don't need this one."

Sunday removed herself from my hold, slipped his shirt over her head, and then carefully walked across the room to put herself right in front of him. Without hesitation, she took the hand Alek had around Noah's throat and brought it to hers instead.

"I'm here. Do you feel my heartbeat?"

Some of the rage seeped from his eyes, their color returning slowly to his normal icy blue. Then she slid his palm down to her chest, right over her heart, before pressing her hand against his.

"This isn't Noah's fault. Killing him isn't the answer."

Alek closed his eyes and took a long breath, a visible tremor racing down his enormous frame. When he came back to himself, he trained his focus on Cashel. "Someone needs to pay. Who needs to die?"

"I know exactly who we need to kill. Those fucking parasites on the Council. They're the ones who sent an assassin after Sunday." Anger seethed in my veins. If I wasn't so worried about my mate, I'd already be out there hunting down the cocksuckers who dared to come after what was mine.

"Believe me, taking out the Council has been a goal of mine for decades. I nearly succeeded once upon a time, but they come back time and again." Cashel stood with his back to the wall nearest the bathroom, the dead vampire's blood seeping over the threshold and staining the edge of the white carpet.

"What's *he* still doing in here?" The growl in Caleb's voice was so pronounced that if I didn't know better, I would have thought he was a wolf. Accusation burned in his eyes as he stared Cashel down.

"It's my house. I'll stay as long as I bloody well want to."

"And you, being the master of the house, could also let anyone you'd like inside at any time."

What the fuck was Caleb smoking, and where could I get some?

"What are you insinuating, Priest? I wasn't anywhere near Sunday when the attack happened. I was toe to toe with you."

Every head in the room jerked in his direction. What reason could those two possibly have to meet up? They seemed more likely to brawl than meet for a polite chat. Then again, looking from Cashel to Caleb, maybe a fight was precisely what had happened.

"My father wasn't part of this, Caleb. I know him better than—"

"Perhaps you should ask your uncle Callum about that. Oh, forgive me, you can't. He's nothing more than a pile of ashes after your father staked him." Caleb was really fucking going for it. "Not to mention the fact that the Council tried and convicted him as a traitor before most of them were conveniently disposed of. People who oppose Cashel Blackthorne seem to end up dead or missing more often than not."

"That's enough. If you're going to continue to insult my father, you can leave. We have a perfect spot to isolate a testy vampire. Perhaps you've heard of it? The well." Noah's tone was icy, his gaze intense on Caleb.

"Fuck, I think I finally see what Sunshine likes about you, Thorne."

He cut his gaze to me and then rolled his eyes.

"Let's give Sunday some time to recover in private," Olivia said, playing peacekeeper before the vampires came to blows.

I bristled. "No. We already have the fae coming after us, and I want to know what you intend to do to keep the Council off our backs. If they won't stop coming like you say, then we're not safe here. We won't be safe anywhere. So, what's the plan? You must have one, big bad vampire boss that you are."

Cashel glared at me. "I am a *king*."

I smirked. "So am I."

"No, you're a boy playing at being king. You won't earn that honor until you prove you'll sacrifice everything for your title."

"Titles are meaningless. It's the people connected to you that matter."

"In that, at least, we are agreed." We held each other's stares, Cashel eventually giving me a brief nod as if I had passed some sort of test. "You were right about something else as well."

"Of course I was."

"Such a wanker," Noah muttered under his breath.

"I do have a plan. If we can prove the child is not an abomination, the Council will have no reason to come for your mate."

"How are we supposed to prove that? A paternity test? Wait until she pops out the kid and see which one of us it looks like? Or better yet, if it comes with its own set of fangs?"

Sunday shook her head. "She. We're having a girl."

"Sorry, Sunshine. We all know she's mine. There's no reason the Council should think otherwise."

She rolled her eyes. "Kingston, there are three very virile reasons they could think otherwise."

Alek placed his palm on her shoulder. "She's a little shieldmaiden. A descendant of Freya herself."

The first genuine smile bloomed across Sunday's face since the accident. "Is that so? And do we all just get to pick which Norse god we're related to? Is that what you did?"

Cashel cleared his throat, killing the mood with a single annoyed glare. "If you're quite through."

"Are you sure you and the priest aren't related? Cousins maybe? You sound exactly like him. You know, without the leprechaun thing." I grinned. "Are you hiding a pot of gold somewhere, Caleb? Maybe a box of cereal?"

"Feck off."

"Thank you for proving my point."

Sunday shot me a stare that said I needed to shut up before she shut me up. I'd make her pay for that later. Loudly. So everyone remembered how much she loved me and my dick. "Continue with your plan, oh mighty vampire king."

Cashel sighed. "Natalie Goode."

"Cousin Silas's mate?" Noah asked. "But she hasn't practiced magic since I was a child."

"If it means the difference between your child living or dying, she will."

Olivia nodded her agreement. "There's no doubt she'll come to our aid. Let's summon her now. The sooner she gets here, the better."

The vampire's expression softened as he glanced at his wife. "Right."

The Blackthornes and their staff filed out after that, but before the bedroom door was fully closed, a cranky little witch stormed right in.

"What the hell? I go to sleep, and you guys throw a party without me? I'm hurt." Moira skidded to a stop. "Why is there a dead guy in the bathroom?"

"Long story short, someone on the Vampire Council sent him to off me. Caleb took care of it. I didn't die."

"Sunday Amadeus, where is your bracelet? This is

exactly why I gave it to you. No one should be able to sneak up on you."

Sunday winced. "I took it off before I got in the tub."

"Why would you do that?"

"I didn't want to ruin it."

Moira's eyes nearly bugged out of her head. "It. Is. Protected. What do you think I am, an amateur?"

"No, you ass, but it's special to me, and I was trying to keep it safe."

"Well your wrist is still naked. Where is it?"

"I put it with my necklace and clothes."

Alek disappeared into the bathroom, likely so Moira didn't have to step over the decapitated body in her search. He wandered back out with a necklace dangling from his finger. "This was all I could find."

"Someone fucking took it?" I growled.

Noah strode into the bathroom and began rifling through the assassin's pockets. "Nothing here."

"Why? Who else would do that?" Alek's question made me unsure if I gave him more credit than he deserved. Maybe the Norseman really was a big dumb Viking after all. "Unless there's another person here who means her harm."

Never mind.

Alek continued his stream of consciousness with more things we already knew. "The fae used shadow to cloak themselves until the last moment. Could they have snuck in while the Council mounted their attack?"

Noah sighed. "At this point, who bloody knows? But it's clear we need to be on high alert at all times."

Sunday's lower lip quivered. "I'm so sorry. I didn't mean for any of this to happen. I loved that bracelet, Moira. I should have taken better care of it."

"Fuck the bracelet, Monday."

"Monday?"

"I'm mad at you right now, and no one likes a Monday."

That got my back up, but Alek spoke before I could say anything. "Hey, now, witch. She almost died, and she's clearly upset. Leave her alone."

"No, she's right. I ignored the warning signs. I was reckless."

I narrowed my eyes at my mate. "What warning signs?"

Alek, Caleb, and Noah were also looking at her with matching expressions of disbelief. She glanced between each of us, not finding a single ally. Even Moira stared her down with her hip cocked and her arms crossed over her chest.

"The bracelet, uh, sort of went off while I was downstairs getting a snack. But I couldn't figure out what it was trying to tell me because it was so sporadic."

"And you just wandered off on your own without letting anyone know? Sunshine, come on. You're smarter than that."

"I didn't want to wake you up. It was the literal middle of the night."

Caleb gave a long-suffering sigh. "Two of us are fecking vampires. We're awake by nature, Miss Fallon."

"If any of us can afford to lose a little beauty sleep, it's obviously me," Alek said, tossing his mane over one shoulder before he closed the distance between them and took her hand. He may have been playing, but I saw the barely restrained berserker flashing in his eyes.

Not to be outdone by these showboats, I stalked toward her and took her face in my hands, tipping her head back and leaning down until our noses were nearly touching. "Exactly, you wake me the fuck up. I don't care what time it is. I don't care if you stubbed your fucking toe. You tell me,

440

Sunshine. Or if not me, one of us. You are not in this alone. It is our job to keep you and that kid safe. Let us do our fucking job."

God, I felt like a dick when her eyes filled with tears. She nodded, blinked once, and the twin tracks streamed down her cheeks.

I wiped them away with the pads of my thumbs. "Don't cry, baby. I'm not mad, but I am fucking terrified. I can't lose you. Ever."

Her lip quivered, and she nodded.

Noah moved to stand behind her, wrapping his arm around her waist and pressing a kiss to her mark. "We all are, dove. Tonight was a close call. Too close. It never should have happened. We need you—all of us—to be on guard moving forward."

Caleb turned his stare on Noah. "When can we expect the Goode witch to arrive?"

Moira gasped so loud I worried the dead vampire in the bathroom had reanimated.

"What the fuck, Moira?" I asked.

"The Goode witch? As in . . . *Natalie fucking Goode*?"

Noah frowned at her. "Yes. She's my cousin's mate. Why?"

"She's only like a fucking rock star in the witch world."

"I didn't realize you had celebrities," Sunday said.

"If we did, Natalie Goode is definitely an A-lister." Moira lowered her voice to a whisper. "Do you think I could get her to sign my party tit?"

"Excuse me, your what?" Alek asked, peering at her like he hadn't quite caught what she said.

"My party tit." Moira pointed to her left breast. "You know, the fun one."

"I'm pretty sure they're both fun," Alek said, his brow furrowed in confusion.

"They are."

He shook his head, likely recognizing he'd entered a losing battle. "Never mind."

*Smart dude.* That giant head of his wasn't filled with wool after all.

"How long until this rockstar witch arrives?" I asked, desperate to move the subject off Moira and her tits.

Cashel stood in the doorway. "She won't arrive for a fortnight. I just hung up with Silas. There's nothing to be done about it."

"What do we do until then?" Sunday asked.

I cupped her face, making sure I had her full attention as I answered, "Everything we can to keep *you* alive."

CHAPTER

# FORTY-SIX

SUNDAY

If my first two weeks at Blackthorne Manor had been a somewhat unwanted, albeit pleasant, vacation, my last two had been an outright prison sentence. Security at the manor was at DEFCON 1. I couldn't sneeze without someone jumping at the noise. The only high point in the last couple of weeks had been the surprise baby shower Moira had thrown me in an attempt to lift my spirits.

It might not have been so bad if I could find my bracelet, but without its magic or my ability to shift, my men didn't trust me by myself. And nothing annoyed me more than being treated like a helpless child.

A large warm palm wrapped around my throat, startling me out of my frustration spiral and reminding me I was supposed to be training. Since the attack, Alek had resumed my daily self-defense sessions with a renewed vigor that bordered on obsessive.

His lips brushed the shell of my ear as he scolded me. "Got you. Again. You need to focus, Sunny."

A little shiver worked its way down my spine, just like it did every time he whispered in my ear. "I'm tired. We've been at this for over an hour. Can't we be done for the day?"

His other arm wrapped around me so he could touch my belly. "Is it the baby?"

"No," I groaned, kicking the ground to alleviate some of my annoyance. "I'm just over these stupid training sessions."

"You need to know how to defend yourself without your wolf."

I rolled my eyes and spun around in his hold. "I spent my whole life without my wolf."

"In a tower. Not defending yourself."

"It wasn't an actual tower," I grumbled.

His eyes were amused, but his expression was set. "I love you, Sunny, but this is for your own good. You can't blame us for wanting to make sure you're safe. If someone gets past us again, all of us—including you—will feel better knowing you're prepared. These sessions, as annoying as they are, could make the difference in whether you live or die. You better than anyone know how precious a few extra seconds can be in determining the outcome of a battle."

"He's right, Sunday."

My chest squeezed at the sound of Caleb's brogue from where he'd taken up position in the doorway. If Alek looked like a golden god, Caleb resembled a fallen angel. His dark stare and head-to-toe black clothing gave him a sexy, sinister edge. Especially with the heat in his gaze that promised if I misbehaved his palm would leave a mark on my ass.

"Show me what you've learned."

Caleb was a streak across the makeshift dojo, blurring

from his place across the room to me. I timed it just right and took a quick step to the side before his arms could snake out and grab me.

He came to a standstill, and I cocked a brow. "How's that?"

His lip curled. I blinked, and he was behind me, his lips at my ear and arm crossing me from shoulder to shoulder. "Not good enough."

I saw the practice weapon, a dull dagger, glint in his raised hand. I couldn't let him prove me wrong. Using a maneuver Alek and I had been working on, I disarmed him as I broke his hold and snatched the blade for myself. The move itself wasn't complicated, but the changes to my body affected my balance, so it required a bit more effort to bend the way I needed to without losing the benefit of speed or surprise.

"False."

"That's my girl. She's got a warrior's heart."

I grinned wide at the appreciation in Alek's voice. Caleb's gaze shone with pride as well.

"I stand corrected, Miss Fallon."

Fuck, I was out of breath. Though that could partially be due to the way his voice caressed my name. I loved it when he called me that. Almost as much as when he called me his good girl.

Frustration and need clawed at me. I was a horny bitch, and they'd been treating me like I might break at any moment. Tensions had been running so high since the attempted assassination my men hadn't been willing to engage in any bed play. They all agreed it was a distraction we couldn't afford, one that left us vulnerable and weak. No matter how hard I tried to initiate things, they wouldn't be swayed. Not even Kingston. Maybe I should act up so Caleb could give me one of his special sessions?

"Whatever you're thinking, little one, put it out of your mind. We're late."

"Late?"

"I came to fetch you. The witch is here."

Anticipation and a healthy dose of nerves sent my stomach fluttering. I didn't know what Natalie was going to do, but at this point, anything was better than sitting here in a gilded cage just waiting for another attack.

Caleb offered his elbow, the gesture foreign from him after our history of secret stolen moments together. I locked eyes with him as I slid my arm through his, the warmth I found in his gaze giving me a glimpse of what a life with him would be like. Now that we were away from Ravenscroft, we could be together this way.

Alek tugged on the end of my braid, leaning in and murmuring, "Once this is over, I'll take care of you. Don't worry, Kærasta. I know what you're wanting. I want it too. It's been too long since I've tasted that sweet cunt of yours."

I practically groaned at the promise.

"Yes, darling one. Once we know the Council won't be coming after you and we can relax, we'll all see to you."

*Yes, please.* A Caleb and Alek sandwich sounded really good right about now. But a whole sausage buffet would be even better.

Now I was ready to get this meeting over with for another reason entirely. Screw what we learned from the witch; I wanted sexy time with my men. What good were mostly soundproofed rooms if you didn't test their limits?

"Come on, boys, better not keep Natalie waiting."

Alek's knowing chuckle followed me out of the room as I tugged Caleb along with me through the winding maze of hallways beneath the house. When we reached the main floor, a thick veil of magic permeated the air, sending tingles skating over my arms and raising the hair on the back of my neck.

Moira and Ash were already in the library, crowded around a woman I could only assume was the infamous Natalie. She looked far younger than I'd expected since she must be in or approaching her fifties. I wondered if that had more to do with her being a witch or her being a vampire's bonded mate. Her dark hair was pulled up in a clean bun, her pretty face unlined, her eyes shining with amusement as she listened to Moira's animated chatter.

Noah stood next to his parents, concern etching a permanent line between his brows. The instant he saw me, he crossed the floor and came to my side. "Allow me to introduce you to my aunt."

Caleb released me as Noah wrapped an arm around my waist and escorted me the short distance across the room. It was all very formal feeling, and I was suddenly self-conscious in my sweatpants and my borrowed T-shirt. Okay, it wasn't mine, and it wasn't borrowed. I stole it from Alek. But these days, anything that smelled like one of my men was fair game, and their shirts just fit better.

"Aunt Natalie, this is my mate, Sunday Fallon." Noah practically beamed as he introduced us. "Sunday, this is Natalie."

"I wish we were meeting under better circumstances, Sunday, but it is still a pleasure. I can see how special your connection with our Noah is."

Kindness radiated from her, instantly soothing me. Thank God. I couldn't deal with another cranky Blackthorne.

"It's nice to meet you too. I'm sorry, I would have cleaned myself up if I thought you were arriving so soon."

She waved a hand. "Please don't worry about it on my account. I think you look lovely just as you are."

"So do I, dove," Noah murmured, kissing my temple.

Natalie was the living embodiment of a hug. I had no doubt her power was considerable. She was likely every bit as scary as Moira's family when crossed. Still, after feeling like I was surrounded by people I couldn't wholly trust, her easy kindness was greatly appreciated.

"I have a gift for you," Natalie said, reaching into the pocket of her skirt and producing a deep green velvet bag.

"For me?"

"Moira and Ash mentioned the charm they made for you went missing. I happened to have this amulet on me. I would have prepared something stronger if I'd known, but it should work in a pinch." She pulled out a delicate chain with a lovely amethyst crystal dangling from its center. "If it comes in contact with magic of ill intent, it lifts the veil and reveals the truth."

"That seems like it will come in handy," I murmured, accepting the necklace and immediately putting it on. "Thank you."

"You're very welcome, dear." Her gaze flicked from me to the doorway, and I followed. Kingston stood there, his hair still damp and curling at the ends from his shower.

"What did I miss? Are we getting presents? Cool." He strode into the room and put himself right next to me, hand sliding around my waist before he dipped his head and whispered, "Sorry I'm late, baby."

Natalie lifted one perfectly arched brow. "Is this the wolf?"

After a sigh, Noah nodded. "The one and only."

She clapped her hands together. "Oh good, then you're all here. It's time to begin."

"What is this for again?" Kingston asked, pulling his hand back as Natalie moved toward him with a small ritual dagger to take some of his blood.

"As I already explained to you, we're performing the supernatural equivalent of a paternity test, which requires DNA."

"So take some of my fur, hair, spit even. It goes against my nature to willingly spill my own blood in a house full of vampires."

Alek snickered. "Someone's chicken shit."

A low growl left Kingston before Alek even finished. "I'm not the one screaming like a little bitch whenever I see Casper the Friendly Ghost."

"It's Callie. If you're going to talk about me, at least use my name correctly." Callie appeared next to Alek, making him flinch.

"Thor's shriveled dick, stop doing that."

She cackled. "Why would I when you make it so much fun?"

He glared at her, and Kingston piped back up. "You have to admit, this is some sketchy stuff. It's dark in here, and we're sitting ducks locked in a room with vampires while they take our blood. This is the kind of thing you start yelling about when we watch scary movies." He put on a fake accent that was supposed to mimic Alek, I guessed. "No, you incompetent idiot, never run up the stairs when the lights go out. That's how you end up run through by the killer!"

"I thought it was only the virgins that got murdilated in those movies," Moira whispered loudly to me.

"No, it's the virgins who survive. I'm telling you, it's always death by dick in those flicks," Ash offered helpfully.

"Shoot, Padre. You almost made it out unscathed. Guess you're as fucked as the rest of us now."

"Literally." Alek chuckled, but Noah shot them all frustrated glares.

"Do you mind? Some of us would like to finish this ritual before Sunday gives birth."

Kingston snickered. "If she gives birth, we don't need the ritual."

Cashel cleared his throat. "But it won't protect your cub or your mate, and isn't that quite the point?"

Kingston sobered and gave a heavy sigh. "Right. Slice away, Glinda."

"Natalie," Moira corrected, horrified that he would purposely refer to her idol by the wrong name. If she only knew about poor Heidi. Or was it Heather?

Natalie, to her credit, didn't look the least bit bothered as she pressed the point of the blade into his palm and sliced down into the fleshy part of his hand.

"Fuck, you didn't say it was silver. That shit burns." Kingston's blood welled, spilling into the bowl she held under his hand. "I thought all you needed was a drop."

"I'd rather take more than have to poke you again."

He pursed his lips. "Fair."

She then repeated the act on Alek, Noah, and finally Caleb. The last of whom was surprisingly more mistrustful than Kingston.

"Witchcraft," he muttered darkly. "I truly am one of the damned."

Natalie winked at him. "Welcome to the dark side, handsome. We have cookies."

"Oh well, if there are cookies," he said, making my lips twitch. His jokes were so rare, they never ceased to amuse me.

"Your turn, Sunday." Natalie turned to me, her eyes gentle. "Into the chalice for this one."

I didn't even flinch as she took my blood, but my men did. Their bodies went taut as tension lined their features. Alek looked like he wanted to fling the knife from her hand, and Kingston's hands were balled into fists. My vampires seemed to be struggling for other reasons. Their eyes flared wide and their breathing changed as they caught my scent. And they weren't the only ones.

Noah's gaze shot to his father and his brother, Westley. The latter had taken a step closer to me, but Cashel had a hand tight on his youngest son's shoulder, stopping him. A shiver ran through me. Maybe Kingston was right.

"Now what?" Alek asked. "Don't tell me we have to drink it."

The innocent comment was a communion joke waiting to happen. I couldn't help it. I snuck a peek at Caleb, whose knowing gaze was locked on me, his lips tilted in the barest hint of a smile.

"No. Each of you will place one drop of blood from your bowl on the point of the pentacle I assign you. Then, after you have done so, Sunday will do the same from her place at the north."

"Uh, Maleficent, what pentacle? Is it invisible or something?" Kingston asked, looking at the floor with confusion etched on his face.

Natalie sighed. "No, wolf. I still need to paint it."

We stood aside, watching her as she poured a small

amount of blood from each bowl onto a plate, then blended them together before using her fingers to draw the pentacle on the floor in the center of the library.

"Nothing like a good bloodstain to really up the value of the house," Kingston muttered.

I shook my head, sighing. "You just can't help yourself, can you?"

"I'm just saying what everyone else is thinking, baby."

"You're really not," Noah said, moving into place as Natalie directed each of the men to one of the pentacle's points.

"Sunday, take your place. Moira, Ash, I'll need to borrow some of your power for this."

Moira looked about ready to fall over with fangirl euphoria. "Of course. Ohmigod. What do you need?"

Natalie smiled sweetly. "Your hands. Join me outside the pentacle. We'll speak the words together five times. Noah, once we start, you begin by letting one drop fall at your feet since you were her first bonded mate."

Kingston grumbled. "Only because we got off on the wrong foot."

"Doesn't matter, wolf. I claimed her first."

"First's the worst. Second's the best."

"Jesus, what are they, seven?" Moira asked. "Next one of them is going to call dibs."

"If you're ready to continue . . ." Natalie said.

I gave them each a meaningful look. "We are ready."

"We will go in order of mate bonds, meaning Noah, Kingston, then Alek. Caleb, you will be fourth, and finally, Sunday. The blood you sacrifice will be drawn to the child's father, and just like that, we will have our answer."

"Please say it's a wolf." Kingston's words were so earnest my heart hurt a bit.

I honestly didn't want to know the truth. Something about it made me worry for the baby's future relationship with my mates. Would they love her less when they knew for certain she didn't belong to them?

"What are we going to do if Noah or Caleb is the dad?" Ash asked. "That will just confirm what the Council suspected."

"Pray," Caleb said.

"That *would* be your solution," Cashel replied.

"Do you have a better one?"

"We run," I said, resolved. "We run and go into hiding somewhere else."

"Or we fight. I'll stand ready at your side. No questions asked." The determination in Kingston's eyes eased my worries a little.

Alek shifted his stance. "If you truly want to run, we could go back to Novasgard. Your Vampire Council has no standing there. And you've seen firsthand how my people deal with outsiders who cross into our realm uninvited."

"They already kicked us out, remember?" I said, touched that he would make the offer. "That one lady, Cora, said fate required us to be here."

"Whatever we do, we do it together. All of us. Noth' changes how we all feel, dove. We belong together."

I took a steadying breath and held the chalice hands, staring at Natalie. "Do it."

She gave me an encouraging nod as the thr linked hands and began reciting the words initiate the spell. Noah dipped his finger ir allowed the blood to drip onto the floor. phrase was repeated, Kingston did th others.

My heart was racing as I waited

repetition, the witches' voices grew stronger and the air in the room more charged. The flickering of the candles no longer seemed natural, but intentional. And was it my imagination, or was the pentagram glowing? Either way, magic was at work here, swirling all around us, preparing to provide us with the answers we sought.

Natalie's eyes glowed with power as the three witches began the final chant. She trained them on me and gave a slight nod. My hand shook as I dipped my fingers into the bowl, then brought them out of the chalice, watching intently as the thick red liquid pooled into a fat droplet. It fell, almost in slow motion, causing everyone in the room to tense as it splashed to the floor.

As soon as my blood made contact with the lines on the floor, the ruby liquid sizzled. My eyes went wide, and I looked up in concern, wondering if that was supposed to happen. But then a series of shocked gasps brought my attention back to the floor. The point at my feet glowed red and black as it began to smolder, smoke rising in acrid curls as the wood charred. The blood bubbled and then caught fire, an actual flame snaking down the path as it crawled toward the center of the five-sided star.

When it turned toward Noah, he looked both awed and ready to vomit. But the flame didn't stop with him. It never stopped, but shifted and kept moving along the bloody lines, touching the point where each of my mates stood, like a fuse slowly inching its way to a grand and devastating finale.

"Is this supposed to happen?" I asked.

Natalie's face paled. "No."

The moment the flame completed the pentacle, my stomach dropped, filled with dread. A wall of fire shot up, ground beneath our feet trembling as pounding hoof beats filled the air accompanied by the blast of what could only be described as a horn sounding an alarm. We all fell to the floor, bracing ourselves until the shaking stopped and the world around us went quiet.

"What in God's name was that?" Cashel breathed.

Natalie stood, her limbs trembling. "The apocalypse."

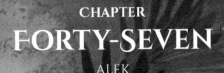

CHAPTER

# FORTY-SEVEN

ALEK

Fear and dread mingled in my belly, my berserker waking up in response to my tangled emotions. I couldn't be sure, I was still too new to its presence inside me, but I think the only thing that kept him from taking over entirely was that there was no enemy for him to fight. Only this soul-deep knowing that something was terribly, terribly wrong.

"I'm sorry, the what now?" Kingston asked, pushing himself off the ground and helping me refocus.

Natalie shook as she pointed to Sunday. "That child . . . it's the end of everything."

My gaze found Sunday, still sitting in a daze on the floor. She rubbed absently at the swell of her belly, eyes shining with tears. "You're wrong."

Moira clung to Ash, her hair now bone-white ringlets. Before the ceremony started, it had been jet black and stick straight. "She's not lying, Sunday. We all saw it."

"What did you see?" I asked.

Her panicked gaze shot to mine. "The end of the world. If that baby is born, not only will Sunday die, we all will."

I stood, legs shaking as my stomach churned and nausea took hold. "That can't be the only outcome. Visions aren't absolute."

"This wasn't a vision," Natalie interjected. "This was the truth. There is nothing good that will come from this baby being born, and there is no way we can stop it. You five put something in motion that has been on the horizon for millennia."

"Us *five*?" Noah asked.

Natalie nodded, reaching a hand out to Sunday. "Yes. All of you were instrumental in this."

"That's impossible. I may not know a lot about magic, but I know how a fucking baby is made," Kingston snarled. "One egg, one sperm. That means one father, not four."

Natalie raised a brow. "And yet here we are. This child is not a mortal, not even a child, really. It is a cataclysm. A growing mass of chaotic energy brought into being by all of you. When it is unleashed, it will destroy the world as we know it."

"It is a *she,* and *she* is *mine*." Sunday snatched her hand back from Natalie's grasp after she helped her to her feet.

The flash of black in Sunday's eyes sent a warning through me. The berserker was close to the surface for both of us. If I didn't get her away from here soon, *she* might be the one to destroy their world. And I might be right alongside her.

"Don't you have anything to say about this, Padre?" Kingston asked. "This fire and brimstone shit is basically your wheelhouse, yeah?"

Caleb's face was stricken, but I wouldn't say he looked surprised by the news. Considering how the rest of us were quite literally bowled over by it, I would have expected at least a little something more from him.

"You fucking bastard," Noah snarled. "You knew. You fucking knew."

He launched himself at the priest, grabbing him by the throat and shoving until he slammed Caleb into one of the floor-to-ceiling bookshelves. Leather-bound tomes fell to the floor in a shower of fluttering paper and heavy thuds.

"I knew it was possible. I didn't want to believe it was true."

"And you didn't think to mention it to the rest of us while we blindly went about our merry fucking way?" Noah asked, his voice rich with the promise of more violence.

"What did you want me to say? By giving her everything she needed, you were bringing about the end of the bloody world? That you loving her was going to kill her?" He shoved Noah away hard enough the vampire prince stumbled. "Why do you think I tried so fecking hard to stay away?"

My gaze went to Sunday, and my heart caved in on itself. We were sad excuses for mates, leaving her standing alone and trembling. In a few long strides, I crossed the now permanently charred lines of the pentagram and pulled her into my arms.

"Alek, I can't . . ." Sunday's voice shook as she tried to speak. "She's real. I can feel her moving. We've heard her heart beating. She can't be some horrible *thing*."

I cupped her cheek, knowing that nothing made in Sunday's image could ever be anything other than perfect. "She isn't. I felt her too, remember? She's ours, Kærasta. Created out of our love. Nothing is set in stone. The path can always be altered. Just because they believe this to be true does not make it so."

Tears splashed down her cheeks as her face crumpled. My words seemed to deepen the cracks in her heart rather

461

than fill them. Damn Natalie, damn Caleb, and damn the Blackthornes. It destroyed me not knowing how to make this better. How to heal the wounds they'd inflicted. How to take away the doubt their thoughtless words had planted.

"What do you need, Sunny? Who can I kill for you? Tell me, and I will bring you their heads."

"Enough. No one is dying tonight." Cashel spoke for the first time since before the ritual, his voice strong and determined. "Take her to her room, Noah. She's had enough excitement for tonight."

"Father, we have to find a way to save her. We can't simply pretend this isn't happening."

Cashel shook his head. "I'm not pretending anything. Your mate looks as though she's about to lose control of whatever creature is lurking behind her eyes. I'm protecting my own. Take her now before I do it."

"I'll take her," I said, just as on edge as Sunday was.

Kingston looked like he was about to fight me over it, but one hard glare and he backed down. Seemed the wolf could be trained after all.

Scooping Sunday into my arms, I cradled her to my chest and murmured, "I know you can walk, but please, let me do this."

She nodded, nuzzling into me. "I wasn't going to argue."

"That's a first."

A sharp burst of pain in my neck made me chuckle. The little minx bit me.

She followed it up with a soft lap of her tongue. "Jerk."

"I was aiming for distraction. Is it working?"

She was quiet for a second. "Not really."

When we reached her room, I was loath to put her down, but I knew I needed to return to the library before decisions were made without me. Someone needed to be down there speaking to Sunday and the child's best interests. And from the sound of things, I was the only one on their side. I couldn't believe how quiet Kingston had been about all of it. As though he didn't care that his child was in danger.

"I'm so sorry," Sunday whispered.

"For what?"

"I don't even know. All of this? What a fucking mess."

"Don't worry about any of that right now. We will sort it out. No matter what they might say, I will not let anyone harm our child. If I must take you away from here, I will. You are not alone in this."

A tear slipped down her cheek, and I reached out, wiping it away with my thumb.

"Do you promise?"

I placed her palm on my chest and matched the gesture on her own. "I swear to you, Kærasta, nothing will come between us."

She let out a watery breath and nodded. "Okay then. I believe you."

"As you should. Only a fool would try to come between a berserker and his mate."

"*Her* mate," Sunday said with a soft smile.

"I stand corrected."

I dipped my head and took her lips with mine, needing the connection, the proof that even through all of this, we were still us. The kiss was gentle, soulful and filled with the truth and love only a fated mate could provide.

As I pulled away, I feathered my lips over her forehead, stealing a final second with her before whispering, "I should get back down there."

"Go. Protect our baby, Alek. I'm counting on you to make them understand."

"With my life."

~

As I suspected, they were already plotting, the murmur of hushed voices carrying through the hallway from the library. The women were gone, likely needing to recover after the ritual they'd performed, leaving only the men still standing around debating things.

"But what do we do in the meantime?" Noah asked as I strode back in. "The Council won't stop coming for her if we stay here."

"Nothing changes," Cashel insisted. "This is still the safest place for you all. *I* can protect you. *We* can protect you. If I need to, I'll call upon every vampire with Blackthorne blood to defend your mate."

"Of course we'll stand with you, brother," Westley said, looking every bit as fierce as his father.

"You'd go to war for a child you think will end the world?" I asked, disbelief heavy in my voice.

"I'd go to war for my family's sake," the youngest Blackthorne insisted.

"And if Natalie was right?" Noah's words were tight with pain.

"We will not let that come to pass," Cashel said.

Something about the promise had my eyes narrowing. I did not trust the vampire king. Not as far as I could throw him. Although . . . I could throw him pretty far. I didn't trust him as far as Kingston could throw him.

"This is all a pointless discussion because nothing is going to happen to my kid," Kingston said.

*Ah, there he is. Finally stepping up to the plate.* Good to see I had an ally after all.

"*Our* kid," I amended.

"I still don't understand how that happened," Kingston mumbled.

"Don't question it. Magic baby. That's all you need to know."

"Maybe, but it still means my swimmers got there first. So she's more mine than the rest of yours."

"You should be so proud to be the first to make a donation to the apocalypse. Bravo." Caleb's words were laced with sarcasm so thick, if I had a knife, I could've sliced through them.

"You're one to talk. If this prophecy or whatever the fuck it is required all of us to participate, then we wouldn't be here if you could have kept it in your pants, buddy. But sure, take shots at me." Kingston crossed his arms and stared down the priest with a level of derision I wasn't used to seeing from him. Mocking disrespect, sure, but outright hostility? That was usually reserved for the other vampire.

"All of you are so quick to lay my sins at my feet, and yet you conveniently ignore your own."

"None of us made holy vows to God that we'd keep our dicks dry. That sin was all on you, Saint Caleb 'I hate myself' Gallagher."

Caleb's eyes burned with anger, and he spun toward the door. "The devil take you all. I've had enough of this."

"Good riddance." Kingston crossed the floor and went straight for the bar cart, pouring a full glass of some amber liquid, leaving it on the cart, and then taking a pull straight from the decanter.

"Why pour the drink at all?" I asked as he came to stand beside me.

"Didn't want to be rude and not leave some for somebody else."

A surprised snort escaped me. There was something about this wolf I found impossible not to like. Whether it was his penchant for chaos or simply his completely unapologetic way of being himself, it was hard not to respect him. Even if he made you want to punch him in the balls from time to time.

"So we stay here, keep her protected, until . . ." Noah began.

"Until it's time." Cashel snatched the decanter from Kingston and drank deeply. "This is a thirty-year-old scotch. I'm not letting you have it all."

"I left you the glass . . ."

"You have that. I paid for this."

Kingston shook his head. "Way to cheap out now, Blackthorne."

"I think you're all missing the biggest point. Just keeping her here and safe won't be enough. Sunday will die if she gives birth to this . . . child." Noah's fingers were wrapped tightly around the back of a chair, knuckles white, the wood and leather creaking.

Kingston paled at the reminder. "So we plan ahead, have healers on hand. The best thing that came out of today is that we won't be caught off guard."

"You're an ignorant fool if you believe that will be enough," Cashel said.

"So you want us to what, just let her die? Not even try to save her? That's never going to happen," Kingston said.

"No, I want Noah to turn her."

CHAPTER
# FORTY-EIGHT
SUNDAY

C ashel's voice washed over me, stopping me dead just outside the library. The door stood ajar just wide enough that I could hear the conversation inside as easily as if I was in there. But, God, I wish I couldn't.

"Turn her? You want to turn my mate into a vampire?" Kingston asked.

"If it's the only way to save her life, would you really question how it's done?" Cashel's words were mocking.

"What happens if it's not successful? What if I lose her to the change?"

"If we don't attempt it, you lose her anyway."

I was barely breathing as I listened to them debate the pros and cons of my becoming a vampire. The thought hadn't ever crossed my mind, so I didn't exactly have an opinion one way or the other. The only thing I cared about right now was keeping my daughter safe.

"So you are suggesting we wait until the baby is born and then . . ." Noah's voice trailed off as his father completed the sentence.

"We get rid of it while you turn her, yes."

"Get rid of it?" Alek bit out, his voice dark with rage.

"There is a way to stop the world from ending, but it must happen in the moments immediately following its birth. We will only have one shot."

"And you're just mentioning this *now*? What is it with you bloodsuckers and burying the lead?" Kingston's question was filled with livid frustration. "How do you know this?"

"I can't say much."

"Of fucking course you can't."

"But," Cashel continued, "Just know there has been someone watching Sunday Fallon since the day she was born. A soul linked to her, charged with keeping this from happening. Fate had other plans, and so did we. With every event that opened one of the seven seals, our plan of attack solidified."

My stomach churned as Cashel continued speaking, each new revelation filling me with dread. Who was this spy? How had I never suspected them?

"And by plan of attack, you mean the murder of this child?" Alek asked.

"One life to save the world." Cashel said it so simply I would have been on his side if the life in question wasn't my baby's.

"How many seals have been opened?" Noah asked.

"Six."

"So there's still a chance—" The excitement in Kingston's voice died as Cashel interrupted.

"No. Not anymore. Maybe before now, but the last seal is known, unlike the others."

"And it is?" Alek's tone was stoic and steady. Too calm. If I could have seen his face, I bet flickers of the berserker would be shining in his eyes. He was fighting to remain in control.

"The birth."

A shuffling noise came right before Noah spoke. "What if we prevent the birth?"

"You mean like an abortion?" Kingston whispered, horrified.

"It's too late for that. Killing the child or the mother ends the same for us all. It's as I told you, the only way to stop this now is during one very specific window and with a ritual I have to complete."

"So you will kill the baby, and I . . ." I hated the resignation in Noah's statement, like he'd already agreed to this horrific plan.

"Will attempt to turn your mate."

No.

They had to tell him this wasn't an option. That there was nothing that would make them consider killing our baby.

But the silence stretched on, not one of them raising a protest. And with every passing second, my heart broke.

My daughter danced in my belly, those once soft kicks now strong and sure. I rested a palm over the place where she'd been moving and closed my eyes, letting myself connect with her. She couldn't be bad. There wasn't a single drop of evil in her. I knew it in my bones. I had to save her, even if it meant leaving behind everything and everyone I loved.

I was all she had.

Swallowing back my tears, I pushed away from the wall and started moving as quickly and silently as I could back to my room. After the last attack, we'd all packed bags, ready to flee at a moment's notice. It had everything I'd need to survive on my own until I found a place to hide. I'd have to figure out how to *stay* hidden later. It wouldn't be easy to evade a bunch of vampires, let alone an Alpha wolf, but that was future Sunday's problem. Right now, I just needed to get out.

I made a beeline for the large walk-in closet as soon as I hit my bedroom. The bag was right where I left it, tucked in a corner next to Noah's. I never wanted to use it, and I certainly never thought I'd be doing it on my own, but something inside me knew I'd have to.

"Where's the fire, babycakes?"

I spun around, finding Moira standing inside the closet door, her teasing smile dropping as soon as she got a good look at me.

"Shit, Sunday, what's wrong? Is it another attack?"

My lower lip wobbled as I worked up the energy to tell her everything. Instead all I got out was, "They're going to kill the baby."

Her eyes widened. "Excuse me? I think I just had a stroke. Did you say they're going to kill her?"

Nodding, I clutched the bag closer and slid my feet into a pair of boots. "I have to leave them."

Moira looked torn. After what she'd seen during the ritual, I couldn't exactly blame her for being on the fence about how to proceed. "Are you sure that's a smart idea? There are a lot of people looking for you right now."

"I can't stay here, not knowing what they're planning to do. I have to keep her safe."

Moira bit her lip.

"Please, Moira. You have to help me. I've seen her in my dreams. I know my baby is good. No one is born evil. Not even Lucifer himself."

"Herself . . . since we're pretty sure she's your mother, right?"

"Moira. Focus."

"She sent you those dreams. What if she was trying to do exactly this? Start the apocalypse, get you to bond with the one thing that can open the door. Sunday . . ."

I blinked back the hot tears burning my eyes. "I *know* she is good. In my soul, I feel her. She is innocent. Please help me or get the fuck out of my way."

Sighing, Moira took my hands. "I can't let you go like this."

"Then move." My berserker was knocking at the door, asking for the freedom to destroy in order to protect.

"That's not what I mean. I can't let you go without something to keep you hidden. They'll find you right away. The second you step foot outside, Noah will be on you if Kingston and that big nose of his don't get there first."

"What do you have in mind?"

"Close your eyes and trust me, okay?"

She was the only person I trusted at this point. Everyone else had betrayed me. Even Alek, after he'd sworn not to.

I let my eyelids fall closed and tried to keep my breaths steady as I let Moira work her magic. I couldn't see what she was doing, but it felt like drops of misty rain sinking into my skin as her spell spread over me. Everything tingled, building to a burn that flashed over me and vanished almost instantly.

"There. That should buy you some time. You're not completely untraceable. There are still other ways to track you. Cell phones. People spotting you. Those sorts of things. But they won't be able to scent you."

"Thank you, Moira." I couldn't manage more than that

as I took my tiny witch friend in my arms and squeezed. "I love you."

"Back at ya, kid." She was trying to be light and breezy, but there was pain in her voice, the same as me. "I'd climb the trellis if I were you. They've stopped talking down there. Someone will be up here soon."

I glanced out onto the balcony and nodded my agreement. "Good idea. Wish me luck."

She laughed. "You don't need luck, sweet cheeks. You've got me. I'll stand outside the door and cover for you. Now go on, take that witchy goddaughter of mine and keep her safe." She pressed a kiss to my cheek, and I felt her tears even though she spun away to keep me from seeing them.

Knowing this was my only chance, I hefted the bag up higher on my shoulder, took a deep breath, and stepped onto the balcony as she left the room. The wind bit at my cheeks, dark, chilly night air seeping into my bones the instant I swung my leg over the railing and onto the trellis.

The bag threatened to unbalance me, and I had one terrifying second where I thought for sure I'd be reaching the ground flat on my back. Thankfully, I hung onto the iron, the thorns from the climbing roses cutting into my palms.

Fuck. There might be a spell hiding me, but surely they'd find my blood.

I couldn't worry about that now. So I gritted my teeth and focused on finding my footing as I worked my way painfully down the wall of roses. When my toe finally scraped the ground, I could have wept with relief. It felt like it had taken me hours when in reality, it had probably only been a couple of minutes.

All I had to do was get to the gate. Then hitch a ride and . . . run.

Easy.

I knew I was deluding myself, but delusions were all I had, so I was going to cling to them as fiercely as I had that fucking trellis. Picking up the pace, I started to walk-run down the gravel drive, trying to stay to the shadows as best I could.

A strange echo accompanied my footfalls, the sound shooting fear through me. I stopped, listening intently. Nothing. Just the pounding of my own heart.

But the moment I began pushing toward the gate again, I knew I'd been too easily fooled. A prick stung my neck, pressure accompanying the pain as cold liquid was injected into me.

"What . . ." My vision grew blurry, eyes sinking shut as a black hood was pulled roughly over my head.

I tried to force my limbs to move, to fight back, but they weren't responding. I couldn't even push the breath past my lips to form words.

Then the world tilted, and the weightless feeling of my body was the last thing I remembered before I faded away in my kidnapper's arms.

CHAPTER

# FORTY-NINE

CALEB

"Father, forgive me," I prayed as I knelt in the moonlight, desperate for strength and absolution all rolled into one. "I've done what you required of me. I'm prepared to face judgment for my part in this, but I need guidance. I'm not strong enough."

My only answer was the whisper of wind through the trees. I blinked up at the star-strewn sky and knew that despite my prayers, He wasn't listening. He'd stopped listening a long time ago.

"What more do you want from me?" I shouted into the sky.

I got to my feet just as the rain started, clouds having rolled in sometime during my prayers. At least it was quiet here. Heavy with the ghost of a life I'd been promised. One that had been stolen from me and painted crimson with death.

I turned in a slow circle, taking in the rolling green hills and the shadows of a small village in the distance, finally coming to a stop when my cabin came into view. The lights were on, a fire roaring in the hearth. Everything was prepared for me. Ready to welcome me home.

What a fecking farce.

This wasn't a homecoming. It was a death sentence.

And I was the executioner.

I steeled myself to face what was waiting beyond the door. The future I'd wanted more than anything dangled before me like a life preserver to a drowning man. Forever just out of reach. I hadn't been home in decades for a reason. Unless I counted the night I spent at *Iniquity* when Sunday gave me a nearly painful glimpse of happiness.

And weren't we all fucking paying for it now.

This place was bloody cursed. What better setting for what was to come?

My damned hand shook as I reached for the doorknob and twisted. The moment the door opened, my favorite scent filled my nose. Lilacs and fecking honey. A reminder of my weakest moment.

My gaze was drawn immediately to the dark and quiet bedroom where my fate taunted me. My heart beat like a death knell, pulling me closer to the secrets awaiting me there. Not for the first time, I hated the sound of it in my ears. It mocked me. Mocked my pain and my dreams.

She lay on the bed, eyes fluttering open, brows furrowed. "Caleb?"

"Good morning, Sunday."

"It's too dark to be morning. Caleb, where are we? I had the strangest dream." She lifted a hand to her head and winced as she sat up. "I thought I'd been kidnapped."

Her gaze moved across the room, recognition flickering in her eyes.

"*Iniquity*? Why are we here?"

"No, my poor lamb. This is not *Iniquity*."

I couldn't give her more than that. I wasn't ready to see the hatred in her gaze as soon as she learned the truth.

"But it looks just like . . ."

And there it was. The knowing.

"Caleb, did you bring me to your cabin?"

"Aye, I did."

"To keep me safe?"

Her hope cut deeper than my shame.

"Are you going to force me to say it?"

Her face paled. "You . . . drugged me. You *took* me."

"Aye."

"B-but, why?"

"It is the only way."

"The only way to *what*, Caleb?"

"Fulfill my vow. Get my soul back. Stop the world from ending. What does it matter so long as it's true?"

"It fucking matters to me. If this was the plan all along, why make me fall in love with you?"

"Things don't always go to plan. But you were a persistent little thing."

That blow landed just as I'd hoped. This would be easier if she hated me.

"Why didn't you just let me die when that demon stabbed me? Then none of this would have happened."

I clenched my jaw and fought a wave of bitterness at the cruelty of fate. Then I leveled my gaze on her, letting the hammer fall.

"It's not you who has to die."

Don't miss the thrilling conclusion! The series will conclude with Temptation. Keep reading for a sneak peek!

479

# SNEAK PEEK
## TEMPTATION: CHAPTER 1
### CALEB

*Ireland, 1922*

"Amen."

I stood, my head swimming with the euphoric rush of all that came to pass this day. My congregation, perhaps small in number to some, had shown up in droves to welcome me back to the island. This time as their priest.

My eyes landed on the small statue of Christ behind the altar as I made the sign of the cross and turned to walk down the aisle. As I moved along, my hand passed lightly over the age-worn wood of the pews, smooth and cool beneath my palm. Once again, nostalgia slammed into me, memories crowding my mind. These were the same benches I'd sat on as a child, restless and eager to run about with my friends and siblings. Knowing if I set a toe out of line, I'd have to face the wrath of my mam and her wooden

As I passed through the arched doors, the bell chimed, signaling the top of the hour, and in this case, the sunset. I surveyed the grounds as I took my time, drinking it all in.

The garden was overrun, and the chapel had seen better days. The whitewashed clapboard was dark with mud and rotten in places from neglect. The many stained glass windows hadn't been washed in years, muting any sunlight that bravely attempted to trickle in.

But the people weren't to be blamed for the unkempt state of their church. Five years had passed since influenza had ravaged our island, taking many, my family included, not even sparing our pastor. There hadn't been a new one to care for this place since. The few surviving priests had been needed in the bigger cities where the parishioners were plentiful. This was the first time there'd been enough new clergy to meet the demands of the people. Which is why I was here now. It'd be my honor to restore this holy sanctuary to its once pristine glory.

I tilted my head back as the bell rang out with its final peal, my gaze traveling to the iron cross standing on the top of the steeple that my father had crafted over a decade ago.

It was good to be home.

Surveying the garden, I bent to pull a few of the weeds I could see in the dying light of day, already forming a plan to clean this up and help it thrive.

"Oh, Father Gallagher, you shouldn't be lowering yourself to dig in the dirt. Not after such a beautiful service today." Maureen O'Shanahan bustled her way down the stairs after locking the church doors. "I can arrange for a few of my children to come tend the garden in the morning. Lord knows they need something to keep their hands busy."

I smiled at the woman who'd already made herself

invaluable to me. "Thank you, Maureen, but I'm perfectly capable of pulling weeds. After all, this is my home as much as yours. There's no job too low for one of God's servants. We are tasked with caring for all of His creation."

She beamed at me. "Look at you. Your mam would be so proud to know her eldest took after her. What a scandal that was. The would-be nun and the carpenter." Her eyes twinkled as she spoke of years-old gossip, but the light in her eyes dimmed as she turned to the small cottage on the hillside. "They were a beautiful pair. God rest their souls."

My heart sank as I followed her gaze. The windows of my ancestral home, dark and cold now, were once filled with the glow of life and happiness. "This plague took so many and spared so few. We must do our best to be worthy in their absence."

Her lower lip trembled as she took in a ragged breath. "When I think of your wee brothers and sisters . . ."

I placed a gentle hand on her shoulder, forcing myself not to relive the moment I came out of my influenza-induced fever dreams and realized my whole family had died. "Let us not dwell on the past, but look to the future we are building."

She sniffled loudly. "Yes. You're right, of course." Pulling a handkerchief from her bag, she dabbed her eyes and then blew her nose. "We're blessed to have you."

"And I you."

Her sunny smile returned at that. "Well, I'll leave you to your settling, and I'll be back in the morning for confession." She batted her teary eyes at me. "Five years is a long time to go without. I hope you're ready, Father Gallagher. The people will be lined up around the church waiting to unburden themselves."

"I can't wait."

She snickered, lowering her voice conspiratorially. "Tell me, Father. Is the listening as exciting as I imagine it would be?"

I pretended to lock my lips, unable to keep the smile off my face.

"Good man, you are."

"Goodnight, Maureen."

She walked away, leaving me with the looming figure of the church as my only companion. I wasn't ready to end my day yet. It didn't seem possible to finally have something I'd worked for be real. Not after everything had been taken from me. But God had His plan, and I was his humble servant. I had to follow where He led.

Pulling the heavy keys from my pocket, I returned to the church doors, wanting one final moment of quiet reflection before supper. I wasn't without options, thanks to my parishioners and their many generous offerings. If the housewives of this island were any indication, I'd be well-fed, and gluttony would be my first sin.

I walked silently, my footsteps barely more than a whisper over the weathered floorboards as I lit a few candles to cast the interior in a soft glow. When I reached the pulpit, I moved to stand behind it, glancing down at the notes from my earlier homily with amusement. What a pretentious arse I could be.

The creak of the door opening had me glancing up, a smile on my face. "Forget something, Maureen?"

Instead of the short but fiery redhead, I found a tall, statuesque woman staring me down, her skin an eerily pale white, eyes a shade of green I'd never seen before. Her long dark hair fell in wild, tumbling curls to her waist. Strange for the fashion of this village. Women here wore their hair pinned back, out of the way, because they needed to be able to work. This was an extravagance.

"My apologies. I thought you were my secretary."

She smiled, her beauty startling and unnerving all at once. I gripped the pulpit hard enough my knuckles turned white.

"Father, I hope I'm not too late to make my confession."

Technically confession was at a set time every day to help prevent these sorts of impositions on my personal time, but I couldn't turn her away. These people had been without for so long; the least I could do was sit and offer her absolution.

"Of course not, my child. Please come in."

That smile again. As though she had a secret she'd never share with me. "Thank you."

"What is your name?"

"Aisling O'Connor. And you're Father Caleb Gallagher, the talk of the town. The prodigal son returned."

She practically glided across the floor as she approached me, ignoring the confessional booth, focus trained on my eyes.

"Aisling . . . Shall we continue our conversation in the confessional?"

Her palm was on my chest before I could blink, alarm bells ringing in my head. "No, Father. I don't think so."

"What are you playing at?" I gripped her wrist, trying to keep her from touching me.

"Immortality." She licked her lower lip, then bared her teeth at me, fangs glinting in the candlelight.

This had to be a trick. A hallucination left over from the nightmares that plagued me since my illness.

"The only immortality I seek is given by God."

"Aren't you precious," she breathed, her eyes taking on

a feral glow. "I think I'm going to keep you. I've always wanted a priest for my collection."

I backed away, but she gripped my shirt, and try as I might, I couldn't break her hold. "Release me."

"I think not. My, my, I had no idea priests could be so . . . handsome. Tell me, Father, are you as hard everywhere?" She slid her free hand between my legs, cupping me, making my stomach turn.

"This is a house of God. You are not welcome here if you mean to defile it."

"I mean to defile *you*. Now you have one more chance to come willingly. I can make it feel so nice, Father. So nice indeed."

"No. Demon."

Her grin turned wicked, her eyes hardening. "Wrong answer. Now I'm going to make it hurt."

Before I could move, her eyes bore into mine, and I felt as if I was falling.

"Stand very still. I'm going to make you mine now, Caleb. And then you'll never tell me no again. But I'll punish you for that later."

I heard her words as if they were floating down through water. I didn't want to obey, but my body was locked in place. Held captive by her evil spell. Panic and fear raced through my blood as half-formed prayers flitted through my mind. *Father, please. Save me. Do not let her do this to me.*

With fingers cold as death, she traced the line of my collar. A sneer curled her upper lip as she tore the white band off my throat and tossed it to the floor. "I bet you're going to be the sweetest I've ever had. I can smell your virgin blood thrumming through your veins." She inhaled deeply and let out a shuddering, sensual moan. "I'll take that too. You'll be mine in every sense of the word."

"No," I whispered, fighting through whatever spell she'd put me under.

Her low chuckle was the last thing I heard before she struck. Fangs I'd tried to deny existed ripped through my flesh and sank deep into my neck.

I floated on a sea of pain and despair as darkness clouded my vision. I think I screamed, but I wasn't sure. I wasn't aware of much of anything outside the agony of her bite. Just as suddenly, she released me. I sagged to the ground, my legs incapable of keeping me upright after losing so much blood.

She followed me down, red smears obscenely decorating her face as she bit into her wrist and held it up to my lips. "Your turn."

I tried to turn my face away, my gaze landing on my collar, now splattered with crimson drops of my blood.

"Eternal life, Caleb. Exactly what your god promised you."

Everything around me went gray, the world turning cold as my life bled from me and into the old bones of the church. Then her blood slipped into my now open mouth, and all I knew was darkness.

∾

*DON'T MISS A SECOND THIS SUPER SPICY PARANORMAL REVERSE HAREM PRE-ORDER YOUR COPY OF TEMPTATION NOW!*

# Also by Meg Anne

**Brotherhood of the Guardians/Novasgard Vikings**

**Undercover Magic** *(Nord & Lina)*

*A Sexy & Suspenseful Fated Mates PNR*

Hint of Danger

Face of Danger

World of Danger

Promise of Danger

Call of Danger

Bound by Danger (Quinn & Finley)

**The Mate Games**

*A Spicy Paranormal Reverse Harem*

*Co-Written with K. Loraine*

Obsession

Rejection

Possession

Temptation

## The Grimm Brotherhood: The Complete Trilogy

*A Sexy & Humorous Urban Fantasy Romance*

*Co-Written with Kel Carpenter*

Reapers Blood

Reaping Havoc

Reaper Reborn

The Grimm Brotherhood: The Complete Collection

# Also by K. Loraine

~

**REVERSE HAREM STANDALONES**

~

**THE MATE GAMES**

**(co-written with Meg Anne)**

# ABOUT MEG ANNE

USA Today and international bestselling paranormal and fantasy romance author Meg Anne has always had stories running on a loop in her head. They started off as daydreams about how the evil queen (aka Mom) had her slaving away doing chores, and more recently shifted into creating backgrounds about the people stuck beside her during rush hour. The stories have always been there; they were just waiting for her to tell them.

Like any true SoCal native, Meg enjoys staying inside curled up with a good book and her cat, Henry . . . or maybe that's just her. You can convince Meg to buy just about anything if it's covered in glitter or rhinestones, or make her laugh by sharing your favorite bad joke. She also accepts bribes in the form of baked goods and Mexican food.

Meg is best known for her leading men #MenbyMeg, her inevitable cliffhangers, and making her readers laugh out loud, all of which started with the bestselling Chosen series.

# About K. Loraine

Kim writes steamy contemporary and sexy paranormal romance. **You'll find her paranormal romances written under the name K. Loraine and her contemporaries as Kim Loraine.** Don't worry, you'll get the same level of swoon-worthy heroes, sassy heroines, and an eventual HEA.

When not writing, she's busy herding cats (raising kids), trying to keep her house sort of clean, and dreaming up ways for fictional couples to meet.

Printed in Great Britain
by Amazon